She Walks in Beauty

by

Nicole Conn

Bella
BOOKS

2013

Bella Books, Inc.
P.O. Box 10543
Tallahassee, FL 32302

Printed in the United States of America on acid-free paper
First Published by Naiad Press 2001
First Bella Books Edition 2013

Editor: Katherine V. Forrest
Cover Designer: Kayleigh Hawes

ISBN 13: 978-1-59493-411-7

Byron's Poetry: Pages 38-39, 43, 105, 257-258, 287, 300-301 from The Complete Poetical *Works of Lord Byron*. Cambridge. The Riverside Press (1905).

Poetry from Nicole Conn: Pages 95, 202, 249, 279.

Other Bella Books by Nicole Conn

Claire of the Moon
Elena Undone

For Gabrielle,
My Bestest BiBi BoBo

Acknowledgments

A very special thank you to Katherine V. Forrest, for her many years of friendship, her ongoing support of my work, and for agreeing to edit this novel. She is truly one of our national resources.

And many many thanks to:

My in-house editor and dear friend, Lisa M. Jones.

To my wonderful and "gentle" readers who have gone through drafts of my dreck to help me find the gems—Jeannie Karaffa, and Faith McDevitt.

And especially to my *Jen-Ben* (Jennifer Bergman) who, as always, pulled out the stops in the final hour.

To my Patron Saint of the Arts, Madeline Lorton, who has been a great source of support—both financially and emotionally for years.

And finally, thank you, dear Gwen, for giving me the greatest gift in the world, our incredible daughter, Gabrielle. May we learn from the past and heal the future.

Special Acknowledgments for Cover

Design Concept & Producer, the Extraordinary & Unparalleled Sue Melke

Photographer: Rodney Bursiel of rodneybursiel.com

Cover Art: Kayleigh Hawes

Styling: Gray suit, gray vest, black trousers, gray shirt—
Androgyny
Men's Clothes for Women
www.wearandrogyny.com

Hair: Jennifer Wright

Makeup: Abigail Hope

Location: WingSpan Films, 4029 W Burbank Blvd., Burbank, CA 91505

Cover Model: Actress Nicole Pacent

Thank you to Melissa Millan for the gorgeous Androgyny suits and shirts.

Very Special Thank you to dynamic duo behind WingSpan Productions; Kim "Rocco" Shields and Rachel Diana.

Nicole Conn—Writer/Director/Editor/Mother

Nicole Conn has been a die-hard romantic and black and white film fan from the age of nine.

Her penchant for adult and dramatic story telling is evident in her latest critically acclaimed feature film, *A Perfect Ending*—"the sexiest film of 2012" (*Curve*) and now the single best selling film of its genre.

Conn's penchant for telling stories that really hit home, is "greatly rewarded" by all the fan mail she gets from viewers who watch her films multiple times. If there ever was an earmark of success, Conn believes it's in "seeing my work over and over and OVER again." It doesn't hurt that her previous feature *Elena Undone* boasts the longest on-screen kiss in cinema history. This classic romance with a twist is "sexy and smart and smoldering."

Conn's previous venture, *little man*, is a documentary she wrote, directed and produced about her own premature son born 100 days early and only weighing one pound. The feature documentary went on to win 12 Best Documentary Awards, along with the prestigious Cedar Sinai's Courageous Beginnings Award and Family Pride's Family Tree Award. The film made three Top Ten Films of 2005 lists and Showtime picked up the feature and ran an Emmy campaign on this hard-hitting story about Conn's son's premature birth and subsequent five-month hospital stay in a neonatal intensive care unit.

In efforts to continue her support of other parents who find themselves thrust into the insanity of the NICU, Ms. Conn collaborated with *Preemie Magazine* founder Deborah Discenza in creating the *The Preemie Parent's Guide to Survival in the NICU: How to Maintain Your Sanity and Create a New Normal* published in January 2010.

Conn's passion for film carried her through her first feature in which she raised the money, wrote, directed and produced *Claire of the Moon*, the maverick film about a woman's journey to her sexual identity. The film garnered rave reviews and paved the way for lesbian themed cinema in 1991. Conn also created a first for lesbian cinema: ancillary in the form of a novelization (in its 15th reprint and 10 Year Anniversary Republish) a making-of documentary *Moments* (best-selling lesbian documentary ever made), soundtracks, posters, t-shirts, etc. She followed these projects with the award-winning short film, *Cynara...Poetry in Motion.*

A two book deal with Simon Schuster produced the novels, *Passion's Shadow* (1995) & *Angel Wings* (1997), a new age love story. The script adaptation for *Angel Wings* won the 2001 Telluride Film Festival's Best Screenplay Award. In another pioneering effort, *The Wedding Dress* was chosen by AOL Time Warner for its new Internet endeavor iPublish, which debuted in June 2001. *She Walks in Beauty* was originally published in September 2001. Not only is it set for re-release as a book, but the feature film is in active pre-production as a transcontinental feature to be filmed in the UK and the US.

Conn achieved industry recognition with her film *Claire of the Moon* and was a finalist in the prestigious Academy of Motion Picture Arts and Science's Nicholl Fellowships in Screenwriting. She believes in giving back to the community and sponsored the Claire of the Moon Scholarship in 1998, awarding second time novelists through the ASTRAEA Foundation.

Well known for her speed, quality and prolific ability to write in many genres, Conn has written five novels, a parent's guide, two teleplays, eleven screenplays, and has produced four soundtracks.

She is currently finalizing her epic tome, *Descending Thirds*, available Spring 2013. She is the co-founder of Soul Kiss Films— *Empowering Women One Film at a Time.*

AWARDS

Best Picture—*A Perfect Ending*—La Femme Film Festival, Los Angeles

Best Feature—*Elena Undone*—Audience Award, Reel Pride, Fresno

Best Feature—*Elena Undone*—Tampa GLFF

Best Documentary Audience Award, Los Angeles Outfest—*little man*

Best Documentary Jury Award, New York NewFest—*little man*

Best Documentary Audience Award, San Diego Film Festival—*little man*

Best Documentary Jury Award, Chicago Indiefest—*little man*

Best Feature hbo Audience Award, Miami GLFF—*little man*

Best Documentary Jury Award, Philadelphia Int'l GLFF Film Festival—*little man*

Best of the Fest Award, Indianapolis G&L Film Festival—*little man*

Best Documentary—Jury Award Chicago Reeling Film Festival—*little man*

Best Documentary—Glitter Award—LA—*little man*

Best Documentary—Long Island G&L Film Festival—*little man*

Best Documentary—WA DC – Reel Affirmations—*little man*

Palme D'Or—Reel Pride—*little man*

Telluride Film Festival's Best Screenplay Award—*Angel Wings*

Courageous Beginnings Award—Cedars Sinai, Los Angeles

Santa Barbara Social Justice Award Nominee

Academy of Motion Picture Arts and Science's Nicholl Fellowships in Screenwriting.

One sheds one's sicknesses in books—repeats and presents again one's emotions, to be master of them.
D. H. Lawrence (1885-1930)

I am afraid.

I can admit it here. I don't want to be a coward...but hell, this is frightening.

My palm itches from numbness. I scratch it but my fingernails are borrowed shavings. I can only guess at the time. It's still light out. Barely. I can see dusk merging with the sea through what remains of the entrance to this cave where I have inadvertently trapped myself.

Surrounded by the ocean—its salty brine so strong I imagine swollen carcasses of crab and deep sea creatures churning in the water below me. Dank. Cold. The rock ledge I have climbed to for safety is a million years old with wet. It never has seen the sun...laden with barnacles and growing microscopic matter in its craggy veins.

I had happened upon this shelter weeks ago, while wandering in a storm. If this were a cocktail party I would describe being imprisoned in a womb-like cave as absurdly metaphoric—lace it with the fashionable humor that permeates the cynical. But I am not feeling humorous. Perhaps only the brave face death with humor. I face it with resentment and defeat.

Hiding my head in the sand has always been a particular skill of mine: But denial is what got me here in the first place. I have made a career of clear-headed negation, sophisticated maneuverings around facing the truth. Reality requires coolly accepting that I am at the end, and it occurs to me I may well fall into the category of those who have tried a little too hard, a little too late.

I am so numb. I close my eyes—feel the inner quiver of my breathing. I am alone. Absolutely. Alone. I feel myself drifting off again, bargain to stay conscious.

Please…let this be a bad nightmare. Make the last decade a bad dream and I will wake up and be in the life I first set out to live.

I'm sinking…tired…NO. Must remember, remember it all. If I do, maybe I can make it until dawn. Maybe they will find my body when the morning sun rises. But it won't matter. Not if I tell you my story.

BOOK ONE
Spencer

Spencer couldn't breathe.

So she had been fired from a show she loathed. It was going to get canceled anyway. But none of this mattered because she had *May You Always* to fall back on. She could pull it and her many other projects—four feature scripts, pitches for TV shows, a children's after-school special—out like a proud grandmother would an accordion wallet showing off all her grandchildren. But *May You* was the talented child she breathed all her hopes and dreams into. It had lived with her for nine years. This meeting couldn't have come at a better time. She had been waiting years. Her entire life.

Tapping her fingers restlessly against the script and budget pages, Spencer sat at an outside table at Le Petit Four on Sunset while a waitress poured her more coffee. For nine years she had cried tears over *May You Always*, a wrenching love story about the obsession of a man for the love of his life. On the brink of consummating their relationship, the woman he loves discovers she has cancer. She won't marry him or sleep with him, because she knows it will only devastate him further. In the end the hero spends the last months of her life with her, selflessly taking care of her as a best friend, but never her lover.

Of course she was nervous about her project—she was an insecure writer, after all—but Spencer had been told so many times *May You* was good, she was beginning to believe it. The praise propped up the never-ending uncertainty of months, days and hours of disappointing rejections—of just about getting there and having the rug pulled—nine years of disillusionment, swallowed like a daily supplement. All she and her partner, Jerry, had to do now was get Lou Sheinberg to put up domestic financing and she would never have to work in TV again.

Spencer checked her watch. Still breathing, and only one palpitation in the past ten minutes. Where in the hell were they? Jerry was always late, but not this late. This was yet another meeting devoted to talking up the latest interest in the project. Suddenly they would find themselves enthralled with actors, producers and financiers they would never have considered—if it meant setting up *May You*. Lunches, dinners. Drinks. This would be the two hundred thirteenth such meeting. She had counted them up last night in her day planner as if to convince herself that all the battles she had fought would make up for the war. She cracked her neck, a habit she had developed since moving to L.A. Her day planner was checkered with chiropractors, acupuncturists, anyone who could help her get rid of the searing pain that shot up into the back of her head. She checked her watch again. Come on Jerry.

When she had found Jerry it had been a mixed blessing. Like thinking you had gotten Kirk Douglas in *The Bad and the Beautiful* but ending up with an Armani-clad *Nutty Professor*. Yes, he wore the sleek black-on-black producer's uniform and yes, he would stab his own mother in the back for a point of net profits—but he was the only person even remotely interested in financing her script. Fortunately, when Spencer hooked up with him, Jerry had separated from his wife and was experiencing a mid-life crisis, and after making nothing but extraordinarily *un*-extraordinary movies he had decided that he wanted to make art house films. Besides, he was loaded and had production deals all over town.

Today's meeting was supposed to be paydirt. Weeks ago Jerry had snagged Lou Sheinberg back into the deal. And that prompted Sondra Roberts to commit to the lead. Well maybe. Her agents said she was still considering but about ninety percent there. If she committed then the aging Alan Elliott would come on board and with his unexpected Oscar win he was riding high. Hollywood loved a washed out comeback story almost as much as they loved gross point deals. It was a well kept secret, but the entire entertainment industry was held together by paper clips and fraying bungee cords. One minor breeze and the whole thing could topple over.

Spencer momentarily wondered why Lou wanted back in. Then shrugged it off. It was probably poignant or perhaps significant that after all this time, she was back to producer zero: Lou Sheinberg. Yeah, she rationalized, it had that synchronicity that was the earmark of all good behind-the-scenes stories. Yes. She could feel it inside. That inner voice that said things were finally going to happen. *Breathing. Yes.*

But now it was getting late, even for Jerry who made "chic late" a fine art.

Spencer took out her cell phone and called in for messages.

"Hey, Spencer, this is Jerry. Uhm…I don't really know how to say this other than to say it. Your underlying rights ran out on *May You* and Lou Sheinberg picked them up this morning and he's killed the Sondra Roberts deal. Now…that's the bad news. He did however get Jennifer Lowell…now don't be upset. I know she's only twenty-two but I think she can play, you know, like up to twenty-eight. But here's the thing. You can't direct. I told him I want you to be an associate producer. Okay? And so we'll talk. Don't worry, I'll take care of ya…you know I always have."

Spencer gasped as she replayed the message three times.

Now her life was over.

Even if she was still breathing.

* * *

I feel the same sharp twist in my stomach I had that day. Held captive by unrelenting terror, I feel an obligation to deny my certain fate. It's called shock, I believe.

"Spencer, what's your first memory of fear?" Therapist asked me that once.

First memory of fear.

My father leaning over a headstone in an abandoned graveyard, carefully snapping the neck of a pigeon, while calmly extolling the virtue of painless death to my older sister. I can still see everything precisely as it was; the overcast windiness to the day, my father in his khaki pants, his mammoth down-filled hunter's jacket. My sister's pale brown hair is neatly braided. She is wearing her little red sweater with the golden windmill buttons as if she is dressed for a playmate's birthday party.

I crouch behind another forgotten headstone, watching them, terrified I will be found out—trespassing on initiation. My father thrusts the dead bird into Rebecca's hands and I feel my limbs go weak and my stomach burn as I watch her eyes widen. She obediently nods, blindly accepting what our father tells her. After all, parents always know best, don't they?

You're not interested in that. You want to know how I ended up in the cave. Get to the pitch. Even here I'm worried about the presentation. The cottage...the cottage might be a good place to start. No—I still have a modicum of story sense left. I shall tell you first how I got to the cottage.

* * *

The next afternoon Spencer sat at a corner table at Aroma's, an outside café in the valley, shielding herself from the sun and the stars with her Oliver Peoples glasses. The pair she'd blithely paid two hundred dollars for. Image really wasn't as simple as looking a part, her good friend Sarah once justified. It wasn't that you cared what the world thought about you, it was telling the world that you cared enough about *yourself* to endorse brand name labels. That expanding the limits of personal consumption to buy the Mercedes, lease the perfect Bel Air home for entertaining, paying outrageous sums to have catered dinner parties was a way of simply saying I'm keeping up with the Joneses and *I'm* worth it.

With a delicate trace of memory she touched a slender finger to the edge of the glasses. She'd worn this set with a cracked lens for two years. It was a great line at parties: *That's why I see the world askew.* Lena had stepped on the edge of them one Sunday when they were on their way out to a screening and the truth was, she couldn't bear to get rid of them.

"Hey." Malcolm leaned over the table, kissing her cheek.

A twitch accompanied Spencer's meager smile as she greeted her friend.

"Bad news?" Malcolm asked as he leaned over and gently lifted the sunglasses. "Ouch."

"Uhum," Spencer cleared her throat "Pretty, huh?"

"You don't have to be brave for me, Spence."

She looked into his laughing, wise eyes. His smooth voice, which wove in and out of a British accent as occasion demanded, always calmed Spencer. She loved the lack of judgment in Malcolm's voice. It seemed all she heard these days were tones of castigation.

"Malcolm…" she began again, tears edging from beneath the frame of her sunglasses.

Malcolm's hand snaked to her own. "Just tell me what happened."

"I never thought I'd say this, but I'm afraid to tell even you." She glanced up into his clear eyes. "How…how in the hell did I get here?"

And then she told Malcolm in broken sentences how Lou Sheinberg had deftly stolen her project. *Her* project! Did he fully understand the irony here? "And because I've been spending too much time 'moonlighting' on Nina's film, I've been fired in the bargain."

"Hmmm, this might just qualify as tragic."

A searing pain shot up under her left eyebrow. She took her glasses off, and Malcolm saw the agony and self-loathing. Spencer gestured for another drink from the passing waitress.

Malcolm intercepted the order with a shake of his head, and pushed his cappuccino toward Spencer. "Take a sip."

"Why? You think I want to deal with this sober?"

"Well, you're going to have to get sober at some point."

"Yeah, why's that?"

"Because I'm not going to AA meetings with you, okay? It's just too Hollywood."

"You think I've got a drinking problem?"

"No. I think you've got a problem and you're drinking over it." He lifted the cappuccino for Spencer. "Come on. Drink this."

Spencer sipped the bitter espresso, let it bite into her senses. She wanted to shower. She'd already had two since she woke, unable to wash the last forty-eight hours from her skin…the stench of failure.

"Come on, let's get you home."

* * *

She woke up in Malcolm's bed sometime the next day, smelling the faint musk of sex in his sheets. So Malcolm had gotten lucky. Good for him. How she wished a warm body could cover her now, soothe the pain. Lena. Missing Lena lived in her like breathing.

She let her mind slip back, ooze into a gentle state of semi-consciousness, but even then, Lena swirled about, yes, the edges of memories sharper now. She had met her six years ago, just as Spencer was beginning to hit her stride. She had just won the Emmy and was even more convinced she could get *May You* made. They had met on a plane back from New York in the most embarrassing of circumstances.

Spencer had sat in first class, clacking out her show's fourth season opener on her laptop when it began. The show was in trouble. Spencer could have told them that. *Lucifer* was a meat and potatoes cop drama losing share to two sophisticated lawyer/crime dramas opposite it. The producers loved the macho lead bad guy who had "escaped the jaws of hell" (prison) to become a good guy. Spencer was attempting to incorporate the seven different sets of notes to revive the story: change the tone of the series, introduce young hip characters, a father figure. No, a love interest. Bring in some kids' music. Make one of the characters a guitar player. But it wasn't working. It was ludicrous and she was angry.

Ba-boom. Ba-BOOM! Suddenly her heart was in her throat like a cement drill. Gripping the edge of her laptop, she made the mistake of peeking out the window and realized she was thirty thousand feet above the earth. Pink stained her neck, rushed up heat-flushed cheeks. Having a heart attack. Her hand grasped the closest thing to her. It happened to be the jacket sleeve of the woman sitting next to her.

"Please," she whispered urgently, "I…I think I'm having some sort of problem here."

"Tell me what I can do to help." The voice was low and resonant and made her feel immediately safer.

"I'm…" She heard the words topple from her mouth, a surreal out of body moment, "I…I think I'm having a heart attack."

"I'll get the flight attendant."

The woman rose, but Spencer couldn't bear dying alone, kept the woman's arm in a vise grip. "All they know how to do is unbuckle a seat-belt."

"They'll give you oxygen. It will calm you down."

Good. A plan. The flight attendant administered oxygen and then discreetly asked among the passengers whether a doctor was on board. Thank God, there was. He took Spencer's pulse, blood pressure and after a few questions, arrived at the same diagnosis as the emergency room doctor had when Spencer had been admitted two weeks earlier with the first of what would become many such attacks.

"Sounds like you've been under a helluva lot a stress lately." He turned to the flight attendant. "Please, two bottles of—what do you drink, Miss?"

"Drink? Jack Daniel's." The first thing that came to mind.

The flight attendant produced two baby bottles of amber liquid and Spencer politely gulped them down. Within five minutes she was feeling better and within ten, quite a bit calmer.

"Anxiety attacks are no fun," the doctor commiserated. "Do you have a doctor in L.A.?"

"No," Spencer answered weakly.

"Well, let me give you my card. Call me when you get settled and I'll give you some referrals."

"So…you don't think there's anything really wrong with me?" Spencer felt like a big baby but she needed reassurance.

"Nothing a few stiff drinks won't cure," he laughed. "Unfortunately alcohol's one of the easiest ways to treat panic. Just don't abuse it. Of course there are much better medicines that could really help you out."

"Well, thank you. I really appreciate it."

The doctor returned to his seat. Spencer's breathing returned to normal and she finally noticed the woman next to her. During her episode she hadn't been aware of the dark brown hair—almost black—the strong pointed nose, the exotic eyes, fine lips. Or the tall and slender build. She was striking. Not at all the kind of woman

Spencer was normally attracted to, but now that she had a moment to appreciate her, Spencer saw she was really quite beautiful.

"Hey...I'm...I'm sorry—"

"Don't worry. It's okay—"

"Sure know how to make a great first impression," Spencer deadpanned.

The woman smiled, and suddenly Spencer felt all the booze hit her stomach at once.

"How are you feeling?" Again the smooth calming tones.

"Much better. Although I could probably use another drink. For safety's sake." Spencer hesitated. "Can I buy you one for your troubles?"

When the flight attendant came by Spencer ordered them both drinks.

"Thanks again," Spencer said and tried out a smile as she lifted her glass to her seat mate.

"Don't mention it. I'm just glad you're okay."

They both took a sip. An awkward silence followed. Spencer supposed she should just let the woman get back to whatever she had been doing, leave her in peace, but she was afraid if she returned to her laptop the panic might reoccur.

"Do you live in L.A.?"

"Yes, well, actually L.A. and the Bay Area."

"Oh. What do you do?" Spencer asked. "Ughh—I hate when that's the first thing someone asks about you. What's your favorite book?"

The woman laughed. "I'm a fund raiser."

"Politics?" She tried to make her voice noncommittal.

The woman nodded. "I'm not much into fiction. I just finished Katherine Graham's biography. Does that count?"

Spencer smiled, more self-assured now "You raise money for the good guys or the bad guys?"

"The good guys of course. Don't worry I'm a Democrat."

"Now what gave me away?"

"You live in L.A. You look like you might be in the film business, no?"

"Yeah." Now Spencer was intrigued. This woman was good. "What gave me away this time?"

"I don't know." Lena narrowed her eyes, assessing Spencer until she felt her throat grow tight. "The Oliver Peoples glasses, the relaxed air—the jeans and black blazer—"

"Please, you're making me sound like a…a—" Spencer didn't even know what to say, but now wondered, had she really grown to look just like one of *them?*

"Some of my best friends are in the entertainment industry," she quipped, then smiled, her teeth straight and white, a smile so sexy Spencer felt her heart quicken, and momentarily feared another attack. "I've always found your world…intriguing."

She wasn't sure whether she should be insulted. "Yes, well politics is pretty intriguing itself."

"Oh we're much more endearing than people give us credit for," she said, a twinkle in her eye.

Spencer briefly wondered if the woman was family. No. She looked too straight, too upper-girls school prep, with a tender aloofness that drew Spencer in.

"Do you have family in L.A.?"

"Yes," she answered, sipping her drink.

"Kids?"

"A daughter. MacKenzie."

Well, so much for that. "How old?"

"She just had her first birthday."

"I'm Spencer." She offered her hand. "Spencer Atwood."

"Lena Kiriakis."

"Greek?"

"On my father's side, Spanish from my mother."

By her fourth drink Spencer found herself revealing her passion for film, waxing poetic about how much better black and white films had been and how depressing it was that people in her industry seemed to have less and less integrity. Lena reflected that their worlds were not so very different, that the idealism of politics rarely matched the process, but she believed in the system and that no matter how cynical people had become, the only thing that made sense to her was fighting for a world in which she could raise her daughter.

By the time they arrived in L.A. they had both gotten tipsy. They walked to baggage claim together, bonded by Spencer's bizarre mishap. Spencer was going to give her a business card, but it seemed out of place and inappropriate. They each gathered their luggage and stood awkwardly.

"God, I never have two drinks," Lena laughed. "I think I'm drunk."

"You? I *know* I'm drunk."

"But you're better?"

"Much." Spencer shuffled her garment bag from one hand to the other. "Hey, I really want to thank you for helping me out. I'm sure you wanted someone yakking your head off all the way back from New York, but the fact of the matter is, talking helped me to keep my mind off…off the other…"

"I enjoyed it. Really. Now I know the true story behind all those Hollywood moguls."

She grinned and her words seemed genuine, or maybe, Spencer thought, they were designed to be so that she wouldn't feel bad. Never had she second guessed so many people as she had since being in this town. In any event, Lena Kiriakis was a class act.

"Well, thanks again." Spencer began to head toward the sliding doors.

"Okay." Lena seemed to hesitate a moment, then thought better of it. "Take care."

"Yeah, you too."

Lena wheeled herself and her baggage out of Spencer's life—

Jesus Christ! The tea kettle shrilled from the kitchen, rousing Spencer from her ether memories. Now she was awake.

Malcolm peeked into the room, silently delivering a large latte with foam spilling down the side.

"Oh, sweetie, thanks," Spencer whispered groggily.

"I live to serve but one." Malcolm pecked her on the top of the head, then headed for the shower.

As she watched him retreat into the bathroom, she thought how well and long they had known each other in these past ten years.

* * *

Malcolm was perhaps the only actor Spencer knew who managed to always keep a level head. She had been immediately drawn to his gentle spirit, his irreverent calm in the face of so much idiocy, his exquisite humor.

She had met him while directing a weekend workshop exploring "the saucy but lovable character actor"—was it technique or something inherent in the actor's own personality that made him or her so recognizable and likeable?

"Like Una Merkel," Spencer suggested to a room full of blank faces. "Did anyone see *Saratoga?* Nineteen thirty-seven? You know, with Jean Harlow? Clark Gable?"

"Yeah," Malcolm jumped in, saving the moment. "You all know her. She was Brian Keith's housekeeper in *The Parent Trap.*" This actress they knew.

From that moment forward, Spencer and Malcolm became members of a mutually exclusive fan club, finding themselves increasingly simpatico and soon inseparable. Spencer first thought he had to be gay. He was too pretty not to be. His infectious smile produced straight small teeth. He had an exquisitely sculpted Roman nose, and beautiful eyes. But as they became good friends, Spencer realized he loved women as much as she did.

With Malcolm, she found consistency. And unconditionality. As was often the case in L.A., they might not see one another for weeks but still managed to check in daily for mood barometers, colorfully supplying the underlying details to the rating.

Metaphors were their favorite thing—a Ping-Pong play of words. Their topics ricocheting from failed relationships to obsessive attractions, to movies, books, and family dynamics, their bond growing with every ten-cent minute. Malcolm even became Spencer's in-house editor, the one she went to first, the kick-butt editor she knew would praise her, but in the same instant, the one person Spencer trusted more than anyone about her work. If Malcolm said it was working it was working, and if he said nothing, well, then, it wasn't.

Now as Spencer guzzled the last dregs of her latte, Malcolm read the *Times.* Folding the paper, he swiveled it around to Spencer. "Look at this."

She stared blankly at a piece of political savagery.

"So?" Malcolm urged. His finger pointed across the page under a classifieds ad for beach rentals. *NORTHWEST OREGON:*

Small but charming two bedroom cottage with ocean view on isolated strip. Perfect for writer/artist.

"What about it?"

"Get out of here. Take a few months off."

"I don't know…"

"Call it a writing sabbatical."

"That would imply I have something to say—"

"Listen Destructo Woman, I'm not going to listen to any self-defeatist bullshit today. I don't have the patience for it."

In all honesty, something about escaping appealed to her, but then the idea of packing up for an expedition of Lewis & Clark proportions, the total exhaustion, evaporated it.

"I think taking some time to get your bearings might not be a bad idea."

"If I run out of town now, I'm finished."

Malcolm's expression said what he was too kind not to say out loud. That Spencer was already finished. The best thing to do was to fade from everyone's memories for a while. In a town devoted to voluntary Alzheimer's she might actually have a chance of reinstating herself in the future.

"Think about it," Malcolm said, finishing his coffee. "I've got to get to work."

"Oh, yeah, you're one of those 'employed' people."

"Someone's got to support your misery." Malcolm's warm fingers gently wrapped about her own, and squeezed softly. He bent, kissed Spencer's forehead, then was off.

Spencer stared at the ad for the coastal properties. A very long time.

* * *

Two weeks later Spencer drove down the gravelly path to the cottage. Without the very specific directions given over the phone, she would never have found the turn-off that wound mysteriously through a darkened glen and then, quite suddenly, emerged into the sun. The ocean appeared between several boughs of evergreen that had met years ago and wed.

Translate *small* to cramped. *Charming* to rustic enough to apply for the historical registry. She knew within five minutes she wouldn't be able to manage for more than a day at the outside. She had to admit it. She'd become a snob, used to bell-hopping attendance, the concierge existing for your sole convenience, room service for royalty. Spencer hadn't always been aroused by luxury. Years ago, the first time an evening maid asked if she wanted the bed "turned down" she had peered at the woman stupidly and said the bed had already been made. But she had gotten used to the small things that made life, if not more illusory, more tolerable.

A heaving tired thing this cottage was. The ceiling sagged, its walls wheezed in the wind, the planking moaned with each footfall up the front steps to the weather-eaten deck. But nothing could have prepared Spencer for its inner soul. She held her breath and simply stood in awe. She couldn't wait to tell Malcolm about it—you couldn't make up this kind of decor. It was the stuff of story-telling—the madwoman's cottage—relics smattered about with no particular motif, a bad beach scene here, a Chinese float there, sea-going gee-gaws, cheap souvenirs from faraway countries. Two opposing variations of still-life bowls of fruit hung over the kitchenette. Rows and rows of age-riffled books tilted and leaned into each other on built-in shelves that ran not quite parallel to each other. The only thing to commend it, really, was the fireplace. Lovingly hand-built with ocean rock, each stone probably scouted one by one during long beach walks, it was huge and comforting. The room smelled as if the last tenant had used it liberally, for it emitted an ancient ashiness that mingled with the brine-musty pervasion of ocean that lingered in every corner. She briefly wondered if she could somehow smother the fresh air with air-freshener.

And then it hit her. She could feel the panic rise in her throat. Where was the TV? This was the age of remedial channel surfing. It must be cleverly concealed within the antique dresser against the wall. No. Perhaps in the back room. Again, no luck. Not even a small black and white. No TV. The term *simply perish* came to mind and then she became embarrassed (only momentarily mind you) by how ridiculous she had become. But the truth was, she could not live without a TV. TV was her soma. Her drug of choice. C-Span kept her warm nights when she couldn't sleep, and when she was too exhausted to think, she sank into yesteryear on Nickelodeon, reliving late nights in New Jersey while Lucy mangled "Vitameata-vegimen." How could she possibly still laugh at that show? She had seen it a million times. She'd give this place one night and then find a room up the coastline that came with HBO.

The drizzle that fell over everything like misted perfume was the perfect backdrop for her mood. Besides, she could not will herself to get back in the car after the horrific drive from L.A. She had left at 2:30 am and her head was still buzzing from the trip. She had been determined to do the drive in one day, afraid she would turn back if she stopped for the night in a hotel.

Her butt hurt. She was dead tired. She sat at the window ledge and peered into the light fog curling off the ocean, becoming witness to a mystical, ethereal beachscape. She gazed so long her eyelids began to falter. She mustered just enough energy to walk to the bed that sat square in the middle of the room and collapsed.

* * *

Where do I begin? At the beginning. Or in my case, at the end. Who is Spencer? Spencer is me.

She is how I remember things. Movie scenes. Third person narrative. So much of my life I have felt like a "she"—I could not BE in the world, so I wrote about it.

"You are quite accomplished at reciting the events of your life with glib indifference," Therapist observes one afternoon when I regale her with my real father's system of reward. (Ten "atta girls" and you got a bottle of your choice. An "Oh Shit!" and you started back at the beginning. I never got past three "atta girls.") "And while you're a fine storyteller, I'm not all that interested in the circumstances. I want to know how you feel about them."

How I feel about them? If I knew that, chances were I wouldn't have been there.

How should I feel about running in quicksand? How could I admit following my dreams had become so painful?

Someone once told me horses only have so many downhill miles before they are cut off at the knees. And while doing research for a character who was trying to have a baby, I discovered a female fetus possesses eight million eggs, but by the time one starts her menses the rate of attrition leaves a mere half million left. No wonder the fertility clock slams into gear by the time a woman is in her mid-twenties!

What if dreams work the same way? You begin with an endless number of precious ideas, visions, concepts all fecund and fertile, a lush womb nurturing their growth but as you work your way through them, much as women miscarry so goes our failure of dreams to thrive. Ninety-five percent of the time your dreams wind up dead on arrival. Take care to snag them quickly before the body and spirit are simply too old and tired to make them work. Before the lush placenta of your soul grows too thin to conceive.

Therapist coos, "You can choose not to be devastated."

But would losing dreams ever, ever be tolerable?

"What I'm saying," Therapist repeats patiently, "is that you have the choice not to be devastated by these things. You can make your life more about you and less about your projects, so that when your professional life doesn't work out, you have other things to fall back on."

"I have plenty to fall back on," I snarl. If nothing else I had memories to fall back on.

"Then it shouldn't be so difficult for you. Remember, Spencer, when I say devastated I don't mean disappointment. There's a mile of heartache between the two."

* * *

The first few days at the cottage I simply sat, wondering at my ability to do nothing. Inertia became me. I sat stunned, shocked that my script had so recklessly derailed. Staring at the waves, I tried like hell to empty my mind of the past few weeks. Hell, the past decade.

I made a few half-hearted vows to find another place with a TV, but mostly gazed through the large picture window that became my screen and found myself as mesmerized by the endless waves as I had been by a dubbed laugh track. This exclusively indoor sport lasted several days, until a minor jolt of ambition finally prompted me to lug the stuffed lime green armchair from the living room to the deck, the flimsy deck rail serving as a foot prop. With the lulling fresh air my lids grew heavy and free-floating associations became wilder and less connected. The undulating melody of the ocean worked itself into the mysterious journey in my mind, lumbering to places long ago forgotten, dark corners that jarred my slumber. I woke with a start, trying to grasp the foggy remnants, but they dissipated before they made any sense.

I looked out at the world. The sun was brilliant, the sky a dazzling blue, the trees an iridescent green, the ocean a deep aquamarine. It was the kind of scene that would inspire swelling violins, or at least a hotel painting. I thought I should meet it halfway. Take a walk. A picture. Anything.

"Nah," I grumbled, returning to the unmade bed. I tumbled into it and fell into a dreamless void.

Now that I had nothing to do my mind had become a vacuum, thoughts hurling into my consciousness…the memories, as relentless as the waves of one crest hitting another, an undertow swirling in from nowhere and an altogether different pattern emerging. Cross purposes and undercurrents slamming into each other to deliver the unexpected and unpredictable.

Those first few days I sat in my chair on the deck, shut my eyes, smelling the earth and sun, snuggling down into memories of my childhood. Recollections—patched and hazy, a peaceful yearning in them for sun-slanted rooms, my mother in white Sophia Loren dresses, knobbly kneed kids slurping on home-made popsicles, my father a booming shadow, and my sisters and I playing silly made-up games.

I tried to think back to my earliest memory. A black and white photo jolted into my mind. I was maybe four. My eyes are staring up and my lips are pursed into a concentration of surprise as if remarking, "Oh, is this life then? Is this what I signed on for…?"

* * *

It was shortly after Spencer turned four that Cal left her mother. For the longest time the only way she could keep him alive was by gazing at the smoothly filtered photos pressed in a worn leather album. She always lingered over a particular black and white photo displaying the best of Cal's muscular GI body. He is heaving her older sister, Rebecca, up by her feet, which are engulfed in his thick beefy hands, while Jill's hair is flattened on his washboard tummy, her knees flopping outward like a rag doll. And Spencer? Spencer is a blur of motion and indiscernible features, caught in mid-flight as she tumbles from a handstand. She had stolen the photo when she left home and has kept it in her wallet all these years. On a rare occasion she will study it and fill with a nostalgic melancholy, but it is more for what is lacking in the photograph, than what it has captured.

Before Cal left her mother, Elise, the family lived in the manager's quarters of the Highlander Motel, surrounded by a constant jumble of people and luggage. The chiming front door bell and outside traffic mingled with a soundtrack of voices as college students and assorted tourists checked in. Though it was nestled against the fumes of one of the busiest strips in downtown Boulder, Colorado, the motel had an awe-inspiring view of the mountains. Seeing those gargantuan forms lift into the sky, painted against the steel blue, was certainty, a stark contrast to the escalating arguments between Cal and her mother. His edict that his own daughters not call him Daddy because it was too "sissy" about summed up his sensitivity. Spencer found him a perfect baseline of machismo for the character Drake Lucifer. She stole some of her best moments for *Lucifer* from Cal.

Spencer's sister Jill—*my little Jilly Bean*—and she shared a twin bed in a slanted attic room. Sometimes in the night she could hear the muted voices from downstairs, and would turn over and snuggle into the warmth of her sister. They slept into the pale indigo of morning, their bodies entwined, limbs akimbo like two puppies, matted pixie bangs entangled, Jill's three to Spencer's five. How did they come out so different starting from the same place? Even more different: Rebecca.

Rebecca was the oldest by three years, but certainly not the wisest. She was fiercely *dependent*. Daddy's favorite girl, even when she was supposed to have been a boy. Since she wasn't, Spencer got the name originally meant for her. She also got all of Rebecca's hand-me-downs, but what second child of lower working class parents didn't in the sixties?

The Atwood girls loved the treasure trove of the motel grounds, a scenic backdrop for any game their imagination could muster. During their waking hours they fought pirates in the motel's pool, helped shipwrecked mates, and time and again switched roles in the *Creature from the Black Lagoon*—with as badly stilted conversation and special effects.

Ojibwa Indian coursed through their sun-stained bodies, and Cal screamed for his "niggers" in the summer as they tanned a deep brown. The old ladies tsk-tsk'd at the word, but Cal seemed oblivious to his redneck insults. The visiting grande dames loved the three unsupervised girls, doting on them after buoying in the deep end of their ocean with their multi-flowered bathing caps. They fed the girls burnt roasted peanuts, like zoo animals, laughing at their antics as they spread Coppertone over shaky jowls.

Fear never entered into the picture in those days. When Cal waded into the deep end and Spencer stood on the edge of the brittle pebbled diving board, he held open his thick beefy arms, and shouted "Make me proud!" What else was she to do, but jump? Swallowed into the chlorine-blue abyss, when she came up for air she doggy-paddled for all she was worth to the safety of his huge Charles Atlas arms. "Atta girl!" he laughed proudly.

"Where is your mother?" Therapist inevitably asks. "You haven't once talked about your mother."

Spencer doesn't remember her mother. Elise is but a hazy image in her white tight-belted dresses, always working, being responsible—doing best what Cal didn't. Cal loved to show off her legs and her talent at the piano. He told her how to dress, complained about her German accent, the way she smiled. Cal was the original control junkie and with all his commands, he stood out in klieg lights—Jill and even Rebecca shared with her the sepia-edged moments of her childhood. But her mother? She's barely a faded photo. It seemed the longer her mother spent with Cal, the more she ceased to exist.

And then the fighting changed, Cal's absence louder than harsh words as the girls picked at silent dinners of macaroni and cheese, hamburgers and gorp (tuna casserole) at the pink-flecked Formica kitchen table in the back room. Spencer could never escape fast enough, excusing herself as the last bite hit her mouth to roam the hotel grounds.

Late one night she ran outside, exhausted by the tension that lived between her parents. It was very dark—one of those black nights in the deep of winter. Her breath furled like a cartoon dragon as she ran to the back of the parking lot. Huge snow drifts planed over the cars, and handrails, and covered the pool. She walked in the gleaming light of the motel lamps and stopped to catch her breath. Crystals glimmered, shiny and adamantine, the snow white-blue, the heavenly sky filled with stationary snowflakes twinkling back at her. There wasn't another living soul around. She was going to flop down and make a snow-angel, but became so mesmerized by the iridescence and perfect sheets of snow, she decided not to ruin them. She was stunned by perfection. It swelled inside her chest with nowhere to go. Here was a spiritual law of beauty and she had just tasted it. And if things could be so lovely, surely nothing could happen to her parents.

"So why do you think Cal left your mother?" Therapist asks.

"Because she was boring," I answer haughtily.

But the truth lies somewhere between Cal being a child and marrying five times before he did finally settle. He was a primitive man. He had even raised his offspring like animals. "You train 'em young, just like a dog," he liked to boast. "As they grow older and can understand things, then you give them rein...but until then—" ZWACK! His thick stubby fingers would whip into a fist like lightning and he would grunt to emphasize his point as he slammed the table.

Lest you get the wrong impression, understand he was only half Neanderthal. He was also master of fun, the king of cackles, and he remained forever young. In Spencer's kinder moments she can give him his due as a man of innovation and brilliance—it is from his genetic pool that she had been gifted with the ability to think outside of the proverbial box.

She kept asking her mother when Cal was ever coming back, but Elise never answered. So she stopped asking and after a while it didn't matter so much to her that he was gone. She had plenty to occupy her mind because with Cal leaving they had been somehow magically transported to the house on Thirty-fifth Street.

It was the era of boxy, cramped houses in a lower-middle class neighborhood, with a zillion kids, that framed the happiest part of Spencer's childhood. Those years were the sanest and most treasured. Just Mom and the three Atwood girls eating yet more abundant portions of gorp and home-made pizza on Fridays.

Poor Mom. With her clunky German accent, and no chance in hell of successfully raising her daughters on a secretary's salary, she could do little more than try to get through each day. She could no longer afford babysitters and enlisted Rebecca to fend for Spencer and Jill.

A thirteen-inch black and white TV sat at the end of the *Jetsons'* Formica dinner table so they could catch *The Munsters, The Addams Family* and *Get Smart,* while dining on leftovers that lasted through the week. Spencer's mother was never the cook she wanted to be, even years later when she had more time and economy. What she failed to understand was that she created the kind of food that made America strong. Meat and potatoes served with intent and love. Her spaghetti always tasted the best to Spencer. Her burnt carrots on the lamb the most flavorful. Even her gorp was the best gorp she ever had. Food isn't the sum of its recipes, it's tradition, memory and love. And every so often for a treat, Elise would drive her frenzied beasts in the little blue Bug to the Dairy Queen for a Dilly Bar. It was a little slice of heaven.

On special nights—like during tornado watch, or when Elise came home late from a party tipsy and in a great mood—they all got to sleep in Mom's bed, snuggled next to one another, Spencer feeling the primal safety she so desperately sought. The next morning she would act all grown up swiping sips of her mother's cold coffee because she'd developed an addiction to Coffee-mate. Could life have been more perfect? But as they swam along, wonderfully content, blissfully naïve about what they didn't have, the first of the crosscurrents rushed in and brought a shark. His name was Jonathon and he became their surrogate father.

* * *

One of the locals told me there was a path that ostensibly belonged to the cottage. It trailed from the cliff top down to the beach. That is, if I wanted to risk my life taking it. The path was a jungle—a thicket of blackberry vines, overgrown sea grass and gnarled roots blocking the sheer drop to the ocean.

"Break a leg ifn' yer not careful," came a codgerly warning from behind me.

Darrell was the only real local on the isolated strip of beach. The other seven cottages, including mine, were rentals, mostly vacant while their absentee owners lived in Seattle or Los Angeles. But Darrell was pure beachbum. He used to run the liquor store and was now retired, both from selling and imbibing. His hair was as white as snow and his curmudgeonly grumbling belied a gentle spirit.

"So how bad can it be?" I asked, impatient.

"How bad depends on how bad ya make it." He looked me over, head to toe. Took his time about it too. "You seem like one a them athletic types. But you can't get through there now. Gotta chop yer way through. Then you can follow the old path by the railroad ties they worked into the side of the hill for stairs. I got a' ax up to the shed you can borrow. I'd help ya myself but I got a bum back." I would later discover during one of our late evening talks that he actually had a herniated liver and had been helicoptered to Portland when it burst forth like a broken dam of Johnny Walker.

I decided I could probably take a whack at it. I followed him to the shed where he handed me an ax and a shovel.

"Good luck."

"Thanks," I said to his swiftly retreating figure then straggled back to where the path began.

I sighed. It would take a lot of work. I had done nothing for ten days. Nothing. Even though inaction was as foreign to me as deep sea diving for pearls.

"The question is not whether you will succeed, but why you are so driven." Therapist revisits this theme at least once a session. "What's behind your need—"

"I don't think it's all that bizarre—"

"Your zeal borders on freneticism."

"It's really very simple. I am driven to succeed because I am a type A personality." My mother had bequeathed me a highly charged nervous system. Cal had given me vision. "Is it really necessary to see everything as some deep-seated neurosis?"

The waves below beckoned to me. Come closer. Come closer from your throne, Queen of Nothing, and step into the tide. My foot hit against the first railroad tie and after that there was nothing but a wall of wild blackberries. I needed a weed cutter. I ventured toward Cannon Beach, the Cape Cod-ian burg several miles north, its quaint artsiness slowly being overtaken by industry. The lumber store was doing booming business. I picked up a saw, a weed cutter and several hundred feet of half-inch cordoned rope.

Since I was in town anyway I stopped at the local grocer, picked up some canned foods, coffee, wine and bread. When I saw the cover of a newspaper I flinched, a surreal feeling floating over me. It was as if my existence, such as it was, was solid, but that the rest of the world was some sort of fantasy. I hurriedly paid and drove like a madwoman back to my refuge from humankind.

I dumped my tools at the mouth of the path and began with the weed cutter. Within a half hour my arms were molten lead and my skin burned with thorn rash and fatigue. I dropped the cutter and assessed my progress. I had only made it to the second step.

I packed up my tools and hauled them back to the cottage and dumped them on the deck. Get real. There were two thousand beach accesses on this coastline. What was the point of clearing this one?

I opened a bottle of cheap generic burgundy, my mouth caving in from the dryness, and sat to watch the translucent hues of sunset, the horizon of luscious peach turning to crimson lavender. I held my breath at the simple beauty. I didn't move for moments, captured by the stillness of dusk. In that moment, I knew I had to finish. This was my goddamn front yard and I needed to take care of it. It was my path and I was going to finish it, if it was the last thing I was to do.

* * *

Now that I have the luxury of revelation in my cave, I realize that purpose is a pure thing. How often we convolute it by attaching erroneous emotion to it. Drive carries purpose to its natural conclusion. Passion is a byproduct. Single-mindedness is the state of mind that makes purpose work. But purpose, in and of itself, is impulse to survive. Without it we wander, lost, abandoned souls with relics of dreams and ideas. I found purpose in the path. And I suppose the path gave me a glimmer at self respect.

* * *

My days took on a semblance of routine. I woke up, downed several murky cups of coffee to fortify my resolve and dragged my tools back to the path. My progress was slow, exacting. But every day I could detect more of a swath in the hillside.

I'd been working on the path for nearly a week now. As I chopped at roots, sawed large branches, swatted flies and spider webs, my mind wandered aimlessly and unprotected. With the feel of the earth under my fingernails, the rigor of physicality, the acrid smell of sun-singed foliage, my childhood came to the forefront constantly, prompting associations about the consecutive purpose of every day, whether it was creating elaborate games of espionage with the neighbor kids, hitting fly balls at the cherry tree, or simply being alone with one of the books I'd "borrowed," sneaking outdoors to read behind the rotting tool shed. Each day was honest.

I perched on step eight and lit a cigarette. When had I lost the honesty? It had been the one trait that had been applied to me consistently. Until the end. Until I became so fearful of saying anything that remotely resembled the truth because I was playing so many ends against the middle.

The sun dappled through the leaves, warming my face as I thought back to when life changed—always referring to my mother's marriage to Hank as B.J.—Before Jonathon, and A.J.—After Jonathon.

* * *

Hank was a salesman at the company Elise worked for. He was a heavyset man with thinning sandy-blond hair, who loved to eat and have a good time. Spencer's mother had finally found someone she could discuss classical music with. Hank played the violin and was only too happy to baby-sit the "charming Atwood girls," as he referred to them, every Tuesday and Thursday night while their mother took piano lessons. It was a good thing because Elise was wasting her hard-earned money having to break from the piano every few minutes to shush her girls as they giggled over goofy Mr. Findelman. He was so skinny he resembled a stork, always stooped over Elise in a shroud of smoke, his shoulder blades poking through his sweat stained shirts as she played. When he passed away from a massive aneurysm Spencer had her first taste of soul-wracking guilt, and would choke before she would giggle at anyone for months afterward.

Hank wasn't a sit-and-study kind of babysitter. He whooped it up with all the kids in the neighborhood. Red rover, ditch it, kickball. He'd grasp tender wrists and "spin the statue," never running out of energy as the kids toppled into one another, dizzily intoxicated. Pretty soon the Atwood girls thought Tuesdays and Thursdays were the greatest days, because it meant Hank was coming to baby-sit. Then one Wednesday morning it looked like he'd stayed for a spend-over. And from that moment on he was there a lot.

After their honeymoon Hank moved his new wife and girls to Portland, Oregon, where Hank's family business was located. Their marriage and all that it entailed, driving their station wagon ahead of the huge moving van to live in a new neighborhood, was like a dream to Spencer. Hank came from an actual family that had aunts and uncles and a great-grandmother and endless loads of relatives. Since they had never had any family of their own it never occurred to Spencer that besides scads of presents at Christmas, becoming part of a large dynasty came with secrets, infighting and the family skeletons. For every wonderful holiday dinner, decked out with roast beef and ham, there was an equal amount of bitter complaints, squabbles and long-time feuds.

Years later she would discover from her favorite Aunt Carol, that no one wanted Hank, especially Jonathon, his younger brother, to take on a wife who had three half-grown kids. He was so young. It was too much. It took him away from traveling for the family business—selling medical supplies—and Jonathon complained about it whenever he got the opportunity. And what about kids of his own, his mother fretted. But once they met the Atwood girls, they must have been perfectly enchanted, for Hank's family took them in from that moment forward.

The girls stayed with Grandma and "Pop Pop" while Hank took his new bride on a week-long honeymoon. They tried to fit into their laconic lives, the steady hours passing by in half-hour chunks of *Petticoat Junction* and *I Love Lucy* reruns. Meals were set up on TV trays and there was never a breakfast without Entenmann's crumb cake and freeze-dried Folgers.

Surprisingly, it was Pop Pop who indoctrinated Spencer into the world of arched-brow acting, the Machiavellian plots of *Another World* and *Days of Our Lives*. While Grandma and Aunt Carol were off to work, Spencer sat with her new grandfather, an overweight and ultra-conservative Republican, who poured them glass after glass of Lipton's iced tea, while they glutted themselves on the deprivation and swooning romance of the soaps. Like Pop Pop, Spencer soon became hooked on the stories, anxious for the following day's melodrama, all fodder for her overripe imagination and the basis of her first terribly overwrought short stories. Oh, how she loved the low-seas drama of it all.

But then Hank and Elise returned and they were moved to Gresham—a working-class suburb south of Portland—into a house that not only had two levels, but bedrooms for days. It was a cheap Colonial built in the fifties, made to look like more than it was, but to Spencer's undiscerning eye it qualified as a mansion compared to their small box in Boulder. Even though she and Jill still shared the same bunk beds, Rebecca had her own room with a new princess bed and Marcia Brady make-up set. There was a living room upstairs and a family room downstairs, with yet another room for Hank's den. Pretty soon the family acquired a cat and a dog and two TV's, and it seemed like the all-American Dream had come true for the broken hausfrau and her three unwieldy kids. And then Hank had a stroke.

* * *

I rustled myself up early, drank my coffee and headed out to the path. Every day now I worked on it, more and more eager to see it finished. Worked until my muscles would not receive another synapse. Worked it until I could see some progress. Darrell hunched over me squawking about how to use a chainsaw.

"Yer gonna end up like hamburger ifn' yer not careful. This is men's work. Why don' ya call the manager and have them do this?"

"I'm enjoying myself, Darrell."

"Yer sure not goin' at it like it's some goddamn vacation. You been out here everyday bustin' hump."

"I know." I insinuated a good day's work might not be so bad for him.

"If it weren't for my bum back..." He let that hang in the breeze. "I'm goin' fishin' later on. You ever go fishin'?"

"No." I stopped what I was doing, lit a cigarette. "I've never actually seen the point in it."

"Well, that's just it. There ain't no point in it."

"Then why?"

"It's just the doin' of it. Bein' out in the boat, in the breeze, havin' a beer. 'Course not me anymore." And then he recalled his glorious career as a drunk, interesting stories really, a steely-edged flame in his eyes, as he reminisced about the bad ol' days. "Kinda like this path here. Hell, you can go down two tenths of a mile to the park's beach access just like I can go to the Mariner and pick up a slab of salmon. It's just the doin' of it."

And with that I got back to work.

I dug until my arms cramped, grasping at tethered roots that had lived on my path for years, digging deeper to remove the growth, exorcising all signs of it, hoping it would never come back. Pulling with all my strength I slipped and fell square on my butt in the slick mud.

How the hell far down did this root go for Christ's sake? I got back up and dug some more. How far back did I have to go?

"You have to go back as far as is necessary," Therapist directs, "to find out when it began."

* * *

She often wondered what poor Hank went through when he had his strokes, and if he could ever know what would happen to his family as a result of them. He was first diagnosed as having suffered a minor stroke. But in those silent hours before dawn, a massive seizure almost killed him. Paralyzed on his right side. In the prime of his life.

The family was devastated. Hank lay in the hospital bed for weeks, making no sign that he knew his wife or daughters. Spencer's heart leapt out to him when Uncle Jonathon drove them to the first of many visits. Pale and crumpled, Hank questioned with a child's fragile simplicity. Spencer had to cover Jill's mouth when she began to holler about Hank drinking his own pee from the hand-held urinal, or eating the flowers someone had brought for him, grunting in pleasure, as English was now a second language next to his aphasic jumbling. After weeks in the hospital, he was transferred to a rehabilitation clinic where he would stay for the next year.

Hank had been the company's number one salesman. With his jovial manner he had made repeat customers of their clients. But with him gone, the business began to lose money. Even so, Jonathon tried to keep things afloat, constantly lending Elise money, until it became clear to everyone that they were at risk of losing their house. It was Uncle Jonathon's idea to move in with them, to pay the mortgage until Hank got back on his feet—even when there was no imminent sign of that happening.

Uncle Jonathon was sweet to Elise, and he treated her girls like his own, playing catch in the backyard, telling ghost stories late one night when the electricity went out, taking them to matinees on the weekend, even if they were films that made their mother shudder, like *The Good, the Bad and the Ugly*. The girls adored him. Jonathon treated them far more as grownups than Hank or Mom did, allowing them a freedom both titillating and terrifying. He let them drive the car in the neighborhood, help him mix drinks and then allowed each of them a sip of his screw drivers, saying it was good for young girls to get plenty of vitamin C.

Sometimes when Spencer and Rebecca visited Jonathon's apartment, before he moved in with them, they would sneak through his things and watch Godzilla movies while he went into the bedroom with one of his girlfriends and shut the door.

"He's got more women on the line than AT&T," Pop Pop who worked for the phone company, would grumble about his youngest son. But in his complaint was a swaggery pride. It was a well known fact that Jonathon was quite the lady's man. Spencer and Rebecca used to wish their mother had married him instead of Hank because Jonathon was far more handsome with his dark brown hair, his hawk-like nose and square jaw. The only thing weak about his features were his eyes, a paint thinner blue, often bloodshot.

Spencer was terribly excited when Jonathon moved in. He became her comrade in a lonely world. He also quickly became her mentor, her Svengali, and, in a strange way, an antidote to her mother's pastel world of *Better Homes and Gardens*. As far as Spencer was concerned, Elise was solely preoccupied by sewing patterns and knitting needles, by long hours in the wallpaper shops, where she exhausted herself with indecision while she tormented her daughters with boredom. Spencer wasn't sure, but she believed there was a point at which she wanted the intimacy of sharing things with her mother—would have done anything to feel as if they could talk about something that didn't have to do with the damn house. But her mother seemed determined not to know who Spencer was.

Jonathon's world was far more fascinating and his interests quickly became Spencer's. He began to pick and choose what she would read. He started her off on books Hank would never have dreamed of letting her read from his library. Like an addict she holed herself up in her room, her imagination running wild as she lost herself in *Peyton Place*, the *Fire Island* books and anything by Jacqueline Susann. She consumed *The Catcher in the Rye* over and over again just to taste the dirty words. Jonathon shared his love of movies with Spencer and began taking her exclusively to matinees with him, much to her mother's chagrin. She didn't think it was such a good idea for him to spend so much time with Spencer and not the other girls. But she never told him that directly—she just complained to Spencer.

Off Jonathon and Spencer would go. They were mad for the spaghetti westerns. Spencer used to tell Jonathon he reminded her of Clint Eastwood. "What? I'm better lookin' than that!" he'd wink. A re-release of *The Graduate*, *Patton*, and as an eleventh birthday present, *Carnal Knowledge*. Spencer was so adult. So urbane. Jonathon and she would discuss the movies and books over dinner, leaving her mother shaking her head. She just didn't get it. Jonathon and Spencer had far more in common than she and her mother could ever dream of sharing. And with that bond she quite naturally took to holding over her mother's head all the things she couldn't possibly understand.

And Jonathon fostered their division. He was different with Elise now. Where he had previously been almost flirtatious— kidding her all the time about "how damn lucky Hank is," pulling out her chair, opening car doors for her—listening to her go on and on about redecorating the entryway he now shut her down as soon as she opened her mouth.

One night Spencer had even caught him cornering their mother in the kitchen, giving her a peck on the cheek as he convinced her to have a drink with him, and Spencer thought her childish fantasies were coming true. Her mother would leave Hank and marry Jonathon and they'd all live happily ever after! But that was when he was still polite—when familial love was still a shining light and they were still children he could be a child with. Before responsibility and food on the table and shackles on his weekends took over. When he realized he couldn't bring a different girl round every few nights and have his way with her. Pop Pop and Grandma set him down and explained his responsibilities. Endlessly. He was only thirty-four to Elise's thirty-seven and ten years younger than Hank. How was he to know, at that tender age, what hell parenting could be and that raising three imaginative and energetic children could break even the strongest man?

The first change in their relationship came when Jonathon asked Spencer to help him fix great-grandma's heirloom chest so that her mother could store extra blankets in it. The trunk's hinges had rusted, making it difficult to open, and Jonathon had winked at Spencer and said, "Come on mate, help an ol' seaman out."

Spencer held his screwdriver, chisel, and hammer, an obedient and fawning lackey handing him his tools as he asked for them. He needed a larger screwdriver to take out the old bracket and told Spencer to wait while he went to the basement to get it. While he was gone she decided to surprise him and fix the hinge herself. He would be so happy. Her chest filled with excitement as she furiously tried to loosen the screws, using her whole body's weight to untighten the rusted works.

THWACK! at the side of her head. She saw black for an instant, as if she had run into the wall.

"Goddamnit, Spence, are you out of your fuckin' mind?" Jonathon shoved her aside. It was his hand—his hand that had slapped the side of her head. "You want to ruin this perfectly good chisel?"

He turned to her, menacing as he held up the tool, its smooth shaft just catching the afternoon sunlight. "What the hell were you thinking?" She was mute.

"You never, I mean NEVER, use a chisel as a screwdriver! Jesus Fuckin' Christ!" Jonathon railed, at which point her mother came in.

"What's going on?" Elise asked tentatively as Spencer began to whimper.

"Get your sissy daughter out of my sight. I knew I couldn't count on you." He glared at Spencer as if he had found dog shit on his shoe, then turned away.

Before her mother could say a word Spencer ran to her bedroom and threw herself on the bed, crying for hours. She didn't feel the welt throbbing at the side of her head. All she could think about was how she had disappointed Jonathon and that he would never, ever see her in the same way. Hadn't she just read a few weeks earlier in one of the books he gave her how everyone, at one point or another, served up huge disappointments to loved ones and once having failed them, could never fully return to a whole relationship? At the time she'd struggled with the concept. Did that mean people couldn't forgive or just wouldn't?

It was in response to all their little human foibles that Jonathon created The System. One night Spencer came home late for dinner and was aghast to learn that for this transgression she would not be enjoying cheesecake that night for dessert. She tried to explain, but Jonathon wasn't in the mood for excuses. A week later he swiped a bowl of ice-cream right out from Rebecca's hands. "Didn't I tell you? You lost dessert for being rude to your mother."

The few times Elise tried to defend her daughters on one of his charges they got double whatever the punishment was, and she quickly retired her defense. Soon TV Marks topped the Dessert Marks. It seemed to Spencer that Jonathon went out of his way to create an elaborate scheme of punishments that would shape the core of Jill's, Rebecca's and her deprivation for years to come. TV Marks cost a half hour of television but they were only allowed to watch a half hour per school night, anyway. A Leaving-on-the-Light Mark at five cents a whack depleted their quarter allowance very quickly. Jonathon's "Marks" were carefully chosen to inflict the most damage. Chances were if Elise had made one of their favorite desserts that night, whoever was the offender would be watching *Star Trek*, mooning about Mom's creamy cheese cake. If it was Wednesday, dimes to donuts Spencer would be missing her favorite show. She lost an entire season of *Here Come the Brides.*

Jonathon knew the TV schedule by heart, and meted out sentences not to serve the crime, but to serve his power, his whim like a torpedo directed at one's desire. Like the finger he flicked at their heads, the velocity akin to a bullet rattling their skulls. Or slamming their heads together to emphasize a point. They never knew when he might strike. Fear ruled. And a daily dose will do you.

Then he began leaving notes all over the house, reprimanding the "Atwood extravagances," repeatedly pointing out the cost of their existence. "Only four sections of toilet-paper allowed," "One teaspoon of mayonnaise per sandwich" "If you haven't gone number two don't flush the toilet for three pees."

And the nice man, the man who had played and laughed with them over at his apartment, the man whose tenor Spencer thought she would never tire of as he sang ballads from The Beatles and Peter, Paul and Mary—his voice began to change. A nastiness crept into his words, a taunting, a warning, a chilling suggestion that cut deep into her spine. And the more he drank the nastier he got.

Teasing became his favorite pastime. It wasn't just the punitive marks, or his tirades at Jill or sneering humiliation of Rebecca's love for dance. He would mock her endlessly over her passion for ballet, a "faggy" occupation he would articulate by licking his pinky and smearing it over a foppish eyebrow. Though Spencer had no way to grasp onto the form that was her mother, she hated the way he belittled her, demanded an entitlement that she serve his needs before those of her children, cheapening her while he clutched tightly to every dollar he allotted her to run the household.

Terror makes people act out in strange ways. Predictably Rebecca, whom he had crowned Princess Summer Winter Spring and Fall, retreated to her princess room, and made plans for her royal escape to move in with Cal, who was now living near Spokane. Spencer dove headlong into the world of books and movies her very savior had given her. Poor Jill had begun to giggle in her chair at dinner, making faces. Like nervous tics they became her constant companion.

Gobbling like a turkey, her cheeks bulging, eyes popping, she began to chew her milk, seemingly unable to stop. Even when

Jonathon's harsh voice rose as he began to count to three—the terror of those simple syllables—she still chewed her milk. He pulled out the belt and whipped her until she could barely walk. Forced to return to the table and finish her dinner, wincing as she sat, Jill nonetheless set her jaw to a tremble of its former movement, a hint of vindication in her sky-blue eyes.

Each of the girls withdrew into her own little cocoon of resentment, separately developing into monarchs of revenge. The more he punished, the more they began to hate him. For Spencer to hate a man who clearly favored her, whose lap she endlessly coveted, wrapping her arms about his stalwart neck and saying "I love you, Uncle Jono," created a twisted sense of fealty—after all he had saved her from her mother and poverty. But whom was she loyal to anyway? How could she love and hate him in the same breath?

How could this gentle man who snuggled them close on the couch and entertained them with Holden Caulfield college-day stories, who taught them about the stock market, cigar spewing nasty smoke as if he were the baron of good will and fortune, be the same dreaded villain each night after seven o'clock? Spencer had once counted on their closeness, the bond of intimacy that she walked like a tightrope, an abyss of pastel on her mother's side, a black hole of inky shame on the other.

The man he became as he drank, his bitterness provoking a belligerent monster... His drinking raged along with his outbursts, long nights of bellowing at Mom—

I shiver even now at the sight of him walking into the room, and I try not to look at his watery eyes, the puffy red skin from his illustrious drinking career, the cruel teeth hidden by thin lips. Here in my cave, decades later, my body flinches at the memory of Jonathon...the tyranny of the unexpected.

And Jill, just sitting there, glazed over by terror. Chewing her milk.

Spencer's fervent prayers began at 4:45 every afternoon that Jonathon would die in rush hour traffic, split in two by a semi careening into him. Years later, over a drunken gab fest, Jill and Rebecca confessed they too silently conspired, though no words had ever passed between them back then. They had all wished him dead. Then they would hate themselves because Christmas Eve would come and he would allow them each one drink, and while sipping eggnog and rum he would read from *A Christmas Carol* in low resonant tones. He'd gather the three Atwood girls in his strong arms as if to protect them from the world. Only he couldn't protect them from himself.

* * *

An inner chill creates muscle spasms in my back and down the sides of my legs. It feels as if I have a fever, but I'm probably experiencing the first creeping stages of hypothermia.

The human body is so delicate, so intricate, and paradoxically equipped with the resources to overcome plagues, broken bones, high fevers. Even memories.

I always wanted to write the female Catcher in the Rye. *Hell, I always wanted to write the female version of anything, because women's voices only whispered in the wind, while men's trumpeted grandly on the bestseller lists of our consciousness. But when I think of writing what I know, knowing what I write haunts me. You know how it goes in the movies—you're traipsing along, minding your own business, having fun recalling the good ol' times—WATCH OUT! you want to scream at the heroine as she goes down that darkened hallway, even after her candles have burned out. That thing, the boogieman—is right behind the next turn. And then the villain leaps out, circles your neck...you can feel his breath at your spine, smell his aftershave.*

As my muscles tremble, I suddenly remember another night. Two inches of bourbon in his right hand, his now paunchy stomach sagging over the broken steps of buttons at his jeans. He insists I join in him a drink. I feel sophisticated and adult and with my bourbon soaked courage, I reveal my secret. With a twinkle of conspiratorial worship I tell Jonathon he's inspired me to be a writer. This would be our lasting bond.

"That's just dandy," he sneers contemptuously, "but you don't stand a chance."

"What...?" I croak.

"You don't have what it takes."

The superior taunt of his brow raises my hackles. "I do too!"

Sometimes the sword whimpers next to the pen. I dash to my bedroom and retrieve my bulging journal. I return to the kitchen and randomly open to read to him from my adolescent observations. He laughs, and in the laughter is a sickness that I am incubating in—the first seed of doubt is planted, and I am exposed to the disease of cynicism.

But I valiantly hold onto my words, as if our dreams could come true, just because we write them down in the pale of a smiling moon. Dear diary daydreams.

Sometimes details get in the way. Sometimes they merely paint black over black over black until we don't care anymore. And I want you to care...just a little. Aren't we a bit the same, you and I? Don't we both wrestle with the need to be good and the desire to survive?

Please tell me we are just a little bit alike.

* * *

Several weeks after I had begun the path, I stood to straighten my back, and realized I had made it down to the first of three naturally graded levels. I sighed and considered the steps above me. Time to celebrate.

I gathered the tools, took a cool drink of spring water and headed back to the cottage. I washed away the dirt and grime in the shower, thinking how pure the water was, right from the earth. No bubbles. No labels. No pretense.

Exhausted from the day's work, I ate a light dinner. I poured a small snifter of heated cognac, letting its delicious heat tickle my nose, glide down my throat, tease my senses and relax my muscles. Something was missing. I scrounged through one of my boxes, pulled out a pouch of CD's. It had been so long since I had listened to my music. *My music.*

Music was the only thing my mother and I ever really had in common. I remember her beautifully sculpted forearms and fingers gracefully sliding over the keys while I lay under the piano and watched her play. It must have saved her life, that piano. Cal had bought it for her while she was in the hospital delivering me. Story has it that when she returned home, she was so astonished that she dumped her newborn onto the bed, dashed to the repair-ridden upright, and indulged herself in hours of her beloved Chopin and Beethoven, reliving all the dreams she had left in Germany when she married my father.

When my mother tells this story she laughs as though it's the funniest thing, and I too have always found it amusing. Being the workaholic that I am, I am only momentarily chagrined at lovers' complaints that I can't leave them fast enough to fly back to my keyboard. Can I relate to her wanting to sit at the piano and make music? Damn right I can. She had just gone through labor, for Christ's sake.

But I am informed by Therapist that being abandoned in my early hours of life, being abandoned time and again have led to the underpinnings of fear and distrust I have of the world.

"I'm not blaming my life on my mother," I resolutely answer.

"I'm not asking you to," Therapist answers calmly. "I'm asking you to tell me how it feels when you hear that she left you on the bed and went to play the piano."

Again, I haven't the slightest idea. All I know is that she gave me my greatest gift—the love of art through her music. I read somewhere that music is the art to which all other art aspires. For me, that means Bach— his music creeps under my skin, captivates me, cuts to my core. Every nuance of emotion lies inside his work. It was in Portland that I began to work solely by his music, hoping that a small bit of his magic would rub off on me. How could I lose my integrity while writing to Bach?

I loved all Solitude; but little thought
To spend I know not what of life, remote
From all communion with existence, save
The maniac and his tyrant. Had I been
Their fellow, many years ere this had seen
My mind like theirs corrupted to its grave,—
But who hath seen me writhe or hear me
rave?

That was the page I opened to after rifling through the glassed-in cabinet that housed the obviously treasured books which lined the Enchanted Cottage. They had estate sales acquisition written all over them, and in most cases were crumbling apart, but I found a student Cambridge edition of Byron's complete works of poetry that was in fairly decent shape.

I took to Byron at first only as a brief jaunt, page by yellow page, but then a title would catch my eye and I would stop for a visit. A student, or perhaps the very same person who owned this cottage, had written copious notes in the margin, just as I had done when I was younger.

Away with your fictions of flimsy romance,
Those tissues of falsehood which folly has wove!
Give me the mild beam of the soul-breathing glance,
Or the rapture which dwells on the first kiss of love.

The first kiss of love! I laughed out loud. Rapture? Only awkward trembling to those ridiculous "first kisses of love" I had experienced through the years. Boyfriends. Before the words *lover, partner,* and then, quite intoxicatingly, *lesbian* came into my vocabulary. First men, and then…oh, yes, then women.

I ask Lena one afternoon after kissing her most kissable lips how she would describe women's lips at contact.

"They're soft…satiny…they melt into your own."

"I mean a description for a book."

"Oh." She leans to me, kisses me, seducing me in her quiet assertiveness. "Well?"

"They feel like the skin at the back of a baby's neck," I say, "but there's no way I can use that as a description."

"Maybe we need to work on it some more," Lena teases and draws me in.

I want her. I always want her. I kiss her lips, nibble at the tendrils of hair at the edge of her neck. She moans, turns on her belly, and waits for me to straddle her from behind. My hand gently trails, then teases her inner thighs. I bend to kiss her buttocks, deftly circling my left arm under her smooth stomach, fingers tracing her soft pubic hair, then tenderly spreading her taut as my other hand teases her, oh-so-gently at first, with small circular strokes. I apply a little more pressure and as her rhythm begins to match my own, I lean over her back, kissing the ridge of her spine, my hands working her, taking her closer, closer now, holding her apart and then slipping my fingers inside her, deeply inside her. As her hips quicken against me, my mouth lunges at her neck and our bodies become one, slithering in our heat, our breathing ragged as my tongue traces the edge of her ear. She screams my name, bucking as my arms caress her body, and I feel every sensation, every thudding pleasure as I rock gently against her…and then as we still…I nuzzle my face into the silken hair at her neck, our breathing sated, and we fall into gentle slumber.

* * *

The summer of her twelfth year Spencer fell irrevocably in love with Clark Gable, greedily scanning the TV guide for any one of his seventy-odd films she had committed to memory. It might take weeks before she would happen upon *Red Dust* airing at 2:40 am, but it was worth it. The alarm set for 2:30, she would tiptoe downstairs, arm herself with whatever could pass for junk food and stealthily make her way into the family room. She'd set the rocking chair about two feet from the set, the volume low so she wouldn't miss, in her clandestine ecstasy, one glance of a narrowed eye, lock of hair as it fell rakishly over his crinkled forehead, one sweet over worked expression as he snarled, "Baby? For a dame you're all right."

Boom Town, Adventure, Test Pilot...these were plots and characters that she cut her teeth on. Joan Crawford, Jean Harlow, and Myrna Loy became her heroes with their gritty determination, their granite hearts laced with gold.

If there was a feeling more pure and safe than oozing into the couch under a natty throw while watching a black and white in the middle of a rainy afternoon, she didn't know about it. She lived to seep herself into the sheer atmosphere of goofy story lines and flesh-raising twirls of Ginger and Fred. Relished the moody chiaroscuro of Orson Welles, the snappy repartee of a handsome Barbara Stanwyck pulling the wool over an "aw shucks" Gary Cooper—a sequined Rita Hayworth tossing "Johnny, let's hate her," with a flip of her luxurious auburn hair. The unabashed swelling of overwrought scores to the sweeping romances, the thinly disguised act of a closing door, when in-between the lines was left to the imagination. A saucy Harlow, the wicked grace of Bette Davis—a cleft-chinned Cary Grant and Bogart's scowl, a torch to Bacall's husky fire. All of this before the frame as an art form became so slick and colorized and too clever for its own good.

Ah...but she had read *Gone With the Wind* that spring, home with the flu, the massive tome weighing heavily in fever-spent hands while she wallowed in the first seeds of pricklingly euphoric deprivation. When she discovered the film version was being re-released for its thirtieth anniversary at their local theater she dove into her first bout of obsessive extremism, greedily consuming Selznick's memoirs, devouring every detail from Clark Gable's collar size to the fact that Vivien Leigh had insecurities about what she considered too large hands. Clark Gable became Rhett for her the moment he graced the screen at the bottom of the stairs at Twelve Oaks, with his jet black hair against blue tanned skin, that wonderful flesh tone only found in film. Chills ran up her spine.

It was the marriage of reality to fiction.

It was still magical when Lena and I saw it on the big screen during its fiftieth reunion. Twenty-eight years since I had clutched fingers to knees, sitting at the edge of my seat, praying that Scarlett would somehow come to her senses.

Lena was the only woman who I believe truly understood me... understood my need for high seas passion, even when she was dead calm in a sea of devilishly dangerous currents. A political consultant, a woman who was as at home listening to opera in her old Hollywood Hills manse, as she was elucidating the subtleties of the political system to harried unpaid interns on the campaign trail. I feel the grimace in my heart and wonder if that is from the mournful loss of Lena, or if around its shell a coldness is developing, the first signs that I will freeze to death.

Perhaps the coldness was there all along.

* * *

Just like in the prison movies, timing is everything, and like an inmate squirreling away crumbs of food to save for a week in isolation, Spencer too, began to save every cent she could to fund her great escape. She babysat, changed every diaper and played every zany toddler game from peek-a-boo to Candy Cane Lane. She flung newspapers at houses on a two mile trek every morning. She worked under the table cleaning construction sites for a friend of Hank's. And at thirteen she got a worker's permit to cashier. In her blue Fred Meyer smock with the cheery red lettering, she bagged, inventoried, cashiered, took extra shifts and became popular with the management, beating every record as employee of the month. She separated all her cash from her babysitting and paper delivery tips into neat little piles and at the end of each week she'd carefully pen her deposit slip, a document of utmost importance, as she watched the sums in her savings book grow. She needed four hundred dollars for her portion of the apartment she and Rebecca planned to rent.

It was a wild scheme, the one she and Rebecca hatched in the pale of moonlight in Rebecca's bedroom. It didn't matter that Hank had returned from the clinic. They had all held their breath as he made his way in his wheelchair into the kitchen for his welcome home meal, Grandma and Aunt Carol falling over polite phrases for fear of saying the wrong thing. So goddamned relieved he had come home and that Jonathon would now go. But Hank was nowhere near getting back to work, not with his broken half-body, his requests still drooling efforts to make the simplest need understood. Cut his meat. Help him drink. Medicate him. He was no help to them. And now they were stuck with Jonathon. Forever. Their mother would never leave Hank now. And there were moments when Spencer wondered how Rebecca and she could leave their mother. She would scrutinize the classifieds for apartments, smoothing a thumb over their destination, then crumple the paper in guilt and frustration. It was Jonathon, in the end, who finalized their decision.

* * *

I saw a drop on the ax and thought it had begun raining before I realized it was a tear. Digging the path had become my therapy, and the deeper I dug, the further back I traveled, the more I had to see my past for what it was.

I gathered my tools, exhausted, then drew a hot bath. I soaked my strained muscles until the hot water gave out. I pulled on some jeans, packed up some bread and cheese and chose a nice bottle of wine I'd gotten a few days earlier, and returned to my nearly finished path. I momentarily froze, for the first time worried about my near future. It hadn't occurred to me before then, but I was almost finished with my path. And then what would I do? Just me and my memories? Not to mention my future?

But I pushed the thoughts aside as the sun was just beginning its magical descent. I cut a piece of cheese, tore a hunk of bread and realized I'd forgotten a glass for the wine, then grinned as I barbarically swigged from the bottle. I was every farmer, peasant, field worker. I was Hemingway and this was my work.

"Jesus, get a load of me," I said softly, shaking my head as I sat upon my throne and awaited sunset. For the first time I felt part of this place. A part of the cottage and the earth, and the sky and the universe. I felt a subtle shift inside. Change. And then heard the soft music of the wonderful silence that is a million sounds of nature woven together in a brilliantly muffled crescendo of forwardness. Nobody ever takes the time to listen to evolution.

* * *

The stars are forth, the moon above the tops
Of the snow-shining mountains.—Beautiful!
I linger yet with Nature, for the night
Hath been to me a more familiar face
Than that of man; and in her starry shade
Of dim and solitary loveliness,
I learn'd the language of another world.

When I woke, crinkled sheets of Byron's poetry covered my bone-weary slumber. I had slept. Real sleep. Not the foggy interrupted swirl of a frenetic mind furious for escape, nor the deadened lethargy of depression. But the slumber of exhaustion. A day's work. It felt delicious.

I watched the sun burn white caps into the roaring tide as I stirred my coffee. The foreboding backdrop of a misty cloud hung like a dense fog out on the horizon. It would probably burn off by noon. The tide was still a good ways out I decided to take my first official walk on my nearly finished path.

A bit steep, but I still had a few good bones left in me. When I got to the bottom I ran to the waves. Foam flirted with my sneakers and I inhaled the clean air. Now and then locals passed by on their morning constitutional or runs. Was this the beginning of each of their days, this absolute perfection?

I walked. Catapulted forward, purified oxygen lifting my lungs, with the pace of a marathon walker. My chest filled with the natural energy I hadn't felt since hitting homers at the cherry tree, or running wildly for the pure and simple joy of it. I breathed fully, enjoying the briny air, intoxicated by its clearness. I wanted to sing. To laugh.

A tear cascades down my face as I think of 'Kenzie, her tender sweetness, her pale ashen hair cupping her fat cheeks as she whips small arms about my neck and says, "Aunnie Spinner, I like playing the beach." Lena and I walking her hand-in-hand, as she topples around on uncertain feet. Her finely-tuned focus as a little finger points at every shell we pass on our way. I watch Lena and her daughter and think, how can it get better than this? How can anything be sweeter than a child's smile of amazement?

I walked, all the while thinking about Lena, MacKenzie, Jonathon, my life in Los Angeles, my distressed dreams, all of it, a stream of consciousness car-wreck. And walked. Like shifting puzzle pieces, somehow all making a larger picture, all these disjointed elements had a theme running through them. A story was brewing. I knew this feeling. Years ago I used to have it quite often. I called it the birthing moment, the coming together of ideas—robust, full of texture, potential—dashing by, bumping into one another, delivering astonishing insights I could barely hang onto. For each project I had ever written or been involved in I could pinpoint when it started. The instant that thought took hold so strongly, so all-consumingly that there was nothing but to see it through. This was such a moment.

By mid afternoon, my legs finally gave way. I slumped against a large dry log that had washed ashore long ago. It had a natural curve in its spine that fit beautifully with my own. I rested against it, staring into the landscape no painter can capture, no writer can describe, the ocean at its limitless majesty.

I fell asleep.

It wasn't until the chill pressed against my skin that I awoke. I had no recall of falling into my coma-like slumber. I blinked, checking around me. I was alone, and the sun was well beneath the horizon, the sky almost so dark I couldn't see. I had slept for hours. I couldn't remember a speck of what I had dreamed. But it was then that I knew.

I was going to write again.

Integrity without knowledge is weak and useless, and knowledge without integrity is dangerous and dreadful.
Samuel Johnson (1709-1784)

BOOK TWO
CYNARA

She did not scream. Her body lay inert, her eyes open. They did not see. She could have been dead had one observed her, the angry body thrusting into her as she lay on her stomach, beneath him. After the first shock of pain—when she knew fighting was futile—she had ceased feeling. Her body became an empty vessel, a hollowed core with him expelling his rank assertion into the deep of her. He kept gasping for air, as if each measure of breath was a price he had to pay. She had to pay. She wished he would be quiet. And after a final animal cry, cured ale singeing her nostrils, he became still. Then he stood and buttoned his pants, his breathing still labored.

"It's better this way." He glanced in her direction. He couldn't meet her eyes, but then he had always found it difficult to face her. He brushed his thick brown hair of which he had always been so vain, to the side with a trembling hand. An air of irrevocability filled the room. They both knew this moment could never be undone.

"Lil—"

The sharp movement of her head jerking toward him stopped his speech. They were no longer bickering siblings. They were enemies.

"You can't always be the winner, Lil." His tone was almost apologetic, as if explaining the hardships of life to a young child. "There are some things even bigger than you. It's better you learn that now. With someone you know."

She glared at him, at his reddened cheeks, his dandified clothing, his air of utter entitlement. A flash of understanding sparked inside her, the first comprehension of an emotion she was just now beginning to experience: Hate.

The silence became deafening.

"Part of you wanted this—"

"Don't you ever"—her voice was barely audible but cut through to his spine—"*ever* make this anything but what it is."

When she approached he flinched as if she might strike him. He almost seemed eager for her to lash out at him, to punish him. But her eyes held no trace of either anger or forgiveness. The brown had turned black. There was no light in them at all.

If there was evidence of regret he soon molded his shame to smug victory. "In any event, you will never be able to eradicate it. That I've had you. You will never be able to escape that, Lilian. I will forever be in the shadow of your heart."

"You may think you are a cancer on my spirit, Charles." Her voice was brittle with conviction. "But you will never be anything but conspicuously benign."

* * *

She slept on the train. A narrow curve disrupted the rhythmic lull of the metal wheels hugging the tracks, jarring her body against the window, waking her. When she peered around this foreign cubicle of moving space, it was as if her senses belonged to another. Her skin was raw. It tingled with sensation she had never experienced. Perhaps it didn't belong to a woman. Perhaps it was merely a receptacle that catered to the whim of ruthless power. As she caught her pale reflection against the tarnished window, she saw a ghost. For she had certainly died that afternoon.

What force of will had gotten her to the train, she could not fathom. She could barely remember walking to her closet, reaching for the weathered carpetbag. She had thrown what clothes she had scattered about in it, three volumes of poetry, her diary, and the necklace from her mother. Trudging through the newly wet sand, her cape snagged against the insidious bramble of weeds overtaking her favorite path to the ocean.

From the same path she had climbed up to the main road, where a neighbor had stopped and offered her a ride. She had told him she was meeting a boarder at the station. When she arrived at the neglected train depot, she acted on instinct alone. She knew there was only one direction she could travel. East. She had stared at the schedule, the numbers melting into cities, mistily evaporating from the threat of tears. But she would not cry. Not yet.

Perhaps in the comfort of a room. A room she would occupy and call her own without the belongings that were part of her spirit, without the scent of her father, the memory of her mother. A room with someone else's life surrounding her, someone who had perhaps left hours earlier and was now traveling to where she was leaving. A room where she could make herself new.

She had taken the money, all the money in Father's tinder box—the full receipts from Bay Cliff's boarders for the month—hidden in his dressing room. With trembling hands she had also grabbed the few bills left in the breast pocket of her father's Sunday suit, which hung crisply pressed in preparation for service the following day. She would not be attending church this Sunday. She would not miss the fanatical zeal of the congregation. But she would miss his short strong fingers holding her own as they walked back from the service. And his pipe, which he let her hold while he lit it, pungent tobacco drifting through her senses, a brief exultant euphoria as she sucked from the stem of his favorite Dunhill. He allowed one puff. He never knew how she loved the cloud of lightheadedness, the delicious dizziness, how she craved their moments of complicit togetherness.

She pictured her father's lips pursing beneath his full white beard when he realized his daughter was absent from breakfast the following morning, then checking her favorite haunts, strolling up the ledge to the cobbled path that overlooked the rugged coastline.

She imagined a frown developing at his forehead as he searched through the swollen cave, the one made smooth by the persistent water swirling through ancient bedrock. Worry would replace concern the moment he discovered that his money was missing. He would be able to track her as far as the station, where she had shoved crumpled bills to an aging clerk who smiled in recognition.

"Goin' on a trip are ya, Miss?"

She nodded. She did not trust her voice.

"Well, and where might ya be travelin' this fine day?"

Again she had gazed at the schedule of cities she had only read about, had dreamed about seeing, when her father had promised visits to San Francisco, Los Angeles. But they were all too close.

"New York," she uttered, as surprised as the clerk was.

"Well you can make a connection in Portland." He checked his pocket watch. "Just in time if ya hurry. Leavin' track three in ten minutes. Where's yer luggage young lady?"

"Uhm...it's being shipped later." She pushed the money toward him.

She barely recognized her voice. Strong, confident. Lying as if she had been born to it. She took the ticket and stepped back then, looking at the parallel rails that would take her away from here. From her home. She grabbed her cape and carpetbag, and when she walked, felt her blood mixed with his seed, sticky on her inner thigh. She must find a bathroom and wash.

With the sigh of the train she was jarred back to consciousness.

An endless span of time passed as the landscape of a continent sped by. Hours, days and minutes all had the same breath, the echoing wheels churning, *no past, no future. No past, no future.* Time was not a passage of seconds and minutes into hours, but interrupted dreams and memories jumbled together until she could not tell real from imagined, truth from fiction.

Sitting on Poppa's lap as he read to her from her beloved poetry, the smells of his pipe tobacco, his aftershave, the soft wisp of beard against her forehead. While he read, she would trace the lines of her father's strong and resolute hands, trusting he would keep, her safe forever.

Her seventh birthday, when she had received that fine color picture book of castles and faraway places from Mother, and Charles had grabbed it from her hands. When she tried to reclaim her new treasure he had slapped her sharply across the cheek. Mother jumped quickly to reprimand him: "Be nice to your sister. You're her brother. You are to protect her, not bully her."

But he would not protect what he didn't love.

Lilian had learned as children do, not by word or concept, but in action and deed that she and her brother were different not just by size and shape. It had to do with getting what you wanted. It had to do with asking permission and then stealing it if it wasn't granted. Somehow in this world of soft, loving women like her mother and Aunt Noonie, big burly men walked into a room and occupied space as if it were their birthright, their movements strong and confident. They owned the air they breathed whereas women merely borrowed it.

On and on the memories flooded, so sharp and clear she could feel the patina of ocean mist against her skin as she dared the waves to catch her, playing tag alone, as there were few children along the isolated coastline. She could taste Noonie's creamy tapioca pudding, her favorite dessert, before being tucked in bed by her father. Further back, yes, she could feel the delicious chills against her neck as the graceful Cecelia Harrington brushed her daughter's hair while she mimicked her mother's gentleness with her doll. And then another lurch of the train would bring her back to her barren present.

* * *

When she finally arrived in Grand Central station and stepped off the train, and then into the streets of New York, she was accosted by a flurry of rapid images, stark and unapologetic, new to her country eye. People bustled about, and Model T's raced alongside one another, somehow choreographed so that they would not smash into each other or the swelling wake of pedestrians. These people looked nothing like those back home, wearing the latest fashions displayed in storefronts: Brooks Brothers suits and velvet gowns, gloves of cashmere and silk undergarments. Huge blocks of concrete structures stretched for as long as the buildings spired high, and as she looked up she felt snowflakes dance on her cheeks, then melt into the grayness of the rush.

She walked slowly and uncertainly at first, straining to take everything in. Where was she going? Where would she sleep? She tried to think of how best to resolve her most dire needs when, in spite of her apprehensions, she began to get caught up into the rhythm of the city, and found herself swinging her satchel with more confidence. But as the hours passed, her fascination faded and she grew hungry. Even with her woolen cloak, she was cold and her boots had burned blisters upon her toes. She was exhausted. The shadow of fear tapped at her shoulder. It grew from an annoying aside to a momentary suspicion that she might be simply swallowed up where she stood and perish on the spot.

"Lookin' for a room, are ya Miss?" The thick brogue belonged to a policeman who stood behind her.

"Yes, sir. I am. But I'm afraid I'm rather lost."

"New to the city are ya?"

"Yes. Very new."

"Have ya no family then, lass?"

"No. No I don't have any family." She pulled her cloak closer.

"Now don't be tellin' your business to just any old stranger, Miss."

"Well, I—"

"Jes' because I got me a fine uniform don't mean I might not be takin' advantage of a situation," the policeman harrumphed. "Ya can't be trustin' anyone in the city. Especially in these parts."

Lilian observed the dirty alleyway strewn with rubbish to her right. Noticed that the people walking these sidewalks looked tired and beaten, their clothes much shabbier than those she had seen only a few blocks west.

"Poor lass. Well, I'll tell ya, me brother has boardin' rooms not far from here. Not much of a palace to be fair, but the rates won't strip ya bare."

"I'd be most grateful," she responded and he directed her to a building several blocks away.

As she wearily walked the remaining distance she came upon a cluttered magazine stand. She stopped, enthralled by the brightly colored images. Gibson girls licking ice cones at the beach while their square-jawed boyfriends dove into the waves, elegant society girls in swirls of taffeta led by men in high tops and tails dancing at a moon-lit ball. Near the sloping newspapers stood a cracked and aging canvas of Paris in the fall, of the crowded Champs Elysees corridor, filled with brilliant yellows, reds and oranges. The painting held a beauty and a sense of mystery she did not sense was inherent to New York. She didn't know yet what it was to be frugal, and so she handed a barrel-chested Italian two bits and bought the painting. It would be a beacon of light for her future as she made her way into this grand new world.

Journal of Parnell Walbrook
France—American Ambulance Field Service: April 1918

It has been quite grueling here of late. Long ambulance runs to the front. This war is tedious and the loss of life angers me. I'm not in the least cut out for this racket—my heart's most violent tendencies run toward overwrought performances at the opera.

I received a letter and package from Mother. Finally, extra socks and tobacco. My new friends and I immediately rolled cigarettes and indulged in our first measure of civilization in months.

I grow ever fonder of my fellow ambulance drivers, most of whom are fresh out of school, and have never given a thought to death and such dire circumstances as we see daily. The grim terror of it all is alleviated by the exceptional acquaintances I have made since our unit joined forces with a group of Americans. Amongst them are two with whom I've become very friendly. Ernest is a grand Yank, all bluster and ego, but in his heart he is a poet. I call him "Hem." I also met the most lovely American woman. She's what the Yanks call an ardent "feminist." But for me her sparkling wit and bon vivant spirit is a refreshing reminder of civilization. Indeed she complained to me that she wanted *to drive ambulance for the Red Cross but they wouldn't let her due to the immutable status of her gender! Not to be dissuaded, Miss Sylvia Beach joined the Volontaires Agricoles and works long hours to teach the peasant women wheat bundling and grape picking to leave the men free to fight. If nothing else she caused quite a stir in her riding togs. The peasants rarely see a woman in pants. She smiled at me and said, "Perhaps if they did they wouldn't be so shy about letting us do a man's work." I'm awfully taken with her.*

Paris: November 11, 1918

Oh glory! The end has come! I sat with Sylvia today as they rang the bells of freedom and we drank champagne for all the friends who have parted our company, and to celebrate joyful peace—there is no end to the singing and jubilation in the streets.

Now that the war is over, I suppose it is time to get serious with regards to my future. Become a barrister or something equally reasonable but the world of business and finance leaves me cold. After sharing a cigarette with Hem, and discussing our futures, he told me he plans to return to Paris, taking up as a foreign correspondent for the Kansas City Star. I just may be able to get on at the Paris Herald.

* * *

The curtains folded indiscriminately, the thick faded material bulging in some places, then tapering to thin strips—narrow here, then a bit wider, then narrow again. From her bed Lilian preoccupied herself with the random pattern of folds, and saw in the furled segments a lifetime of ups and downs, and thought she had only survived the first few tucks and that there were so very many more to go.

She thought about her new life and what she was to do with it in this tiny square room in the dilapidated boarding house. Hidden down a dark narrow alley behind what had once been part of a grand hotel, it was now amongst one of the many previously fashionable parts of New York that had rapidly degenerated into block after block of dreary flats. Elegant old brownstones with brass railings now housed the vermin of the city.

The money she had taken from her father was running low. Just that morning she had stretched her limited budget from coffee and a doughnut to the runny hamless pea soup at Bariff's Grill, which she had wolfed down at sunset. She had placed the few remaining dollars and coins into a porcelain bowl and stood in the center of her "box," to survey her meager belongings.

She had persuaded O'Brian, her new landlord, to let her have the small wooden table she had discovered at the base of the stairwell. She used it as her desk, placing it under the cracked window. She fashioned a chair from two milk crates she had found littered in a back alleyway. A broken lamp with a torn shade sat clumsily on her desk, its merit not function but design, to instill an ambience of artistic endeavor. The rattling dirty panes provided light until the pale glow of a gas lamp began to flicker the coming night. Stingy O'Brian shut down the gas by nine, after which Lilian sparingly used candles.

Daily she convinced herself that her box provided all she needed: a desk, chair, and, of course, the bright and glittering Champs Elysees canvas cast its light on her simple abode. But now her stomach cramped with tightness as she lay on her cot, hunger her familiar bedmate.

She prayed for sleep.

* * *

Journal—Parnell Walbrook
Paris: July 1919

I was very impressed to discover the delightful Sylvia Beach has started a lending library by the grand name of Shakespeare and Company.

This store is the most ingenious idea as American literature has a limited representation—and reputation!—and now she has all the Yanks and Brits and fascinating Parisians meeting in her shop for a copy of William Blake, Shaw and Henry James. I discovered quite by accident that Ernest also frequents the shop. I've asked Sylvia to pass a message onto him that I've returned from London and am here to stay.

Although I might rely on my allowance, it is with great pride that I have found gainful employment as "Critic Heard 'Round the World" for Mr. Conde Nast of Vanity Fair. Can you just imagine!!

Paris: January 1920

Enjoyed a most intriguing outing at one of the notorious Natalie Barney's salons. The evening was filled with witty conversation, delicious gossip and an exquisite repast of foie gras, marinated white asparagus, roasted squab with truffles, a delightful platter of fresh fruit, all topped off with champagne and Pernod. Her abode is replete with wild garden and an homage to Greek Doric temple. On Friday afternoons it is rumored to be filled with…lesbians!—and receives a great deal of attention because of it.

An openness exists here that enthralls me. It is as if a genie had floated from a bottle and asked me what favors I wished granted, for here I can live as who I am. Discreetly, but accepted.

In fact a fascinating debate arose between Hemingway and the notable Miss Gertrude Stein on the merits of male homosexuality. The rugged Hem is the last to make comment on this topic, so he listened passively as Miss Stein posited, as if she would have the faintest idea, that the sex act between men was so apparently repulsive that men were consumed by self-loathing after engaging in such atrocity. I couldn't help but reply, "Dear Miss Stein, it is surprising to me that you, who are so very clever about women, show not the slightest inclination of the same toward men."

Natalie quickly grabbed me by the arm and although secretly pleased, admonished me not to make an enemy of Gertrude for she casts an inexorably long shadow. I know everyone claims her to be brilliant—a truly innovative thinker. It is peculiar then that she presents none of this modernity to her own relationship—she treats her own lover like a man's wife, better seen than heard.

As near as I can tell, Miss Barney heads up the exotic and intriguing, Miss Gertrude Stein is the self-proclaimed leader of the modernist movement, while Sylvia and her bookstore bridge the chasm of the veritable rainbow of colorful personalities bursting at the Left Bank's seams.

In spite of my little run in with Miss G, I can't think of when I've enjoyed a more enchanting evening.

* * *

Lilian walked miles through the city she now claimed as her own and though she took care to avoid the seamier elements, she came to find New York nowhere as frightful as she had once believed.

The first few months she had only ventured several blocks from her room, absorbing a constant barrage of sights, sounds and smells. The exhaust from model T's, the dirty streets, the exotic ghetto odors, were all so different than the ocean brine mingled with the sharp scent of pine. But the smell of the city never failed to produce excitement and energy within her.

At first she invented each day as it came, jumping from her narrow bed, stretching her cramped muscles, hurriedly dressing and then getting out of the boarding house as fast as she could make it. She'd wander the streets until hunger drove her to a small café where she had her first deliciously bitter sips of coffee. She soon developed a sense of how the city was laid out and slowly began to widen her radius, adding street numbers and as many additional blocks as she could until she exhausted herself. Often she would head to the library, where she spent a good deal of time researching and reading. But she rarely ventured out in the evenings, fearful of being accosted.

Lilian began to see New York as an urban landscape representing the conflicts in man. She marveled at skyscrapers that yawned into the clouds—the opulence of man scaling new heights—their exquisite oak and maple scrolled interiors, marble pillars, brass and gold fixtures. Only a few blocks east immigrants flocked in record numbers to scabby tenement shacks in the very shadow of those achievements floating in the sky. The bright lights of Broadway, the city's museums and libraries filled with man's greatest accomplishments, coexisted with grog shops, darkened opium dens and drunken prostitutes. City sidewalks were thick with confidence men, panhandlers and dopers clashing with the cymbals of a band of Salvation Army redeemers. The granite highway of Wall Street was backed by banks filled with newfound riches where a man could make a fortune with a bit of muscle and ingenuity. Minutes away children labored fourteen hours a day in suffocating sweat shops, gluing envelopes or stripping feathers for a measly few dollars a week. Lilian wondered at the extremities between those lives and yet how little tangibly separated them.

Whether she traveled by foot or omnibus, her desire for knowledge was unquenchable and she knew she was finally at home when the flurry of cars racing by no longer flustered her, but droned into the background as she window-shopped. She'd even made a friend or two along the way: the newspaper boy, Scotty, the waiter at the restaurant where she ate most of her dinners and a fellow boarder, James, a young gentleman who studied law.

She spent a great deal of time studying the character of the people with whom she came into contact, making up stories in her head about where they came from. At the café where she had her coffee every morning, she gazed surreptitiously at the other patrons, studying their manner, clothes and speech, so unlike the slow squalid figures who had peppered much of her previous landscape; lumber and fishermen, Indians and farmers. Lilian and Charles had always been excited by travelers from Portland and Seattle and occasionally they'd had guests from San Francisco, and even as far south as Los Angeles. But these New Yorkers were different. They had a distinct style and refinement about them, an elegant aloofness to their movements that Lilian found intimidating.

She spent hours in the evening mimicking their gestures, their turn of a word. One night she nabbed a pack of cigarettes a young man had abandoned at the table next to hers and later tried them out. Assessing her reflection in the small warped mirror she had purchased from a sidewalk vendor, she narrowed her eyes mysteriously, lifting her hair and gauging its fullness.

"Not exactly the flapper look." She cocked her head, then shoved a cigarette between her lips with mock sophistication, maneuvering it this way and that, inhaling with panache. Then she laughed and wished for another voice besides her own.

Those were days that sent her to bed exhausted, sleep that clung to her like a heavy shawl. Often, the following morning, when the gray of a new day peeked its way into her room, she knew getting out of bed was impossible. She couldn't move. Perhaps she had had a dream, or she would find her hand upon the flesh of her body and it would remind her of him. She could smell his rank odor, the air of brute power. She imagined the stench of decay emanating from her own body, until her own skin was foreign matter and it was as if someone else touched it altogether. She would turn her face to the wall until she succumbed to sleep once again.

In the beginning there were many of those days. Days without time. She could not will herself from bed, and would lie as still as possible. But then one day she woke at five in the evening, and sick with over-sleeping she realized she had wasted an entire day of her life. For the first time it frightened her. She needed structure to order her day. In any event, she must find gainful employment. She had no skills to speak of, even if her father always called her "my bright, shining star."

How she missed her father, his gruff exterior, so poorly covering his sweet charm, his tender heart. How she ached to lay her head against his silky white beard, to hear the comfort of his voice as he told her one of his funny stories. A pang of guilt swept through her body, thinking how angry and hurt he must be. She had wired him shortly after she had arrived in New York and then written him a long letter explaining, "…you have always told me to follow my dreams, to seek adventure. And now it is time. Please forgive me for taking the money. I shall repay it—every cent. All I ask from you, Father, is your blessing. Please do not try to find me, for if you do I shall certainly lose my resolve. Do not worry. I am well and safe. Your loving daughter, Lilian."

But now the money she had taken was dwindling to nothing and she had to find a way to pay her rent. She systematically walked up and down the blocks, shaking in the doorway until she could bring herself to speak to the manager of the haberdashery or the owner of the bakery. Always the same answer: Skilled workers only need apply. She had received several lascivious offers from fat gents who slunk in alleyways, perspiration clinging to their garments while they preyed on the promise of naïve flesh.

One morning, as she was finishing her coffee, she overheard the manager tell Scotty that he was going to have to let the counter girl go for "uhum, reasons I'd rather not elaborate upon, if you catch my meaning. Know of anyone who can help us out?"

"I can!" Lilian shouted, then slapped her hand over her mouth. "What I mean, Mr. uhm, Mr—?"

"Baker, young lady. And who might you be?"

"This here's Lilian. And she's a right good lass," Scotty chimed in, smiling. "She's smart too. Wouldn't be windin' up short the end of a shift."

"Hmmm." Baker rubbed his chin. "Looks a bit young."

"I'm eighteen," Lilian lied. Well, she would be in a year or so.

"Right, then." Baker nodded. "You'll start tomorrow."

The tension in Lilian's neck eased and it was only then that she realized how frightened she had become. She had a job. And free food. She could finally pay O'Brian, whom she had been dodging for the past week.

The work wasn't really so different from tending to the boarders at Bay Cliff. She worked long shifts hauling dishes to the kitchen, and serving coffee and dinners of stew with bread, a side of pickles and a piece of pie, all for thirteen cents. She could now enjoy more food on the menu than she ever had as a customer. It wasn't the Waldorf Astoria serving peppermint creams and hand sandwiches, but how she loved her scrambled eggs and Irish bacon, biscuits smothered in gravy. Since she was only allowed one meal per shift, she ate with "the appetite of a sea lubber," Scotty teased.

She would flop herself upon her cot the minute she returned home and fall into the slumber of the wicked. Of course she wouldn't be a counter girl forever. With three shifts a week, she just covered her rent with little to spare, so she timed her one free meal at the end of the day to stretch it out as long as possible. With her spare time she could write. She was devoted to her work, and would write, as she had always written, whether lulled by sweeping waves, the wind shuffling her papers wildly about her, or in solemn quiet, late at night, a single candle burning at her claptrap desk, the words flowing as quickly as she could put pen to paper.

Lilian lived for poetry. Her father used to bring her volumes of Shelley, Keats and Wordsworth as well as the latest modern verse when he returned from business trips to Seattle or Portland. She would dash to his den and snuggle into the form he had imposed upon his chair, to warm herself by the roaring fire, consuming words and phrases as if they were food and wine, never sated, always desiring more.

Later she would pack up her new volumes in a small leather satchel and head out to Devil's Point. She rode Aragon, her palomino, up a winding trail that led to open fields, giving him his head to race through tall stalks of sea grass, her braid unraveling in the wind, her eyes shining with tears from the wind and euphoria. She'd tether him to a pine and then hike up the craggy rocks that jutted out and gave the point its name, infamous for the many ships that had found their prows gashed against the unsuspected ridges that stretched fifty yards out from the surf.

Lilian often read aloud, emoting with theatrical flair, extolling for the creatures in the sea the words that sung to her from the page. She bellowed until she became hoarse, filled with the magnificence of her surroundings, the best that nature gave with the best that man had to offer.

In her early years she had written silly poems and melodramatic plays. Now her love of the word drove her to write all the pent-up feelings she had had since that night, sometimes merely as a release, other times as a structured sonnet, but mostly to fight the fear, anger and hurt she couldn't understand. She wrote late into the night, the flickering shadows punctuating the movement of her fine-veined hands as she worked with the rudimentary tools of her trade, pen on rustling paper. A flinch in her cheek, a gentle tremor of candlelight in her eye, yes, a new way of seeing things. The more she wrote, the more she craved writing and soon her days were filled with hours that had no measure, days that could have been colored by rain or sun for all she knew. Oftentimes she wrote deep into the night until she fell asleep, her head flat on the small table, the candle burned to dark.

Within a year she had completed a small volume of poems she felt could only be entitled *Naked Truth*, a journey as seen through a woman's eyes. There was nothing she left out or to the imagination. Birth, sex, rape and death were all handled with unflinching imagery. When she was finished she hardly knew what to do and very shyly paced her room while James, her fellow boarder, read it in his.

"I can't believe this, Miss Harrington. This poetry is, well, it's...it's uhum, unbelievably daring." James was still blushing even though they had been sitting at her table and having tea for nearly ten minutes. "I mean, it would seem to me you have talent. I'm afraid I've read nothing of this nature, so I'm scarcely qualified to critique."

"But do you like it James, and please, do stop calling me Miss Harrington."

"It's not a matter of liking it, uhm, Lilian." He acknowledged the proffered intimacy with a slight bow. "It's more as if, well, should one read something so private?"

"Private? What is private? Things happen to all of us. Things that perhaps we don't speak about in public, but surely we understand that we all have knowledge of. For instance the marriage night—"

James choked on his tea. "I'm sorry, Miss Harrington. I really must be getting on. I have to go to the library and finish a paper."

"James, please, I'm sorry. I didn't mean to frighten you." But she couldn't help laughing, because it really was too idiotic. Here he was, at least five years older than she, yet acting like a child.

"No. It's just I must be going."

And that was the last she spoke to him. He would tip his hat coming and going, but she never again prevailed upon him to read her work. Lilian was undaunted by his reaction and she spent the next day in the library copying the addresses of the publishers she thought might be interested in *Naked Truth*.

Applebury & Crone was the last of seven publishers she had singled out. When she left the library, she had a plan. She would write each of the publishers and show up on their doorsteps if necessary.

The paper promised a bachelor pad. It turned out to be a basement dwelling. The kitchen pipes were broken and the heat worked infrequently. But it was theirs. Their "groovy digs." Spencer supposed it could be called the first sign of adult-onset denial. You don't want to see what was leaking down the concrete block wall of the kitchenette? Cover it with a Salvation Army blanket. You want to believe Max is going to marry you? Blind yourself with the bedazzling diamond on your hand.

It was the afternoon they were waiting to pick up the key to their new "pad," that Rebecca dropped the news on her. After slumming for drinks at a dive bar and working some poor schlub into buying them Tequila shooters and then dumping him, Rebecca informed Spencer that she had become engaged. She had grown more princessy, and with her long auburn hair, diet-ridden body, and wicked grin, she resembled Jane Fonda a bit—but only in *Julia*. She had always been Spencer's hero, so grownup and mature. She was forever trying, unsuccessfully, to catch up to those three years Rebecca had ahead of her.

"Ta...da!" She thrust her hand in Spencer's face, a huge diamond limping awkwardly to the side of her ring finger.

"Uh...what's that?"

"I'm engaged!" Rebecca shrieked a little too enthusiastically.

"What?!" Spencer screamed. They hadn't even moved in yet and Rebecca was already abandoning her.

"Max and I are gonna get married. Probably next spring. After his divorce."

Spencer may have been young, but even she had read enough books and seen enough soap operas to know that married men who were a hundred years old didn't leave their wives for teenyboppers. Besides, what about her? What about their plans?

"I decided to skip my predictably messed up twenties," Rebecca sniffed self-importantly as she told Spencer about her latest beau, Max, who was twenty-three years her senior, and so obviously a Cal replacement Spencer was surprised Rebecca didn't see it herself. She continued gabbing furiously, constantly referring to how wonderful it was going to be to be on their own. But didn't she realize by marrying Max she wasn't on her own?

"Do...do you think we're going to miss Mom at all," Spencer asked tentatively, realizing that she, in fact, was desperate for her now.

"Oh, sure. But I'm tellin' ya Spence, we're going to have a blast."

But later that night as they drank Maxwell House drip coffee from a run-down vending machine, Spencer had no choice but to weave a new set of dreams into her bright shiny Christmas globe, as the swirling snow had become little clumps of plastic raining on her parade.

While Rebecca spent almost all of her time with Max, leaving Spencer isolated in the bowels of the city, she squared her shoulders and braced against the big bad world. They had no furniture. No TV. No one knew her. She would simply stare at the floor, or lie in bed, occasionally reading, but mostly she slept, her skin chilling at the foreign noises in the night. She could never get warm there, even in the height of summer.

Sitting in the dank chilly basement she began to write lists of all the things she planned to do to rectify her situation. It was called *Fix My Life*. She found a waitressing job at Carrow's, a twenty-four-hour coffee shop, trained by Rhonda, a "kiss-my-grits" hard-ass Harley gal with, you guessed it, a heart of gold. Like with her babysitting and newspaper route money, she'd spill tips from double shifts onto the chipped Formica table and smooth out the crumpled dollar bills and stack coins in neat rows, counting the fortune that would presumably send her to film school. Dining on Cracker Jacks, Macintosh apples and Gallo rose wine, she ate the stingy allotment of calories Rebecca had dreamed up in her anorexic mind, smoked a couple of cigarettes and stared at *Fix My Life.*

I am an adult. I am an adult. It was a refrain she played over like a bad melody. But it wouldn't fix the toilet that refused to flush and the strange smell emanating from somewhere behind the small empty refrigerator. Here she was, standing in the middle of the splotched vinyl floor, queen of her domain, without a clue. *I am an adult.*

God, how ill-equipped we are for living on our own. No one teaches you what laundry soap to buy, to keep extra light bulbs on hand, that without a three-to-two-way plug adapter most modern appliances won't run. Can openers don't suddenly appear when you are starving for that sole can of tuna and a plunger doesn't miraculously coalesce around stuck toilets. Those ridiculously tedious things your mother did, that bored the tits off you, price shopping and comparing Tide's whiter whites, quickly begin to make sense. I owe you one, Mom. And as you finally grow up, you begin to have conversations about this stuff instead of the meaning of life, only to find this is the meaning of life.

Her independence terrorized her. She felt like an impostor, dressing herself up, splattering makeup on her face and learning to wear nylons and three-piece polyester ensembles poached off the nearest JC Penney mannequin. She really hadn't the foggiest idea about how...well, how to live.

Her early twenties were a blur. She worked hard. Damn hard. Played hard. But for the life of her, she didn't seem to be getting anywhere. Perhaps because she never stuck anything out beyond her first yawn of boredom. Especially school.

Embarrassed, she stopped counting how many jobs she walked away from, simply unable to stand the ennui a minute longer. Chagrined to think of how clever she always thought she was. If she had so many brains, why did she continually seem to be at the beginning of a one-way road with no turnoffs? She took over Rebecca's job as service secretary, playing grownup with her associates all in their early thirties. Friday nights were a drunken revelry down at The Brewery, topped off by smoking hash by the railroad tracks.

Yes, one of those nights she lost her virginity in a distinctly non-novelesque scenario. After spilling her third glass of red wine on herself and her paramour's white carpet he grabbed her hand, hauled her to his bed. Appalled at her arousal, he dabbed her wetness clean with one of the many boxes of Kleenex in his apartment...a humiliation all the way around.

She soldered cabling for medical machinery with a bunch of nerdy science guys, packed produce, sorted cherries. Mucked stalls at the horse track, and dropped acid with fellow excavators from the archeological digs one summer down the River in Bonneville. She waited more tables, stuffed envelopes, and drove a delivery truck.

The only thing she did consistently besides schlep her meager belongings from apartment to apartment (Rebecca had long since married and divorced Max) was to sleep with men she would never see again, or men whom she would see way too soon on Monday morning. And every night she wrote in her journals, capturing the nuances of futility that had become *My Life*.

She pored over the fall and spring catalogues for courses every year, yet she kept putting off enrollment, quarter after quarter. The two times she did sign up for class, the ponderous group pace squelched her enthusiasm. She couldn't sit still and wait. She had great things to achieve—unable to wait for anything, even when she wasn't going anywhere. Impatience. Her nemesis.

After five, six, seven years—a slow burn of working, shopping for groceries, drinking with abandon, partying like she had all the time in the world—slivers of doubt began to creep into her being. She hated to voice it to herself, but maybe she wasn't going to be a writer, or a filmmaker. She couldn't even get through one course of creative writing. What ever made her think she had what it took to be a writer?

While Spencer struggled with her indecision and morbid lack of self-esteem, her mother phoned her one day to tell her that Hank and Jonathon's business was finally thriving again and they were willing to help Spencer with school, as long as she majored in something practical. It was the perennially attached string, about the size of those cables on San Francisco bridges, but she thought, what the hell? She wasn't doing anything meaningful with her life, and if she could at least get a degree of some sort, perhaps she could make a living that would support her creative endeavors better than waitressing tips. How many dreams turn to this logic in the naked city?

She became a business major and one afternoon turned to the help-wanted boards at the college and found an ad for a temporary typist needed for a business proposal. Perhaps it would warm her fingers up. Perhaps by sitting and typing she would get into the groove of writing. She didn't know why, but when she called the number she expected a man to answer and was pleasantly surprised to hear the warm husky voice of a woman.

Adrienne Curtis was using a small inheritance to open up a women's café/restaurant and was in dire need of someone to make her rat-scrawled notes legible for interested investors waiting on the sidelines. Spencer agreed to meet her at a small café the following day.

She had just gotten out of possibly the most sleep-inducing material of Statistical Analysis, and not even the double latte was having any effect. She laid her head on the café table daydreaming about movies when her droopy vision ran headlong into the steely blue orbs of one of the strongest looking women she had ever seen. The woman sat three booths away from her. Energetic and frazzled, she appeared to be waiting for someone. It took several moments for Spencer to realize this was Adrienne.

She was right out of a Renaissance painting—strong, earthy and thick-limbed with the patrician features of a time past. The only thing contemporary about her was the slight crook to her otherwise straight pointed nose. Adrienne was all business as she handed Spencer a packet filled with papers and a hand-scribbled profit and loss sheet that would take her three days to decipher. Adrienne swept her hair out of her eyes. They were clear, and deeply intelligent, but it was the veneer of anger in them to which Spencer found herself drawn.

Two weeks later Spencer handed Adrienne the finished documents. She was impressed and wrote her a check.

"You know, I'm just about to head to one of the restaurant properties to check it out. Wanna join me?"

Spencer didn't think twice. She followed like a puppy dog.

They pulled up in front of a hole in the wall called Ladies Galore, a strip joint that had been in the neighborhood for years. It was pitch black inside save the bar lights. A tinny juke-box wrangled "Your Cheatin' Heart." Sour beer and stale cigarettes assaulted Spencer's senses as she watched Adrienne assess the merits of the layout. She watched her from behind, noticing the firm shape of her buttocks, the strong back, her wide shoulders bristling with a fierce energy. She had never been around someone she could actually feel from feet away. And when Adrienne turned and gave her the thumbs down with a sardonic smile, a jolt went straight through to her solar plexus and she found herself gritting her teeth as she smiled back.

Spencer had never considered being attracted to a woman. If you don't know about those divine maple walnut scones at Starbucks, how could you ever think to eat one? Having spent her twenties between a workaholic frenzy to nowhere and dumping herself into the nearest bed that made the kindest offer, women had simply never been on Spencer's radar. In moments of severe self-reflection, it frightened her somewhat that her propensity for lovemaking and romance was nowhere near the mark of the trembling passions she had read about from her early teens. She adopted what she considered the healthy attitude that what made for good story-telling had very little to do with reality.

However, Adrienne was unlike any other woman Spencer had been around. In fact she described her as distinctly male to Sarah, a fellow film student who was becoming her closest confidant.

"Something, I don't know, very—"

"Assertive?" Sarah supplied.

"Yeah." That's what it was. And it was extremely attractive on her.

* * *

Donald Paris was everything Spencer was not. Punctual. Tidy. Focused. On a charted course and nothing would steer him from his goals. His strength of commitment was a breath of fresh air next to Spencer's lack of direction. With his misted eyes (he suffered from chronic hayfever), thick hair the color of sage honey, and an unconvincing mustache over fine lips, he faintly resembled Errol Flynn.

Most people remember the finer points of a relationship by their special calendar dates, but every milestone Spencer and Donald passed pivoted on the success or failure of the Portland Trail Blazers. If they lost they had pizza. If they won Donald was gracious and charming, treating Spencer to a wonderful pasta dinner at Opus II.

They didn't make love until the Blazers' first playoff success. That night they dined at Donald's favorite steak house, his eyes dancing over the oil lamp's rancid flame.

"Donald," Spencer asked well into her second glass of wine, "do you ever do anything…you know, other than basketball?"

"Sure, silly" Ah…an endearment.

"Like what? What do you like?"

"Oh, lots of things. I'm just busy you know? Law school isn't for the frivolous." He launched into a tidy lecture about responsibility while she studied his jaw line, the way his teeth were so perfect they didn't look quite real.

"Yes, I know. But like, what's your favorite thing to do? Besides basketball?"

"Philately."

"Stamps, right?" she asked queasily, for Jonathon was obsessive about his stamp collection.

"Yes. I've got an amazing collection. Handed to me by my father, and his father before him. Worth a small fortune," he laughed. He was in a good mood. The wine had softened his natural tightness, making him quite handsome in that moment. "What about you?"

"Films. I'm just wild for films. Watching them, studying them. Making them. I want to be a filmmaker some day." Only then did she hear how ridiculous, how pompous it sounded. Like when you're a kid and say you want to be an astronaut. A brain surgeon. A Scotland yard spy.

"You're not serious." He teased good-naturedly. "You can't make any money doing that."

"It has nothing to do with money," she responded loftily.

"All I'm saying is, what are the odds? It's like all these dreamers on campus who are writing the great American novel. How many of their manuscripts are ever even going to get finished? Find their way to a publisher? Maybe one? And how many more of them will finally realize they can't write their way out of a bucket, that their dribbly little ideas are so cliched and naïve…" His voice trailed off. So a poet's heart beat beneath that pristinely ironed oxford shirt and a single rejection had sent him on the path of respectability.

"Donald," she sympathized.

"Come on, it's so goddamn predictable." He threw his napkin down in disgust.

"And you're not?"

"Yes. I'm very predictable and that's why I'm going to be successful."

When Donald drove her home in silence she had already decided good riddance. But when he killed the motor and leaned to her, his eyes were sincere. "So. We've had our first fight. Want to make up?" He kissed her tenderly, sweetly, and when his tongue found her own, the anger she was fighting to maintain dissolved into a force stronger than the will to dislike him.

Fast forward two years. Donald graduated with distinction, passing the bar and forging ahead with Buckman, Buckman, Steele and Witherspoon, while Spencer changed her major four times and continued to struggle with part-time accounting jobs.

Donald and she had very little in common but their disparities did not stop them from moving in together after their first anniversary of paper-bagging it between his apartment and her studio. She moved into his fashionable loft in the northwest believing she would get to know the real man behind the façade. But on the rare occasions they spoke over dinner the conversations pertained to the practical and affordable. Or law.

Sameness. How quickly time passes—how sameness, routine and safety flicks life away in a New York second. How quickly one grows old when there is no change. And how little one is aware of it. Our lives had become the drudge that Malcolm and I would later refer to as "practicing at life."

"You know, there's an opening at Massingers," Donald mentioned one afternoon, his penis slack against his thigh after they had made love. Extremely large penis, not altogether comfortable.

"Assistant to the vice president of marketing." Those were the jewels he muttered after their passion.

"What are you saying?"

"Come on Spence, how long do you plan to be a professional student?"

"I *am* working toward something you know, Donald."

"Yeah? What's that?"

"I've told you." Truth was she could no longer remember her game plan. "I'm just trying to find the right niche so I can make some quick money to support a small film project."

"Right." Donald was maddeningly calm. Then he leaned over and gazed into her eyes, searching. This was new. Penetration of the soul. Her heart beat a different waltz until he said, "If you were going to have made a film or be a writer, you'd have something to show for it by now. Even a rejection letter."

He rolled over and got out of bed. She lay there, stripped of any comfort, churning his words over in her head again and again. She lay there until it was dark and he returned to remind her they were meeting his parents for dinner.

"I'm not going. I don't feel well." She couldn't face those words *and* his stuffy-back-Eastern-Republican parents.

She was curled in the same position when he returned two hours later, heard him softly go through his routine, the one he performed every night with the precision and exactness required of a shuttle launch. When he finally climbed into bed and before his breathing calmed, she said in a small voice, but one that she knew he heard from his sigh of satisfaction, "I'll take it."

* * *

For a time success brightened her world. She forgot the dreams that still beat lightly through her veins. If she wasn't directing a movie, she was directing the housewives of America into purchasing Client X's Line of House and Home with their enticing ad campaigns.

"I'm so proud of you," Donald cooed at dinner one night. "Success becomes you."

"Yeah, I'm such a star," Spencer replied grimly.

"What's the problem?" Donald flipped through the menu, annoyed.

"No problem."

"Spence."

"OK. I just didn't think it...it was going to be like this."

"Like what?"

"Dog-eat-dog. Someone always has to lose. I just cost Jim Butterfield his promotion."

"Butterfield is a loser."

"No he's not. He's kind of a dignified asshole, whose ideas aren't as sharp as they once were."

"Sweetie, just do your job. Don't worry about Jim."

"That's why I wanted to make a movie. Nobody gets hurt."

Donald cocked an eyebrow as disdainful as it was incredulous. "You are so in dreamland, Spencer, sometimes it scares me."

"What? What did I say?"

"You think the film business—hell, any business, is any different? You don't think it isn't all about winning whether you're making cars or pushing little home-made baby booties? Don't be so naïve. It is *all* about winning. Winning and then winning some more. Because as soon as you start losing, like Butterfield, you're over. Come on," he brightened, "this is supposed to be a celebration."

She weakly held up her champagne glass. "Cheers."

Two months later a rumor leaked that Jim Butterfield was on his way out He invited Spencer to play handball that week. Grunting, sweating, smashing point after point she knew it was his balls they were knocking about without mercy, his guts on the line. He saw Spencer falter, walked over to her, beads of sweat dripping from his brow.

"Hit this goddamn thing like you're serving it to me for breakfast."

They were kindred spirits. Neither of them wanted the killer instinct, but it was a necessary evil. She hit the ball so far into the corner he shattered his knee diving for it. On the way to the hospital he muttered, "I didn't say breaka ma leg," in a silly Brando Mafioso squeak. Then winked at her and they shared a smile. Not unlike the initiation of the dead bird, so many years ago in that cemetery, she had now trespassed into the world of cut-throat reality. Little did she know how well it would serve her.

* * *

It was during her second year at Massingers that she ran into Adrienne at a bookstore. She was at the check-out stand buying *How to Make a Movie on a Shoestring*, *Ten Thousand Dollar Flick*, and *Kamikaze Film-Making*, along with several industry rags when she heard a voice from the opposite cashier.

"Spencer?"

She looked up and right into those eyes.

"Adrienne! Wow…how are you?" she stammered.

"Great. What about you?"

"Same." She took her change and walked out of the line where Adrienne joined her.

"So…did you get your, uhm, your restaurant?" Spencer nervously grappled with her purchases while Adrienne stood, confident and poised.

"Well, yes and no. I actually own a bar. All the money's in booze."

"Oh. Where is it?"

"Over in the northwest. I found an old warehouse and remodeled it. It's got a great dance floor."

"Oh…well, Donald and I will have to come by some time."

"I don't know about that." She grinned, reflecting crooked white teeth in a crooked smile that twisted down at one part of her mouth. Spencer remembered now how it warmed her face, softened the animal drive.

"Pardon?" she asked, confused.

"It's a gay bar, Spencer."

"Oh." She wasn't sure if her response was audible, or if her mouth just formed the letter.

"Here's my card." Adrienne pulled one from her blazer pocket and handed it to Spencer. "I've gotta run. It was great seeing you."

Adrienne smiled one more time for the benefit of the adrenaline pumping through Spencer's stomach and raced off, Spencer's eyes following her strong back until Adrienne was lost in the crowd on the streets. An inexplicable sadness washed over her.

* * *

It had been nearly three years since she had seen her younger sister. Jill had come to visit from Seattle to meet Donald and join Spencer for Thanksgiving that year, and Spencer noticed that her body was a bit rounder than usual. She was so used to seeing it without an ounce of fat, almost identical to Cal's—short, thick and muscular—and could never see her without thinking of him. Rebecca had always been the beauty queen, Jill was handsome, with her angular Italian nose, and Spencer...she was the one with the brains and energy. Even though the three learned to love one another like soldiers stuck in the same bombed-out bunker, they had spent far too many hours arguing over the same ridiculous and petty concerns that drive most dysfunctional families.

It was Jill, in her brutally honest way, who had nabbed Spencer in the women's room when she first met Donald over dinner and hissed, "You're not going to marry him, are you?"

"Well, I...I really don't know."

"You're kidding, right?"

"Why? What's wrong with him?"

"Spence, come on! He's a gweeb." Subtlety was not Jill's strongest suit.

"Look, he's not a bad guy. He's a bit nervous around you. You know, he's not used to you yet."

"He's not used to *you* yet," she snorted.

On Thanksgiving the three of them sat at Donald's formal table amidst a forced gaiety while they devoured the turkey and dressing in a desperate attempt to stuff themselves into a false sense of celebration. Later, they struggled into the living room to rest until they could make room for dessert. But Donald couldn't wait. He emerged from the kitchen bearing a silver service tray with his famous pumpkin crème brulee, and just as he presented a ramekin to Jill, she projectile vomited all over the table.

"You idiot! You've ruined my—" Donald bellowed. "—Do you have any idea? It took me two goddamn days!"

Spencer jumped up and herded Jill into the bathroom while Donald fumed. Spencer urged Jill to the guest bedroom but she assured Spencer she was fine.

"I just can't believe this! What—do you have the flu?" Donald whined in protest "You're going to make everyone sick."

"I'm not sick," Jill replied. "I'm pregnant."

"What?!" They both stared at her.

"I'm pregnant"

"Well, who's the father?" Spencer asked.

Jill put a napkin to her mouth as she belched. "It's artificial insemination. I'm pretty impressed Mom didn't tell you. I didn't ever think she'd be able to hold out."

"But—" Donald began.

"My lover and I decided we wanted to have a baby."

"Your lover?"

"Yeah." Jill held up a drumstick. "We decided it was turkey baster time."

Donald and Spencer sat there like children who had just discovered Santa Claus was a figment of imagination perpetuated by Macy's and The Gap. Jill laughed with a trace of vindication. "Jesus Christ, you mean Mom didn't tell you that either?" Then, smiling proudly as if embracing a holy religion, "I'm a lesbian."

Donald was silent and befuddled the entire day, but that night he paced their bedroom, muttering, "I can't believe it. I can't believe that she would do it."

"What, be a lesbian?"

"Oh, give me more credit I know she can't help what she is. I'm talking about the pregnancy—that she would bring a child into this. A *turkey baster* for Christ's sakes. It's not even sanitary."

"Oh, and penises are?"

"You know what I mean. Those germs are normal."

Spencer laughed at that. It struck her as funny. "Look, Donald, I'll admit it took me a few hours to get used to the idea. I mean Jill's always been different. And if she's happy being a lesbian, great. My worry is that she's too young to have a baby, that she doesn't have the resources to take care of it properly. When I have a baby—"

He shot a glance her way. "Don't even—"

"Oh, Donald, I'm sure. We have no room in our lives for a baby." And that struck her as an odd sentiment as well. He climbed into bed and snuggled close, as if Spencer was a measure of sanity against all that Jill represented; a world that didn't want or need men.

"Oh, honey, I'm so glad at least that you're..." But the word hung in the air. He couldn't say it, not after he'd been telling her how *not* normal she had been for the past few months. She supposed he had to count his blessings. At least she wasn't pregnant or a lesbian.

* * *

In an effort to show her acceptance, Spencer decided to take Jill to Adrienne's bar, Girl's Town. She had done a great job renovating the space, with a late eighties chic interior, tastefully framed Nagel artwork, and a giant revolving disco ball. Madonna boomed from the loudspeakers and several patrons drank at the long bar that faced the dance floor.

Spencer grabbed for Jill's arm as they walked up to the bar. It had seemed like a good idea at the time. Get Jill out of the house, away from Donald. Separate them as much as possible for the remainder of her visit.

"Hey, how did *you* know about this place?" Jill asked.

"I get around," she croaked over the music.

"Well you know I can't drink but I can buy you a beer."

"Sure."

As they perched themselves on two bar stools, Adrienne came striding through swinging doors, holding a clipboard, heading their way in her abrupt business mode.

"Hey, Adrienne," Spencer called, but she must not have heard her over the music as she continued through a counter-door behind the bar to check supplies. It wasn't until Adrienne turned toward the dance floor that she saw Spencer sitting in front of her.

She did a minor double-take and when she smiled Spencer's knees quivered.

"What are you all doing here?"

She looked surprised but a part of Spencer felt as if it was no surprise to her at all—as if she had expected her. Spencer introduced Jill and Adrienne and they immediately fell into a comfortable rapport. They spoke the same language, after all. Spencer glanced around and saw women sporting short haircuts, dressed in flannel shirts and jeans, and immediately knew she was the outsider. As her eyes continued to rove she saw two women fondling one another on the dance floor. Another dressed in leather from head to toe shot pool. Her left arm was obscured by tattoos and she smoked her cigarette as if it were her last. The woman next to her looked every bit as rough, and as she bent to take her shot, the woman in leather leaned over her and began to dry hump her.

Spencer's head quickly spun back to the bar. Adrienne's eyes caught hers and she gently put a hand to Spencer's. "Can I get you something to drink?"

She nodded emphatically.

"Well?" Adrienne's mouth crooked down, a tender teasing.

"Martini. Tanqueray."

Adrienne made it herself and set it in front of Spencer. She gulped the drink and desperately dug through her purse for a cigarette. She inhaled deeply and her head began to spin. Thankfully, after about a half-hour, Jill began to feel nauseous and asked if they could go home.

Adrienne walked them out to their car. Once there, Spencer stood awkwardly fidgeting with her keys.

"It was good to see you," Adrienne said. "Think you'll come again?"

"Oh…I don't know. I just, you know, brought Jill. Thought she would like it."

"Oh." Adrienne put a hand in her pocket. "Well, I guess I should get back to work."

"You did a great job, though," Spencer added quickly. "I mean with the bar. It's nice."

"Thanks."

"Well…" *Why couldn't she just say goodbye?*

"Goodbye Spencer." Adrienne turned and walked back into her bar.

* * *

After the Thanksgiving weekend Jill returned to Seattle and Spencer went back to her life, as deprived of meaning as it was. She had taken to silently stealing away two nights a week to The Voice of Independent Film, a class where eager dreamers sat raptly listening to Perry Van Houten, a washed up screenwriter who had script-doctored a big hit in the late seventies.

Squandering large portions of class time, Van Houten rebuked his students for imagining they had "a snowball's chance in hell of making it down there. This little class here is nothing more than fun and games, but I'm here to tell you not one of you here has the balls to make it. If you did you'd be down there. Not here."

The students squirmed in their chairs, sheepish and chagrined. But the woman sitting next to Spencer turned, and rolled her eyes, then grinned. Exotic. Beautiful. What had gotten into Spencer? She had started noticing women everywhere. In the market, at the video store. Running through the park she had passed an athletic blonde and thought the woman had given her a flirtatious smile.

"So why are you here?" Van Houten's rhetoric drilled through her thoughts. "Because we all have this little voice in us that says, 'I'm different. I'm the one who's gonna make it.' " He drew heavily on his cigarette as the class waited, hoping for that one clue, that one piece of the puzzle that *would* make the difference.

This class was the only important thing in her life, and he was ruining it. She got up and began to walk out the door.

"Excuse me, Miss?" Van Houten called after her, but she didn't answer him.

"I guess that qualifies as mutiny," Spencer said cryptically as she sat in her car waiting for the heaters to begin to thaw the frost on the windshield. She couldn't go home and face the empty apartment. She decided to take a drive to clear her mind. Of course she was heading there, but when she found herself parked outside Girl's Town she let her car idle.

"What the hell are you doing?" she asked herself under her breath, gunned the motor and sped away.

* * *

Heavily armed with the defense of bringing a "bar-warming gift," Spencer returned to the bar the following day at noon so there could be no confusion as to her intentions. Broad daylight. The bar should be empty. No ambience by which to confuse the issue.

Adrienne was receiving a beer delivery, directing the driver to the storage pantry in the back of the bar when she saw Spencer holding a square package that reached to her knees.

"What's this?" She came from a storage locker, walked up the stairs and joined Spencer in the sunlight.

"A bar-warming gift. I just think it's great what you were able to do. After all, I know what you went through—you know, all the numbers and stuff. It was pretty ambitious and you pulled it off." She stopped, scratched the side of her lip. "Anyway, I'm impressed. Here." She handed Adrienne the package.

She took it and motioned Spencer to follow her inside. She led her to the office, a small cubby filled with liquor receipts, bar tabs, ashtrays, new drink concoctions and general disarray. She offered Spencer a chair, but she remained standing as Adrienne unwrapped the present, a framed black and white photo, circa nineteen twenty, of women in drag in a Parisian salon. Adrienne shook her head, then laughed.

"This is great. It really is." She kept staring at it. "And I know right where to put it. Follow me."

Down a tunnel and into the bowels of the forbidden. It was dark as night until Adrienne switched a knob that turned on the dance floor lights. She headed behind the bar and took down a nondescript painting that hung over the cash register and replaced it with the Parisian *Les Femmes Dangereuses*.

"God, I just love it. It's perfect." She cocked her head appreciatively. "And now you must let me make you lunch."

"That's okay. I've got to get back to the office."

"Come on, you've got to eat."

Spencer hesitated for a moment, then agreed.

Over lunch they sat in one of the dimly lit booths and Adrienne talked about the problems she'd had finding the right investors, how crazy the bar business was, and how she wasn't sure she had made the right decision.

"Then why did you do it?"

"I wanted to have someplace nice for the dykes to go to, you know? But they don't appreciate it. Complain, complain, complain. That's all they do. I don't know. Maybe I'm just having an off day."

"I'm sorry."

"Don't be. You've made it perfect." She grinned at Spencer, and her direct gaze did not waver. "So, Spencer, what are *you* doing here?"

Spencer bit her lower lip.

"You just passing through? Curious?"

"Well, you know my sister Jill—she's a les...les—she's like you and everyone here all..." She ran a nervous hand through her hair. "Let's just say I'm trying to adjust—and you know, figure it all out."

"So what's your story?" Adrienne leaned back, assessing her.

"Story? Not much of one I'm afraid."

"You're interesting. Something about you."

"It's been so long since anyone found anything about me interesting," she responded without thinking. "I guess that sounded pretty lame."

"Not at all." Adrienne's smile radiated across the table and Spencer found herself digging her fingers against her jeans.

"Let's see." Adrienne leaned across the table. "Here's the deal. You're from a rich family, desperately misunderstood. All anyone wants for you is success. Junior League Poo-Badom. But you have dreams. Filmmaking, right?"

She nodded, fascinated by Adrienne.

"Your family and boyfriend"—she waited for Spencer to supply his name, "Donald find you maddeningly wild and histrionic. Donald is a great guy, but uptight. He wears plaid golfing clothes on Sunday and has a Roman numeral trailing a cumbersomely long name. He's not bad to look at if you like the chiseled blond Aryan thing, but the family has had you married off to him since the second grade. The only thing that keeps you from jumping into the Willamette is the secret lover you have stashed in a trailer park in Gresham who rides a Harley, smokes dope and whispers poetic nonsense in your ear. And of course, this one scintillating conversation."

She was laughing. Adrienne was a jewel.

"See? It's not so hard to talk about yourself, is it?"

And then Spencer did. She talked her head off. She told Adrienne about her past, her childhood, her daydream desires to be a filmmaker—a writer. She kvetched about her job, and Massinger and the whole screwy corporate system. She had stopped checking her watch sometime after she knew she was already an hour late back to the office, and then she spoke about Jill, and her unexpected declaration.

"That must have come as quite a surprise," Adrienne mused, grinning.

"What came as more of surprise is that she's pregnant."

"Turkey baster?"

Spencer nodded.

"How did what's his—Donald take it?"

"Oh, like most men. He found it threatening and titillating in the same breath."

Adrienne sipped the last of her coke. "And how did you take it?"

It was the way Adrienne asked, the lowered huskiness to her voice that made Spencer glance up, but as soon as she caught her expression, she felt compelled to play with the salt shaker.

"Well. Well, I'm…I'm fine with it. I love my Jilly Bean." But they both knew she was trying too hard. "I just don't have a lot of experience with—"

They peered into one another's eyes for a very long moment then. "And you?" Spencer finally asked.

"I've been a lesbian for as long as I can tell," she stated simply and again contemplated Spencer with unnerving directness.

"Oh my God." She gathered her things too quickly. "I can't believe we've been sitting here all afternoon."

"Yeah, well, don't be a stranger," she said cryptically as Spencer got up and walked out of the booth.

* * *

She kept reminding herself that life was good. Solid. Donald had made the leap to partner. They lived in a wonderful apartment. They had IRAs. But she had begun to feel like pick up sticks—a chaotic mess all tentatively and interdependently resting against one another. As if impending doom lay right around the corner. Why was she fretting? Things were, if not exactly gripping with Donald, at least status quo. And Massinger was thrilled with her work.

He made a habit of entering her office toward the end of a long day, heaving his girth upon the corner of her desk, giving himself license to finger the familiar objects. "I sure know how to pick 'em. No, no"—he'd raise his hands as if Spencer was about to interrupt—"women are better than men. Have to be. But what really puts you a cut above the rest is you know it requires sacrifice. You know your personal life comes second."

After the last such encounter Spencer stared at the pile of work on her desk and simply got up and walked from the office, telling her secretary she was coming down with the flu. She drove to a video store near their apartment and asked the gangly youth with a Van Halen T-shirt behind the counter for a movie. "I want a... something...well, I don't know, emotional. I don't know, romantic, maybe, but it isn't necessary, I just want it to be really good, you know?"

He turned with intent, walked a couple of steps and then with an almost poetic gesture removed a tape and presented it as if he were handing her the translation to an ancient religion.

When she got home she quickly shed her clothes, closed all the shades, slipped the video in and sat on the couch in her slip.

When Donald came home she was on her third viewing of Moira Shearer's balletic dive to her death in the tortured conclusion of *The Red Shoes*. Donald turned on the lights, but stopped when he saw her tearstained face, the half-finished bottle of Jack Daniel's on the end table.

"Spencer, what's wrong?"

She turned to him with puffy eyes.

"Oh, God, it's your stepfather."

"No." She could barely choke out the words. "It's Moira Shearer...she's...soo...sooooo...saaaaad," she wailed.

"What?" Donald's shock transformed to annoyance. "Who's Moira—whatever?"

"The dancer." She pointed to the TV set. "In the movie. *The Red Shoes*."

"What the hell is going on here, Spence?"

"It's just that she had...had to chose between her passion for dance...and and"—she *was* drunk—"and the love of her life."

"Look, I know you've been working too hard lately, but this isn't the end of the goddamn world, you know. You're just tired. Go to bed."

"No."

"Go to bed, Spencer."

"No."

He slumped a bit until he targeted the Jack Daniel's. "You're drunk."

"An apt ober-servation," she giggled.

"This is going too far." Donald began to pace. "You need help, Spencer. I suggest you seek therapy. You used to be a sensible person who had goals, met them and was happy with life. Now you're an emotional roller coaster. Every day it's something else. I can't take it anymore. You know that? I want the woman I first met."

"This *is* the woman you first met. The one you've been living with is an impostor."

"Great film dialogue, Spence, but this is real life."

"That's what I'm afraid of."

He picked up the bottle, then set it back down. "Don't let your stress make you a statistic."

"See, Donald? Movie dialogue feels pretty good, doesn't it?" she snapped back. He stalked out of the room and down the hall to the bedroom.

But this wasn't a movie set, and Donald and she weren't in the throes of heady romance. No soundtrack foreshadowed the next stick plucked from her wavering equilibrium. As she stared at the frozen image of the impassioned Moira who could not live without her world of dance, she realized her life was too real.

It had no illusion. No fantasy. No romance.

She turned off the lights, sat back down on the couch and hit the remote.

The next day she sat in her office with a killer hangover and pretended to work. Donald was right. She had to get a grip. She was actually beginning to see her spinout and was about to call Sarah, but when she picked up the phone she dialed an entirely different number.

* * *

When Adrienne opened the door to her bar Spencer stood paralyzed. Adrienne led her to a bar stool, went behind the counter, and poured a healthy shot of heated cognac.

"Here. It's cold outside."

"No, it's just that—" Spencer's hands trembled as she lit a cigarette. She was giddy with rebellion yet in the same breath terrified to be sitting in Adrienne's bar. "I...I guess I'm sort of stuck."

"So. What's the problem?"

"Me. I'm the problem...my life...the fact that I don't have one. Or not the one I planned on anyway."

" 'Life is what happens while you're making other plans' ?"

Spencer raised the glass in a touché gesture, gulped back the cognac. The warmth began to spread through her limbs, fended off the sense of peril. She studied Adrienne as she leaned against the bar. So goddamn compelling with her dangerous, angry blue eyes. Alive.

"How do you do it?"

"Do what?"

"Hold it all together. Put yourself out there. You seem like you have all the answers. Like nothing musses you up."

"Believe me, I get mussed." She smiled sympathetically. "Why don't you start from the beginning?"

Spencer didn't really know how to say that a video had toppled her over the deep end. That by watching the heroine's ordeal, making the age-old choice between one's art or love, she had been sent reeling. "The thing is, I can't even compare myself to her. It's not like I've been suffering for my art."

"No, it sounds like you've just been suffering."

And with that simplest of truths, Spencer began to cry, alternately hating herself and feeling sorry for herself as she told Adrienne about her life. "I'm sorry. This is so ridiculous. Here I am blithering about all my problems and you barely know me—"

"I know you," Adrienne stated. "Don't you think I know you, Spencer?"

Spencer tried to catch her breath, wiping the last of her tears. "Ughh...I'm exhausted. I'm exhausted until I could just lie down and sleep forever."

"Well, I wouldn't go that far." Adrienne moved from behind the bar, steered Spencer by the elbow, directing her to the dance floor. She went inside the DJ booth and expertly flipped a turntable. Slow lazy jazz sifted through the speakers.

Adrienne walked directly to Spencer, stood a moment, a gentle smile in her eyes. She put her hands up, waiting.

"I don't bite," she teased.

Spencer reached for her and the instant she touched Adrienne she knew.

Adrienne's right hand moved to her waist. She wanted so badly for Adrienne to touch her, yet...

Adrienne's body began to sway to the music. Spencer stood ramrod straight, refusing to bend until Adrienne's hand pressed gently against her shoulder blade...trying to breathe, as Adrienne's arm circled her waist, leaving her no option but to follow Adrienne's lead. Her commanding lead, as she moved Spencer against the length of her body and Spencer's knees buckled. Literally.

Spencer could barely stand, so swift was the rushing of blood to her head. She held onto Adrienne for fear of falling, smelling her perfume from the heat of her skin, mingled with breathy cognac and she knew she wanted to taste her tongue, her lips and feel the skin of her cheek touch her own, the heat of desire at her neck. Adrienne did not move any further toward her, simply guided Spencer around the dance floor, the puppet to her string.

Spencer wrapped her arms about Adrienne, latching on for dear life, the pounding of her heart making itself known in every region of her body, blackening out thought as Adrienne's lips neared ever closer to her own, her hands at Spencer's neck, holding her fast, her mouth demanding an answer that became an agony of bitten lips, crushing teeth, a swimming of tongue and saliva—a searing through of Spencer's body. Adrienne pushed her against a wall. She fell limp as Adrienne's body pressed against her own, her hands unfastening buttons, bruising Spencer's skin, tongue in her ear, and then her pants loosened, Adrienne's hand down between her thighs, and then, yes, where she wanted her, deep inside her, pushing through her, and as soon as she felt Adrienne's thumb on her clitoris, her head fell back...she was coming, coming hard as Adrienne panted her name...she thought it was her name...She couldn't hear, see...she could only feel Adrienne filling her up and letting herself surrender, she shuddered into her power.

* * *

They lay in Adrienne's bed in the pale of dawn, in an apartment several blocks away from the bar. Spencer was exalted. From lack of sleep and pure adrenaline, from adventure and fear. She was loved. She was adored. She had been ravaged.

As Adrienne dozed Spencer studied her profile, her strong nose slightly bent from a childhood accident, her skin a pale alabaster, her lips thin with tension even in sleep. She dared herself to gaze over Adrienne's half-naked body. She was as close to Amazonian as Spencer had ever seen with the deep crevasse at her spine, her massive back muscles taut and defined, swimmer's shoulders. Strong calves led to the promise of well-defined thighs, just hidden beneath the sheets that caressed the form of her narrow hips and full breasts. As Spencer gently lifted the sheet she thought Adrienne, in fact, had a man's body, with just enough curve to be a woman's. Suddenly she caught a reflection of her own face in a warped mirror that hovered above Adrienne's bed, amused to see the smile that lit her face. When she turned to her, Adrienne was watching her.

"Hey."

"Hey," Spencer returned.

"Feel any better?"

"Yes." She grinned. "I should say so."

Adrienne was silent for a long moment as she studied Spencer. "Spencer. What do you want to be when you grow up?"

Spencer played with the sheet in her hand.

"I'm serious."

"I want to be a filmmaker," she responded timidly and pulled the sheet closer to her.

"Then you're going to have to jump in all the way." Adrienne took in the sight of their naked bodies. "Like you did last night."

"What do you mean?"

"It's great you're taking these courses. One here. One there. But you're just standing on the fringes where it's comfortable. Trust me I know. It took me a couple of years before I could get off my duff and buy the bar. If you really want to make it, in anything, you gotta be inside it. All the way. Not just an evening here and some weekends."

"Yeah, well I still have a national deficit to contribute to."

"You can do it much faster making film. Believe me."

Then Adrienne leaned over, kissed her. Thoroughly. "Know one thing about me Spencer," she whispered as Spencer gasped for air, "I'm ruthless. When I know what I want, I go after it. Take no prisoners. Do you know what I mean?"

Adrienne's eyes narrowed as she peered into Spencer's and she nodded obediently.

How could I know women's lips were tender, their skin like liquid fire. That I would be moved by the hollow flutter at their throats, the soft inside of their thighs…the grace with which they moved, the gentle touch of slender fingers on my face…eyes in which I saw deeper into myself. How could I know what I had been missing all my life, that I had a quaking desire and it was called woman?

* * *

She spent Wednesday and Thursday nights with Adrienne before she returned to close the bar. Spencer told Donald that she had a new documentary film class that met both nights, and further convinced him that she had to stay late to work with her film partner after class. Lying. And quite artfully. The one thing she had prided herself on never doing. She told the truth even when it could be omitted, even when it hurt her.

But she couldn't help herself. From lying or from being with Adrienne. She counted the minutes until she could be with her, time ticking by like glacial plates molding a new earth, a new Spencer being molded as she lay beneath her. Adrienne owned her. Moving over her body, caressing it not with mere kisses but a hunger of embraces that unleashed the wanton in her. She had never been so wanted, so ached for, and it was a potent elixir to her bludgeoned esteem, an opiate that led to addiction.

For how could she let go of Adrienne's desire for her—lips upon her, moving her, making her come in an assault of sensation. Her tongue melding into her swollen need until one became the other and Spencer fell into an abyss of pleasure, ever building, ever mounting…Adrienne's mouth teasing as Spencer neared release— but not until Adrienne so demanded. Adrienne's command grew stronger, her control ever more dominating.

Spencer lay splayed out before her. She would do anything. Whatever Adrienne wanted in those moments where she took her outside of herself, fingers flicking at the direct source of her pleasure in an endless repetition as precise as a pianist's drill, one arm wrapped around Spencer's thigh, her hand holding her open, the other inside. Adrienne possessed every part of her, created every nuance of sensation, and the more she exposed herself to Adrienne, the sharper Adrienne's voice rasped in her ear, the tighter her mouth became, the narrower her eyes as Spencer bottomed out to her over and over again.

Even after Adrienne kneaded her flesh until it was bruised, kissed her mouth until she drew blood, yanked Spencer's hair and then gouged into her neck, leaving the mark of an angry lover's hickey—camouflaged by powder for days—she came back for more. Adrienne's caresses a roughening shove, a slap at her buttocks as fingers traveled from what Spencer knew to what Adrienne dared her to know—thrusting into her anus as she came, trembling at the impact. Adrienne took her places she never knew existed, Spencer's fear swallowed up by Adrienne's control, her machinations.

One night Spencer knew as she lay there after Adrienne had left for the bar, blood drying between her thighs, that this was no longer lovemaking. They were in her primary domain, a world of ever-widening foreplay, a dangerous world of stretching the boundaries, exceeding the speed limit. Adrienne's bookshelves were lined with erotica, S&M novellas; a strap-on dildo lay beneath the bed, and shackles for her lovers' wrists. And Spencer couldn't say no.

Who was this woman? Could Spencer create her character from the snatches of a tragic past? Thrown from a car at two weeks of age, left squalling in a ditch until Adrienne was discovered, many hours later, as the only remaining survivor of the accident that took her mother's life. Raised by her sternly religious widower father, Adrienne began acting out as soon as she entered adolescence. Drugs, drinking, playing around. She was caught with an older woman at seventeen and flung from the house. Roamed the streets until she ran into the first sign of comfort, a drifter who quickly got her pregnant. She gave her baby up for adoption, and her father sent her away to school, hopeful for rehabilitation. Adrienne's rehab was LSD. But she was brilliant and educated Spencer on many subjects, not the least of which was sex. But the majority of Spencer's lessons ran to the kink of Adrienne's choice, S&M, and it was difficult for her to understand the manipulations, the facades, the bifurcation of humiliation and trust.

"This isn't an intellectual exercise," Adrienne reminded her one night as they lay in bed after a particularly athletic performance involving Adrienne's dildo and whip. "You aren't supposed to understand it. You're supposed to feel it."

"I guess…" Spencer was so uncertain of herself in the face of Adrienne's experience. "I guess I thought feeling was supposed to come naturally. Without the gimmicks, you know?"

"Some people enjoy a little extra sensory stimulation." Adrienne placed her fingers across her pubic hair. "Some people need to have all their senses fired up." Adrienne continued to rub her pelvic bone, and then watching Spencer watch her, slipped her fingers over her clitoris, moving them in a slow rhythmic pattern.

Spencer swallowed, afraid to watch, afraid to turn away. She had never seen anyone do this to themselves, and a part of her was fascinated. And the little girl in her was filled with shame.

"It's okay, Spence…it's fine…feels sooo good," Adrienne's voice was husky with arousal. She licked two fingers of her left hand, tweaked her nipple, then reached for Spencer and placed her hand over Adrienne's to let her feel Adrienne masturbate, so that she would know her, feel her, feel herself becoming more and more aroused, and then Adrienne turned Spencer over, grinding herself into the fleshy part of her upper thigh as she came, then angrily shoved fingers into her, fucking Spencer harder and harder until she felt herself go numb.

"So, basically you were living with your mother and having an affair with your father figure," Therapist points out one afternoon as I sit in her office.

Of course I had never thought of it in those terms, but I could see that that was precisely what I had been doing. By light of day I let Donald belittle me, make mincemeat of my dreams, and by night I allowed Adrienne to strip me of my spirit. My shoulders inch up in discomfort as I feel the guilt over my double life with Adrienne, the shame that spread over me like a rash when she was through with me.

I wonder if that is where I began to fragment. Began to see more and more someone else playing the role of me—Spencer, executive, and clueless lover, succeeding wonderfully at failing miserably, however successful I was at punishing myself.

As I curl inward, my muscles shuddering to produce heat, I hear a rustle and realize I have my notebook in my back pocket. Can I wrinkle the pages and light them to a few pieces of soggy driftwood? I hunch up and scavenge around on my knees, feeling my way in the dark with trembling hands, gathering kindling and finding two larger pieces, feel their dampness and with it a sense of futility. With stiff and uncooperative fingers I laboriously crinkle the pages and stack the little pieces of wood crossways, lamenting my haughty dismissal of camping.

I waste one match, then another. Miraculously, however, a fire starts, my chilling breath fanning the miniature flames, and for thirty seconds I have hope, but almost immediately the papers' edges curl black, and helpless, smoke fumes kiss my cheek. I keep blowing. Another spark catches and I feed it more paper, huffing a whooshful thinking into the cinders. It takes and a pathetic camp-fire girl's fire becomes my key light. I rifle the pages I have left in my notepad and wonder how long I can keep this thing alive.

Taking inventory can be the simple act of counting, coveting, or as in the Twelve Step program assessing all your past failures. Or as I am now appraising the most basic of elements that may keep me alive. Or in despair of that, gleaning lessons from the widest array of memories that may prove to be my salvation. If I can just put it together, like one of those party gifts—untie the knot without pulling the strings—perhaps I will finally understand what became of me.

In the movies people always have what Sarah and Malcolm and I refer to as "cinematic epiphanies"—Clark Gable's newborn infant is dying so he finds religion, Cary Grant suddenly survives his incurable undocumented illness when Carole Lombard decides to fight for their love, and Scarlett only realizes she loves Rhett when he walks out the door.

In real life we may attempt cinematic moments to push us beyond our safety zone. But for me it was the small things in life that led to my epiphany.

* * *

Jill had returned from Seattle, sans lover with nowhere to go, so Spencer and Donald took her in until she could get on her feet. Since Donald quickly became absent working on a case in San Francisco, Spencer had no need to confront all the issues bubbling beneath her surface. When she shared with Jill that she had a secret lover and the secret was a woman, Jill eagerly became coach, cheerleader and therapist all wrapped into one. They alternated between being sisterly and loving and Bette Davis siblings from hell. Her pregnancy and Spencer's general depression rubbed salt into old wounds. But Jill was resourceful. She fell in love with Kat before things got too bad and moved into an aging but beautiful Victorian in northeast Portland. The few times she could convince Donald to have dinner with them Donald seemed to like Kat well enough, but he couldn't get over that "they" had somehow taken the world by the balls and created their own rules.

As Adrienne had created her own rules. Rules that terrified Spencer more and more. She spent fewer evenings with her, slowly understanding that what she had initially perceived as unlimited passion was not desire, but Adrienne grasping for her own salvation through power and revenge.

Spencer droned on at Massingers, loathing her job and wanting to blame Donald for her life. He had always been so solid and focused, so she listened. Adrienne was built of Amazonian savagery, so she listened. They, after all, knew what they were doing, whether they had chosen a path of cautious predictability or one of darkened coves, chains and leather.

Spencer had to take responsibility and participate in a resolution. She decided to write again. If she just wrote, whatever— type the same key over and over, string silly sentences together, perhaps, just maybe, she would begin to feel better.

The chief tenet in every manual on writing she had ever read was *write what you know.* So she did. She wrote every evening and weekends. She canceled dates with Adrienne so she could write. She wrote in the pitch of stillness before dawn. She wrote gibberish, mixed metaphors, and screwed up syntax as she spewed every thought racing through her mind on paper, alternating between wretched drivel and moments of literary insight.

And then one day, that final straw was plucked from her carefully contained bundle of pick up sticks and it all came crashing down.

It was during a writer's high—inside one of her climactic scenes—when she experienced one of those altered experiences every writer cherishes. A writer's version of being in the zone. Your fingers can't type fast enough, your head doesn't even know what your subconscious has instructed you to write. You have no idea if it's day or night, rainy or sunny, because you only exist inside that screen, the scene inside the deep of you, and what has transpired can be attributed less to your brilliance and more to the muse. If someone interrupts, it's like waking from a coma.

It was during such a moment that Donald sauntered in, leaned over her shoulder, and harrumphed sarcastically. Spencer could smell his disgust, feel him checking his watch and then saw in her peripheral vision that he was gingerly leaning down and pulling the plug. Her screen went black. For several moments she was too stunned to move.

"What the hell do you think you're doing? Jesus Christ, do you have any idea how much I just lost?"

"Do you have any idea how much you're going to lose? It's ten-thirty."

"I don't care if it's...it's—" but she was too upset to be clever.

"Spencer, Massinger called me yesterday. He's been worried about you the past couple of months. Thinks something is affecting your performance."

"Do you think that macho jerk move you just made is going to stop me?"

"Maybe it'll make you think. This is serious now. You've been late three times in the past two weeks." His voice wavered as she began to approach him, fists clenched in rage.

"I *will* write, Donald. I will write when I want, for as long as I want and if I want to stay in my bathrobe all day and skip work there's not a friggin' thing you can do about it."

"Spence—"

"Don't say another word. I could hit you right now, Donald. I mean it. I could smash your smug little face in."

He smiled then, coy and apologetic. "I'm sorry. I guess that wasn't very nice."

"Very nice?"

"Oh, Spencer, grow the fuck up."

She blasted him, knuckles sinking into his smooth-shaven face, producing a thwacking sound—the exact sound she heard when Jonathon hit her.

Donald sprawled backwards onto the sofa, too shocked to speak. She was mortified. She had never hit another human in her life.

"Pulling the plug isn't going to stop me. So keep the hell out of my way." And with that she returned to the bedroom and dressed for work.

It was Friday and she was already three hours late. She stared out the window and at the work before her. She moved through her day in a fog. The instant the second hand peaked at Five O'Clock, Spencer robotically filled her briefcase and left. She almost got in an accident as she drove to deposit her paycheck.

The bank line crawled. Donald had asked her to get loan applications for houses. The house they were purchasing not as a symbol of their white-picket fence perfection, but as a tax break. What was she doing picking up loan forms for a house she was desperately against? She glanced at the clock. 5:30. An obscenely long queue commanded the attention of three tellers. Stuffy and uncomfortable, she searched the lifeless, bored faces around her. She swallowed several times. Heat pushed its way from her neck over her face. Maybe she was coming down with the flu. The weary faces swam before her like suffocating flotsam.

5:36. What was she doing with her life?

5:40. She could change it. Sure…there was time.

5:47. Why didn't she leave Donald?

5:52. How did Adrienne fit in?

5:56. What was she doing with her life?

5:59. "Next."

She walked to the teller, a disenchanted Benjamin Savings clone wearing a pink bold lettered pin bearing the acronym: TGIF.

"May I help you?" the teller asked rotely. Spencer glanced at the line, no shorter than when she was at the back of it. Secretary, executive, construction worker, nurse, Domino's pizza delivery boy, waitress; all with the same dismal pall in their face: TGIF.

"Excuse me, Miss, but it's closing time."

She put her check down with the deposit slip.

"If you want to deposit this, you have to fill out the slip."

Spencer filled it out, acutely aware of the dulled, but hostile line behind her.

"Here's your receipt. Have a nice weekend."

She stood there. Then stared at the teller's face, as she waited for the next person.

"Miss, there's about a thousand people behind you."

"I don't want to deposit it."

"What?"

"Give me cash."

"Your transaction is complete," the teller huffed impatiently. "If you want another one, you'll have to go to the back of the line."

Spencer leaned over and bore down on her. "Look, *Miss*, I've already whacked someone today so just give me the goddamn cash."

After the teller counted the last hundred she gazed right through Spencer and said, "Have a nice weekend."

She returned to the office that night and wrote a letter of resignation to Massinger, citing her irretrievably lost enthusiasm, that she didn't, after all, have the sacrifice it took to be a "player." As she signed her name, she felt as if she was watching someone else's life unravel, craning her neck at the scene of an accident, terrified, but unable to tear herself away from the willful destruction.

She scribbled a short letter to Adrienne, telling her she had been right. That she needed both feet involved in whatever waltz she was dancing to and she was heading to L.A. and that she would contact her once she settled. A third letter went to Donald.

It occurred to her she should be signing this letter *Chickenshit*, but the coward in her was smart enough to know he would integrate the information more concisely if it was in writing and if she cited, numerically, the pros and cons of their relationship. Surely he must see that the con list far outweighed the pro list. She wished him well and said that she would send for her stuff.

She cleaned out her office drawers, drove home, packed as much as she could into two suitcases, stuffed her computer and as many books and treasures as she could into her car. She drove to Jill and Kat's, told them a woman needed to do what a woman needed to do.

She then, quite simply, drove out of her life.

Naked heart, lies flat and still, the beating breast no more...
Silent are the tears that paint
in a thunderous roar
the black of blood, my frozen blood...
its arid landscape raw...
My naked heart is still in love
but can beat ne'er more

Lilian sighed, huddling in a raveled woolen blanket, and stared intently at the page before her, frustrated, searching to find the precise word. She wanted something that would describe exactly a particular nuance of desperation. She peered about her room, the stained walls seeming to grow closer together. Remnants of food lay untouched on her small desk, drying undergarments swayed in the chilly draft, books and papers cluttered every free corner of space. Scrutinizing her bleak environment she reconsidered her lines and then gathered the pages thoughtfully to her breast.

She brushed slender fingers across the cover page and turned to study her curtains, their time marks ever changing. She finally stood up and took great pains to dress in her finest frock. Clutching her manuscript to her chest, she walked out the door.

An hour later she was ushered into the small offices of Applebury & Crone, Ltd. by a sickly male clerk, a stark contrast to the beefy Robert Applebury who thrust a hand in her direction. Although Applebury possessed a portly figure, he was quite handsome, with salt and pepper speckles painting his thick hair and mustache. She was led to a hard wooden seat opposite an oak desk piled with submissions.

He sat down, pulled her manuscript from a stacked pile, placed it deliberately in front of him and pursued a dramatic silence for some moments.

"Absolutely daring," he ruminated as he turned the pages of her manuscript. "It's been such a pleasure, I cannot tell you Miss Harrington. A rare pleasure indeed."

Lilian waited.

"A rare pleasure." He played with one end of his mustache. "Unfortunately—"

Lilian raised her eyes, expecting the worst.

"My dear Miss Harrington, the truth of the matter is I've never read such poetry. And in a form I've never quite seen—all rather free flowing, isn't it, but with the mark of one evidently acquainted with the classics. It's unique, Miss Harrington, and I see very well what you're striving for. An ambitious undertaking, yes. Not to say it's finished. Still needs a good deal of polishing. You are young and with time, I'm sure you will hone your craft with the best of them." He cleared his throat. "But even if you were a man, it's simply too raw. It would make the reader quite, well, I don't know any term to use other than uncomfortable. Never to my recollection have these issues been explored with such…frankness. Perhaps more accurately, unrelenting honesty. Regrettably, Applebury and Crone publishes books that entertain the reader. This, my dear, would scare them."

A silence fell over the room as Lilian's shoulders slumped. She was gripped by a familiar fear but willed her face into a mask of nonchalance.

"Thank you for your time, Mr. Applebury." Lilian got up to leave and Robert Applebury rose and approached her.

"Miss Harrington, do you mind my asking a question?"

"Not at all."

"This work, it's from personal experience, I take it."

"Yes."

"Perhaps this poetry was a necessary journey for you, to fight your demons. But, if I may, a suggestion."

Lilian met Robert Applebury's gaze and saw that he was very kind.

"Maybe for yourself, you write your poetry. But for Applebury and Crone, perhaps you would consider bending your talents to a romance. A mystery even. They do quite well. You are a very talented young woman. I would love to pay you for that talent."

"Thank you, Mr. Applebury." Lilian shook his hand. "I will consider your kind offer."

* * *

March 4, 1920

Greetings Dorothy,

Herewith, I am submitting my piece on Paris's opium dens and with a bit of delicate arm-twisting I'm sure you can convince our dear Mr. Crowninshield to publish!

Speaking of opium dens...met the ravishing Djuna Barnes—she's the talk of the town. She has the most scandalous past—married off to an uncle, and having an affair with the photographer Marsden, yet is weaving her glistening web for every lesbian of the night. I rather say she and Natalie are in direct competition for the suffragette's vote!

I have the most delicious gossip to share with you when I dock next week. Until then, you have my greatest affectation!

Yours ever so, Rabbit.

* * *

"Damn Rabbit all to hell!" These were the first words Lilian heard walking into Dorothy Parker's office. Before her paced a mite of a woman, tiny but fierce, her large, expressive eyes dancing with mock anger, short brown hair enveloping her attractive face. "How can he leave me hanging like this?"

Lilian stood just inside the door, not wanting to interrupt. The woman stole a glance in her direction then tossed the letter across the desk in disgust. She got up from her seat, muttering not quite under her breath, "I'll just have to resolve it myself and start a wicked rumor."

Lilian cleared her throat, "Mrs. Parker?"

The woman's lips were pursed in amusement as she mused over possible recriminations, then she turned to Lilian. "Yes."

"Are you—"

"Dorothy Parker. In the flesh."

Lilian walked forward. "Lilian Harrington. Robert Applebury recommended I make your acquaintance. He also advised I submit my work to Mr. Crowninshield."

"Crownie's gone for a couple of months I'm afraid." Mrs. Parker leaned forward and peered at the bound writings. "What do you have there? Tales of jealous wives beaten by their no-good philandering husbands? Or essays on our beleaguered war heroes? And please, just don't tell me you're another critic. New York is astonishingly full of critics. Like a big plate of scrambled eggs while the talent is the poor parsley wilting on the sidelines." She stopped a moment. "Hmmm…maybe I'll just clean that up and put that in my next review."

"I wouldn't know how to be a critic," Lilian said self-effacingly.

"Bully for you. Then what is it?"

"Poetry."

"Oh, dear Lord. Any good?"

"So I've heard."

"Well, hearsay's everything." Mrs. Parker deftly removed the manuscript from Lilian's hands and unceremoniously dumped it upon her desk. "There, now that's taken care of, we're just heading off for lunch. That's Mr. Benchley and myself. Care to join us?"

At that moment a slight gentleman with thinning hair and sandy mustache whisked into the room.

"Ahhh, Mr. Benchley, just in time. Did you know we are simply ravishing?"

"Ever so." He smiled appreciatively as he tipped his hat, presenting both arms to escort them from the room. "Ever so ravishing."

* * *

Three hour lunches. Glass-clinking, flask-guzzling, laughter-choked lunches. As Dorothy's new pet and project, Lilian joined her when she could, fascinated by the array of characters that were drawn to the Rose Room of the Algonquin, a musical chair parade of the famed literati of New York. Alexander Woollcott, known to his friends as the master of bitchiness, initiated the rapier-edged banter of one-up-manship that darted between the "round tablers" as they discussed—"darling it's a debate not a discussion"—the latest theater event, book, opening, and broken love affair.

It was several weeks after Lilian had first met Dorothy Parker that she noticed every time she joined them at lunch, no matter how early she might arrive, their table was already half full, and several cocktails ahead of newcomers. And no matter when she left there were just as many people straggling behind. When did these people do all the work they talked about?

"That's the secret, Lil," Dorothy offered one afternoon. "They're a great bunch of talkers. You know what they say about children being better seen than heard? It's just the opposite with writers—most of them are much better being heard than read."

"Hey Ho!" someone bellowed. All eyes turned to a tall and remarkably handsome man who entered and gracefully bowed, hat in hand. "It's Rabbit!"

Dorothy pursed her lips. "Has naughty child finally come home at last?"

"Naughty boy has returned to the scene of the criminal who's taught him every trick in the book."

A round of howls followed and general pandemonium as the man was assaulted with a flurry of questions. He was impeccably attired in his tailored Brooks Brothers suit, crisp white shirt and Guard's tie, and with his doe-brown eyes, delicate mustache painted at his upper lip and wavy brown hair, Lilian thought he was the most beautiful man she had ever seen.

"Lilian Harrington, you must meet our very own Parnell Walbrook," Dorothy purred, "whose tongue is only slightly more forked than mine own."

When he bowed to her, she caught his eyes and sensed a deeper wisdom and gentleness she had not as yet witnessed in this bunch. "But you must call me Rabbit, as all my favorite people do."

Lilian immediately loved his voice. It was not just the low and melodious timber, but the precision of his impeccable English accent. He kissed her hand.

"Oh, my. Chivalry is not dead," Dorothy quipped.

"At least not in Paris," Rabbit responded with a disdainful nod toward the disparate group.

"Sit and I'll fetch you a drink," Dorothy insisted.

Parnell sat next to Lilian, and then smiled. "I've been dying to meet you."

Lilian found it difficult to believe that a man of such urbane sophistication would be interested, much less dying to meet her.

"I hope you don't mind, but Dorothy let me take a peek at your work last night when I flopped in her apartment."

"Oh…" Lilian's voice sounded far away and not her own.

"It's damnably impressive. Quite unnerving, little one," Rabbit said gently.

Lilian pinkened at the revelation in this overbearing crowd.

"How absolutely delightful," Parnell said, astounded. "Someone can still blush in this town."

Dorothy placed his drink on the table. "I see you have already fallen in love. Again."

Dorothy was soon nabbed by Benchley. "Now you know Mrs. Parker, it's simply far too long that I've been deprived of your attentions. I must talk to you of a matter of great importance. Great importance—"

"Well, dear man, I'm not promising a thing. You can lead a whore to culture, but you can't make her think."

Laughing, he put a hand to her elbow and led her out of the fray.

"So, Lilian," Rabbit asked, "did Crownie snap his suspenders and say something like, 'To be perfectly frank the only reason I agreed to meet you is because Dorothy speaks so highly of you—

and since she seldom speaks highly of anything, I didn't want to miss this rare opportunity.' "

Lilian laughed, for Rabbit's impression was remarkably close to the distinguished publisher she had met at Dorothy's behest.

"'I'm impressed.'" He continued mimicking Crowninshield, "'Your poetry's, well, raw. 'Goes for the guts' is how Benchley described it—'"

"But, how did—"

"Oh darling, there are no secrets in play land. Unfortunately it doesn't really matter how much we might like your poetry. The question is, will the little old lady in Dubuque?"

"Perhaps you've missed your calling, Mr. Walbrook."

"Please, it's Rabbit. Crownie thinks that if anyone shows the slightest bit of intelligence he'll lose half his readership. Which is a point well taken here in the States. Even when Dorothy's being a goddamn intellectual snob, she's so utterly charming about it that it's sheer entertainment."

Lilian checked her watch and began to gather her coat.

"Dear me, was it something I said?" Rabbit tossed.

"Oh, no. Nothing like that. I should be getting back to work."

"What do you do?"

"I mean my writing."

Rabbit's laughter momentarily stopped the hum of the conversation. "That's so enchanting. Someone here who actually works. Tell me, did Crownie ask you to write captions?"

"Yes, something like that." Lilian cleared her throat.

"Well, it's how Dot got her start. Brassieres. I believe her crowning glory was 'Brevity is the soul of lingerie.' "

"Hallo everyone!" a voice broke through the din. "Listen to this review if you can bear it." The gentleman stood and read a scathingly sarcastic review of a new writer's debut novel. Laughter and boos competed for domination.

"Might I ask you a question?" Lilian asked in a lowered voice.

"Only if I supply a brilliant answer."

"Why must they be so hateful?"

"Who?" Rabbit queried. "The critics or this bunch?"

"Well, both I suppose. I mean everyone in here is a writer. Why would they want to tear each other apart?"

"Oh, my darling, you are naïve, aren't you?" Rabbit's voice was pained.

"It just seems so self-defeating."

"Touché."

"And that makes them feel better?"

"Yes. It's all relative. If someone else is being ripped to shreds, perhaps what they're laboring over isn't quite so bad. Misery not only loves company it adores indulging its perpetual excuse to stay sodden."

Lilian bit her bottom lip and fussed with her gloves to hide her discomfort.

"Don't worry darling," Rabbit said earnestly. "There really is a lot less to us than meets the eye."

* * *

An angry ocean swells gargantuan waves toward the shore as a young girl struggles in the water, the waves crashing ever closer. She can barely withstand the elements, the waves slapping her body like a toy doll against a jagged cliff.

A hand stretches out to help her as she climbs to safety. It is her mother, thank God, it is her mother, come to save her, grasping for her tiny hand and pulling her up with all her strength, but as Lilian reaches the top, she's pulled face-to-face with her brother Charles, now fully-grown.

"Noooooo…" Lilian struggles to free herself and in her victory, begins to fall, very slowly, into the oncoming waves.

Lilian awoke. She grabbed at her stomach, then peered at the cracked panes, the curtains with her foolish markers of time and wondered how long she would have to be hungry. She moved from the small cot and walked to the cupboard to assess her rations. An end of a loaf of bread. She picked it up. Moldy. She let it drop to the floor.

When Lilian met Rabbit later that day she tried desperately not to appear as eager as she felt. It had been a full day since her last meal and as Rabbit pored over the menu, extolling the virtues of Jack Horner pie, veal cutlets, steaks, and deviled eggs, saliva swirled against her tongue. And when the veal cutlets with potatoes and peas were placed before her she ate as slowly as possible, soaking the last of the dinner rolls in thick gravy.

Rabbit flagged down the waiter. "Sir, would you be so kind as to bring another plate of biscuits with gravy. And more coffee?"

Lilian appeared stricken. "Am I that obvious?"

"Nonsense." Rabbit extracted his gold cigarette case. "Do you know what a delight it is to see a woman with a healthy appetite, rather than one nibbling like a polite little church mouse?"

"Don't think we're all a bunch of untamed heathens from the Northwest. Once upon a time I had manners."

"And what are manners but a fool's way of coping with position and money?"

Lilian smiled appreciatively as she polished off yet another helping.

"Starvation and rejection are the artist's paradox," Rabbit offered as he drank his coffee and smoked his cigarette. "They stoke the fires of genius while bleeding the humility right out of you."

* * *

New York: September 1920

I have met the most exquisite creature, who would turn more than a few heads in our fair city. Her name is Lilian. Although she's quite slender, she brings to mind a Greek statue—a strong face with a regal bearing, but she is indelibly female. If given the opportunity to fatten up she will grow into her full breasts and the kind of curvature most idiot men make fools of themselves over. A long chestnut mane covers half the length of her body, but it is her eyes that are her finest feature. A slate blue-gray, the color of an angry sky, graced by a fierce intelligence. A light struggles to shine there, covering secrets, to be sure, but it is this vulnerability that draws me to her.

I'm thinking I shall bring her back to Paris with me. She is in dire need of a mentor, and who better than the tortured Lavinia to bring some well-placed torment into a young poet's life? I'm sure I won't be met with too much opposition by Lavinia to mold a young and beautiful poet in the shadow of her better self.

New York: November 1920

Ahhh, there was never more excitement as dear Lilian's when Dorothy and I took her to the theater last night. Her eyes were the proverbial wide saucers as she took in the tails and tops, women glittering in their gowns. I rather doubt she blinked once after the lights dimmed and the velvet curtains lifted. It was all prattle and nonsense—a dreadfully long affair. When Dot asked what she thought, Lilian stammered, "It was wonderful."

"What so drew you in?" Dorothy barked.

"Well, not the play. It was wretched."

Dorothy and I burst out laughing.

"It was the sets, the lights, the actors. I wondered what their lives must be like. Wondered if they knew the words they were speaking were awful, and yet they bravely marched forward. It's courageous, what they do."

"Dear Lord, Dot—better be careful or she'll have your job. Very eloquent, my dear."

"Quite right. I'll simply call the review an ode to courage: How wrought, they fought—and all for naught."

Moved by Lilian's enthusiasm, or perhaps a hangover, Dorothy did not desecrate the play in her column, graciously proclaiming she "was not going to tell on them," and instead wrote her review about the woman next to her who had lost her glove.

The same wide-eyed wonder persisted the next day when I called for Lilian after work and we took a cab to visit resident painter, Neysa McMein—the only one of Dorothy's lot who isn't utterly hopeless. Her studio, cramped at the best of times, was positively bursting. While Neysa, all delightfully smudged with paint, continued on at the easel—nothing comes between her and her work—not even her ever competent still!

I do enjoy—with a certain Pygmalion satisfaction—watching my little sparrow. Such a delightful student of life, though I detect a secret buried beneath her naïveté. But she's not one to complain. Indeed, if anything, she pretends that her circumstances are far better than they are. She's quite the most charming little person I have encountered since Sylvia. I can't wait for them to meet. How she will thrive and blossom under the nourishing City of Light.

* * *

A grazing nib flew across the final sheets of paper as Lilian sat amidst basic chaos. Clothing littered the cot, while papers and books were stacked next to a steamer trunk Rabbit had provided for her journey.

The nib stopped.

Over a completed manuscript, Lilian placed a blank piece of paper and scrawled, *Naked Truth*, by Lilian Hal—

She quickly crossed out her name and hurled the paper aside.

She was damned if she would use her own name on this manuscript for further submission. She had gotten nowhere as a woman poet, and even Rabbit had suggested they find a new persona for her introduction to Paris society.

Suddenly something caught her attention. She leaped up and grabbed at one of the books, toppling over a stack. She leafed through "The Romantic English Poets," trying on name after name, until she arrived at the perfect passage.

Aloud she read,

> *"This bosom, responsive to rapture no more,*
> *Shall hush thy wild notes, nor implore thee to sing;*
> *The feelings of childhood, which taught thee to soar,*
> *Are wafted far distant on Apathy's wing."*

"Well put, Lord Byron," Lilian observed wistfully.

She reached for a clean page, and under the title she boldly scripted her new nom de plume: *Byron Harrington.*

She packed up the manuscript. On her way out the door, she briefly stopped to admire her fading Paris canvas. A brief smile of excitement could not fully camouflage the faint traces of cynicism, just beginning to curl at the corner of her mouth.

* * *

Lilian's life feels so much like mine. Where does the writer end and her creation begin?

Memories recreated, written on the page, manage their very own brand of reality, and who's to say they're any less valid? When Anaïs Nin says writers write to live twice, perhaps it would be more accurate to say that we write to finally understand what we have already experienced.

What I know is writers live to write—and in doing so write to live. Nothing is sacred, so don't be telling us your secrets. We steal everything we can get our grubby little hands on. I've had conversations with friends who have said something sublimely witty that I will scratch unabashedly on the side of a used envelope, stolen scraps for my next script. We are hoarders of life, even if we do not feast on it. We hear and watch people in an unnatural way, soaking up details and nuances, witness to great joy and wordless agony—often editing in the midst of reality a more ponderous statement, a snappier comeback—Where does the writer's life end and the page begin?

I still hear the Bach in my head, keeping me company, giving me solace—I know…I know. I have to go back to how it unraveled. It's simply so much cozier revisiting that other world, the world I have been living in for the past weeks, the world of perfection…my new world of writing Cynara.

Climbing out takes time. It doesn't happen overnight. The movies always make it appear as if some backlit catharsis is what plucks one from the abyss of depression and hurtles one toward a new frontier. Excitement and adventure replace the darkened eyes, the stubble-bearded discontent. A new life. Through a new lens. But the reality of depression is like any discomfort…disease. It's one step forward, two back. Your days may never be as black or as unforgiving as they were at the absolute bottomness of it all, but it actually takes a helluva long time before you have a week of good days hung all together like a string of Christmas lights.

Years later, when Byron was asked, she would be hard-pressed to say what it was she loved most about Paris. From the moment she had arrived as Rabbit's little orphan, she was instantly captivated by the sights, sounds and smells of a city electric with energy. It was as if Lilian's canvas had come to life—with its horse-drawn carts, its ancient architecture, cobble-stoned poplar and elm-lined streets—and was now populated by an exciting mix of artists, writers, painters and poets who were single-handedly changing the face of literature and culture.

Would her favorite thing be so simple as the smell of fresh air during springtime, as the rains fell, posing a sweet melancholy during her lengthy walks? Or the silent moments she stood before the small window in her quaint attic garret, bundled in Rabbit's cast-off cloaks for warmth? Perhaps it would be the early mornings when she lay hugging herself for warmth, and could hear the sounds of the old shepherd's pipe as he herded his goats in the street below her window. Or her favorite bistro, where the kind owner, an aging gentleman with an old gendarme's mustache covering half his face, would pour her a café au lait so that she could begin her work.

Yes, all this would be in consideration for what she most treasured.

The eager strolls along the Seine, past the square with its benches filled with lovers, pigeons pecking greedily for cast-off crumbs, the quickening gait as she became inspired for her morning writing sessions. The afternoons she might spend there, reading avariciously every book given to her by Rabbit or loaned to her from Sylvia's bookstore. The sun-soaked warmth made her sleepy as she watched the river barges, their billowy clouds of smoke painting the sky. The fishermen lined up on the banks with their lengthy poles made of cane, were so much a part of the scenery that they blended in with the stately elms. And as the sun began to fade she often strolled home through one of the many gardens overflowing with color and texture, fountains and statues heralding the glory of the past.

The music, perhaps, that floated from the cafés and bistros, Josephine Baker's clear vibrato, the eager accordion expressing the joy of creation—or the plaintive violin, the darker side of the muse—one did not exist without the other—a daily backdrop to the artist's plight. She could never hear these melodies without becoming a little sad.

One of the places that might top Byron's list was Sylvia Beach's bookstore, for that was where she learned the difference between art and commerce. She couldn't wait until she could escape inside the cramped interior of the notorious Shakespeare and Company, indulging herself in Sylvia's latest shipment of books. Sylvia single-handedly provided the latest in American literature for the French—translations, critiques and experimental works. More importantly, it was Sylvia and the unusual coterie of female artists from whom Byron began to understand the power of feminine persuasion. How she enjoyed Sylvia and Adrienne's dinner parties, where Adrienne cooked simple but satisfying peasant dishes, applying her earthy lust for food to the printed word, seeing both as imperative nourishment for the soul.

She loved debating and gossiping with the then unknown Ernest Hemingway, the generous Ezra Pound, the fascinating Scotty Fitzgerald, and anyone who came into Rabbit's general vicinity, for Rabbit was never far from his next meal, or too terribly distant from a challenging debate. Eating at Hemingway's favorite café, the Closerie des Lilas. Lively conversations were the staple at the many drinkeries, sidewalk bistros and cafés they happened upon in their travels. Michaud's was reserved for only the most elegant of celebrations with its expensive wines. And early mornings spent at the intriguing Dingo Bar—littered with paint-speckled artists, jovial philosophers and furrow-browed writers, all drowning their sorrows in vintage melancholy.

The rains that cleansed the city, made fresh and alive with smells of newly baked bread streaming from the bakeries; the piquant flavors of produce lined up in stalls at the market; or walking on newly minted gravel along the paths of the Luxembourg gardens or the perfume of fresh blooming flowers teasing her nose while old ladies hawked their wares—she would fondly remember any number of these things.

But the truth would be, of all the things that made her feel alive and aware and full of potential—of all the exciting places and fascinating people—the moments she would not have given up for anything were those first and few she spent alone in her cramped and drafty garret. Those precious moments before she adopted the façade of indifference to attend parties and readings, before she meshed into a persona that served her well, but suited her ill. It was in the drafty garret, where she sat bundled at her desk, her hands clumsy in fingerless gloves, scrawling the words that were in her heart, when she still believed in a thing called possibility. To be certain, that is what she loved most.

* * *

Rabbit had settled Byron in her "little nest," as he referred to her garret, which he had found through his endless circle of connections. After giving her a week or more to become "suitably acclimated," he arrived one afternoon with several packages.

"What's all this?" Byron asked. She already felt indebted to Rabbit for whisking her beneath his wing and acting as her escort.

"Well, darling, we simply can't have you tramping about in those." He pointed at her peasant's skirt and one of the few shirts she owned which had become tighter as her breasts filled out. "Gertrude might get away with it, but no, not for you young lady. We want to create a, shall we say, certain insouciance…" He handed her a cigarette case. "A certain image of flair, elegance, and most importantly, mystery. Go on, open them."

Byron unwrapped the brown paper which held a very smart shirt, pinstriped tie and tie pin, and a jacket with a tailored cut more suitable to a man's coat than a woman's.

"Slacks are optional of course," Rabbit offered, then gestured to her skirt. "Personally I would find all that material hanging around my legs a great deal of trouble. Not to mention dangerous."

Byron laughed. "Rabbit, I can't accept all this."

"Of course you can. Now, skedaddle. We're running late— fashionably so, but it doesn't do to arrive after everyone's left."

"Would you mind?" Byron gestured for Rabbit to turn his back. As she put on the shirt, stiff and formal, a shiver snaked down her back. These were clothes meant for someone of substance, someone to be dealt with and she found herself growing excited as she knotted the silk tie.

"Okay, I'm ready," she whispered.

Rabbit's face beamed with pleasure. "*Mon Dieu*! An exceedingly tasteful improvement, if I do say so myself. Now to my barber."

"Your barber?"

"Darling, whatever else, you can't be seen running about Paris with hair the length of a horse's mane. You will be mistaken for an Indian." Rabbit smiled encouragingly and took her by the elbow. "Trust me, sweety-heart. If there is one thing I know, it is fashion. And what it means to be all the rage of it."

* * *

So it was that when Rabbit presented Byron to Natalie Barney et al. that afternoon at one of her infamous Friday salons, Byron stood before some twenty-odd people feeling like a prize steed about to receive a prod and a poke and a check of the teeth. Byron could not help but gawk at the Persian decor of Miss Barney's home with its exotic accents and the elaborate garden, graced by a replicated temple of Eros. The infamous, the elite and the frankly bizarre all joined Natalie at her house. People's names and careers were made and destroyed, dissected and analyzed and thoroughly gossiped over. "As an artist displays paintings, so our dear Miss Barney presents her menagerie of personalities," Rabbit had explained as they arrived by carriage. "It is an experience not to be missed under any circumstances. Besides, we need to get you properly introduced to Parisian society."

As Miss Barney approached to greet them, Byron noted that the woman, now in her mid-forties, was elegant and still quite beautiful.

Natalie graciously offered her hand. "So wonderful to meet you. Rabbit tells us you are to be a rare new talent on the scene. Just what we need. More women's voices."

Natalie bussed Rabbit's cheek. "Be a dear and introduce Miss Harrington around."

"My pleasure." Rabbit drew Byron protectively to his side and before venturing forward, whispered in her ear, "Now don't worry my dear. I shall tell you the truth behind these luminaries and they won't appear nearly so frightening."

Byron smiled weakly.

"For instance, standing beneath Natalie's nymph painting there"—he pointed to an attractive woman with flushed cheeks, auburn hair and a cigarette dangling elegantly from her hand—"is the ultimate nymph herself, Miss Djuna Barnes. She writes in bed wearing nothing more than a cape, reportedly a gift from Peggy Guggenheim. She's all Irish and can drink Joyce under the table!

"And over by the potted frond—the tall rather mannish looking Disraeli is Janet Planner and her beautiful friend with the enormous blue eyes is Solita Solano. Solita ditched her husband to become the *New York Tribune's* drama critic. And the party of the third part is the shipping heiress from Britain, Nancy Cunard."

Rabbit watched Byron take in their clothing, all three dressed in white tailored linen suits with white gloves. He added, "Yes, our three fates!"

Swiveling her about, Rabbit pointed out a slight gentleman, a black patch covering one eye and goatee sprouting from his pale face. He was so stooped over he seemed as if he might fall if not for his cane. "That is our very own resident genius, Mr. James—"

Byron clutched Rabbit's sleeve. "Oh…it's Mr. Joyce."

"Yes. But before you go limp with awe, remember half of Paris thinks his sprawling masterpiece wouldn't do to wrap fish in. Just the other day Miss Virginia Woolf touted his work as that of 'a queasy undergraduate scratching at his pimples.' And lest you be carried away by his fragile and sensitive poet's stance, know that he lives off half the women in Paris."

Two sides existed within every hero, Byron supposed, but she was finding it so difficult to absorb the heavy burden of celebrity in the room that her head began to swim. Natalie returned and stole her away from Rabbit. She crooked an arm in hers and walked Byron to a cluster of women chattering furiously about someone apparently not present.

When Natalie cleared her throat they turned to Byron and appraised her. Two of the women were so masculine in their attire and bearing they could have been men, and Byron's lip tremored slightly as she was keenly eyed for inspection. The most feminine of the group, with black hair bobbed above her shoulders, but with such delicate features she could never be mistaken for a man, simply cocked an eyebrow at Byron.

"Now don't be a pout, Lavinia," Natalie admonished, "or you will make our guest feel unwelcome."

"Charmed," Lavinia mocked and skulked out of the room into the gardens.

"Don't mind her. She doesn't mean a thing by it. She's—"

"Sulking." Rabbit intervened. "Lavinia's not happy unless she's in the throes of a tragic breakup. It inspires the muse."

Byron's mouth went dry and she could feel her palms sweating.

"Oh, dear, it's the Steins." Natalie waved at two women entering from across the room. Byron's gaze followed Natalie's and she was momentarily taken back by the odd pairing. The first was a stout creature, with the frame and garb of a robust peasant, her hair tightly pulled into a topknot. She dwarfed the bird-like sylph beside her, whose features were dominated by a large nose and more than a whisper of hair above her upper lip. "Gerty said she might drop by. And the thing of it is I didn't know Joyce was going to be here."

"Ohhh." Rabbit primped his mustache. "'Company, villainous company, hath been the spoil of me.'"

Byron swallowed with difficulty. She didn't belong with these sophisticates; people who quoted Shakespeare and made conversation like the witty dialogue she had read in books.

"Gerry!" Natalie called out to her, then hissed under her breath. "Let's make the best of it."

Rabbit leaned to Byron. "It's Gertrude and Alice. Or better put, Mrs. Husband and the wife."

Byron could feel the undercurrent of tension and was finding it difficult to breathe as the stout powerhouse strode toward her. Silence befell the group as if royalty approached. Byron's upper lip twitched. The room began to spin and before she knew it, she could no longer feel her knees.

She tumbled to the ground.

"Oh dear," Gertrude muttered, "I guess you should have given her more warning that I was coming."

* * *

Paris: January 1921

Lord, what an afternoon! Took Byron to meet the ladies. Perhaps I pushed a bit early to introduce her to our mercurial lot of expatriates, but I think it's important that she make friends and feel at home here in Paris as I do. I believe her natural talent will soon shine among them.

In any event, she made quite the impression, in spite of her need for smelling salts. The women rallied around Byron after she fainted, flitting about with fans and brandy to outdo one another with their newly acquired nursing skills. I rather think Byron made a mark, for rarely have these cronies seen a woman with such a balance of womanly curves and striking handsomeness—the kind that makes one look twice to experience pleasure yet again. Even Lavinia gave her a careful appraisal once our poor girl had been resuscitated.

After several brandies Byron became herself again and spoke with the women, unaware that it is her naïvete and curiosity, her vulnerability and the unsuccessful mask over evident pain that makes them so attentive. None of them know her as I do, nor see her talent yet, but they will. If there is one strength I possess, it is understanding the nature of one's gifts and limitations, including my own.

As for my poor little sparrow, I later discovered the true reason for her fainting as we supped on a rare treat of oysters followed by a wonderful steak at the Lilas. It was not due to her poor appetite, as she had professed to the clucking hens, but rather that she had caught one of the more masculine women kissing Cherie upon the mouth...

"Not as a token of friendship," Byron blurted as she and Rabbit sat finishing oysters for dinner.

"Byron, I'm certain it's rare where you come from, but surely you understood those women were...are..."

Byron seemed perplexed.

"Oh my dear one, you are really quite divine." Rabbit began to chuckle. "It really is refreshing to be around someone so guileless and please, know I mean no harm. Do you not know about women and women together, then?"

She shook her head.

"But you have heard of such relationships?"

Byron cleared her throat. "I've only heard of men. I read about such matters in New York."

"Ahhh," Rabbit responded. "You make it sound all rather clinical."

"Oh, no. I didn't mean that at all. Please, I'm sorry if I expressed myself badly." Byron sat up, eager to explain herself. "Please understand, I have no objection. It is not for me to say what I don't understand."

"It's difficult to read you Byron, so I'm just going to come out and say it. Are you intimating that you are not aware of my own proclivities?" Byron nodded, her brows furrowed in sympathy.

"Do you understand, child, that it does not make a man less a man?"

"Do I understand that you are such a man?" Byron's eyes reflected the wisdom of a woman much older than her years or experience would indicate.

Rabbit was inexplicably shy. "Suddenly I feel I want to explain my situation—"

"You needn't," Byron assured him.

"It's just...I rarely talk about it. It's a given, well, here in Paris anyway. But I've been this way since I was a lad." Rabbit's jaw tensed as he lit a cigarette.

"Rabbit, you are my dear and good friend." She smiled lovingly as she put her hand over Rabbit's. "And nothing will ever make that otherwise."

Rabbit studied Byron, realizing he had grossly miscalculated. Byron was only naïve in ways of the world. Not in matters of the heart. For so few had made him feel as unsullied as Byron did in that moment.

* * *

Byron took great pains with her appearance the morning she had been invited to assist Sylvia. So anxious was she to be a part of Shakespeare and Company that she stormed from her garret and ran the two miles to the bookstore, arriving a half-hour early. That Sylvia would think enough of her to invite her to her shop, let alone to help wrap and ship the underground copies of the Mr. Joyce's *Ulysses*, was an incomparable honor.

Byron was simply in awe of these people. It astonished her that Sylvia had devised this bookstore to become the melting pot and central meeting place for the cultural elite. That her partner Adrienne Monnier was doing the same for the French with her bookstore across the street. That Miss Stein with her gregarious and emphatic positions had male writers quaking in their shoes for an introduction, and that the beautiful Natalie Barney had created one of the most sought-after milieus at her frequent salons. All this proved to Byron, as nothing could have in her isolation at Bay Cliff, that women could do anything they set their minds to—anything a man could do—and often made the difference between success and obscurity. Why, if it weren't for Sylvia, James Joyce's *Ulysses* would have been banned "unto obscurity where in my ever so humble opinion it belongs," Rabbit had prophesied. And now here she was involved in selling subscriptions to Joyce's mountainous and ever-changing tract, witnessing first hand the delicate perseverance of women's desires and the hard work they must sustain to carry off the smallest success.

As she paced back and forth beneath a portrait of Shakespeare, hung from an iron finger above the door, she stared into the store windows, daydreaming of a future when she could chatter nonchalantly next to these powerful women at a party, discussing items of great import, pretending that her book sat displayed in one of the showcase windows.

"You are Mademoiselle Harrington, no?" a large woman with a thick French accent asked.

Byron jumped, almost tripping over herself. "Yes, I am." She blushed as she turned to look into the lively and intelligent visage of Adrienne Monnier.

"Sylvie's running late a little. Do you mind to wait?"

"No...not at all. I would be more than happy to wait," Byron eagerly agreed.

"Please to help yourself," Adrienne insisted as they entered the bookstore. "I must attend to some paper and Sylvia will come shortly."

Once inside, Byron had an opportunity to take in the book-lined shelves, the corners crammed with antiques, and art. A beige sackcloth masked old walls and Serbian rugs covered the floor. *New Republic*, *Poetry*, and *Egoist* lined the racks on one wall, while portraits of Oscar Wilde and Walt Whitman dominated another. It offered a quaint coziness for anyone who loved books and Byron believed it was that very warmth that lent itself to the bookstore's success.

Byron reverently touched the bindings of works by William Blake, Henry James and Ezra Pound. She tiptoed cautiously through the aisles and stopped, gingerly pulling an old book from the shelf, the binding loose at the edges. She opened it. The smell of weathered pages engulfed her senses. She had loved this smell since childhood when her father allowed her the rare treat of leafing through his book collection, the old books he kept behind glass and key.

The door opened and Sylvia blustered into the store, her thick bob of hair wind-blown and astray.

"Oh, dear, I'm sorry I'm late. I had a bite with Ernest this morning. He told me all about his new short story and I'm so excited I could spit. Well, let's see." She dumped several parcels on a table, over-laden with books, and glanced at Byron as if she were another item on her task list she had almost forgotten. "Yes, then, let's come along and go to the back and get started."

As Byron began to follow, Sylvia stopped in her tracks and turned around. "Have I completely lost my manners? How rude of me. Let's begin this properly, shall we? A spot of tea and then we'll be on our way."

As they worked the morning flew by. Since the book was being banned in the States, Byron helped disguise *Ulysses* for an underground shipment by masking it in a fake cover of *The Complete Works of Shakespeare.* "Rather prophetic, don't you think?" she asked Byron.

"I think it's very clever," Byron acknowledged shyly.

"*Merci.* Now, Miss Harrington, what are your plans for Paris? Rabbit tells me you're a writer."

"Well…" Byron immediately felt presumptuous. "I—I've been working on my poetry."

"Ahhh, a poet," she said, but not unkindly. "We shall have to introduce you to our very own resident poet laureate, Lavinia."

"I've met her," Byron whispered.

"Oh, well, don't let her fool you. Under that dreary façade of moodiness beats the heart of a wonderful woman who is kind and generous when she's of a mind. She might be able to help you. Mentor you, perhaps."

Byron would discover that Sylvia was constantly introducing writers to publishers or the press, painters to models, and she was known as the gatekeeper to Miss Stein. It was the few and privileged who attained a letter of introduction or a personal meeting through Sylvia to Miss Gertrude Stein. "Yes, and for those unlucky enough to have a sitting with her," Rabbit observed later, "they are likely to hear no end of her genius and very little of their own."

"So, Byron," Sylvia now asked, "maybe I could read some of your work?"

Byron shifted uncomfortably.

"Only when you are ready," Sylvia reassured her. "Oh, my, what a lot of books you've put together. You are industrious."

Byron bent her head, overwhelmed that *the* Sylvia Beach had asked to read her poetry.

"I think we're due for some more tea, what do you think?"

When they returned to work, Sylvia showed Byron a stack of library cards for her lending library and asked Byron to find a way to organize them. "I seem quite incapable of doing it myself. I have no idea what I've lent to whom. I can never keep track of all my little bunnies."

"Bunnies?"

"Oh yes." Sylvia explained, "We call all our subscribers bunnies, for the *abonne*—which means subscriber in French. Didn't you know? That's how Rabbit got his name. He said, 'If you must call us bunnies, please spare me and let me be called a rabbit.' He's been our head Rabbit ever since."

"It's interesting," Byron mused. "There are moments when I feel as if I've known Rabbit all my life. But it seems every day I find something new about him."

* * *

Paris: April 1921

I don't know how much longer I can tolerate the anguish that insinuates itself between Etienne and myself at almost every meeting. Father Time is not generous with many, and in our case is downright frugal. Between my being abroad and his wife's condition, it is a cause for celebration when we may string two hours together—but lately we have managed to stifle all but the last of joy and warmth even then.

What has happened to us since that first time…Lord when I think of it now, it punishes me with its beauty and tenderness.

I first encountered you, dear lover, while searching for a barrister to consult with over my contract with Vanity Fair. But I did not hear the words of money and terms of engagement because my engagement was with your muscular hands and their delicately clipped nails, your rugged face with its blunted boyish features…your hair so thick and curly that I longed to bury my face in it.

And then you appeared at the door of my flat like a Brontean character, all windswept and dampened from the mist, and stood there with the unlikely excuse that you needed a signature which very well could have waited until morning. But desire does not work according to schedules and the heart does not dictate the terms upon which we fall in love.

You stood before the fireplace, your wet hair shining. You had beads of water at your forehead, and I wondered if they were from the mist or from nerves. But I should have known in an instant you are not a man who suffers nerves. You held my hand a little too long as you received the glass of sherry, your eyes direct and certain as you placed our drinks aside. You touched my collar, gently unfurled my cravat and drew me to you. How tender your lips, your kisses so gently teasing—not as I expected. I thought you would be rough and all man—a Hemingway type, with a swaggering right to your prey.

But you moved inside my arms, searching for a safe place to be nothing more than who you are. The backs of your hands caressed my cheek, then, gently grasping me to you, you waited for me to quell your agony. Your hands explored as you tore inside my shirt, smoothing over my chest, your face nuzzled into my skin as you slowly dropped to your knees. You didn't ask permission as you unbuttoned my pants—tenderly grasping me as if it were your right, then slowly stroking me, quickening my desire…the heat of your breath on me, taking my own away. My legs quivering I reached out for your arms, and could feel your hard muscles taut and defined beneath the silk of your shirt…You pushed me back into my reading chair, and then your soft brown eyes looked into my own, and I could see the boy of your youth, innocent with need, awaiting permission to take me in your mouth, glutton for my seed as I spent myself in abandon…in joy.

And so we have carried this clandestine affair of ours far too long. While I would love nothing more than to imagine waking every morning with your face next to mine, the truth is you are married, dear one. And your wife is feeling miserable with this pregnancy and your time is ever less affordable.

I feel trapped.

I suppose there is only one thing for it—raise hell and wreak havoc!

* * *

Over the following year, Byron set herself to task. She arose before dawn, rushed to her first sip of café au lait, lit a cigarette, and settled over the pages of her manuscript. If she was under the presumption that she had labored in New York, it was nothing like the challenges Lavinia set before her. For as Rabbit had predicted, Lavinia "could no more be kept from the allure of shaping one's genius than she could stay away from the opium dens." Lavinia would not accept something that approximated perfection and Byron was eager to please the dark and commanding poet. She labored as she had never dreamed possible to produce the most accurate and yet subtle nuances to her words and phrases.

She wrote first by hand, dipping a quill into black ink, then typing her first revision using carbons. She did not edit with a red pencil as she had seen many do—it was too violent—no thought should be annihilated. Instead she used a blunt yellow artist's pencil so that her previous thoughts might remain, in case she chose to revisit them. The very accoutrements she used were like the painter's brushes and like a painter she loved the tools of her trade, the feel of her smooth slender pen, the smell of dank ink.

She religiously spent her mornings dedicated to reaching a pre-assigned goal. She would not leave until she finished, and then, weary but elated, she would throw a cloak over her shoulders for a long walk along the Seine. She would pace anxiously waiting for comment as Lavinia read her pages, and often dashed to Rabbit's flat or the bookstore in order to put off one of Lavinia's many tirades. Or worse yet, the brooding poet's silent displeasure. "My, my, my," Lavinia would mutter as she smoked her cigarette. Nothing further. Or: "So, tell me, *ma cherie*, what is 'fretting rain'? I wasn't aware rain could fret. Do you really mean to tell me you know how rain *feels, ma petit météologue?*"

Byron attempted to defend her work. "I…it's a metaphor."

"A *metaphor*? Oh, is that what this is then?" Lavinia appeared amused.

"Yes, it was supposed to be," Byron responded.

"Well is it or isn't it?" Lavinia pushed. "It might help if you stopped trying to make everything so serious. So damned important. So deeply moving." Lavinia swallowed her sarcasm with a gulp of her wine. "What the hell is really all that important, anyway? Now. Go back. Write about the rain—tell me all about it. Tell me how it feels on your skin after you have held your dying lover in your arms. Tell me how it cleanses after you have tasted the breath of a traitor in your kiss. But for God's sake, do not tell me how it 'frets'!"

When Byron returned to her apartment she paced angrily. What made her think she had the talent it required to be a poet? Even a lousy poet? She paced until she slumped against her cot, biting into her bottom lip so that she wouldn't cry. If she did she would think of her father, feel the wrench in her stomach, no less severe as time passed over missing him. Even with the never-ending excitement she longed for home. So many nights she lay in her garret and ached for the chilly morning walks, watching her shoeprints in the sand, the warmth of the fireplace in the den, the burnt rust of a sunset. And her ocean.

It made her think of the rain as it met the angry, tempestuous ocean, the rain at the coast in all its moods and mystery, and she picked herself up, sat at her desk and reshaped her work, taking Lavinia's comments and making them welcome friends as opposed to the enemy. She honed the lines again and again, much like the grizzled Chinese sculptor she passed every day in his shop, shaving his delicate figurines over and over as he exposed the intricate design only he saw inside his pieces of ivory.

"I can take an éntire day to write a single paragraph," Hemingway pointed out to Byron as she and Rabbit lunched on the terrace of Negre de Toulouse.

Byron set her fork down immediately. "Really?"

"Yes. I must get it completely right. I don't want to move forward until everything is just as I want it."

"That's exactly how I feel!" Byron exclaimed. "Thank God. I thought I was the only one who took so long to work on a simple line. It's just that I want to make it—"

"Sharp. Precise," Hemingway supplied. "You know when I see things at their clearest?" He buttered a roll. "When I am absolutely famished. I walk along the streets when the smells of the bakeries and cafés are at their most distinct. The light on the Seine is at its brightest, the sky its bluest. Hunger best hones the senses."

How true this had been for Byron all the many days the acids gnawed at her stomach as she roamed the streets of New York. She had never defined it before now, but she recalled having seen the sharp angles of the buildings, the sheer contrasts of light and shadows and feel her thinking was filtered by the perfection of clarity. Those evenings she felt her work took on a raw, more edgy tone.

"Yes!" In her eagerness, Byron almost knocked her glass from the table. "It's as though with hunger comes a level of immediacy— an imperative."

Rabbit tossed his red and white checkered napkin to the table. "Dear me, why I'm so full I must be positively dumb."

Much as Hemingway would spend an entire day on a paragraph, she now understood how intent one could be on a single word or idea. She thought of this as she and Rabbit later strolled through the Luxembourg gardens. Miss Stein had made a similar point at one of the last salons they had attended, although

Byron confessed to Rabbit she found it difficult to comprehend much of what Miss Stein wrote. She suspected she was too simple to understand the mind of someone so advanced.

"Rubbish," Rabbit replied, "that's all it is. I don't know why she intimidates you. Yes, she may be the harbinger of modern prose." Rabbit plucked a rose and fastened it to his lapel. "But 'a rose is a rose is a rose' is perfectly redundant."

"But don't you see, she's trying to express that it isn't just a rose. It's an endless and infinite number of things. It may simply *look* like a rose, but it's so much more. It's one thing one day and quite another the next."

"Why, Byron, I believe you understand Gertrude's work better than she does herself."

"Oh...I didn't mean to sound—"

Rabbit's huge laughter silenced her.

"Darling, you are such a gem. Ready to take the world all in one huge gulp, aren't you? Just remember. Don't let yourself be taken in by this lot and promise me you will never become too impressed by anyone. We all possess warts, my dear one, so let discrimination be your guide."

* * *

"I can't go!" Byron clenched her hands together as Rabbit lounged on her bed, his legs crossed, a sweet grin tugging at his mouth. Sylvia had sent a message by way of Rabbit that Byron was to join her for afternoon tea so that she might discuss her manuscript.

"Darling, this is just opening night jitters."

"But what if Sylvia says she hates it? That it's the worst pulp she's ever seen? That I have no business—"

"Byron, do you trust me at all?"

She turned to face him. "Of course I do."

"Then get your shapely bottom out of here and go meet your destiny."

"Will...will you—"

"When have I not been by your side? But of course I shall escort you to said rendezvous and then meet you at the Lilas after. How's that?"

But after Rabbit had delivered her as promised, Byron felt all courage seeping from her limbs. She paced outside Shakespeare and Company smoking a cigarette. And then another. Several times she headed into the store, but she couldn't quite make herself pass the threshold.

Finally Sylvia opened the door. "Shall we have tea out on the sidewalk, then?"

Byron grinned queasily.

"Come on in," Sylvia said, hiding a shadow of a smile. "I don't bite."

Byron followed Sylvia into the shop and took the proffered seat while Sylvia fixed tea.

"Byron, I'm not going to beat around the bush." Byron accepted a cup and saucer. It rattled furiously. She wanted to run, afraid her world might collapse if Sylvia uttered a word one way or another.

"Oh my, please don't be discouraged. Byron, I think it's extraordinary." Sylvia sipped her tea and smiled. "Yes. It's really quite remarkable. I think your work with Lavinia has paid off. I know it hasn't been easy."

Sylvia's words hadn't quite sunk in until Sylvia got up and embraced her. Byron felt something fall loose inside, as if she could finally relax the tight rein on her nerves.

"Do you…I mean, do you really think—?"

"Think? I know! My dear I haven't been in this business and not learned to see the forest for the trees, although I'm sure my harshest critics might disagree. I do not publish because I think I might sell a thousand copies. When I read something that begs to be seen by others—no, *must* be seen by others—I have no choice but to follow my due course."

"And?"

A delicious glint of victory twinkled in Sylvia's eyes.

"Then you mean—?" Byron was still in shock from the praise.

"Absolutely. I intend to publish your *Naked Truth*."

For a moment I feel the excitement of when I left. Of traveling all night at breakneck pace to escape one reality for another. No idea where I was going. I was new. If I had fears they soon faded away as a russet pink filled the California desert sky and I could smell a million years of blooming jasmine mixed with the dusty warmth spreading over the sun-baked terrain.

When an infinite number of paths with an infinite number of variations present themselves to us how do we stumble onto our specific journey? What if I had stayed in Portland? With Donald? What if I hadn't met Adrienne? Hadn't quit Massingers? How different my life would be. If I had never made my escape, I more than certainly wouldn't be here, in this cave. What if I hadn't decided to take a break this afternoon, at precisely 3:11 by the digital computer clock, proud to descend my finished path to this isolated strip of beach. Because it was mystifying and the surly weather was like Heathcliff on the moors and I wanted to research my cave for Cynara.

Thinking of Cynara *gives me a brief uptick in the assessment of my survival. Makes me feel hopeful.*

Creating.

Creating was in my blood before I could crawl. My life has always been about making things, right down to my path. And as I cherished the finished landscaping, a tangible accomplishment I could see, I began to understand that living in L.A. became not about the process but about the product. How easily I had gotten swept up into the game.

* * *

How acutely aware she became after a few short weeks in L.A., of the divergent soul. From the first moment Spencer entered the heat-scorched, smog-ridden, beauty-fading Hollywood an erosion of the most subliminal order began, and she could not be aware of the microscopic abrasions that cut at her soul.

Only in L.A. do you hear women comparing the price of collagen per ounce while they weigh produce at Gelson's. It used to be drug deals.

You must learn the language of *industrese* to navigate simple conversations—picking through the tundra of the endless shorthand terms of L.A. jargon. *Turn-around*—your project was huge in the trades last week, but now means nothing because the studio exec who green-lit it has been axed. *Cute meet.* Means a little too precious. *MOW.* Movie of the week. It's just been transformed to the much more comprehensible *MFT*—movie for television. *MoPicLit*—Motion Picture and Literature department. Must save the energy of those few extra syllables. *Flavor of the month. Fifteen minutes of fame. That's so five minutes ago.* And then this vernacular ends up as "clever dialogue" in a movie that everyone in America picks up and it soon becomes part of the ever changing lexicon. See—movies do change lives.

Only in L.A. do people act like lesbians at a potluck, sharing their most intimate secrets when they've just met at a sidewalk café, bound tightly together by a too highly pitched version of reality—a frenzied lust for the impossible, the improbable, so right around the corner.

And only in L.A. do you sell your soul for the price of a bit part.

That is the milieu in which Spencer had spent the last decade —nearly a quarter of her life in L.A. A frittering away of Franklin-Day-Planner days where achievement was the goal and getting nowhere was the result, until she began to feel like an only mildly interested spectator of her life. Getting up, brushing teeth, the same hazelnut creamer—cloying sweetness to disguise bitter coffee. Endless hours in meetings, meetings with producers who had barely graduated from high school, swimming through a sea of 8 X 10's of the same perky-nosed blonde with varying shades of collagen and silicon, partying through premieres. Late at night awaiting the blank computer screen that buzzed at her, waiting for direction. Everything seemed so utterly uninteresting.

"A classic case of depression," Therapist insists, scribbling on a pre-scription pad for any one of the anti-depressants creating major revenue streams for Pfizer and Eli Lilly. "You're just overwhelmed," Lena offers gently. "You're burned out," Sarah snipes. "Join the crowd!"

Sarah, Spencer's other dearest friend next to Malcolm, had by financial necessity tossed her aspirations of becoming an independent film producer for something that paid the rent. She had spent the last year staring at a tarry-hued monster with eyes dripping sulfuric acid, watching its face blow up. Sarah had long since passed being affected by the gore; debating in her new role of special effects supervisor whether the blood dripping from the cartilage should happen before or after the ripping of skull-bone through the cheeks.

Over lunch Spencer would listen to Sarah's utterly perfected cynicism squeezed out between slightly swollen cheeks. Sarah's new regime of Xanax chased by four beers a night for dinner had finally shown their presence. Spencer swore to herself that she would never become as jaded and bitter as Sarah and if she did she would leave the business. But Spencer had also sworn the moment she stopped seeing the smog she would leave L.A.

Disinterest has a way of creeping up on you. Apathy is like anything you abuse, you need more and more to really satisfy you. In those final weeks Spencer could not recall a time when she cared less about the moments of her life than right before she created her own self-destruction. It wasn't a huge effort, this amelioration of her life, but rather a testament to her endurance. Her ability to hang around long after her heart was no longer in it.

* * *

Sarah had followed Spencer to L.A. a month after Spencer arrived and together they rented a small two bedroom house that lay nestled in a cul de sac in Studio City in the "happenin' " part of the Valley. It was cramped but it had the prerequisite kidney-shaped pool necessary for the tan of success.

Spencer's year of savings had dwindled to less than a quarter of what she had left with, and she had only been in L.A. for a half a year. She had, of course, figured finances based on Portland's cost of living, never imagining how expensive things were in the big city.

She began to spend time at Café Bistro, where unemployed writers, directors and actors do what has become an uninspired art form in L.A.—hanging out. Only Derrick, a devilishly handsome blond-haired producer had ever had any kind of success in this group. He fancied himself their leader as he sat amongst his minions at the large table, a group of ever replaceable members who came and went depending on the turn of fortune; a bit part here, an option there, a gig writing for a pilot that would never be produced.

Even though Derrick had only one credit and was now languishing in obscurity, he languished with panache. It's far easier to languish with something under your belt. Nothing more humiliating than responding to the question, "What do you do?" at an industry party, followed by the even more diminishing, "Would I know anything you've done?" Production personnel are not among this group. They are the thriving economy of L.A. Only creative people muse, dream and plan, and then pontificate with ever-increasing frenzy after several cappuccinos.

It wasn't unusual when returning home from such non-events or an industry party for Spencer to find seven or eight business cards gnarled into pockets of her purse, scribbled over with their new numbers and of course the several other phones where one could be reached by message. Never has networking by so many netted so little.

After loading herself up on mocha-inspired dreams at the bistro, a ray of hope lightened the screen at her computer, Bach faintly elevating her muses in the background, the click of keys her only company.

Yes, she became lonely. Lonely for the smell of Portland's rainy fresh air. Lonely for Jill. Desperately missing Adrienne's body hovering above her own, day-dreaming about her, her skin, her lips, her eyes—and then she would shut herself down. Her sexuality was a complication she couldn't bear confronting. She missed her family. Yes, even Mom. She began to think of visiting Jill, but called her instead. Jill informed her that Donald had been phoning relentlessly, desperate to talk to her. She decided she would do the honorable thing and contact him.

"How long are you going to do this, Spence?" Donald's voice was stoic.

"How long am I going to do what?"

"Be down there. Do this—this thing you're doing."

"This *thing* happens to be my life!"

"You know what I mean." Donald's tone softened. "Massinger keeps calling me. He says you're welcome back any time. He knows he might have pushed you too much—"

"No, Donald, that's not—"

"I've spoken to your folks. They're worried sick and I've got to agree I'm a little freaked about the crime down there. Single women get stalked, mugged, murdered all the time."

"Come on Donald, don't go over the deep end. I'm careful."

"But why? Things were great here."

"Did you even read my letter?"

"Uh…sure I did." She could hear him sniff the way he did when he was lying. "I just don't get why in the hell you would leave such a good thing."

"Where have you been the last few years? I was on a slow track to insanity at Massingers and our relationship had about as much passion as a rice cracker. Did you ever once hear how miserable I was? Did you ever understand that I had a dream that got shuffled away between paying the bills and acting like I was a responsible adult, whatever the hell that might be? Life isn't just something you go through so you can stand at the end of some bank line. It's about making those dreams come true. Or at least trying to."

A long silence crackled over the phone. "What about us? Are we just over?"

"Oh, Donald." She shook her head. "Tell me one thing about our relationship you even miss."

"Is it that Adrienne person?" His voice tightened in anger. "You think I don't know she's a dyke?"

"Yes, she's a lesbian. And no. I'd love it if it were that simple. I'm happy to report the only person I left you for is myself."

With Donald gone from her life she felt renewed hope. No waning lost female on her radar. Purged from the last remnants of her old life, she could settle down and really get to work. She pulled out *May You Always*.

She spent weeks and weeks rewriting *May You* and then asked her pals at the bistro what they thought. She got rave reviews. Well, that wasn't so difficult. Armed with the high opinions of those low on the totem pole, she was prepared to cold call producers in the *Hollywood Creative Directory*, the Bible of producers. Only she didn't know that to solicit a manuscript without an agent simply swooshes that script into a huge pile that gets taken out with the recycling every Thursday. She sent *May You* to ten producers a week, approaching her strategy as she had the details and tasks of the business world, applying the cool logic that at some point someone's interest would spark. She would then go in for the close.

But that's not how Hollywood works. Hollywood is a morass of connections and networks, cliques and power bases and until you know who's who, who's not, and who's not really who they think they are, you are forever lost.

Regardless of her lack of self-confidence, she had always considered herself a smart woman, a fast learner. She had to come up with a plan. Money was pathetically scarce. She was beginning to feel like a has-been without having been had. If someone would at least take advantage of her. Like every other waitress, temp worker, and Starbucks counter person, she finally had to put her script aside, on the night table next to her stacks of *Hollywood Reporter*, *Variety* and *Dramalogue*, where the help wanted sections were now more compelling than the production schedules.

They were hiring PA's—production assistants—on a small indie film. What better experience than to be on a film set? The wages were paltry but she got fed well from the craft service table. Ironically, it was her business background that saved her. She understood budgets, line items, how to rob Peter to pay Paul. She was quickly promoted to assistant to the accountant. One thing about production; cream rises to the top quickly. They liked

Spencer so much that on the next film she assisted the producer. The film after that, she got an Associate Producer's credit.

And then she got her big break. She was hired to work as a line producer on a television pilot with the understanding that she wanted to work into writing. She knew she was heading in the wrong direction from film to TV, but since she was on a condensed version of suffering for her art she wanted to make a decent living while doing it. She had long been accustomed to a modest six figure salary and yearned for her luxuries again: hardcover books, CD's, a laser disc player.

She had to have an agent to close her first deal. Let's call him Lou. Let's call all agents Lou for they are by and large completely interchangeable. He drove a decent deal on *Lucifer*, the cop drama about a redeemed convict turned avenger. It didn't take long for the exec producers to see that Spencer had great ideas—as well as an unflagging work ethic. They offered her a slot as one of the three women on a team of fifteen writers. They were finding it difficult to round out what there was of the lead heroine's dialogue.

Spencer spent three frenzied sleepless nights pulling together a sample script. They made some changes, some that cut deeply, but for the most part that script made her mark on the team and she had finally realized a part of her dream. She was a working writer.

She was in nirvana. A surreal state of L.A. chic. When she drove over Laurel Canyon into Hollywood, she was a part of the thriving machine. When she ordered a cappuccino from a waitress she was magnanimous—oh was she an actress? Send her headshot to the show, perhaps she could hook up the struggling actress with *her* casting director. She partied with abandon. Hey, those industry parties were a blast when you had a real business card to hand out along with empty promises: *I'll call you, let's do lunch*. When you had something to say to fill up the endless *walla walla* chatter. Hey, she was a writer on a show.

During this heightened sense of awareness, her sexuality ran into her like a Mack truck. She had been starved for so long that she ran rampant from one liaison to the next, a greedy child unable to keep her fingers out of the cookie jar. A quickie hand job in the other woman's car, late at night in a parking lot. Going down on an actress in her trailer between takes. It was dangerous, exciting and a thrill to be making it with a high profile guest star, even if her career was waning. Making out with the script supervisor. And then she had a string of mini-affairs with the Vickies. Sarah and she kept them straight by calling them "Vickie-Gelson," because she had met the perky Italian at the deli counter of Gelson's; "Dark Vickie" an actress who was as moody as a badly lit noir film; and "Vickie Lane," a dead ringer for the pretty Lois Lane in the old *Superman* series.

None of these entanglements held the same fury of infatuation as her affair with Adrienne. Nor the sweet and tender exploration of any softer side of herself. Most of her exploits were with like-minded individuals all on the fast-track to the slow-no, driven by the same need—their own intangible dream, and relationships ran a far second. But she heard the common complaint from lovers as she sprinted from the bed to her computer, that she had no time for cuddling, romantic dinners, reading the Sunday paper. She had spent long enough putting herself second. She was cultivating the fine art of selfishness.

And then, suddenly the season was over. It crept up on her so unexpectedly, she found herself bereft. Having poured heart, sweat and tears into her work—the loss of working every waking hour left her in a wasteland of numbing indirection, a sense of unworthiness once she'd stopped producing at that eager pitch. The saturation of moodiness, the leaching depression that inevitably followed.

She had planned to really perfect *May You* during her summer hiatus but the listless malaise followed like a stubborn shadow. She rationalized she was doing more important things. Taking meetings, doing lunches. It was through one of those nefarious connections—one of those two degrees of separation where an actress's friend knew a cousin whose husband was a producer seeking fresh material—that she hooked up with Jerry.

"He just loves *May You*," Jerry's assistant gushed.

"Oh, did he get a chance to read it?"

"Well, no…but he loves the pitch."

She met Jerry for lunch at Cantor's—one of the original *doing lunch* eateries. Jerry's claim to fame was the stellar *Flush Tones*, about a teenage boy who gets advice from his talking toilet. It had scored with the prepubescent male demographic it was intended for and had held the box office lead for seven consecutive weeks.

Jerry had one of the lousiest reputations in a town where many had to stand in line to reach the heap of pretty lousy people. He was the quintessential producer dressed in a jet black blazer over black Armani shirt, and permed silky hair that was woefully thinning. He had just finished making *Bongo Bikini*, a retro beach blanky fest with lots of floating objects popping up on surfboards. For someone who was trying to change his reputation, Spencer had to wonder at his choice of material. Even more confusing was his interest in *May You.*

She identified the problem with Jerry right away. He was genetically incapable of good taste. He thought *Bongo* was artistic because they shot part of it in black and white. But for whatever bizarre reason when he read her script something in it resonated for him.

"She's got balls," Jerry said as he bit into a French fry.

"Well, yes…it takes a lot of courage—"

"But she's gotta be younger."

"I thought we discussed this over the phone—"

"And not Tara Wilson. Her butt's like a float and she's flat as a surfboard."

She envisioned eighteen months of *Bongo* vernacular but held her tongue. *May You* had been shopped all over town, and even with her inroads at the network, she could not get anyone to say more than they thought it was well written.

She had twisted her cocktail napkin into little shreds and now scooped them into a neat pile. "Do you mind if I ask why you want to do this?"

"Look, I've made over fifty films. Most of them forgettable." He shrugged. "I'm just at the point in my life where I wanna make a film I can take my kids to."

Jerry was the only one who was willing to put up the option money. In fact, he was so cash rich, he offered to buy the project outright, which meant that he would actually own *May You*, but she would make a tidy bundle.

Lou hammered at her to take the deal.

"But what if he destroys the material?" Spencer asked, sitting across from Lou in his very Lou-like office, hedged by mounds of scripts behind him, headset at the ready. He took a phone call during the middle of their conversation, making faces while sweet-talking a client, and then holding a mute button as he rolled his eyes. "She's such a cunt!" He winked and released the mute. It made Spencer feel oh so secure.

"Just tell me you're going to be a team player," Lou cooed into the headset.

Spencer impatiently waited for him to get off the fourth interruption of this meeting, frantically searching her soul to determine whether she wanted to let go of the one script she treasured. It was hers. Even if she couldn't sell it.

"Well?" Lou snapped.

"Oh, you're talking to me?"

"Spencer this is a great deal. You're gonna get a lotta money— meaning *I'm getting ten percent of a lotta money*—and you haven't been able to set this up anywhere else, and if you really want to get outta TV—I mean it's a no brainer."

"But, Lou, what if he takes it and mangles it and just...and what about my wanting to direct? I mean that's what I've been holding out for all this time."

"No sweat. We'll make the deal contingent on best efforts to let you direct."

"Best efforts. Right. And I believe in the Easter Bunny."

"Look—at the very least you'll get a chance to pitch your vision to whatever lead he gets."

"I don't know."

"If you wanna be like that, fine Spencer. But I think it's bullshit."

Lou was right It was all bullshit Why didn't Jerry just option it and at the term of expiration he could then have first right of refusal to purchase the project outright?

"Well," Lou sighed dramatically, If that's the way you want it. But you'd be making a lot more money up front if you'd just let the damn thing go."

Yes, maybe she should have. But that's twenty-twenty hindsight and in the meantime every six months she would be pleasantly surprised to get the check in the mail for his option rights and remember they were no further along than they had been from the very beginning. As she came head to head with this reality, it was the first true heartache she suffered in L.A.

But her obsession over getting her film made soon came to an abrupt halt. While she was opening her mail late one night while stuffing a taco down her throat and blipping on her message machine, she stopped in her tracks as she heard Lou's voice, oddly enthusiastic. Ecstatic even. "Hey, Spence—did you see today's trades? You did it You've been nominated for your *Lucifer* script. Thunderdome babe! We're callin' the shots now. Fuck yes!"

* * *

Charles Ives said: "Awards are merely the badge of mediocrity." I don't know about that. Even if you feel a bit like an impostor, they feel pretty damn good when you get one. It's later that you feel the void. The night I won the Emmy I remember with crystal clarity. The limo, red carpet treatment, flashing strobe lights as fans and reporters scream at the stars—of course they have no idea who the hell the writers are. Ushered to my seat where I cannot breathe for two hours.

Suddenly a blanket of calm lays itself over my shoulder and I watch the proceedings in an altered state. When my name is called from the five nominees I do not hear the actual winner. But I know from the expression on Lou's face, the thrilled expression from fellow crew members, the producer leaning over to kiss me. My mother's tears of pride. I am getting up, walking through a maze of tuxes and designer gowns, up several steps where my knee caps turn to jelly donuts, to Judith Light, who is presenting to me, and I lean to her, kiss the side of her handsome face. I hear someone make a speech, short and sweet, reciting the required list of people to thank, producers, the networks, the voting members—thinking there is someone special I should be thanking, isn't there? That one person? Who is it? Oh, but it doesn't matter now, because there are lights and a million people in the audience and thundering applause.

We head to a swank chi-chi restaurant the producers have booked and everyone proceeds to get wildly intoxicated. Everybody's my new best friend. Singing, dancing, congratulations, so many people pecking at my shoulder. My publicist with coke residue on his upper lip. Lou popping up with one person after another "you just have to meet." I can't take it in, simply float through the unbelievable, the fairytale night.

My parents are adorable in their naïvete and blush of pride. Gone are the terrible memories of yesteryear. Several glasses of champagne later I sit between my mother and Hank and we are all gay as if there is no tomorrow, because we can all unload a huge sigh of release, an unwrangling of nerves. Old grudges evaporate.

And when there is only a last handful of us, Hank pulls the crumpled L.A. Times *article—the same one he has taken out with his one good hand to show over and over—that heralds his stepdaughter as "a new and important voice." He glances at me, then nods in that way he has, a shy I've-got-something-to-say-smile, winks and says, "I'm proud of you, Spence."*

But when all the glittering lights fade and I lie in bed still pinching myself in disbelief, I know there is something missing.

Where is she?

* * *

Of course Cinderella always has to contend with her pumpkin, and it was only a matter of time until the bells chimed her fairytale away. By the time her hiatus was over her fifteen minutes were not only up, you would be hard-pressed to find anyone who remembered she ever had them in the first place.

Lucifer got canceled. It had never been very good to begin with and it had simply run its course. Lou sent Spencer out for three series, all of which were crime dramas. But she didn't want to continue the same tired genre and was afraid she would be pigeonholed as a certain kind of writer. Little did she know it was easier to get work being something an agent could describe in half a second than a versatile writer who wanted to try her hand at some of the new *thirty-something/L.A. Law* type series. All the producers asked her in for meetings, liked her writing, but she just didn't have enough credits in a new genre. And she had heard through the grapevine that as a *thirty-something* writer in a gen-X world, she was already considered "old." She ended up working on a terribly intrepid prime time soap that truly stretched the limits of credibility.

But nothing would get in her way. She would not give up hope. She had won an Emmy. Proof positive that she was accomplished, on a road to ever-higher achievement. To prove it to herself over the next few years, she woke at four am to work on more spec scripts before heading to the studio, then drooped over by two in the afternoon. She sent out some pretty bad stuff, changed agents, went to parties, and took meetings.

"Love your work, but it's soft," was a comment she got a lot.

"What's that mean exactly?" she finally asked a producer who simply stared at her open-mouthed in response. Well, he didn't know exactly. It was just the term they used for her kind of work.

"Soft equals woman. Equals emotional," Sarah explained offhandedly "Emotional means not commercial. Means 'soft' box-office."

"Oh." What could Spencer say?

She ventured into commercial scripts and wrote a serial killer story, with a stupendous opening, a new turn every ten pages, blood galore, a surprise ending. She gave the supporting characters a gimmick, you know, had them suck lollipops, addicted to sunflower seeds. It was formulaic and completely predictable.

Lou sent out the script and it got a great showing. Optioned, developed and even financed a couple of times, but it never made it to the screen. In the meantime *May You* languished on Jerry's desk. Every time she called him she got the same runaround.

"How long are you going to let this guy represent your material?" Sarah teased one afternoon while they shared cappuccinos at Cravings.

"Underneath that smarmy veneer lies the heart of a man who loves the movies."

"Oh, for God's sake, do you really believe that?" Sarah demanded.

"Sort of?" she responded, forced to believe her own rhetoric. She was Dorothy following her yellow brick road and if Jerry and his cohorts were the bumblingly inept companions in the road movie of her life, she had to believe that at the end they would all get a heart. A brain. Integrity.

But her wheels were at the soft edge of mushy mud, beginning to spin—walking that fine line of passion versus desperation. The parties, meetings, lunches, the movement, motion of her life in fast forward, the pushing, pushing, pushing that kept her in the playing field. All of it made up of equal parts fear and excitement, fight and exhaustion, hope and denial, hope and rejection. There was a certain symmetry to it and the mariachi of manic behavior became the balance of extremes.

If only...if only. There was a law of averages and if she talked to every goddamn producer or studio head in this town, eventually she had to make it. Somewhere.

* * *

I try to pinpoint the precise moment I knew there was no turning back—when I began wanting things so badly that I stopped seeing the underneath.

There should be a bigger word than desire. "Burning desires" they call it in AA. How can one be consumed by a focus so intent and not get it? Stories of withered souls, bitter with disillusionment and resenting the forces of destiny—they had no place in my picture. I simply refused to suffer disappointment when it was slapping me in the face. Is that will? Or stupidity. Is that the mark of a survivor? Or someone in denial. Is it all the same thing, split by the vagaries of hairline cracks?

All the things we work to attain for our lives are conveniently sold in separate packages. If we want to be an architect we struggle through school with spatial perception problems. We want to be a doctor and develop algophobia. If we want to have children we're infertile, or we have them and they are the reason we cannot become a classical pianist.

I once asked Malcolm, "Now why can't I just have the life that I want? I just write a few screenplays and someone pays me a million dollars for a spec script and then I'm the hottest thing going—I land a three-pic deal and soon I'm directing and taking meetings for my Saturday morning cartoon series that will spin off into a kids' clothing line and then I'll buy a mansion in Malibu away from the smog."

"But you are doing it," Malcolm insisted during one of our marathon phone calls.

"How is this doing it? Struggle, struggle. Wait, wait. Get rejected. Struggle some more. Ooops, more rejections. No sex. Let's not forget that—"

"Oh, please, you've had sex with three different women in as many months. Besides you are so unavailable. For as long as I've known you, you've been one of the few people who make a living at what you love to do. You won an Emmy for God's sake. So you're not a director. Nothing, but nothing is going to happen on your time frame. You are the most impatient person I have ever met, but don't forget for one second that you are, indeed, doing the life you set out to do."

To have ten more minutes with him on the phone. To tell him how much I love him. Just to tell him how dear and precious he is to me.

* * *

"You fucking cunt! I can't believe you went behind my back and went to another agency. After everything I've done for you? No one in this town even thinks you have talent. If it wasn't for me you would never have gotten your goddamn Emmy. And if you think you can sign with another agent, you can just kiss your career goodbye."

Lou's voice screamed epithets from Spencer's machine as she stood there, mail slipping from her hands, mouth open. She couldn't swallow. How had Lou at ICM found out she was leaving him and going to Lou-Anne at CAA?

Trembling she dialed Lou-Anne.

"Yeah?" Lou-Anne's terse Brooklyn accent. "What's up?"

"Did you say anything to Lou about my coming over there?"

"No way. Jesus!"

"Well, he's found out and he's being ugly about it." Spencer replayed the message over the phone for her.

"Christ what a schmuck! The guy's harassing you. If he sucks at what he does that isn't your fault. Besides, he doesn't get your material. You need a woman taking care of you. Someone with some sensitivity. If he threatens you one more time, tell him to suck his dick and in the meantime, I'll get Gary to rush your contract over here."

"Well...I'd rather end this on good—"

"Fuck it. Ain't gonna happen. Don't worry. He'll be kissing your ass in a few weeks."

After she hung up she felt like she did so often these days. Was she winning the battle and losing the war? The phone rang again. It was Malcolm.

"Hey, where are you?"

Oh shit. She had forgotten she had promised to go to his fundraiser. "Is it black tie?"

"Just wear what you've got on."

"Just tell me there are cocktails in my future."

"I've got one right here with your name on it."

* * *

Spencer dashed out of the cab feeling breathless and hungry. She hadn't eaten since breakfast and after Lou's nasty message couldn't put anything in her stomach.

As she and Malcolm hobnobbed amongst the sea of black tails and red cummerbunds, Malcolm spotted an old friend he knew from his Project Angel Food days. Exhausted and hungry, Spencer sifted through the crowd in her new Armani suit, darting from one hors d'oeuvre tray to the next. She knew she would run into someone from the "biz" and began to scan the crowd. She might as well make the most of it and network.

She saw her from behind. Tall, taller than Spencer was attracted to, and quite slender. But something about the way the woman stood, her lanky grace was reminiscent...And then she turned around. Oh my God. It *was* her. The woman from the plane.

Even when she wanted to run, Spencer couldn't take her eyes off the darkly exotic beauty and wondered if...if—that's right, Lena—would remember her from their strange first meeting. Apparently she did, for after several seconds of catching her eyes, she cocked her head a bit as if trying to figure a matter out, and then a dawning of recognition brightened her face. Slowly she smiled, and nodded in Spencer's direction.

God, she *was* beautiful, Spencer thought. Striking. She projected a sense of self-possession, a detached ambivalence toward the crowd. In a world saturated with desperation, Lena's autonomy was a beacon of light and as Spencer approached she could see the professional warmth with which she engaged those around her.

Lena extended a hand. "Spencer, right?"

"Yes. You remembered." Spencer blushed.

"Kind of difficult to forget."

Spencer's finger traced an eyebrow as she tried to hide her humiliation. "That was, what, over two years ago?"

"Yes." Lena nodded.

"How are you?"

"I'm really great. How about you?"

"Pretty good."

Lena made her shy. Especially given the circumstances. Spencer, soft butch extraordinaire, suddenly stumbling, bumbling. She wanted to speak like her characters, but giddy chatter came out instead. Malcolm reappeared and introductions were made, and Lena mentioned their meeting on the plane.

"Oh, so *you're* the one." Malcolm spoke before he realized what he had said.

Lena arched a brow toward Spencer.

"I told him how kind you were to me..."

She smiled then, directly at Spencer. "I have to go."

"Oh...well, I'm...I'm so glad I got to see you."

Lena dug into her neat little hand purse and pulled out a card. Without a word she slipped it to Spencer, then gave her a chaste hug good-bye.

But she hadn't been able to summon the nerve to call her.

"Malc I just can't. It's like, genetically impossible for me right now. I'm too...too exposed." Spencer was still wobbly over her last affair, which had created an excellent opportunity to thrust herself deep into the nadir of workaholism. "Besides, I can't even tell if she's gay."

But a few months later, they met again at a lesbian cocktail party. That night Spencer was celebrating. Jerry had interested some Russian financiers and after several martinis Spencer boldly sought out Lena. Still, it was Lena who asked if she would like to continue their conversation in a quieter spot. They left the glitz of the Mondrian and had cocktails in a darkly lit corner of the St. James Hotel.

"So it's very serendipitous that I ran into you tonight," Lena stated half-way through her drink.

"How's that?"

"Well, I heard a rumor about you today."

"What?!" Spencer had barely paid attention to their conversation which had focused on the gay political scene. She had been too busy staring at Lena's Hope Lange physique, her beautifully sculpted arms, strong slender fingers.

"Yes, a friend of mine is a producer at Dream Works." Lena bit into her olive. "Said you're like a 'dog with a bone.'"

"That's flattering," Spencer responded.

"Actually she spoke very highly of you. Just said you were on a mission."

"Hmmm." Spencer took a sip of her martini. This wasn't exactly how she had planned this conversation going. "I don't really want to talk about work."

"But it's very important to you."

"Pretty much."

"What else?" Lena asked, her eyes narrowing.

"Well," Spencer cleared her throat again, "I love my little niece, Heather. I call her Pookerdoodle. She's like my star. When she was born, I just...I just fell head over heels."

"You like kids." Lena said it as a positive statement.

"That's right—you have a daughter."

"Yes, whom *I'm* head over about."

"Does she look like you?"

"Yes. She's got my eyes."

Which prompted Spencer to study Lena's, dark and intent.

"They must be beautiful." Did she just say that? Was that like a bad line of dialogue? *See, editing the moment again.*

"Thank you," Lena answered graciously.

"I'd like to meet her," Spencer said without thinking.

"Would you?" Lena smiled and as she began to lean closer her cell phone rang. "Sorry. I've been waiting for an important call from a client in Australia. I've got to take this. Do you mind?"

"Not at all. Would you like some privacy?"

Lena shook her head and Spencer caught the shimmer of Lena's necklace in the "V" of her throat, the tendons arched and graceful, her neck begging to be kissed, her eyes glimmering with a smile at Spencer as she talked politics over the phone. Spencer could feel herself falling.

What, was she crazy? She had just met her.

Lena ended the call, tenderly touched Spencer's collar, her dark brown eyes penetrating and warm. "I'm sorry, I have to cut this short. I have a crisis."

"I'm sorry." Spencer tried to control her lip from twitching. "Hope everything's okay."

Lena leaned to kiss her, her lips fitting perfectly with Spencer's own. When she was finished, she gently rubbed her thumb under Spencer's bottom lip erasing the trace of lipstick.

"I'm sure it will be," Lena picked up her sweater. "May I call you?"

"Please…please," Spencer stuttered, "I'd like that."

* * *

Lena was not in the least her type. Spencer had always been a chump for what she described as lovably Botticelli. But here she was sitting across from her on their first date. Lena had called her before the standard two-day wait rule. And when she phoned she was direct.

"Would you have dinner with me?" she had asked in a low husky voice.

Within moments of their first cocktail, Lena's knuckles nonchalantly grazed against Spencer's forearm and Spencer saw Lena's clear eyes, void of coy flirtation. She didn't maneuver, nor did she play games. That was also against type. Spencer had thrived on the hunt and chase. It made for exquisite capitulation. But here was Lena, direct and uncensored and Spencer felt her body begin to yield to her magnetism, warmed to the tell-tale movement from within her neglected interior.

It was only later while she paced her living room, unable to sleep, that she realized what it was about Lena. The attraction wasn't just sexual. She *liked* her.

"Now that would be a completely foreign concept, wouldn't it?" Malcolm asked as they had lunch the next day.

"Entirely."

"So are you going to see her again?"

"We'll see." Spencer tried to sound noncommittal.

"Why don't you call her?"

"Because I'm too steeped in insecurity."

"But she's already made the first move."

"You think that makes me instantly confident? Besides I…I'm not quite sure how I feel about her yet."

"Know what I think?" Malcolm asked with a knowing smile.

"I'm sure you'll tell me."

"I think this is the first decent woman you've ever come up against and you're shitting your Victoria's Secret skivvies."

"I knew you'd tell me."

But the truth was, Spencer had no frame of reference for someone like Lena.

Lena was just plain and solidly good—a lesbian Jimmy Stewart. She had been born into and raised in wealth. And because of her philanthropic idealism she gave a great deal of her money back to her political causes. She was a woman of extraordinary convictions and Spencer was just a little intimidated standing next to all that wholesome wonderfulness.

The other thing about Lena was her breathtaking beauty. Spencer loved the gentle grace of the way she moved, her beautiful brown eyes, and those arms—which she took every advantage to expose, wearing sleeveless V-necked tops that also exposed her sexy neck and collarbones.

In her short but accelerated history of dating creatures from Venus, Spencer had never slept with one she would actually consider being friends with. Besides, she was almost too nice— "yes, nice would be a tragedy," Sarah had smirked. It was difficult for Spencer to believe she deserved this level of quality in a lover. Wonderful friends she could cope with, but the Lenas of the world simply didn't fall for someone like Spencer.

When she called a few nights later to ask Spencer to the movies, Spencer knew she was sunk. At the mere sound of Lena's voice Spencer's heart tasted a moment of freedom, a liberation from the dull gray disillusionment of her life.

"How I know a movie works," Spencer explained later that week over cappuccinos and cheesecake, "is that I'm unaware I'm watching it because I'm *inside* it. If I'm not judging all the elements of craft going into it and it appears effortless and seamless, that's my criteria for a good movie."

"I never thought of it that way." Lena took a bite of her cheesecake. "I only know that I like a movie—or I don't. But for you it must be kind of disappointing. Loving something, but then being so aware of it, it takes you out of the experience."

"Occupational hazard." Spencer glanced away, and stared at the floor.

"You okay?" Lena asked.

"That's the problem with the movies," she said after a moment. "You begin thinking they're real. And you imagine that you too can be swept off your feet, explore where no man has been before.

They make the unattainable reachable. They make true love seem graceful. But when you discover they are not real, that it's all done with movie magic, smoke and mirrors, your reality is dented, and you begin seeing your dreams a little differently."

"It's lost its magic?"

"I remember seeing Spencer Tracy and Lionel Barrymore in *Captains Courageous.*"

"Rudyard Kipling," Lena nodded.

"Yeah." Beautiful *and* smart. "So there are all these great shots of the kid and the fishermen out at sea, but if you look closely you realize they're not really swaying about in a fishing boat on the ocean. All the boats behind them are the product of a blue screen, the sun glinting shadows in their faces are from carefully rigged lights, and you're no longer transported to the lusty life on the high seas but to an overheated studio set. You start to hunt for where the lines of reality break off and make-believe begins and stop watching the scene."

"So your craft has betrayed you," Lena offered quietly.

Spencer found the empathy in Lena's eyes almost too much to bear. How could this woman know her so well, understand her pain in the span of hours?

"Yes…I suppose it has."

transatlantic review
Aug 3, 1922

Harrington's Truth Raw and "Naked"

"...and the phrases are exquisitely succinct. This reader can state without equivocation that Harrington, while certainly unseasoned, is a brave new voice. While the savagery of Mr. Harrington's tone may indeed offend many, it will, nevertheless, elicit strong feelings in all. It is precisely what is needed to reveal this writer's inner truths, the most raw and explicit material to have been published in recent years."

Dear Dot,

I thought you of all people would enjoy the enclosed of our very own Lilian's first review. Although she is only known as B. Harrington and her true gender is a secret but to a small few, her book has become the chatter of the Left Bank!

Indeed with Sylvia's publication of Naked Truth, *Byron has become an instant cause celèbre. Her newfound success, albeit currently contained within the obscure world of the 6th arrondisement, has put a spark of fire in her eyes. She positively glows. Sylvia plans to keep Byron a mystery and since Byron quite by her own nature keeps to herself she shan't have too difficult a job of it.*

By the by, Etienne and I have arrived at a new agreement which allows us more time in each other's company. I suppose if I allow this arrangement to expire in its own time, much like milk left out to spoil, it shall turn us both quite sour. But enough gloom. Our very own wounded bird has become quite a grown woman now and I for one am so very proud of her!

Your ever faithful, Rabbit

Journal: Paris. November 1922

Things have settled somewhat in the past few months and Byron is no longer in the whirlwind of celebrity that took her quite by surprise, poor thing. Suddenly everyone wanted to know who she was—or more precisely from where this mysterious Harrington fellow hailed. Men were suspicious, women were intrigued. But it was only a matter of time before it came out. In the instant that Janet whispered to Gertrude that B. Harrington was the timid child who had fainted at her footsteps, it was known throughout all of Paris that B. was indeed a woman.

Certainly, like most poetry, it will not make Byron rich, but it has elevated our little bird to one of those exquisite substratas in our caste system. Though not a man, she enjoys the kind of critical acclaim reserved for the Joyces and the Eliots, so has secured the men's respect. As for the women, to a certain set, she is greatly admired. Lavinia told me Byron was all the chatter at Natalie's "women only" salon yesterday.

And finally, even Miss Stein broke silence. I'm sure it nearly killed her but she must have determined that brevity was the better part of jealousy for she made her proclamation of respect in one word. "Important." Now if she would only exercise such restraint in her own work!

Oh by the by, there's a Russian painter, Pilieskov something or other, who's making quite a pest of himself over Byron.

* * *

Rabbit and Byron became known as "Le Pair" because they were almost as inseparable as Gertrude and Alice. They rarely missed an opportunity to spend time together. If Rabbit was seen waiting for Hem at the Lilas, Byron was not far behind. If Byron found herself in the middle of a heated debate at Natalie's, Rabbit's strong opinion was sure to follow.

So it became somewhat of a strain on their friendship when Byron met Pilieskov. Sylvia and Adrienne had invited Byron, Rabbit and Ezra Pound to celebrate Sylvia's birthday at Michaud's. As the evening wore on they went round and round with toasts, each topping the other with a story about Sylvia.

"...and the dear parrot who often partook of Sylvia's tea, while perched upon her shoulder, flew out the window and took a dive in the Seine."

"Miserable bunch of feathers," Sylvia grumbled.

"There's Sylvia, tossing off her shoes and diving into the river. Anyone who can rescue a parrot from the Seine should certainly be awarded the *Légion d'Honneur!*" Rabbit raised his glass.

"Hear hear!" echoed round the table.

As Ezra began his toast Byron noticed a tall somber gentleman clad in black making his way to their table.

"Excuse for me," he bowed. "I must ask to say celebrations to the wonderful Miss Beach."

His voice was low and resonant and thick with his native Russian tongue. After bowing to Sylvia and then the rest of the table, he stopped at Byron, allowing the barest smile as he raised her hand to his lips.

Byron caught Rabbit's distinct displeasure when Sylvia invited the stranger to join their party.

Over the next few weeks Pilieskov called on Byron, inviting her to the theater, a reading at Sylvia's bookstore, and finally to a museum showing his work. Byron enjoyed spending time with the Russian, drawn to his darkness for reasons she couldn't fathom.

"He's so...so black," Rabbit protested as they shopped for flowers to bring to Natalie. "Doesn't he own anything but funeral wear?"

"I know he's a bit, well, eccentric I suppose, but he's very clever and his work is—"

"Oh Lord, if one more tortured eccentric is equated with genius I will shoot myself. And if you start with his views on cubism I shall scream."

"Why don't you like him?" Byron asked as she picked at some roses in a stall.

"I don't trust him."

"You don't even know him."

"Dear Lord—do women such as yourself have no comprehension of their commodity? This man is known as the greatest philanderer in all of Europe!"

"Rabbit weren't you the one who told me to 'not believe the things I heard from others and even less from the horse's mouth?' "

"*Mon dieu!* I've created a monster."

"Please, Rabbit," Byron said as she took his hand. "Be happy that I've found a new friend, for if you can't be, it will ruin the whole thing."

Rabbit sighed, nodding resignedly.

"I'm meeting him for dinner. Will you walk me?"

He kissed her hand. "*I to be overjoyed,*" he taunted, mocking the Russian's accent and manner.

That night while watching Pilieskov cut his meat while they dined, Byron wondered what he looked like as he worked, how he held his brushes, worked paint into the canvas. Did he forget that his hands were wet with color as he ran strong fingers through his thick black hair? Did his skin bristle with the heat of composition? She imagined his large body as graceful as a dancer's in front of his canvas.

"Would you sit for me?" he asked abruptly.

"Pardon?" She started, afraid he had been reading her thoughts.

"Will you?"

"But I—" She would be lying if she said she wasn't flattered.

"Good." In the only lightness she had seen from him he winked. "Tomorrow then."

The next afternoon Pilieskov led Byron into the center of his studio. Cramped and in disarray, it was not unlike her own workspace.

"You are…" Pilieskov appraised her with his painter's eye. "… *Krassiva.*"

"What does that mean?"

He didn't answer but his eyes narrowed appreciatively. He took her by the elbow. "Come. You may change in this room. There is robe."

Byron entered a small closet where Pilieskov's clothes, painting supplies and several robes hung. As she undressed she thought how bold she had become. To think of sitting for an artist. But then, art had become something altogether different since she had been in Paris. A purity existed in the work of those around her and it made her feel if not entirely unselfconscious, at least willing to experience the muse in all its shapes.

As she reentered his studio, Pilieskov was immersed in mixing colors, preparing his canvas. She walked slowly forward. He turned and pursed his lips, shut one eye, then directed her to a chaise lounge where he manipulated her position, placing her weight against an elbow, putting two fingers of her right hand above the material of the robe, the rest of her hand resting softly beneath the folds.

Pilieskov continued to fuss with a precision bordering on the fanatical as he prepared to render his vision, tweaking the material of her robe this way and that, brushing a lock from Byron's forehead, even creating her expression by massaging the muscles of her face with his thick fingers, her cheeks flushing with objection and, to be fair, a twinge of arousal. When he finished placing her just so, he returned to his canvas and began to work. Quickly and quietly.

At first Byron was only aware of her own breathing, the slight fluttering of her heart, her flesh rising with the teasing cold, her nipples growing erect. She was exhilarated by her own boldness. With the exception of Rabbit, she had not been alone with a man since Charles. No lips had touched her own, no man had touched her since…since that night. After leaving Bay Cliff her focus had been on survival, and relationships were a luxury confined to friendships. The few men who had shown any interest in her at all she immediately avoided. She simply didn't entertain the idea of romance.

After she had rejected a number of persistent suitors since she had been in Paris, she would lie in bed nights wondering if she was a freak. Wondering if what Charles had done to her made her like the women she had read about, cold and unfeeling. Frigid. What was wrong with her? She thought of the men she knew: Hem, Ezra, even Mr. Joyce whom she so greatly admired. Not one of them did she find attractive. When she dwelled on the women and thought of their partnering—Sylvia and Adrienne, Miss Stein and her "wife"—she would let her mind wander over their bodies, and was relieved that she felt nothing akin to desire for any of them. Not even for the beautiful Natalie and her handsome lover Romaine Brooks. But did she for men?

As she watched Pilieskov, watched the sureness of his hands, the slight sway of his feet as he worked his creation, she felt a warmth and a sensuality to her skin beneath the satin sheet, an awareness of her body as a potent tool. The idea of inspiring the muse was a heady prospect. It was some time before he looked up at her and when he did she saw a new glimmer in his eyes.

"I'm finish. For today."

As he washed his hands in a bowl, Byron began to move.

"Be still. Please. Stay there one moment." Pilieskov dried his hands and approached her. His eyes grew dark and the light was of a different nature. He kneeled beside her and took her hand.

"Thank you. *Krassiva…*" He kissed her hand, whispered in husky lament, "…beautiful…beautiful." His mouth branded her, his lips soft and hot, sending shivers up her arm, teasing the strands of hair at her neck. She was entranced by his homage, moved by the spirit of their creation.

He nuzzled his head into her neck, kissing and then whispering into her ear, more Russian and fire, and she felt herself becoming more aroused as his hand found her waist and he pulled her to him. His adoring gaze smoldered into lust. How she wanted his full lips to embrace her own.

In one swift motion he scrambled on top of her with a rough tenderness as he spread sloppy kisses over her face, the taste of stale cigarettes and wine—his mouth became a brutal motion that soon devoured her neck, shoulders, her breasts. She wanted to feel, to be stirred as he unbuttoned his pants. He pulled his cock free with an abruptness that startled her and, coaxing her hand around it, implored her to stroke him. As she was accustoming herself to his size and enlarging stiffness, he pushed her hand aside and with little finesse thrust himself into her. Gone was her arousal. All she felt was a void, her body numbing as he grunted into her.

She stared dumbly at Pilieskov, his eyes closed as he peaked in a guttural roar. Her arms hung limply by her sides. He wiped saliva from his chin, while quickly pulling himself out. She searched for something in his face, a moment of tenderness, but he would not address her, muttering briefly she should dress, that he had to be somewhere in a few minutes. Their coupling had had nothing to do with their shared experience this afternoon. Nothing to do with her.

Byron dressed and without a word parted Pilieskov's company. As she wandered the streets of Paris she thought, *I have now lain with a man.* Feeling much like a student learning a required subject, she was hard pressed to find what aspect of the act had inspired volumes on the matter. Oh, so this is how this feels, and that is how that works. She supposed the rest was really all rather innocuous. She did not feel compelled to repeat the experience so she would conclude her relationship with Pilieskov as simply as if she were wiping crumbs from her hands.

Paris: July 1923

I walked down the escarpment to meet Byron for lunch and it wasn't until I found myself whistling that I knew why I was so happy. It seemed ages since I had seen ma petit piaf and she is suddenly available again for making merry and wreaking havoc. When I asked her what happened to the gloomy Russian, she merely shook her head and said "Don't let me ever not listen to you again."

Her smile was a bit brittle and I thought it would be a matter of bad taste if I asked, as I suspect, whether our Russian was an oafish sort of lover.

* * *

After the incident with Pilieskov, Byron found herself split between brief trysts with men who were more refined, almost effeminate, and recommitting herself to her work. She slept with her lovers as if they were a necessary experience in proving she was, if not a woman, at least a member of the human race. She could not justify her affairs with rapture or maudlin poetry and so they dissipated as quickly as they came into being. She devoted even more hours of her day to her poetry. She was all too happy to resume late lunches and dinners with Rabbit, all too happy to be in the warm and witty company of her dearest friend.

One of their more favored pastimes was their unquenchable curiosity for true crime stories, an obsession they shared with Hemingway. Unlike the American presses, which only provided brief synopses of events, the French press provided detailed accounts, and once one became involved with a murder story, it was impossible to let a day pass without reading the paper. Lest one should swipe the rod, Byron found herself arriving earlier and earlier to nab the paper as soon as it was hung, eager to get to the next installment.

Over the course of weeks she joined Rabbit and Hem to follow the investigation of the grisly murder of an infamous actress, who had enjoyed more success behind stage than in front of it. The three of them could be seen bent over the paper as they greedily consumed every last bit of information in the daily serial. Their raised voices could be heard blocks away as they argued heatedly amongst themselves and other café patrons about motive and intent, suspect and victim.

"I know this is journalism, but you would think they might create more of a cliff-hanger—like the serials in American matinees," Byron noted one afternoon. "They have so much opportunity to make this more fascinating. They already have the audience."

Hemingway nodded. "I'm in complete agreement, Byron."

"Well, darling, you could always apply for a post," Rabbit offered.

"If it *were* me," Byron nodded haughtily in Rabbit's direction, "I would expand a bit on the director—flesh out his personality so that we could attest to his motive. After all, she left him right before the play became a huge success. Suppose she had used him? Suppose others had used him before and this was the last he could take? Suppose she had a lover in the wings, and this was her opportunity to escape the over-bearing—"

"Well, listen to you," Hemingway chuckled. "You've certainly given this a lot of thought."

Rabbit tapped his Gauloises upon his wrist, then snapped to attention. "Byron, I say, why don't you give it a whirl."

"What do you mean?"

"Well, you're already proven yourself to be the best detective of the three of us. I have no doubt you could write a better yarn if you put a mind to it."

"Do you mean a short story?"

"Yes!" Hemingway thoughtfully scratched at his beard.

"But I don't write short stories," Byron protested. "I'm a poet."

"Of course you are," Hemingway agreed, "but this will give you an opportunity to take your natural talents—to expose the raw underneath, the edge of the knife—and write a real story. What could be better material for exploring the human condition than murder, greed and lust?"

"I don't know," Byron frowned.

"It's settled. Now all we have to do is find a title." Rabbit extracted a pen from his jacket and began scribbling on a scrap before him. "Let's see, The Luxembourg Lynching, The Parisian Phantom—no, alliteration is so gauche. I've got it—The Mystery of rue Cardinal Lemoine —"

"That's no mystery," Hemingway interjected, "it's horse dung that causes that smell!"

As they laughed, Byron glanced from Rabbit to Hemingway, their voices raised in approval and excitement, but for Byron it was simply the silliest notion.

* * *

She didn't take the suggestion that she write the short story seriously until she strolled that evening, as she often did to clear her mind of the day's events, and she let herself speculate, all in good fun of course. If one were to put an intriguing twist to a motive, and add the alluring elements of the seamier side of the Paris underworld, perhaps it would make for a rousing and suspenseful read.

She shook her head, trying to return to thoughts of poetry, but found herself again and again returning to a mystery creeping into her imagination. For fun she began to follow the premise through and two hours later she had a grisly murder, a dashing detective solving all number of clues, a damsel in distress, and a killer whom no one could possibly suspect.

By the time she reached her garret, she was ruined to work on her poetry. Damn, her time in the evenings was so rare. She really needed to be more serious. Perhaps she should address her finances since she had spent the evening in such expensive folly.

The royalties from *Naked Truth* were dwindling, and although it had been critically successful, poetry did not sell well, and there was no denying that it had only allowed her to scrape by primarily because Rabbit insisted on paying for almost all their dinners and lunches.

Perhaps it was time. Time to instill a little fiscal responsibility.

Paris: November 1923

Well, I think it is finally over for Etienne and myself. His wife returns from holiday tomorrow, and my hopes for a passionate good-bye turned to silence as we both accepted that this was the last time we would spend together for the foreseeable future.

I wandered the streets for hours feeling lost and yet a great weight seemed to slide from my shoulders. I headed to Byron's, knowing she would be at her desk, ever industrious.

When she saw me, she knew immediately what I was about and opened her arms to me. She held me for a long time as we sat on her bed, and she comforted me without words. I should be quite lost if anything happened to my dear one, for she, in her own quiet way, gives me far more strength than I give her.

"Enough of this dark despair," I said, straightening my tie. "Tell me good news. If you don't have any, make it up."

But as it turned out, Byron had not only good but excellent news.

Damn if she hadn't gone and gotten herself a publishing contract. Mayhem at the Montparnasse *was such a success with readers of* Vanity Fair *that Knopf as well as Faber & Faber have contacted her about making the short story a full length novel. I picked her up, twirled her round and round, "See ma petit piaf…you are ready for flight!"*

To lessen the blow of Etienne's departure and to celebrate Byron's grand news we set ourselves to the task of celebrating until the wee hours.

* * *

Byron's father arrived for a week long visit before he headed to London for business. As Francis grew more accustomed to the changes in his daughter, he relaxed as Rabbit kept the three of them delightfully entertained on a whirlwind tour.

"How I love nothing more than to show off my fair city," Rabbit puffed as he gaily swung his new cane. "Rather than bore you with sights overflowing with goggle-eyed tourists, I shall take you and *Monsieur* Francis to, shall I say, the off-beaten Parisian treats—the real Paris."

"That's just what I'd like," Francis replied, holding his daughter close. "Of course—now that I've come to appreciate my daughter's transformation—all I really care to see is what's in front of me. This happy smile on my very accomplished daughter's face."

Rabbit bowed in acknowledgment and added, "Of course a little culture never hurt anyone so how 'bout we begin this tour and feast upon the Monets and Cézannes at *Musee du Luxembourg.*"

After spending the morning in the museum they were all famished and dined quite simply, in the noon-day's sun, on sausage and freshly baked bread, accompanied by a fine bottle of white Macon wine. Having sated all the senses, Francis promptly fell asleep.

Byron watched her father adoringly.

"It must be difficult for you," Rabbit said. "I can see how much you miss him."

"Yes, I do. Terribly."

"Yes. Well he's a wonderful chap."

"My father..." Byron's lip trembled.

"I felt much the same way about my mother before she passed on. Otherwise I don't know if I ever would have been able to stay in Paris."

"I wasn't given that choice," Byron stated cryptically.

"But whatever do you mean?"

"Let's just say, had things been different, I would never have dreamed of leaving my father." Byron got up, brushed off her slacks, ending the conversation.

Later that afternoon they caught up with Hemingway at Sylvia's and he invited them to the races.

"I rather thought he stopped gambling," Byron whispered to Rabbit.

"Apparently he's returned to the sport for our benefit today," Rabbit concluded.

Byron put her arm in her father's, feeling safe, really safe for the first time since she had arrived in Paris. She felt a lightness in her chest and a spring to her step and knew that she would never have been able to leave Francis if she had been given the choice.

They headed into the decayed part of town to the Gare du Nord, sat upon a blanket Hemingway had spread upon the fresh spring grass and watched as the horses took to the track, jumping stone walls and hurdles. They drank a good deal of wine, Hemingway jumping up rather suddenly as his horse might trip or make folly, and then as the sun began to fall, Francis and Hemingway shared stories of Spain and their passion for bullfighting.

Byron thought it might well be the happiest day of her life.

Paris: April 1924

The word is out. Mayhem *is a huge success. Unfortunately the reviews are not.*

Sylvia and I try to keep them from Byron—when she sees one, all the blood drains from her face. Sylvia insists she only read the good reviews and dispense with the less kind. But every artist I have ever known could give a fig about good reviews. They narrow in and focus on the bad and that is all they take away from the experience.

I did show her the lovely review Dottie wrote which Byron dismissed as charity. Janet took quite a shine to Mayhem, *calling Nate Venable "a delicious sort of detective...*Mayhem, *while not the most important book of the season, is certainly the most scandalous. A delightful read." Janet is about to begin writing a fortnightly newsletter for* The New Yorker *under the name of Genet.*

Paris: August 1924

I worry about Byron of late. She's become rather withdrawn, perhaps a bit depressed, even though Mayhem *has made her a tidy little sum. She frets that no one will ever again take her writing seriously. I remind her that she not only enjoys the respect of the inner circle, but is now a huge hit with her public. So the critics don't like her work—Pah I say . Look at me! What do critics know?*

I assisted her in finding a new flat. She held onto that cramped little garret like a baby unwilling to leave the womb. I kept telling her it simply wouldn't do. It was so tiny and she has so much correspondence and business to attend to now—she needed a desk bigger than a milk crate.

"Besides," I teased her, "Whatever shall you do if one calls to—ahem" which caused a pillow to be tossed at my head.

Dined with Natalie and Djuna. Those girls are so busy. I do believe they are the two most promiscuous women in all of Paris. Byron's eyes kept wandering to a new member of their little enclave. Marie Salavier is a stage actress, and though she enjoyed the flattery of several who had just seen her last performance she was not all bluster and dramatics as so many theater people are, seemingly unable to turn off the stage lights. In fact, she was quite refined and disarming.

Later in the evening I discovered Byron and Marie out in the gardens, hunched over in earnest discussion and if I didn't know better, I would think I saw a spark of interest between them.

* * *

Byron didn't think she had ever met anyone quite so pretty as Mr. Scott Fitzgerald. His golden-blond hair, his aquiline nose and sensual mouth gave him the kind of elegant beauty that could easily belong to a woman. She found him fascinating because she, like most everyone else, had devoured *Gatsby* in a single sitting and, as a writer, was taken by his brilliance.

"But I've been trying to work, I tell you," Fitzgerald moaned as he swiftly downed yet another brandy while they all sat around a table at the Lilas. "It's this city. I just can't write here."

They were a fascinating study in contrasts, Byron thought as she assessed them. The slender Fitzgerald, his face bright with drink, whining like a fishwife. The masculine Hemingway, his eyes narrowed intently, his intoxication a controlled illusion.

"If one can't write in Paris, old man," Rabbit offered, "I suspect they can't write anywhere."

"Parnell is right," Hemingway barked. "Damnit, Scott, you're writing rubbish with these short stories. You wrote *Gatsby*, for Christ's sakes."

"Look, I take the stories," Fitzgerald defended plaintively, "and it's really not so very bad, Ernest. I only make them tawdry for submission. Then I can change them back again. Voila."

"That's like saying if I clean myself after sleeping with a whore, it's no longer whoring but making love."

"Hem, please," Rabbit warned.

"No! I've had it with this conversation. If you write your work beneath you—mutate your words to sell to this audience or that—you take your self down with it. You can't split integrity into pieces and say I chose it here and not there. It's no time at all before you destroy your talent."

"I...I really think I've heard enough," Scott snapped, then blanched as he sank into his chair and slumped over the table.

"Is he ill?" Byron checked to see that he was still breathing.

"He'll be fine in an hour." Hemingway plopped Scott's hat upon his head. "Sweet dreams."

Later, after long shadows were cast by the emptied wine bottles, Fitzgerald came to. Hemingway picked him up by his elbows and grasped him about the waist. "A very good evening to you both," he said resignedly, dragging Fitzgerald off with him.

"Tally ho." Rabbit raised his glass, and when they were out of earshot, he mused, "How dreary. Poor Hem. He's taken it upon himself to be Scott's keeper due to his unshakeable belief in Scott's genius."

"But don't you think he has a point?" Byron asked, Hemingway's earlier words cutting into her good mood. "I mean, after all, he has already proven that he can write magnificently—"

"As have you—"

"You didn't let me finish. He needn't sell out with his work because it's commercial as well."

"As is yours."

"My commercial work is no better than the stories he's talking about."

"But darling, you're making a dreadful mistake. You're applying an ill-conceived judgment to yourself and, quite frankly, to Scott. Your circumstances are entirely different and the point is you have a magnificent gift to tell a rousing good story with a helluva lot of class."

"But it's not what's in my heart."

He took great pains to light his cigarette. "Let me tell you something, little one. It's not a disgrace to be successful in spite of what all the l'Odeon elite conspire to make one believe. Yes, there is art for which one must starve and suffer. You've done that. You've suffered quite enough."

Byron stiffened in her chair. What did Rabbit know about her suffering?

"Don't get flustered, Byron. I have no earthly clue what it is that torments you, but any fool who spends time with you can see the pain. Something happened and you turned it around with *Naked Truth* so stop bludgeoning your pretty little skull. Now you deserve a time where you can enjoy your life. Enjoy your success. It doesn't have to be the ugly stepchild that you don't want anyone to see. Let Nate make you filthy rich and be admired the world over, and you shall be the wiser."

* * *

Byron decided to follow Rabbit's advice and allowed Nate another outing. She gave him all the freedom anyone had ever dreamed of, so that readers might live vicariously through his adventures. "He's so damnably charming, and mysteriously handsome that the fairer sex find themselves all swoony and such," Rabbit gushed. "I say, Byron, you've based your character on my finer attributes."

Rabbit wasn't too far off the mark. For she had indeed fashioned the glib detective upon Rabbit's more outlandish personality traits. Nate was a sophisticate who charmed women and men alike and after the publication of her second book, *Phantom of Delight*, much was made of Nate Venable. His character soon grew to be a celebrity and Byron Harrington a sensation.

Nate's adventures were peppered with excursions to Paris's underworld, to foggy streets with villainous characters who might hold the very clue Nate needed, only for him to discover these nefarious parties floating in the Seine. Nate's latest victim was found in the back alleyway of the Hole in the Wall Bar whose rear door used to be a one way ticket to the sewers, leading the story to a grand climax in the catacombs.

Because the material was increasingly scandalous, the publishers found it more and more necessary to shield the public from Byron's true identity. "No it wouldn't do at all for your fans to discover who you really are, Miss Harrington," insisted Mr. Abercrombie, who was meeting her on behalf of her publisher.

"But what if they do find out?" Byron asked, afraid of the charade. "We've been through this once before with *Naked Truth*, and somehow the truth finds a way of rearing its head when least expected."

"That was a different case entirely. Very few Americans are familiar with *Naked Truth*, and if they are, they belong to the literary set which wouldn't likely read the Venable series in any event."

"Not to put too fine a point on it." Byron pursed her lips in resignation.

"Since you live here in Paris it will be easier to keep your press at minimum while we rally around the publicity of your character. Soon, in the public's mind, B. Harrington will be synonymous with Nate Venable."

"That may well work in the States, Mr. Abercrombie," Sylvia piped up. "But you understand that my partner, Adrienne Monnier, plans to do the French translation. Miss Harrington is quite known to the literati"—Sylvia nodded encouragingly at Byron—"as well as to her reading public—and she is known as a woman."

The publisher, duly noting Sylvia's denunciation of the publishing world's hypocrisy, offered, "Then let's work around the matter for the time being. Since Miss Harrington's appearance is not altogether"—he cleared his throat—"conventionally female, perhaps we could make it less so. Would you have any objection to that?"

"Absolutely divine!" Rabbit remarked later when she and Sylvia told him of Abercrombie's suggestion. "Why this calls for champagne and, lo, I just happen to have some!"

Rabbit presented a bottle as Sylvia gathered tea cups. "Darling, this is positively enchanting." His eyebrows rose in delight.

Byron shook her head. "I don't know. I mean, won't I feel a bit foolish?"

"What's foolish in Paris?" Sylvia asked.

"What if news gets back to the States that I *am* a woman?"

"Darling, don't tell me for a moment you don't know that's exactly what the publishers are hoping for."

Byron's confusion was evident in her expression while Rabbit's brows raised in mock consternation. "It is precisely what *Monsieur* Abercrombie expects to happen. A bit of press here and a rumor there. Ohhh, yes, how very intriguing." He lowered his voice to a hushed whisper. "Why, the porter at the hotel swears the writer of those detective novels is a —"

"—No. You don't say!" Sylvia feigned shock.

"But a woman could never write that kind of"—Rabbit slapped the back of his hand to his forehead—"torrid material. No I simply don't believe it. Well I'll just rush right out and buy it and decide for myself." Rabbit began to pour champagne. "Ahhh, it's the kind of publicity money can't buy."

Byron turned to Sylvia. "Is that true?"

"I'm afraid to say it is."

"Oh Lord."

"Come on, one and all. It's time to make merry and wreak havoc." Rabbit raised his glass and cajoled Byron to do the same. As the three of them stood to toast, they were all aware they were experiencing a moment of reckoning. Rabbit winked at Byron.

"To Nate Venable. May he live on in infamy!"

Journal: May 1927

We all sojourned to the Lilas for a hearty celebration. Byron's latest Venable novel is out. It's her best one yet. America's gone mad for that damn detective!

* * *

Shakespeare & Company was so packed with patrons they were drinking champagne in the streets around a placard which pronounced "Celebrated Novelist, Byron Harrington, In Person with the latest Venable Mystery, *To Heir Is Divine*." Besides the cultural elite, the shop and streets were overflowing with curious fans, for it had become something of a sport, amongst the

American tourists, to spot the real B. Harrington. A week didn't pass that there wasn't some mention of just such a sighting in the French and American papers.

Sylvia had invited her entire library clientele for the occasion. Hemingway leaned against a bookshelf as he argued with Gertrude. Natalie and her crowd flitted amongst the patrons, Genet was there covering the event for *The New Yorker*. Even Scott and Zelda showed up.

Stacks of the fifth and latest Venable mystery were displayed in stylish covers in the window. One copy was propped open to the cover page with Byron Harrington's elegant autograph, dated July 1928, gracing the page.

Rabbit watched as Byron finished signing books. As he smoked his cigarette, it struck him suddenly how few traces of Lilian remained in the elegantly sophisticated author as she stood to accept an accolade paid to her by Ezra Pound. Her tailored trousers and tweed jacket struck a perfect balance for her androgynous, but graceful carriage. Her long and luxurious hair had long since been replaced with a chic bob. Her eyes, at once aloof and unfriendly, in the next instant sparkled with amused assurance as she sipped a glass of champagne.

As he wandered through the crowd, he heard snatches of conversation filter from the ambient hum in the cramped, smoke-filled book store. *"Nate Venable is delicious…He just gets better and better…darling do you really think so…no, I'm certain this is her fifth novel…I hear she's staying with Genet and Solita in the country…"*

Rabbit made his way to Byron. "You wouldn't believe all the many different places you lived, and how many lovers you enjoy."

Byron rolled her eyes.

"There are so many stories floating 'round you'd have to be three people to make even a fraction of them true."

Byron grinned sardonically as a young woman approached them, nervous and trembling. She thrust a book at Byron. "Mrs.—I mean, Miss Harrington, I know you've finished signing, but would you mind awfully? I ran all the way from Church to get here on time."

Byron smiled and graciously signed the girl's copy.

"Oh, thank you! Thank you so very much." The girl was so flustered that Rabbit gallantly steered her toward the refreshments.

"Such adulation," he remarked to Byron when he returned. "I'm sure it is far more rewarding than hearing from God!"

Byron was intent on a conversation taking place behind her and held up a finger. A wealthy Parisian, who stood holding her book, was shaking her head. "Well really, what do you expect from an American? They have no talent, except to make money."

"And they do it in such a singular fashion," her male companion responded as he held Byron's book before him. "Fun, but utterly forgettable."

As the pair cackled, Byron retrieved her cigarette case with utter cool, although Rabbit could see a tremor at her jaw. Hemingway and Gertrude's voices rose above the din and saved the moment.

"Darling, Hem and Gerty are becoming quite tedious in their never-ending debate over all this integrity rubbish. One person's artistic standard is another's flaw. It's all relative and I want you to recognize that. After all, I do believe more of the reading public would rather be entertained in high style than to be courted with philosophical ephemera." He paused to gulp champagne. "Really such a bore. Sweetie-heart, you are all the rage."

The woman behind them turned and appeared to recognize Byron, smiled condescendingly. Rabbit protectively steered Byron aside.

"Intellectuals are so dreadfully incompetent when it comes to jealousy."

Byron smiled weakly.

"Darling, please wipe that cocker spaniel expression off your face. Any fool knows that success breeds contempt."

"Oh, Lord." Byron finished the last of her drink. "If you're going to be philosophical, I need more than champagne." She linked her arm in his. "Come. To the Dingo we shall go."

* * *

As they entered the drinkery the melancholy tones of classical piano set an incongruous tenor to the scene of the packed, rowdy crowd; patrons celebrating with abandon, all fighting for their voices to be heard in the smoke-filled bar.

Rabbit squeezed through the crowd to the pianist, Jake Wilmarth, one of the newest American imports. Rabbit leaned to the scrappy-looking fellow with a tangle of sandy hair, and whispered in his ear. "Might we have something just a wee bit more tormented?"

Without blinking an eye Jake jumped into frenetic ragtime.

"Much better."

Edging her way between two artists drawing sketches of one another, Byron nabbed a couple of chairs, one of which yawed to the left from a broken leg. No sooner had they sat when Pierre appeared behind Byron's shoulder and shouted over the din that he was going to get a drink.

"Dear Lord, what alleyway did he just creep out of?"

"Please, not tonight," Byron pleaded. "No quarrels please. Besides, I thought you were going to give Pierre a second chance."

"I might if he wasn't always draping himself over you like an unattended shawl."

Byron frowned. Is that how he saw Pierre? She supposed she didn't pay him a great deal of attention. He was extremely jealous of Rabbit. As for Rabbit, he treated Pierre with aloof disdain.

As the evening wore on, the smoke became heavier, the laughter more boisterous. Byron could barely hear herself think. Rabbit must have said something funny for everyone was laughing hysterically, comrades in arms, the entire bar a union of hilarity and pain.

Such revelry was an activity Byron had become more and more adept at over the last couple of years. She put a cigarette to her mouth and drew the smoke deep into her lungs, an act of utter sensuality, but as she caught her reflection in a cracked mirror on the wall, she started at her own air of haughty sophistication.

Who was this masked stranger?

She turned from her own curious gaze and lifted a bloody Claret to her mouth.

* * *

As the night progressed, Byron, Rabbit, Jake, and Pierre were joined by several others who debated and argued into the evening, their ever-proliferating group moving from café to bistro to restaurant, journeying toward a long slow inebriation. En masse they walked off a hearty dinner of marinated potatoes and sausages until they passed through "one of the more charming parts of

Paris," as Rabbit observed, and somehow found themselves at the entrance of the Hole in the Wall Bar.

Home to the miscast, the disenchanted, prostitutes and opium pushers, the cramped bar enjoyed a thriving business behind what was a barely noticeable red door in the narrow street of the rue des Italiens. Drinks flowed freely as a strange and motley crew of circus performers piled in and joined their group.

As Byron's eyes fell to half-mast, the room began to list and sway. She grasped the table, trying to make sense of the bizarre setting, feeling much like Alice at the Mad Hatter's tea party. The rambunctious band of performers cajoled and enticed as they led Byron's straggling group to another party. Singing terribly out of tune, they careened through so many narrow alleyways and winding blocks that Byron stopped trying to figure out where they had traveled.

They entered a low-ceilinged barracks packed to the brim with men and women dancing, some half-naked, some costumed in elaborate dress, from the mystical to the macabre. Masked phantoms, a Minotaur, a salacious Pan pawing a large-breasted Ophelia. A woman with hair down to the floor whisked past Rabbit and when she turned to smile she revealed a full beard.

"Well, I suppose, when in Rome—only Byron, do keep your wits about you."

"And those might be where?" Byron slurred, tipsily.

Rabbit turned to her in concern. "Truly, Byron, do take care. I've heard many a tale about circus people and they're not usually repeated in polite company."

"Well, don't stray too far."

But it was difficult to stick together in the mass of dancing people, undulating like a roiling snake, moving and slithering through the room. The noise was deafening, a disharmony of laughter, music and shouting, and as Byron fought her way through the rabble to rest against a wall, she realized Rabbit had disappeared. She disentangled herself from a drunken reveler and bumped her way through the crowd searching for him when she felt a hand on her sleeve.

She turned, relieved, thinking it was Rabbit but found herself staring straight into the dark mask of a stranger garbed in black tie and tuxedo, shadows thrown by the top hat concealing his features. He leaned to her and whispered in French, "Do not be afraid."

"Pardon?" Byron asked.

"I said there is no need to be afraid," he repeated in English with a heavy French accent, his voice soft and husky.

Byron peered at the face, but all she could see were enchanting hazel eyes with curiously long lashes. As the stranger leaned into her she could smell a delicate cologne mixed with scented cigarettes, heady and compelling.

"I'm not afraid. I'm simply trying to find my friend."

"The man you came in with, yes?"

Byron hesitated. Something about the darkly clad figure commanded attention.

"Please, permit me to correct my faux paus," came a silky whisper. "Come with me."

"Where?"

"Not far. Just down the hall."

"Oh, dear Lord." Byron began to laugh. "Are you—? Well, I'm not interested. I'm not here for business."

"This is all pleasure, I assure you."

"No, you don't seem to understand, I'm just here—"

But the stranger pressed Byron's fingers and again she was filled with the exotic scent that radiated from his skin. "Come."

Byron was unaccountably intrigued. Perhaps she could chalk it up to Venable research. She shrugged and allowed herself to be led through the thick press of bodies to a darkened hallway where she could hear noises from behind closed doors, echoes of pleasure, release and remorse.

The gentleman pulled her out the back door down a very narrow alley through a darkened cove. For a moment the hair on Byron's neck prickled and she wondered if she had made a grave mistake.

"Very dark, be careful," the gentleman offered, then suddenly a door opened, and they were in another building with smoky halls. A tart smell assailed Byron's senses as she stared at the velvet contours of furniture, the lewd paintings on the walls—tassels and fringe heavily laden with eau de forbidden. The gentleman extracted several bills, folded them, and pressed them into the palm of a shrunken, toothless Chinese woman. He ushered Byron up a stairwell to a room that was dimly lit by a Tiffany shrunken lamp, casting the room in rose-colored pink.

Byron knew she was quite drunk, which perhaps was the reason for her calmness. She expected to be scared, yet found herself increasingly intrigued by her situation and the person who had led her here. Pulling Byron close, his mask intact, the stranger murmured something she did not understand.

He led her to a battered sofa and pulled up a chair. "Oh, how I have waited."

Byron frowned, yet more confused as he struck a match against the wall and placed it at the end of a long coil, one amongst several other coiled tubes that swirled from the base of a contraption in the shape of an oval vase. He brought the end of the snakelike tubing to his mouth and inhaled, briefly, as if starting a pipe then offered it to Byron.

"What is it?"

"Better than brandy."

"But—"

"No talking." The gentleman's voice was softly entreating as he placed the pipe to Byron's lips, and when she peered beyond his mask she saw gentle encouragement in his eyes.

A sweet burning rasped along her throat and as she drew the rich intoxicant into her lungs, a fierce terror suddenly overtook her. But before she could wonder what she was doing her arms turned to liquid, the tension in her jaw melted, her entire body eased into a state of utter and weightless grace.

The dark figure took an extended inhalation and as he swallowed the smoke, Byron took notice of his slender physique, how the black trousers and tails framed the lines of his body. She found herself strangely aroused. A primal attraction. For some reason the idea made her giggle.

He turned at her laughter. "Why do you laugh?"

"You. Me. Whatever are we doing here?"

"We taste the best of life."

Byron floated in a fairyland, and when the stranger sat close beside her, she did not object. When his warm hand stroked her neck she did not resist, for his fingers felt as soft as satin; so curiously soft were his hands as they wound their way to her hair, then slowly traced the arch of her brow, sending a shiver that felt like a long uncoiling snake through her outstretched torso. Byron closed her eyes, overwhelmingly sleepy, and yet electric within her body at the same time. The stranger leaned Byron back until she lay fully upon the bed, then stretched beside her, his hand carefully loosening her tie, unbuttoning her shirt. She shook her head, knowing she should stop this… stop it now, but her seducer lifted Byron's hand and slowly kissed every part of it. With each contact of his lips against the tips of her fingers she felt a tight ache in her stomach that traveled down her groin. As he placed her middle finger in his mouth and he delicately licked it, his teeth grazing the edges of her palm, she shuddered helplessly—a puppet, utterly at the whim of her master.

As Byron felt the edges of reality fade in and out she had only one thought. She must feel the hands again. She entwined her fingers in his, exploring the mysteries of his palm, seemingly forever, then boldly slipped his hand just beneath her shirt and gasped as those soft slender fingers stroked her stomach, followed by the heat of the stranger's mouth caressing her neck, her nipples growing erect so suddenly it hurt. With an urgency she had never felt before she wanted that mouth to play upon her, upon every part of her, ached to have the warm liquid of his tongue against her breasts, and as he sucked upon her nipples, her desire rose, so that she wrapped herself in the stranger's arms, now eager to feel his skin.

But somehow he kept himself at bay, his mouth moving slowly over her stomach as his fingers continued to stroke her nipples, so tightened that she knew she would break apart if he were to stop, his mouth edging toward her waist, nibbling at the top of her trousers, teasing her as he nudged the material aside, but still did not move to unfasten her pants until Byron could stand it no longer and whispered her need.

"It would be my greatest pleasure," the stranger murmured, his hand rapidly unbuckling the belt, unbuttoning her pants and then his head moved to her arching pelvis, his sweet breath hot against her soft hair. She could feel the wetness of her desire, as strange as the rest of this evening, for she had never been like this before— had never been this full, this thick with want. His lips gently massaged to the center of her, his tongue now flicking against that which she touched only when her body ached for release, that which until now had been an annoying hunger, but had become a fierce raging that begged to be answered, his tongue continuing to send quivering waves through her body until she finally felt him go inside her. But no…wait, it wasn't *him*, it was his fingers thrusting into her, filling her up, with two, then three fingers until she only felt the fullness rocking her against her own pent-up need. She began to keel under a long shattering release, gasping, shuddering as she peaked, then trembling until the waves finally abated and her body went slack, then still, and she knew she could not move. If her life depended on it she could not move.

Byron lay hazily spent as the stranger stood. He returned to the coil and sucked greedily from the pipe, then walked to a chair, his back to her. He removed his mask and tie, and freed himself from his coat, then let his shirt drop, revealing narrowed tapered shoulders. Byron's head momentarily swam in disorientation, for something was wrong. A terrible misunderstanding. She tried to form words, but none would pass her lips. And even though her Prince Charming of the underworld had blurred to a hazy shape, when he turned to Byron, she was very clear that what he exposed to her were the very full and beautiful breasts of a woman.

* * *

Her skin was warm, and Byron could see little beads of sweat lay between the woman's breasts with small, pink-flushed nipples that Byron bent to kiss. The taste of woman was so new, yet it was as if she was born to it. She wanted more. More of this woman's skin beneath her hands, her hands now slowly roaming about the slender physique with the arching ribcage, responding to her touch, an awakening cat, slithering to meet Byron.

In the dim light, she looked at the form beside her—a woman's body—no longer an inanimate object. This new image was flesh at its most highly combustible, the touch of a woman's skin bristling beneath her palms. And as the woman reached for Byron's face and brought Byron's lips to her own, she was quite suddenly suffused with the searing ache in her groin she had felt moments before… salt-kissed meshing of tongues, laced with the tart sting of the opium pipe…directing her to the sweet musk of her new desire… and it was called woman.

* * *

She came to in the stark light of the noonday sun, in a room littered with books and prints. It took her several seconds to recognize the small but fashionable flat as her own. Still fully clothed, she looked thankfully at her belongings. She was back in the safety of her own abode. But how had she gotten home?

Last night bore some explaining. She shook her head. Gently. So she had tasted the fruits of opium. When her legs were strong enough she got up carefully, walked out onto the balcony and tapped a cigarette on the ledge of the railing. The exquisite view of the city never failed to take her breath away, even in her current condition.

As she lit her cigarette she suddenly saw the Chinese opium pipe, felt a rush inside, a flush over her body. What had she done? The images were so vague she could very well have dreamed them.

"When in Rome," she murmured. She smoked her cigarette and closed her eyes, hoping the morning sun washing over her would cleanse her, return her to her former self. And then it struck her. The person she had been with, indeed had been so frankly intimate with, was not just a woman. The woman she had eagerly wrapped her legs around was the actress Marie Salavier.

As she tried to integrate the myriad elements and ramifications of the previous night, she heard footsteps galloping up her stairwell, followed by a pounding on the door. Before she could open it, Rabbit bolted through.

"My Lord, you don't know! I've looked everywhere." Rabbit's hair was uncharacteristically mussed, his clothes askew.

"Please…" Byron moaned, cradling her head.

"Byron." Rabbit walked directly to her, clutched her by her shoulders. "It's your father."

A spinning dizziness washed over her, and before she could sink to the floor, Rabbit held her upright, led her to the couch.

"Rabbit."

He grabbed her cigarette before it fell. "A telegram arrived at Sylvia's last night. He's ill. You must leave at once."

"I must pack—"

"Hurry, darling. I've booked us passage on the next steamer."

The magazine photo of Lena captured her arch strength, I thought, as I sat gazing at it for nearly an hour, sitting by the dying fire in the cottage. I had gone through a box of mail Marcus had forwarded me, catching up with bills, attending to correspondence in order to re-venture into the world at some point.

Adrenaline shot through the pit of my stomach when I first saw the photo—I was nonchalantly leafing through *The Advocate* before throwing it in the trash can. Lena was standing next to several politicos who were awarding her for tireless efforts on behalf of the *glorious cause*. When I came across the photo, I realized that in the time I had spent at the cottage I had begun to feel—if not better about myself—that there was a pinprick of light making itself seen through the tunnel.

Lena was not a good idea to muse over in the light of consciousness. I had tried to be a good soldier, never breaking my cardinal rule. No pining allowed. But now I was faced with Lena, and no matter how hard I might try, I could no longer shove her into the overladen sack of denial.

* * *

Lena invited Spencer to her house for dinner shortly after their first date. Spencer left work early, to whirl through the racks at Nordstrom's. She tried several different shirts and jackets. She wanted to look new for Lena. Handsome in a soft butch way. Wanted to impress her, seduce her. She was running late, but found just the perfect cerulean Faconnable shirt and a tailored black blazer to go with her black dress jeans.

From the moment she arrived at Lena's Mediterranean villa, her throat tightened in anticipation, her hands began to sweat and she knew she was poised for a panic attack. As she rang the doorbell, she struck a suave pose. The door opened.

"Hi. Are you Spinner?"

A silken blonde munchkin stood dwarfed by the large door. She wore miniature red sneakers, a bunched up pair of Osh Kosh overalls and T-shirt, clasping a gnarled Curious George in determined fingers. She had the largest, most expressive slate blue eyes Spencer had ever seen. A pug nose and a little mouth shaped like a heart. It was love at first sight.

"Yes. Yes I am."

"Mommy says come in and go to da kitchen." She waited at the door as Spencer entered.

Spencer leaned down to her. "And what's your name?"

"'Kenzie."

"Nice to meet you."

A spontaneous grin. A smile to bring world peace, little white teeth flashing. Years from now, she was going to knock them dead.

As MacKenzie led her to the kitchen Spencer noticed the nicely understated Tuscan décor, a warm ruggedness edged with elegant touches. Lena was wearing an apron, and as she straightened from the oven door, Spencer was struck by how hearth and home transformed her. Gone was the edgy handsomeness of the power player. In its place was a soft-edged warmth, a quiet beauty that was maternal and wholesome.

"Hey, I'm sorry, I've been running a little late." She walked to Spencer and gave her a friendly embrace.

"No problem." Spencer nonchalantly presented a Merlot.

"Thanks. You mind watching MacKenzie while I finish up?"

MacKenzie led Spencer into the living room, shuffled herself upon the couch and turned expectantly. "Mommy says you make movies."

"Well, actually I work in TV."

"Oh, like *Sesame Street*?"

"Sort of. I write for TV shows that are on at night."

Mackenzie rubbed her nose. "The bad ones Mommy won't let me watch?"

"Uhm, probably."

"If they're bad why do you do that?"

"Well, we try to make them good…it's just that—" Like Spencer was going to explain to a four-year-old child the vast mysteries of the Hollywood machine?

"I gotta friend, Emily, and her mommy is a paducer on TV. What do paducers do?" MacKenzie wiggled her tiny red sneakers.

"That's a very good question, MacKenzie."

Lena walked in. Having discarded her apron, she stood in black slacks and a white silk tank. Spencer felt beguiled by daughter and mother.

"I think your daughter's got a career in the making."

"MacKenzie is one curious little camper, aren't you sweetie?" Lena bent to her and ruffled her hair. "You better go get your bag, sweetie. Uncle Bobo is going to be here any minute."

"Okay." MacKenzie dashed from the room.

"We'll be alone tonight." Lena leaned her head to one side, appraising Spencer.

"Sure we don't need a chaperone?"

* * *

After Lena's friend picked up MacKenzie, Lena brought wine and two glasses along as they moved out onto the deck that overlooked green hills dotted with Spanish architecture. The sun was just beginning to fall when Spencer turned to Lena, as she leaned against the railing, her dark hair shining in the gilded light.

Spencer was enchanted. She couldn't keep her eyes off Lena as she pointed out landmarks and talked about the area she had lived in for ten years. She had spent the past decade doing political work, but now that she had MacKenzie she wanted to raise her in a better environment and was planning to move back to Northern California where her family lived.

"Where's her father?" Spencer asked.

"Somewhere in deep tundra. She came from a sperm bank."

"You just decided to have a kid?"

"No. I've always wanted children. A family. While I was pregnant with MacKenzie my lover cheated on me. I've been single ever since."

"That's hard to believe."

"Not celibate," she grinned. "Single."

Spencer cleared her throat.

"You're not very comfortable with me are you?"

"Of course I am," Spencer stated too loudly.

"Are you?"

"I'm just…well, I'm not usually…I guess I feel a little shy."

"That's sweet."

"Is it? I think it's pretty damn humiliating."

Lena grinned. Charmingly. Then moved a step closer to Spencer. "A lot of the old stars lived in these hills when Silverlake and Los Feliz housed the whole industry." She looked out at the view and without skipping a beat added, "I'm trying like hell not to fall in love with you."

Spencer wasn't sure she had heard her correctly.

Lena turned to her. "I'm planning on moving in the next year or so. You sound deeply entrenched in your career here. But I find myself thinking about you…" Her eyes were clear and bright.

"I…I'm…Lena…"

Lena set her glass aside, moved within Spencer's arms and slid her hands up to Spencer's neck.

Lips on lips for the first time can be awkward, clumsy, foreign, but with Lena, Spencer felt as if they had been kissing for years, were meant to kiss one another, were a perfect fit, and as their lips engaged in exquisite foreplay Spencer finally understood how kissing could be its own end. Enrapturing. Spencer had never been enraptured before and she found herself wanting this woman in a way she had never wanted until now. It was more than sexual desire, it was a need from deep inside, a need to be met, to be answered, and in a single kiss Spencer knew Lena might well become the love of her life.

* * *

Lena took Spencer's hand and quietly walked her to the large master bedroom. The moment they moved inside the room, they turned to reclaim each other. It only took a second to reconnect, gentle nibbles that led to an eager exploration, tasting the pleasure of each other, melding into that perfect fit, an intensity growing to the kisses that led to ragged breathing, measured sighing. Lena walked them backwards in their embrace to the bed where they continued kissing, completely engaged in that simple activity, both standing until they could no longer, tumbling onto the bed, fully clothed, unwilling to part company until Lena finally pushed herself away.

"I've got to stop…a second." She flopped back against the bed. "I've got to catch my breath."

Spencer's eyes roamed Lena's lanky body, the silk blouse fluttering above her breasts from her rapid pulse. Spencer leaned to kiss the edge of the blouse, nuzzling between Lena's breasts, tenderly grazing the soft part of her skin, then moving to Lena's stomach, slipping a hand to the waistband of her pants. Lena's hands rushed to Spencer's head, luxuriating in her hair, then pulling her up to her mouth so they might find each other again.

Spencer's hand moved beneath the shirt, to caress Lena's waist, kneading the skin, teasing the edge of her pants, and slowly, very slowly, slipping fingers beneath the cotton of Lena's slacks, gently ruffling the hem of satin underwear, tracing a finger along her inner thigh, Lena's body arching to Spencer's hand, giving her permission to explore further, Spencer's fingers gently massaging the satin…closer…closer—

"Touch me," Lena gasped. "Oh God, go inside me."

Spencer moaned as she felt the pearly wetness, pulsing her fingers between swollen folds and then teasing once again, until Lena groaned and Spencer's fingers thrust deeply inside of her, again and again, defining a rhythm of pleasure given and pleasure received.

"I want to…" Spencer's hot breath tickled her ear, "I need to taste you."

"Oh, please," Lena choked.

She deftly slipped Spencer's blazer from her shoulders, kissing her neck as her hands skimmed beneath the folds of her shirt.

Spencer raised the silk blouse over Lena's head, burrowing her face into her deliciously dark skin, her hands roaming up her back, over her ribcage to the tender swell of breasts, her tongue tasting the salt-sweet of her skin. As they toppled to the bed, they both worked quickly to remove Lena's pants, and tossing them aside, Spencer moved between Lena's legs, an inch away, teasing her with hot breath against Lena's underwear, feeling Lena's ardent desire; then pulling her panties aside, she greedily put her mouth to Lena, loving the taste of her, luxuriating in the wet of her.

Lena's pelvis moved in rhythm with Spencer, her breathing quickening until she gently pushed her aside and pulled Spencer up to her. Her eyes pierced Spencer's as she began to undress her, but as she tried to remove her chemise Spencer stopped her.

"Are you okay?" Lena asked softly.

Spencer grasped Lena's wrists in reply, pulling them over her head as she straddled her body. Spencer slowly lowered her body until it was a whisper away from Lena's own, waiting for Lena to slide up to her until the heat of their bodies met.

She kissed Lena's eyes, her cheeks, lips, chin, leaving small brands upon her neck as she devoured every inch of her body. Her mouth traveled down beautifully sculpted arms, sucking at the tender inside of Lena's elbow, the curve of her hip, the arch of her pelvis, and finally...finally returning to the inside of her thighs, her tongue trailing ever closer at the tender inner skin. A tingling agony of wait as Spencer traveled the contours of Lena's soft and silky matted hair, gently thrusting her tongue into her vagina, pulsing and swollen now as Spencer answered her need, her suckling and torturing tongue melting into her, fingers easing deep inside her at the moment that Lena came, screaming her new lover's name, Spencer a heartbeat away with her own cries of release.

* * *

Unlike most encounters, where Spencer rushed to the climactic moment, she wanted to absorb and enjoy every moment with Lena.

And Lena let her roam her skin freely, languid under her touch, as Spencer's desire reawakened.

Lena bent to remove Spencer's chemise.

"I'm...I just want to keep it on."

"Whatever you want. Are we going too fast?"

"No...not at all." Spencer bit her lower lip, self-conscious.

Lena smiled as she massaged the cotton material. "I thought you were a butch."

"I am." Spencer could barely breathe, she was so aroused.

"But we both know who's in control here, right?" Lena teased, and swept the chemise from Spencer to reveal full breasts, gently cupping them in her hands, then flicking a tongue at tender nipples.

"I'm still the top—"

But the rest of her words were swallowed up in a kiss and then she fell victim to Lena's powers of persuasion.

* * *

They made love for two weeks straight Spencer called in sick for days on end while Lena canceled appointments right and left. Bob took MacKenzie for a long weekend. They lived between Lena's bedroom and her kitchen. Standing in the kitchen, tugging the skimpy robe from Lena's body bending her over the counter, Spencer taking her from behind. Midway back to the bedroom, tipping her onto the couch, opening her legs, partaking of her hunger, Lena's power. All day long, into the night, into the wake of dawn until Spencer wondered if they were sick. "I mean, I know a lot of lesbians who really pour it on the first few weeks, but Len... I think we're one for the medical books. I'm not sure this is even possible."

"Let me show you how possible it is," Lena purred and mounted her body over Spencer's, aggressive and sure of herself, needful and mindful of Spencer's insecurities, almost as if she knew her before Spencer ever had the opportunity to reveal all the dents, her many vulnerabilities. She honored Spencer's body, about which Spencer was painfully shy, with a desire that matched her own.

Through it all there was only one sign of desperation from Lena but it was the one that counted. She wanted Spencer. Desired her. Needed her. It felt wonderful to be a part of something. As Spencer walked in with coffee, enveloped in a huge flannel robe, that was soft from years of wear, smelling indelibly of Lena, she would move to her, and slide her arms around Lena from behind, as easily and naturally as if they had been married for years. When Lena turned and smiled, the goodness in her eyes sent Spencer reeling. So this is what it *could* be like. It didn't have to be about playing games, and torture and endless deprivation. It didn't have to be, as it had been with Adrienne, about punishment, or self-loathing, or erosion.

* * *

A searing pain cuts into my center. I touch my skin. Numb. But I taste the tears streaming down my face. If there are regrets, and I have plenty, the worst is that I will never again see my family...never again touch Lena or hold MacKenzie. Kenzie-Bug. That's what I called her because she was so small, so delicate.

How could I know she would be the moon, the stars and all the revolving planets in my universe? She became the daughter I never had, and as I one day accepted, never would have. She taught me about primal love; instinctual, soulful, pure and magical.

I picture her round face and upturned nose, the huskiness of her child voice, the pudgy fingers that produced tears in me every time they sought mine unsolicited. Her fierce jaw and too small chin. Her translucent blue-gray eyes, and sharp pumpkin angled eyebrows, thick and beautiful.

I feel the wealth of memories, MacKenzie moments, lying over me like a cuddly-worn blanket...

* * *

One night Lena worked late and called to ask if Spencer could pick up MacKenzie from day care.

"You sure you trust me? I've never really been much of a babysitter."

"I have faith in your skills," Lena said. "Besides, 'Kenzie adores you. In fact, it's kind of giving me a complex."

"I'd love to pick her up. We'll go catch a bite. Girls' night out."

Lena laughed. "I'll bet. Maybe we can have girls' night in when I get home."

"You're on."

The day care was a zoo. Kids were everywhere, weaving in and out of Spencer's ankles with mustard and Kool-Aid stains from head to toe. The day-care gal informed her that MacKenzie hadn't yet awakened from her nap. Spencer was exhausted. She had spent the entire afternoon arguing with producers over two lines of dialogue. When they finally came to an agreement, the actress decided she didn't like them after all. Traffic had been a bitch and here she was knee-deep in toddlers and MacKenzie wasn't even awake.

"I'll just go get her," Spencer offered, and tiptoed into the back room. MacKenzie was curled on a mat on the floor. Her cheeks were bright pink from the heat of slumber, and sweat married the fine strands of hair at her cheek. Spencer lay down beside her, her nose inches from MacKenzie's and watched her shell of an eyelid open lazily, close again, and then open…and with a small smile in them she whispered *Aunnie Spinner, it's you*, and then leaned to kiss the vicinity of her mouth. Innocent and real and completely without reservation. Spencer's heart began to crack into a million pieces from the force of loving this precious human thing almost beyond the capacity to endure.

After she woke sufficiently to understand Spencer was going to take her to dinner, Spencer offered a visit to the Disney store beforehand for a gift.

MacKenzie chose a clever little marketing gimmick of *101 Dalmatians* that had a stuffed puppy packaged with the book and tape, and when Spencer loosened it from its shrink-wrapped bondage, she asked, "Aunnie Spinner, would you please zip up Lucky?" She had worn her favorite sweater for the outing, a stylish German affair Jill and Heather had picked out for her during their last visit.

And there MacKenzie sat throughout dinner at Hamburger Hamlet, with Lucky zipped inside the sweater, propped beneath her chin. Spencer cringed every time she picked up her gigantic hamburger, certain it was going to splatter from hell to breakfast, but each time MacKenzie carefully maneuvered her napkin so that it covered them both.

They took a short stroll to get ice cream for dessert, Lucky still popping out from beneath MacKenzie's sweater, her vanilla cone gripped with determination in her little velvet fingers. She perched on a stool twice her size, and as she devoured the cone with utter focus, a fine blue vein stood out on her cheek near her temple. Spencer's throat tightened as she realized how precious and fragile she was, with the inner strength of innocence. She was in that instance, quite simply purity of life. The essence of appreciation.

Spencer surreptitiously wiped a tear, then turned to MacKenzie with a bright smile. "So 'Kenzie-Bug, are you more into movies with cartoons or ones with real people in them?"

"Quite actually, Aunnie Spinner, I like cartoon movies for things like *Beauty and the Beast* and, oh yeah, *The Little Mermaid*." She stopped for a moment to consider and then dove into the cone and got some on her nose. They both laughed. "But for things like *Free Willy* I like real people."

"You know your Aunnie Spinner was a co-producer on a movie."

"Yeah, Mommy told me."

"You can see it when you're a little older."

"Okay." She was noncommittal.

"I mean, I really want you to see it." Spencer found herself oddly desperate for MacKenzie's approval.

"Okay." She was intent on lapping up the dribbles. "But it's not like you made *Jurassic Park*."

Spencer sat stunned. Where had she come up with that? How could she discern gradients of fame and success at such an early age? Spencer didn't know whether to laugh or cry. "Yeah. I'd need a lot more money for that."

"Yeah and own a really rich house." She licked her fingers. "I told in show and tell that my auntie makes really good TV shows." Spencer heard the pride in her voice and she was instantly overwhelmed by the new standard she had to live up to.

MacKenzie had two bites left. She looked at Spencer with a twinkle in her eye. "Here Aunnie Spinner. You can finish." Spencer made a show of gobbling it up. Then MacKenzie leaned forward. She had a wise grin on her face as she whispered in Spencer's ear, sweet child's breath, soft as baby powder, "I love you Aunnie Spinner." She wrenched Spencer's neck in a hug and then as quickly jumped off her stool, ready to go. They'd just had a Hallmark Moment and she was done with it. It would stay in Spencer's heart forever.

* * *

In those days Spencer came to believe it was her love for MacKenzie that fueled the passion to continue pulling together *May You*. Her love for Lena that gave her hope for a future.

Even though life settled down and Spencer returned to her workaholic regime, Lena would often have a bed-picnic waiting at two, even three in the morning, offering hand-fed Greek delicacies. Pouring her a hot tub, rubbing her shoulders, kissing the bruises of her psyche at another disappointment, Lena loved her well into the early morning hours. Spencer had never felt so alive, so fresh, so utterly cherished. She couldn't get enough of Lena's skin, Lena's soft lips on hers, of staring into those soulful brown eyes, listening to her resonant voice, the way Lena rubbed her feet after hours of lovemaking, Spencer giddy with deliciousness. Lena was a drug and addiction soon followed. One afternoon, stuck in traffic, trying to get to her, she found herself screaming at every driver, every moment she had to wait. She stopped and puzzled over herself in the rearview mirror.

"What is going on with you?" she asked, and then saw the smile that started in her eyes and soon spread to her mouth. "You're in love, you fool."

Later that night as Lena lay on top of her, her artful hands cupping Spencer's cheeks, eyes narrowed and serious, Lena moaned as she came, "I'm so in love with you Spencer."

Spencer grasped her in her arms, holding tightly, as she felt Lena's spirit wrap up into her own and she knew that this woman owned her heart—her soul. She heard herself say the words, but never had she meant them as she did now. "I love you, Lena. God, how I love you."

I miss her. Ache for her. For them. I could tell you hours and hours of theory, but the plain and simple truth was I wasn't ready.

How could I have foreseen that the take-no-prisoners battle I was fighting on the outside would quickly break the borders of our moated island of love—begin to leave the ruin and wreckage of a fundamental truth I had not yet faced? I could no more allow the calm and consistent love of a good woman than I could give up my dreams. Did they have to be mutually exclusive? In hindsight, I'm sure there was a way to have worked it out. It wasn't Lena. It wasn't her impatience. It was my inability to choose.

It doesn't take long for life to unravel when you're not paying attention to it, and the unspooling quickens when you give it a nudge. Until I arrived at the cottage I had faithfully followed the pact I made with myself. Thoughts of Lena and MacKenzie were off limits. No sweet indulgence of memories. It was only as my mind began to clear as I worked on the path that I became strong enough to relive it. And here I relive it, because it may well be the last time. Every touch, every whisper, every night we spent talking until the light blue sky filtered in and we enveloped our bodies together and finally fell asleep, rushes back to me. Perhaps that is the way to end it. Fall asleep thinking of Lena. The sweetest dream imaginable.

* * *

Would Lena have saved me, I wondered as I continued to work on the trail. It had taken the entire summer, but the path was almost finished, even if it was still a bit rough and difficult to tread down. I decided to border the sides in ocean stone, so I hauled huge boulders from the wash-up below, lugging them all the way up the steep incline like a tight wire act. I had even planted ground cover on some of the less seemly areas and had begun to cultivate a little garden on the last level section that held a scenic view. I planned to buy a swinging wood bench. I would hire some locals to have it lifted down and installed.

Sometimes, after I had made decent headway, I would give myself a reward, sit on a step, smoke a cigarette and gaze at my ocean, memories of Lena and MacKenzie breaking more and more into my thoughts.

And then Sarah called one night. Toward the end of a two-hour catch up she mentioned she had run into Lena at a Melissa Etheridge concert.

At first I didn't know what to say.

"Did you hear me? I ran into Lena," Sarah repeated.

"Yes. Yes, I heard you."

"Well aren't you the least interested in what she had to say?"

"Was she with anyone?" I asked instead.

"Yeah, some guy. I think his name was Rob. No, Bob." Uncle Bobo. Well that was safe.

"You know what I mean. Was she with anyone else?"

"Well, there were like four or five in their group."

"Great," I hissed under my breath.

"What?"

"Nothing. How did she seem?"

"Great. Very tan. She had just gotten back from Hawaii."

Sarah must have read my thoughts because she sneered, "Now Spence, you don't know that she was there with anyone. In fact, she said it was something to do with the Hawaiian marriage stuff."

"Yes, but you also don't know that she wasn't with someone."

"No. I didn't give her the third degree if that's what you mean."

"Shit. I'm sorry." I took a deep breath. "So, whatever…how was the concert?"

"Spencer, I know you're being all nonchalant and everything but Lena did ask how you were. You know…what was going on with you."

"Please tell me you didn't tell her." But I knew in my heart, Lena was already aware that I had fallen from grace.

"Oh yes, I said my good friend has gone down the proverbial tubes and is having a nervous breakdown—give me a break! I told her you were working on a project, isolating yourself up north to attend to your writing."

"Thank you. At least part of that's true." I told Sarah that I actually *had* begun writing.

"God, Spence, that's so great. It's what you need to do. Just write. Forget about all this shit for now. It'll all be waiting for you when you return."

"Thoughts that warm my heart."

"Seriously, shugie." Sarah's warm and supportive voice was what I loved so much about her. "I'm so happy you're back to work."

The next morning I returned to my path, sitting with a mug of coffee on the level view spot, wondering how best to place the swing. There was very little space in front of a sheer ledge that dropped to the rocky wash-up thirty feet below.

"Heard ya plan to put in a swing thar."

Darrell's voice startled me out of my thoughts. "Yeah, I'm not sure it's going to work though."

"Yep, kinda got a problem," Darrell commiserated, gazing out at the ocean, several steps above me.

"Any suggestions?"

"Could try to move the rock to Mohammed, or go another way."

Was Darrell trying to get philosophical on me? "What do you mean?"

"Jes' mean, if you cut the path up round this stump the grade's a lot easier to walk down. Then you get more room for yer swing. 'Course ya gotta restructure a few feet, chop down this tree."

"Thanks." I was elated even though I realized it would take a good deal more work.

I considered Darrell. He seemed like the most contented man on the earth.

"You git that cleaned off, an' get your bench delivered and I'll set a spell with ya when you're of a mind."

"What? You're not going to help me chop down the brush?"

"I learnt somethin' a long time ago. Fool's paradise is the easy way and you're lookin' at a helluva fool!" He winked at me, cackled a bit, and trundled back up the path.

The Easy Way.

Had approaching things the easy way ever entered my mind?

When I returned to the cottage, an incredible sadness enveloped me, as if the melancholy had been swept in by the rolling fog creeping over the horizon. Darrell's words echoed through me. The easy way. Perhaps I had believed the only path available to me was to struggle, push, and torment my way to success. The easy way was certainly the last avenue I had considered.

A rattletrap brougham wound its way through the gray bleakness. Sodden piney landscape passed on one side, the ferocious and rugged Northwest coastline on the other. Through a parting of branches here and there Byron could see a span of ocean to her right. The sea air, the dense fog up in the hills, the dank sand—all familiar smells and sights to Byron as she drank in the scenery. It wasn't long before they passed the weather-beaten, carved wooden sign, *Bay Cliff*, shrouded in mist.

The truck came to a stop and a portly farmer turned around to her. "Aint no problem takin' ya on up to the house ma'am."

"The fresh air will do me good."

"Alrighty, I'll come up along with your trunk when it gets into the station."

Byron wound down a narrow trail that led to the beach, retracing the path she had taken when she had left. She clutched her bag tightly as she walked steadily along the dampened sand. She breathed in the rich sea air. So long. Almost twelve years since she had been back here. How would it be changed?

She pondered the ragged cliff-line. That would not change in her lifetime and gave her a certain measure of security. From where she stood her view encompassed the majestic volatility of the Oregon coastline to Bay Cliff, the towering Victorian with the Harrington family crest just visible above the main entrance.

As she made her way to her childhood home, she thought better of entering the front and slipped in unnoticed, up the back stairwell that ended on the second floor. She tiptoed silently to her father's room, entered slowly and walked to the bed.

Her throat tightened. She could not remember the last time she had cried, but tears threatened when she saw Francis Albert Harrington's gaunt frame, the lines of chronic suffering etched into his gently handsome features. As she bent to touch his once strong hands, she could see they had withered. Gripped inside his fingers was a smoothly worn piece of wood, carved in the shape of a heart, which he now caressed as his eyes began to flutter open.

"Cecelia!" Francis gasped.

"Father?" Byron momentarily wondered if her father's mind had been affected by his illness.

"Cecil—" he stammered and then recovered. "Good God in heaven, I thought I'd dropped dead during my nap. You do so favor your mother."

She rushed into her father's arms. He held her tight, embracing her fully, as she smelled his pipe tobacco, traces of his cologne, but something else as well—sickness, decay.

He held her at arm's length and they studied each other. He shook his head, as if he still couldn't believe she sat before him.

"My how you resemble your mother." He grinned appreciatively. "Like a mirage, you standing there quite suddenly in my room."

She saw his eyes were still bright and she smiled.

He pressed her hand. "Especially when you smile."

"No mirage, Father," she responded. "Flesh and blood, and perhaps a bit too much gin."

"You look wonderful," Francis said. "A little weary maybe. When did you get in? Did Charles meet you at the station?"

Byron's shoulders edged up. "No...I didn't want to bother anyone. I hitched a ride. Then came up the back way. Straight to your room, like a covert spy."

"Right out of one of your books, eh?" He studied her carefully, as if he were afraid she would disappear. "Lilian. I am so pleased that you came."

"Father." Byron's voice turned serious. "Father, how are you?"

"Like an old man in his bed."

"I want to know how—what we're facing here. And I want no more talk like that. We'll get you out of here in no time."

He pulled at the full white beard that matched his beautiful silver hair. "I'm afraid not, my dear."

"Nonsense."

"Stubborn as ever."

Francis began coughing and when it appeared he could not stop, Byron became alarmed, but just as she was about to call for help, he recovered. After wiping his eyes, he appraised her wistfully. "Stubborn *and* beautiful. Yes, your mother's daughter. I only wish she had lived to see you grow into such a fine young lady. So smart and clever with your stories—and how well your name is received in Paris."

Uncomfortable with such praise, Byron moved from the bed to the window, pulling the drapes further apart to allow more light.

"I'm aware you've built a new life for yourself, Lilian, but I have often wondered—especially after my visit—why you haven't come to see me. Just once even."

A silence hung between them for a moment.

"I've been busy, Father. Really, I don't know how to find time these days, what with deadlines—"

"It's quite all right, Lilian. I'm aware Bay Cliff is not your cup of tea, but it is, after all, your birthright."

"Yes, and, well, here I am."

"And that's all that matters."

"Lilian!"

Even though she hadn't heard that voice in over a decade, the moment it reached her ears she went back to that night, could feel the hot breath upon her, the grunting aggression. Her jaws clamped tightly as she turned to him. His powerful frame filled the doorway. He was a large man now, tall and thick, his once handsome features yielding to the battle of excess. His eyes caught hers and she held their challenge until he drew his own away, made a slight bow of deference. He entered the room, his finely-trimmed mustache curling in a charming smile directed at his sister.

"My, my, what a surprise! It is Lilian, returned from her travels." As he moved to embrace her, she turned abruptly. Without missing a beat, Charles sidestepped to their father. "Oh, how foolish of me. It's Byron, isn't it?"

"And quite a name your sister's made for herself," Francis exclaimed.

"Well I'm not surprised. Byron's always had a talent for make believe."

Byron maintained an even gaze at him, but a slight twitch at her cheek belied her confidence.

"It's been far too long." Charles briefly touched his mustache. "You shouldn't have been such a stranger all these many years."

"Yes, well I should hardly call this a social visit, Charles."

A tense silence ensued until Charles laughed and returned to the door. "Nonetheless, I shall have Mavis set an extra plate for supper."

"I will take my dinner here. With Father."

"There will be plenty of time to visit. Father needs his rest." Charles stood at the door waiting for Byron to join him.

"Father is very capable of chewing and conversing at the same time, Charles," Francis remarked. "Lilian's company would be a tonic."

"Very well." Charles smiled obsequiously. "I want you to feel welcome here, Lilian. This is, after all, your home."

He bent to take her bag. "I'll show you to your room."

Byron walked to him and removed her bag from his hand. "I remember the room, Charles."

* * *

Byron lightly traced her bed frame with her fingertips, stopped, then clutched the wrought-iron rail until her knuckles turned white. She momentarily had a vision of another bed frame she had grasped in the strangely tinted room filled with opium dreams, and the intense pleasure she had experienced making love with another woman.

She lit a cigarette, a trace of arousal stirring in her as she recalled the evening, replayed time and again since leaving Paris. She closed her eyes, swallowed, as the two very different memories juxtaposed in her mind and struggled to play themselves out.

She heard the thudding of hooves from outside and turned to the window. From her second-floor room she could just make out a horse and rider racing close to the ocean's edge. As she watched the figure disappear into the night, she rubbed her neck, stiff from the traveling. A weariness washed over her. Seeing Charles again made her feel as if the woman she had become, the woman of confidence and power, had all but washed out with the tide.

* * *

She woke to the murmur of sounds below. It was a comforting sound of old, the hum of boarders that filled the rooms of the great Victorian. Byron's room was positioned squarely above the dining room and she used to wake in the mornings to the tenor of the voices and invent conversations for the unique and interesting travelers who passed through their small town. She briefly wondered how full the house was, and what faced her below.

She glanced at her watch. Last night she had fallen deeply asleep fully clothed, and had missed dinner entirely. She must go to her father straight away. She quickly washed and then stepped lightly before his door, but when she peeked inside he was fast asleep, still holding the worn wooden heart. She wished she could sit with him, but instead she braced herself and headed for the dining room.

Much like the rest of the mansion the dining room was large and stately, filled with Cecelia Harrington's many warm touches. Small totems filled the charming built-ins, and a graceful elegance softened the bold strokes of the mid-nineteenth century Victorian. The dining room was adorned with a crystal chandelier her father had brought from his European travels and it hung above a table that comfortably seated sixteen.

Byron stopped before entering the dining room. She had a perfect view of the boarders through a large mirror that not only reflected the dining room, but the front half of the sitting room on the opposite side of the arched entryway.

Charles sat at the head of the table, reading the paper. Seated next to him was a large and dissolute looking man, and beside him a woman, presumably his wife, disinterestedly picking at her food. Her red hair, high cheekbones and beautifully shaped mouth suggested she had once been quite beautiful, but she now appeared haggard and pestered.

"Such wonderful food!" squealed a younger woman who resembled the redhead, but she was far more plain and possessed an excitable and nervous manner that contradicted her mouse-like features. "You never mentioned you ate so well here, Ginger. Why, according to Mother, you've simply been starving yourself—and I can see myself, you have lost a bit around the middle—but darling, you've only yourself to blame for looking so gaunt."

A thin, frazzled serving woman with disheveled hair began to pour Charles coffee and then attended to several of the guests' needs. Charles caught her by the wrist and whispered emphatically in her ear. Byron realized that the woman she had mistaken for a maid was her brother's wife, Mavis, whom her father had told her about during his visit. Her scattered demeanor and veiled eyes betrayed her station as the lady of the manor as she nodded briefly to her husband and continued about her ministrations.

"Would you like some biscuits, Ruth?" Mavis offered the basket.

"Thank you Mrs. Harrington," Ruth chittered. "I don't know how you do it. One feast after another."

"Yes, I can state categorically the food here is quite superior," an overweight matron interjected. An aging dowager with a high-bridged nose and pinched expression, her dress and jewels indicated wealth and station. "So many of these family-run organizations cannot offer the same excellent cuisine of the hotels, but I should say you have outdone yourself. However, I should like to ask if we could trouble you to supply prunes in the morning. They are most advantageous to the health."

"I'll see what I can do, Miss Falstaff," Mavis responded, then whisked back out the swinging door to the kitchen.

"Mark, please pass me the biscuits after Miss Barrett is finished, won't you?" Miss Falstaff asked of the expressionless youth seated next to Ruth. Clean-cut and lazy-eyed, he reminded Byron of many people of wealth. Well groomed but without an ounce of intellectual curiosity.

The rest of the table was empty.

"Why, here you go, Miss Falstaff," Ruth said as she offered the biscuits. "I'm perfectly capable of passing them myself. Why, I'm practically independent. Well, I will be, anyway, once Mother sends me to finishing school."

"And when shall that be?" Miss Falstaff sniffed.

"Well, it's open-ended really. Mother thought it would be nice for me to visit Ginger. Make sure she's minding her P's and Q's. Besides, she wanted me to get out and travel a bit before I'm all boarded up at boarding school." She laughed nervously at her bland pun.

"Sound advice," Mark agreed with a mouth full of food.

Miss Falstaff cast an appalled grimace at her nephew's manners.

"I've been waiting my whole life to see New York," Mark continued, not quite finished chewing. "Get it out of the way now, while I'm young—then settle down to serious business."

"And what might that be?" Byron asked as she entered the dining room.

All eyes turned to her. Miss Falstaff wrinkled her nose in obvious distaste at Byron's attire. Clad in men's slacks, a French white blouse and black pinstriped vest and satin tie, she walked to the buffet. Byron filled her coffee cup and nodded briefly to the various boarders. "Good morning."

Everyone nodded and greeted her with a polite hello, but as they glanced at her surreptitiously, Byron felt an awkward tension, as if they had been previously coached by Charles that there was a new boarder amongst them, his eccentric sister visiting from abroad.

"Mark Templeton." Mark extended a hand to Byron and then indicated his aunt, "And my aunt, Miss Verity Falstaff."

Byron gallantly stretched out her hand. "Byron Harrington."

"*Chahmed*," Miss Falstaff barely hissed through clenched teeth and then peered through her spectacles at Byron. "But how very odd. You have the same name as—"

"I don't believe it." Ruth bolted upright in her chair "Do you believe it Ginger? I simply don't believe it!"

"What's the matter?" Mark asked.

"I suppose you don't know who sits in our very midst?"

"I'm afraid I don't," Mark responded.

"Then to be sure you haven't picked up a paper in the last five years," Ruth replied excitedly. It's Byron Harrington! *She* is Byron Harrington!"

"But I thought he was...I mean—"

"But that's just it, don't you see? *He* is a woman! Byron Harrington is a—what do you call those—you know a...a..."

"Pseudonym," Miss Falstaff dryly supplied.

"Well, Miss Harrington, I can't tell you how pleased we are all to meet you. I'm Ruth Barrett and this here is my sister Ginger. Ginger Brown." She indicated the unshaven man next to her. "And her husband, Clay."

Byron nodded in greeting. Ruth nudged her sister.

"Pleased to meet you."

Byron glanced from Ginger, who half-heartedly returned to her toast, to Clay, who seemed to be on the unfriendly side of a hangover. Byron sat as her brother finished.

"Well! I just can't get over this!" Ruth shook her head.

"Byron, this is my wife, Mavis." Charles stood as Mavis entered the room and made the introduction with little fanfare. "She will see to any needs you might have during your visit. Now if you'll all excuse me, I must attend to the accounts."

"Nice to meet you Mavis," Byron acknowledged her sister-in-law, but Mavis kept her eyes downcast and only nodded rotely as Charles exited through the archway.

"I can't wait to tell Mother," Ruth continued. "I've read every one of your books at least three times, haven't I Ginger. At least three times!"

"At least three times," Ginger sighed.

"I should rather think the fun would go out after you knew who did it," Byron observed.

"Oh, no. Nate Venable's—why, he's practically a national hero!" Ruth nudged Ginger again. "You're brilliant!"

"You must mistake what I do for literature, Miss Barrett."

But it went right over Ruth's head as she prattled on. "I simply can't wait to tell mother. She'll be the darkest shade of green—she's practically in love with Nate Venable! Tell us, where's he off to next?"

"Oh, yes—how daring!" Mark placed his hand over his heart. "We promise, we won't breathe a word."

Byron considered Ruth and Mark, both giddy with anticipation. She lit a cigarette. "I haven't quite decided. It's between saving an Italian heiress—"

"Yes?" Ruth leaned forward.

Byron took a deep drag, building the suspense. "Or discovering an American statesman is really a well-known transvestite in Paris."

Ruth's eyes bugged from her head. Miss Falstaff dropped her fork.

"Perhaps Nate will drum up a nasty opium habit. Or too much bathtub gin. Find himself washed up alongside the Seine."

Mark choked on his muffin as Ginger's jaw flexed in amusement, the first sign of life Byron had seen from her.

"Mark!" Miss Falstaff distastefully pushed her plate aside. "I think I've heard quite enough."

"What do you think?" Byron addressed Ruth.

"Well…I really couldn't…I mean, I don't know anything about such—"

Clay finally came to life as he heaved himself from the table. Ginger snaked out a hand to stop him.

"You going to the mill?" she asked.

He shook her hand off. "I told you I was, didn't I?"

"Yeah. That's what you told me," Ginger replied acidly.

He snorted as he walked out the arched entryway.

"Well! I really think I should get busy and write Mother." Ruth scurried from her seat to join the others.

Byron inhaled deeply from her cigarette.

"You sure know how to clear a room," Ginger said, then smiled. "Care for a cigarette?"

Ginger got up and moved to the chair next to Byron, accepting her offer.

"So, how long are you staying?" Ginger asked as Byron struck a match.

Byron raised her eyebrows. "I don't know. How long do you think I can tolerate it?"

* * *

Byron stoked the dying fire in her father's room. She was out of sorts, unused to the torpid pace of Bay Cliff. In Paris she was always busy, attending salons, writing, meeting Rabbit. Lord, how she missed her Rabbit.

"Darling," Francis whispered. "Come sit next to me."

"You're awake." Byron moved to the bed, and took his hand.

"So. Tell me a story. What's Nate Venable up to these days?"

"Oh, not very much lately."

"You come up with such fascinating adventures." Her father sighed. "Although, I must say Lil, the last one had a bit of color in it, eh? Made me blush under this rag." He tugged at his beard. "You have such talent, my dear. So very clever."

She smiled briefly, then let his hand drop, and stood to retrieve her cigarette case. "Yes. For parading a cynical detective around who wears women the way most men do a cheap pair of socks. That's not talent, darling. That's corruption. Hypocrisy. A living, in short." She patted his hand. "But we have more important things to discuss."

"Yes? And what might that be?"

"Well, I thought it over last night and I've decided you simply must come back with me."

"What? To Paris?"

"No. First we'll go to New York until you have your strength back. Then we'll book passage. First, Italy—the sun and pure enchantment of Villa Bellarosa will do you no end of good. Then we'll return to Paris—"

"Lilian. I appreciate what you're trying to do, but your lifestyle would hardly suit a bedridden invalid with a heart condition."

"You're not an invalid and I'm serious, Father."

"So am I."

"But you can't be!" She tossed her cigarette case on the bureau, then wandered listlessly to the window, flipped open the curtain. "I've only been here one day and already this—this paisley prison feels like one of my wretched novels."

"This is where I belong now, Lilian."

"It…it chokes me. It feels…like…like—"

"Death?" her father asked gently. "It is."

A silence hung between them.

She swept to his side, pleading. "This isn't you! You're not one to lie around in gloom. You loathe inaction. We'll book a room at the Algonquin. Rabbit's in New York right now and you adore him. He'll keep you in laughs. And there's so much to do. Museums, plays when you feel up to going. Besides, I need an escort. They're beginning to call me an old maid."

"Lilian, please. I know you find Bay Cliff tedious. But I'm afraid it's time. And this is where I need to be. My home." He momentarily grimaced in pain. "Please stay on...make me laugh at your awful stories...just a few more days."

"Father?"

"Just a few...days." He nodded into slumber.

Her stomach wrenched and she felt a burning in her chest. Of betrayal, then anger. How could he do this to her? How could he expect her to stay here? With *him*? How could he expect her to act as if nothing ever happened? As she paced the room, she knew she was being childish. Her father needed her. She must put her loathing of Charles to the side.

She walked to him then, saddening as she saw his once robust health so diminished. A softening acceptance filled her eyes. She laid her head against his chest. Memories flooded her. Times of old. A summer picnic with Mother when the wind flicked the blanket around them, and they fought to save their food, all laughing that they had picked such an unlikely day for an outing. Even Charles had been fun and happy in that moment.

Her breath came more slowly as she entered slumber, dreaming of her mother lit in a golden hue. And suddenly it was her mother who lay in the bed, the last time she had seen her alive, hollow-eyed and pale.

She was young again, watching Francis, stoic with grief, sitting with her mother's lifeless hand in his. Then a coffin slid into the ground. Lilian looked up as the coffin disappeared and her eyes met her brother's: Though his grief was plain, it was not without a trace of victory. Their mother would no longer be able to protect Lilian. Dirt thundered onto the lid. And all Lilian could see was black.

* * *

Lightning flashed through the darkening sky as Byron walked along the water's edge. She had run outside without her cloak. The late afternoon still held the glow of the sun, but suddenly a bank of clouds roared over the horizon and the rains fell.

Byron ran to the cave for shelter. Her cave. She had found it one summer when she was ten and it had become her special place, a place where she could escape Charles's taunts. Now as she entered the damp cave she brushed the rain from her shoulders. As she climbed the edge of several rocks she marveled at the strength of Mother Nature; the ageless tide that had carved the unusual contours through the center of a rock, scoring a large doughnut hole in its center through which the raging ocean was visible. She sat on one of the upper ledges, lit a cigarette and waited out the thunder and pelting rain. But as dusk came and went, the rains did not cease and Byron knew she had to return. Surely before the tide came in.

She lunged up the stairwell, sopping wet, almost running into Charles who stood blocking her way. She stopped and waited for him to pass, but he did not move.

"Ah, there you are. I forgot to warn you about the weather."

"Do you think I've forgotten everything?" Byron snapped.

Charles took a step closer to her. "It can be extremely unpredictable this time of year. And dangerous." His eyes followed the contours of her wet clothing.

"Move." Byron held his direct gaze.

He faltered, then let her pass.

Byron let herself into her room, fell back against the door, and slid downwards into a neat little puddle.

* * *

When Byron entered her father's room the next day, she was met with the warm smile of Dr. Edward Dutton. He was a tall and sturdily built man with a pleasantly handsome face. Gray dappled his thinning hair, and a wise twinkle in his eyes was born not just of studying life, but learning from it.

"Ah, Lilian," said her father. "Please come in. I want you to meet the most civilized man in the Northwest. And Doctor, I'm proud to introduce my daughter, Byron Harrington."

Byron moved forward to extend her hand which he firmly grasped in his own. He smiled. "I'm a great admirer of yours."

"Then you're not as civilized as my father thinks."

Their laughter spurred a coughing jag in Francis. Byron rushed to him, helped him to sit upright as the doctor administered his medication.

"Rest now, Father." Byron tucked the blankets around him and he almost immediately fell asleep.

She glanced to the doctor who motioned her outside.

"How about some tea?" he asked.

"I'll have Mavis bring us some in the sitting room," she replied.

Later she and Edward sat deeply involved in a chess game in the large sitting room, the warmth of the sun filling the parlor with stillness and repose, its conservative furnishings dominated by a mammoth hearth and a piano.

"Your father's a new man since you've arrived," Edward said as he contemplated the board.

"I don't know. Charles seems to think I'm wearing him down. And judging by the way he simply drops off to sleep at a moment's notice, perhaps he's right."

"I think you're the best medicine the doctor could have ordered." Edward picked up his white queen from the chessboard, and studied the battlefield before him. "We had a standing chess game every week."

"Is he still cheating?"

"Yes...and still losing." He replaced the queen and moved her forward several squares.

"Would you settle for a substitute?"

When he regarded her, his smile was direct and forthright. "I'd like that very much."

After a long while only a few pieces remained in the fading sun as Byron and Edward sat in rapt concentration, unaware that Charles had entered the sitting room. "My good man, I had no idea you were here."

"Good evening, Charles," Edward said without looking up.

"Hmmm...appears to be a tight game."

Neither of them answered, but Charles remained hovering over Byron as she moved her rook.

"Well, I shan't get in your way. I'll go and have Cynara fetched 'round."

Byron glanced from her brother to Edward.

"No. Please don't bother." Edward's eyes never once left the board. "I will call on her later."

"It's no bother at all. I'll have Mavis run—"

"Charles, it's quite all right." The doctor's voice sharpened. "I'm in a very delicate situation here."

Charles surveyed the board as Byron moved the black queen and removed one of Edward's pieces.

Edward sat back and caught his breath. "You've done it then."

"Nonsense," Charles intervened. "It's not over yet. You've still got a fighting chance."

But it was apparent to them all that he did not. Edward glanced from Charles to Byron.

"I'm afraid not. She's captured my queen."

* * *

A sunset torched the sky and lit the waves like burning embers. Byron was mesmerized by the brilliant red on the sea as she strolled along the trail of a sloping precipice a mile south of Bay Cliff, unaware that a woman sat on a berth just below her path. Byron lit a cigarette as she continued down the trail, gathering in the extraordinary beauty of her surroundings. This was what she had missed and longed for while in the heart of Paris. This part of Bay Cliff.

She stopped quite suddenly, now aware of the woman sitting in profile not twenty feet from her, rich auburn hair cascading down her shoulders.

The woman was striking. Beautiful, but in an unconventional way. She had what Rabbit referred to as strong English features—a straight pointed nose, high cheekbones. Slowly, as if sensing her, the woman turned and faced Byron to reveal soft and sensual lips, and she appeared to have been crying, for tears rested on her cheeks.

Byron stood a moment, uncertain, then began to approach cautiously, but the woman didn't seem to see her, or if she did, she stared straight through or beyond her. Byron sensed the tears had come from a release borne of the sheer majesty of their surroundings and realized, quite awkwardly, that she had interrupted a private reverie. She was about to offer help, but then a defiant glare, and abrupt dismissal of her as the stranger turned from her, made clear none was required. Byron hesitated for an instant, then walked from the clearing.

* * *

Byron entered the house long after sundown and was heading up the stairwell when she heard Charles's angry voice hissing from the sitting room. "I've told you before, if she cannot attend dinner, she is not welcome to the food."

"She isn't feeling well."

Mavis's voice was hesitant and fearful. Byron backtracked just enough to catch sight of them around the edge of the entryway.

"We're not running an infirmary here."

"Charles, please—"

"Besides, her health doesn't keep her from traipsing all over the countryside."

Byron frowned, confused.

"I'll talk to her," Mavis promised.

"Yes. Do that. Because if you don't, I will."

Byron could hear Charles's footsteps as he walked from the room. She quickly continued up the stairwell and headed to her room, planning a quiet evening to write. She had been so inspired by nature's aesthetics she thought she might actually get in her first night of work.

Byron took off her cloak and moved to the typewriter that had finally arrived from the station earlier that day along with her trunk. She placed a hand lovingly upon it, then rifled through her clothes in search of a special case. She pulled out a flask, filled with Framboise from Genet. She took a small drink and then settled at her desk.

An hour later she continued to stare at an empty page.

* * *

Byron awoke from another nightmare, flailing under her covers, drenched in sweat, her body wracked as if she had run for miles. Trembling, she got up, threw on her robe and made her way to her father's room.

She pulled a chair to his bedside. It was going to be a long night. When she opened her eyes some time later, her father was gazing into her own with thoughtful concern.

"How long have you been here, dear?"

"I don't know." Byron stretched, her body stiff and sore. "I couldn't sleep."

"You look pale. I'm worried about you."

"Don't be." Byron smiled reassuringly.

"What is it, Lilian? What is it that plagues your dreams and causes you to spend your days as far away from here as possible?"

Byron rubbed the back of her neck.

"You know, you never told me why you 'escaped—'"

"But Father, I did tell you."

"It has been convenient for you to say that to write about the world you had to see it first. I have always supported your decision." Francis shifted in his bed. "God knows you and Charles have never gotten on, but I was hoping this visit would ease the bad blood between you."

Byron stood. "That will never happen."

"Whatever else he is, underneath it all, he is your brother."

"Consanguinity is no excuse for boorish behavior, and that is all I know of him." She heard the sharp anger in her voice, and thought it best to change the subject. "Father, how in the world did Charles and Mavis ever manage to come together? When you wrote that Charles had married, I rather suspected someone, I don't know, more…more—"

"Spirited?"

"Yes, that's it."

"Mavis has a wealth of spirit." Her father pulled at his beard. "It runs deep and is well hidden. Don't be taken in by her—shall I say, flustered manner. She's a very bright woman. She's had a rough life. I dare say, no one knows for sure what goes on between a man and his wife, but I rather think they were in love—at one point anyway. I think Mavis's strength of character reminded him of your mother."

"Strength? The woman looks like she's about to topple over from nerves."

"Yes, she is nervous. It's developed as a kind of condition shortly after her sister came back."

"Her sister?"

The bell rang for breakfast and Byron jumped in her seat.

"Off you go then."

"Perhaps I can come later and read to you?"

"That would be lovely."

Byron went to her father and saw him take the wooden heart from beneath the sheet and rub it like a worry stone. She eased his furrowed brow with a kiss.

* * *

Several nights later Byron sat at her desk in a burgundy, pin-striped robe, pecking furiously at her typewriter. A thudding crash stopped her mid-rhythm. Hearing a woman's muffled scream, she bolted upright and hurried through her door.

It was dark in the chilly hallway, but she saw a light emerge from one of the rooms opposite hers. A door flung open and Clay stumbled into her, barely maintaining his balance.

"Steady on there, old boy!" Byron caught him, steered him back into his room and caught sight of a woman administering to Ginger's swollen lip.

"No one...no one tells me what...what I can and can not do." He hiccuped loudly. "Do you hear me?"

"I'm afraid they hear you in Portland, my good man." Byron held him off as he tried to push through her to Ginger. "A tad pie-eyed, aren't we?"

Clay attempted to focus on Byron. "She ca...called me a l-lout...a go...good for nothing lout."

"Well, we can't all be so well loved."

"She hates me...my own wife...hates the sight of me..." he sobbed. "I...I hate the sight of me."

"Imagine," Byron responded dryly.

"Since you seem to be quite practiced with the drunk and disorderly," said the woman who held an ice-bag to Ginger's mouth, "perhaps you can get him out of here."

"No. It's all right," Ginger said. "He's gone into his blubber stage. He's harmless now."

As Byron ushered him to the bed, he collapsed backward, out cold. Byron removed his tie, shucked off his shoes. As he began to snore Byron surveyed the mess, then Ginger's bruises.

It was the woman from the beach who turned and faced Byron, assessing her as Ginger went to her besotted husband.

"If you need anything, you know where to find me," Byron assured Ginger and walked from the room. The other woman followed.

The two stood awkwardly in the darkened hallway until Byron pulled her cigarette case from her robe pocket and offered it to the woman. She accepted and as Byron lit both cigarettes, shielding the flame against the draft, she could see in the stranger's intelligent deep-set eyes, a unique blend of vulnerability and strength.

"The other day…" Byron inhaled and then her voice trailed off as the woman turned aside. "I didn't mean to intrude."

The woman turned her head slowly, gazed directly at Byron.

"Byron Harring—"

"I know who you are."

"So, I imagine you are Cynara. Mavis's sister."

Cynara inclined her head. Byron cocked her own towards Ginger's door.

"Heart-warming slice of domestic bliss."

"Yes. Isn't it."

"Let's call it 'Romance and Courtship,' " Byron mused. After a moment's thought she nodded her head and began:

"Pale lads and winsome lasses,
with the blush of love on their cheeks.
How it fades into black eyes
and the flush of liquor reeks."

Cynara smiled cryptically. "Ah, yes. The writer who thwarts her vision with cynicism."

As Byron was about to defend her position, the woman held up her cigarette, mouthed the words "Thank you," and walked past Byron, who in turn watched her fade into the enveloping darkness.

Silhouettes crystallized into their actual shapes as dawn faded into the first rays of sun. A half a pot of coffee was finished and several lit cigarettes had gone unnoticed, leaving neglected arcs of ash cradled in the ashtray.

By now my regular routine of working on the path had been replaced by writing. I awoke before sunrise, sat at the kitchen table I had moved right before my scenic window and wrote with the kind of mesmerized focus I hadn't experienced since those early days in Portland. Words tumbled out fluidly. Effortlessly. Perhaps because it was the first time since then that I was writing only for myself. I had two inspirational quotes taped to the corners of my laptop. "Write the Truth," and one I had scribbled in bold letters on the back of an envelope while talking to Lena long ago, the two of us commiserating that neither of us could find a good book to read: *"Write the book that you want to read."*

Now when I went on my daily constitutional, my mind lived inside my world of words. I could see Bay Cliff up on the rugged hillside. I discovered a path that led to a tumbling waterfall that I circled time and again trying to figure out how to play its geography into my story. When I discovered the incredible cave with a carved-out doughnut hole, on the other side of Hug Point, I knew it would be the perfect setting for a pivotal scene.

Pent-up energy invigorated my walks. I was bursting from the excitement of my work, and my days were filled with the execution of what I could truly claim as writing. *I am a writer.* How I had longed to say it again. And mean it. By late afternoon, after my third writing session, I would navigate the path and after a long and exhausting trek on my private beach end up at my favorite spot, my swinging bench up on my highland.

As I swung gently back and forth, I was filled with a peace I had never known possible. I was, quite simply, happy with myself for the first time in my life. Happy with just me. Even in the face of my history, I was able to stand up to my failures, meet them square on. I could now peacefully watch my "lady in the cape," a craggy rock shape just out of reach of low tide, as she melted into the sunset.

* * *

Yes, I had gone far afield. Wandered astray. It became so clear in the cottage and here in my cave to see my life as the disjointed mess that it had been. How we think we can tidy it up into a three-act structure, or a well-rounded novel. But that's not life. I see all the scenes spinning about like European cinema—life's little moments strung together by a unifying theme, which shifts as the character changes and evolves, hopefully, into a better person.

I suppose it's just our nature to want to be liked, in spite of it all. And that's why I cringe when I get to the last of it, for it's the hardest to tell. The downfall.

Making up stories is easy. Telling your own is horrifying—scraping away at crusted-on denial, burrowing for the facts in the face of tilted memories, understanding who you really are, and how much of a figment of your imagination your life has actually been.

* * *

She met Nina Delvecchio at the screening of her latest short, *Brave One.* Nina was a director Malcolm wanted to work with and he had invited Spencer to the screening and then introduced her to Nina after the Q & A.

"It was intriguing." Spencer didn't gush. Had she, Nina would have known she loathed it.

Nina smiled. Sincerely, with very small if crooked white teeth that fit with her beautiful Italian eyes, dark and mercurial. "Thank you."

"Where did you find the little girl?" Others were milling about trying to gauge consensus; was this piece brilliant or just another piece of doom—their discomfort in not knowing what they were supposed to think discernible from twenty paces.

"Off the streets," Nina yelled over the din.

"It worked," Spencer stated simply.

Nina flashed a smile at Spencer as she was thrust into a semi-circle of adoring film students from USC. Spencer gathered her coat to leave.

Nina excused herself from the group and caught up with her as she was exiting the lobby doors. "You have a card?"

"Don't leave home without it." Spencer handed her one. "You?"

She shrugged, then smirked. "I think you can remember who I am." Then turned and left. Spencer laughed. What an arrogant piece of work.

* * *

She got home, tossed her keys on the kitchen table and the phone rang. Eleven p.m. She thought it was Lena so she answered.

"Hey," Spencer purred.

"Hey yourself."

"Oh...uhm..." She was caught off guard. "Yes?"

"Nina."

"Delvecchio?"

"The same." Nina paused a moment. It sounded like she was taking a drag off a cigarette. "Do you want to produce my next film?"

Spencer sat a moment, stunned. "Why do you want me to produce it?"

"Because you see my work." There was a pause. "Besides, aren't you getting sick of the shit you're making?"

She almost slammed the phone down. Nina was an asshole, way out of line. But something about her brutal honesty was alluring. Exciting even.

"Call my office in the morning. We'll set up a meet—"

"Fuck the meeting. You either want to do it or you don't."

"Listen Delvecchio, if you want an answer I'm going to have to see the script, know what we're doing, what the budget is, who's —"

"Spencer. Stop. I'm asking if you want to produce me. Yes or no. All that other shit is the crap that gets in the way. This is where it starts. It's like making love. You don't first ask how much goddamn grocery money you're getting every weekend. You operate on the mutual illusion that it will all work itself out because you want to fuck the bastard. Or not. It's as simple as that."

She heard the whishing sound again. She was smoking. Pot.

Every terrible scenario imaginable flashed through her mind.

"Okay," Spencer finally answered.

"Good." She sounded cocky but pleased.

"By the way," Spencer asked, "how much grocery money are we talking here?"

* * *

They met for coffee at Cafe Luna on Melrose. Nina was a short woman, with a thick but proportionately gorgeous body and exquisite bone structure. Strong. That was the best word to describe her. Strong face, strong hands, overbearing personality. You could tell she would be more comfortable naked than clothed. Primal. Her dark hair was thick and curly. Her chocolate brown eyes turned black in an instant, and thin lips twisted easily in anger. Far more pleasant in a smile. But she saved that for rare occasions.

They talked film throughout the afternoon, during which Nina consumed an entire pack of Marlboros. She smoked her cigarettes with utmost concentration, as if it were a holy experience. Spencer couldn't take her eyes off her. God, she was powerful. Troubled. Nina turned to her, knew she was being watched.

"When will you read it?"

"Tonight"

Nina began to pack her notes and files back into her briefcase. "Do your people know you're doing this?"

"No," she replied briskly.

Nina crooked an eyebrow. "How did I know that?"

"I'll tell them."

"When? During our acceptance speeches?"

Spencer picked up her briefcase and stood as well. "Yeah. That would be a good time."

* * *

That night she canceled her dinner date with Lena and told her she had way too much work to do.

"That's getting to be a habit," she teased on the other end of the line.

"Well, it's always been a habit, Lena." Spencer hated the bite in her voice.

"I was just joking, sweetie."

"I—this is who I am. My work is important. Sometimes I don't think you really know me that well."

"I thought I did."

"You know me in bed." Spencer instantly regretted the barb.

A long moment of silence paused.

"Spencer, is everything okay?"

"I'm sorry. I'm just tired, and I have a budget to go over tonight and then…then I got this script last minute I have to read. I didn't mean to take it out on you."

"If you came over, I could tuck you in and let you read and not bother you for a moment," she offered.

"I can't, Lena," Spencer sighed. "I really need to focus."

"Okay. I guess I could catch up on some paperwork myself."

After they signed off, Spencer poured herself a glass of wine and picked up Nina's script. She read it twice, back to back, the first time racing through. The second time wanting to get all of it, the nuance, the subtext. The texture. It was so personal she found herself almost embarrassed to read it.

It was a love story of sorts. Not unlike *May You*. Maybe that's why Spencer got hooked from the first page. It was about the obsession of a man for the love of his life. In a lesser writer's hands it would have been trite and sensationalized. But in Nina's it was real and human.

Spencer felt torn. One half of her wanted to dive head first into the project, because it was good. Because of its similarities to *May You*. Because of Nina. She kept trying to convince herself she wasn't attracted to her, but the other half knew better, and already she wanted to flog herself for the transgressions of her mind.

She phoned Nina at three in the morning. "I would be honored to produce your script."

"Thank you," Nina muttered sleepily, but humbly.

"No. Thank you."

Their mutual admiration society had begun.

* * *

"You seem so distant," Lena sighed. After an attempt at uninspired union, they lay inches away, not touching in bed. "I don't know where you were, but it wasn't here with me."

"I'm sorry," Spencer spoke softly. "I'm preoccupied."

"You're always preoccupied these days."

It was true. Spencer had given herself completely to the project, working herself to the bone. Not only did she still have the terrible series, but now she was going to produce Nina's film during her hiatus. Tons of prep had to be attended to, so she began her early morning stints breaking down Nina's script, creating feats of magic on production to save Nina money.

Lena moved closer, curled a leg over Spencer's, massaged her waist. "Have you ever tried letting the universe come to you?"

"What kind of platitude is that. Isn't it here? All around me— happening?"

"Why are you working so hard on this when it isn't even your project—when you already have a job?"

"Because the job's not the job I want. I'm no further along than I was in Portland."

"You are too. You now work in the profession you love. You've won an Emmy. How many people can say that? In the two years I've known you, I don't know that I've ever seen you satisfied. You always want to push the river."

"It doesn't move fast enough for me."

"What does?"

Spencer wondered if anything ever would. At first all she had wanted was access. Access was truly the Holy Grail in her industry, but now that she had it, now that people returned her calls, it still had gotten her no further ahead. She was still struggling and more times than not she felt unfulfilled. She had begun questioning not just every value she ever had, but whether she ever had any at all

"I...I've got to—" Spencer tried to move from Lena's grip, but Lena held her in place, lacing arms about her neck, kissing the side of her face, and then fully upon the mouth.

Again Spencer felt divided. How easy it would be to sink into Lena, her warmth, her steadfastness. Tonight, like many lately, she was beginning to see that perennial fork in the road ahead. One arrow pointed up a 12 percent grade hill, the other out to a pasture. You don't hit this fork until you're old enough to feel the fight. Weighing the balance of what the fight is doing to you and what will happen if you don't have it to hold onto. There was a reason you heard "I got outta the business" from so many people. There was a reason they couldn't make it. But she needed to make it. What else did she have? She would do anything.

Anything.

Spencer disengaged herself, started to dress.

"What are you doing?"

"I'm sorry. I've got to go."

"I thought..."

"Look, I know we were supposed to have the whole night. But only a third of Nina's money came in. We have to do this film for peanuts and Nina expects miracles from me. The only way I can do that is get some studio time at night. We'll just have to make it tomorrow. Promise."

"How many tomorrows do you think I have?"

"What do you want from me?" Spencer spat, exasperated. She had no patience for this. She had important things to do. A movie to make.

"I think the question is, what is it that *you* want?" Lena put a robe on and walked to Spencer. "I'm serious. What in the hell is it you're fighting for so damn hard?"

"Let's see, a few hundred million to run my own studio—"

"Spencer, please don't." Lena's voice was kind, empathic. Just what Spencer loved about her. Lena faced adversity with calm, whereas Spencer had to create a maelstrom to find the calm within the center. Lena grounded her in the worst of circumstances, only this time Spencer wasn't sure anything would work. "I'm trying to have a real conversation here. I just want to know what it is you need. If there is anything I can do."

"I don't know if there is anything anyone can do." Spencer sighed, buttoning her shirt. "I keep getting close—so goddamn close, and it's pulled from me."

"Maybe you're trying too hard."

"What the hell does that mean? I hate it when people say stupid shit like that." Spencer ran hands through her hair, couldn't stop herself. "What the hell would you know about it? You've got it made. You're at the apex of your professional career. You've got a child and the white picket fence. You've got enough money to make your own goddamn movie. So don't patronize me with a bunch of easy words, Lena, because that's not how the real world works."

"Do you want out? Is that it?"

"Lena, I don't know why you have to make a federal case out of this."

But the truth of the matter was, Spencer struggled with the options. If she walked with Lena's blessings she would be free to fall deep into the bottomless pit of Nina's film and, from the way things were trending, into her arms. Lena was just too damn perfect. Spencer needed some churn. She required edge to be creative. Lena would never understand that.

"I'm not I'm trying to tell you I see a pattern emerging here. I have tried to have this conversation with you for the past three months. We go along fine and I guess when you feel like you've fueled up enough on our relationship you have the resources to go out and burn the candle at both ends. Between your show, Jerry, and now Nina's film I never see you. I understand about deadlines and projects. I've been there. But even when you have a moment to touch down, you don't take it."

"I took MacKenzie to the zoo just last Sunday," Spencer replied defensively.

"Yes, the few moments you have, you give to my daughter and while I'm thrilled that you love her, it's not very flattering for her mother. The last time we had a date, you were so goddamn exhausted you fell into bed with a migraine. Or you freak out with a panic attack. Then you scurry back into my arms. For a few moments your guard is down enough to let me back in. But I'm not a goddamn pit stop, Spencer."

Spencer pulled on her blazer.

"Did you hear me, Spencer?"

"Of course I heard you." She checked her watch. "I've gotta go. We'll finish this later."

Spencer walked to Lena to kiss her goodbye, but Lena gently warded her off.

"You should say goodnight to MacKenzie," Lena said quietly. "She waited for you all evening and I told her you would see her when you came in."

I remember that night so clearly, walking into MacKenzie's room, dark save the Curious George night light. I hear her tender breathing and lie on the bed next to her, careful not to wake her. When my eyes accustom to the light, I can see the faint traces of her high forehead, her small pug nose, her heart-shaped mouth falling to one side.

I lightly touch her silken hair, having stroked it a million times. My body jerks with a silent sob.

She shifts, waking slightly. "Aunnie Spinner?" she mumbles.

I try to steady my voice. "Yeah, it's me."

"I just had a weird dream." She curls her body against mine and wraps a slender arm over my tummy.

"Yeah, what was that?"

"We were out by the ocean and we were hunting for starfish like we did this summer and you found this, like, golden penny. But it turned into one'a those blue Christmas balls you like a lot. It shined really bright. You gave it to me and said, 'Here, now you can be whatever you want.'"

MacKenzie wipes a hand over her face. "Weird huh?"

"I think it was a good dream, sweetie."

"Would you sing that song, Aunnie Spinner?"

"What song?"

"The one about the wine and the blossoms."

In my cracked voice I sing two choruses of "Today" and remember the many nights I have crooned this song for MacKenzie. How can I walk out of her life? In the short time I have known her she has given me back the ability to feel again, the joy of spontaneity—a glimpse at redemption.

Her breathing deepens. I kiss her sleep-flushed cheek, and feel a new anguish to put into the vocabulary of my heart.

From behind her paper, Byron watched the sensuous play of fingertips around and around the rim as Cynara dangled her hand over an emptied cup. As the two of them sat alone in the dining room Byron advanced a cigarette to her mouth, and exhaled nonchalantly as she watched Cynara walk to the buffet, pour herself more coffee, and place a muffin on a plate. She made no sign that she was aware of Byron as she topped the muffin with marmalade and continued to fill her plate with eggs and sausage. Byron frowned, curious and baffled. This woman was utterly out of context to the boarding house. She no more belonged here than did Byron herself. She dressed simply, but elegantly; her style and bearing were uniquely feminine and decidedly urbane. She returned to her seat on the far end of the long oak table.

"You live in the cottage up the hill?"

Cynara barely nodded.

"Last night. What did you mean?"

Cynara made a great show of buttering a biscuit, but still did not respond.

"It's not polite to insult someone without giving them benefit of an explanation."

"It wasn't intended as an offense. Merely an observation."

"Based on your many years as a literary critic, no doubt."

"Based on my good taste and judgment."

"Oooh...now that sounds far more inspired than years of educated objectivism." Byron fidgeted at her collar. "Tell me, what is it that you find so undesirable?"

"In general or specifically?"

"Why not both?"

Cynara's eyes met hers. "Are you sure?"

"I'm quite certain." Byron placed her elbows on the table, pressed fingertips together below her chin. "In any event, it couldn't be any worse than I've already heard."

"Well, to begin with, Nate Venable's a stick figure. Even when he's being wonderfully droll, allowing his readers a glimpse into his glamorous and sophisticated world, he's aloof—not real. He's one note—sarcastic and cynical—which I suppose passes for entertainment. Also, given his creator, I've always found it strangely ironic that his escapades do nothing to advance the cause of women."

"Well," Byron responded dryly, "I see you've put a great deal of thought into this."

"I've read the Venable mysteries to your father a number of times."

"A great source of pleasure, no doubt." Byron tried not to sound defensive. "And in general?"

Cynara's expression softened as she looked at Byron pointedly. "Simply, that his adventures will be buried long before your readers are."

With that Cynara finished her coffee and stood. Byron remained nonplused as she walked from the room.

"Let's not let these friendly chats become a habit," she whispered under her breath.

* * *

Tendrils of smoke wove a murky plateau over Byron and her lifeless pages. A rap on her door did nothing to help her mood. She had been sitting, as she had most every night, wordless.

When she opened the door, Charles entered presumptively, with an aggressive air of entitlement. It was the first time they had been in this room together in twelve years.

"Not interrupting am I?" He cast an amused expression toward her lack of industry. "I thought surely our landscape would inspire the muse. As you've certainly been partaking of it enough lately—"

"Is that all?"

"This is not an inquisition, Lilian. I've simply noticed you spend far more hours out and about than you do inside. I hope we haven't made things unpleasant for you."

"Being outside helps me think."

Charles raised his eyebrows as he noted the empty page in the typewriter, "Hmmmm…yes well—"

Mavis tapped on the opened door and Charles turned in exasperation.

"Yes! What is it?" he demanded.

She glanced nervously from one to the other. "It's your father. He's taken a turn."

They quickly made their way to Francis's room where their father lay in bed with labored breathing, his face ruddy with fever.

"I'll go for Dutton," Charles said.

Byron nodded and pulled up a chair. Waiting through the night as her father's strength visibly ebbed from his body, a chill slowly working its way up her spine, she knew that she hadn't been fully prepared for the inevitable. Seeing her brother across from her sharing the tightly stretched anxiety brought home the reality that her father was indeed dying. It was only a matter of time.

When the doctor arrived, he excused everyone from the room. Byron paced in the library until Mavis brought word that the fever had broken and that Dutton would come and speak with her shortly. Byron collapsed in a chair next to the hearth, exhausted from worry.

"Byron. Byron?"

Byron snapped awake. She woke groggily to the early dawn and looked into the kind visage of Edward Dutton.

"I'm sorry. It took me much longer to attend to matters than I thought. And then you were sleeping so peacefully I didn't want to disturb you. But we're out of the woods for now, now that his fever has broken."

"May I see him?"

"After breakfast." Edward laid a gentle hand on her shoulder. "I'll say one thing for your father. He's tenacious."

"Or stubborn. It runs in the family."

"An admirable trait," he said quietly and smiled warmly at her.

She ran a hand through tousled hair. "Where's Charles?"

"He left shortly after the fever broke. Said he had business in Portland."

"What can we expect?" Byron rubbed her forehead as if pained.

"Your father's a fighter and now that you're here he has something to hold onto. But I'm afraid it won't be too much longer."

"Is he in pain?"

"He has medicine for the pain. And I have full faith in Mavis."

"Mavis?"

"Yes." Dutton smiled as if Byron must know. "It is Mavis who has cared for him all this time."

The more she learned about her brother's wife, the more confounded she became. Because of her work, she had always prided herself in being more observant than the average person, seeing the underneath of a matter, not just what presented itself. She studied people, used their quirks and what made them tick in her characters, but since Mavis was Charles's wife, Byron had not bothered to get to know her, and since the woman seemed incapable of meeting her gaze squarely, she had not given her a second thought.

"And a damn good job she has done," Dutton continued. "If it wasn't for Mavis, I don't know how Bay Cliff would get on."

* * *

"Yes, I'm telling you I heard it from my cousin." Mark's hushed voice slipped through the walls of the sitting room as Byron made her way into the dining room, bundled up for her daily walk.

"Oh, but it's too dreadful," Ruth hissed. "I thought it was the city of beauty—the city of light."

As Byron nabbed an apple from the fruit bowl, she turned to catch Cynara's amused expression, as captured by the reflection in the buffet mirror, while she watched Ginger, Ruth, Mark and Miss Falstaff sharing tea in the sitting room. They were engaged in a rather heated exchange.

"I do wish the two of you would exercise some control," Miss Falstaff insisted, although her own voice quivered with anger.

"Why, there she went, right into the dining room." Ruth's voice could be heard above the others.

Byron turned as Ruth shouted from the other room. "Miss Harrington? Miss Harrington, could we bother you for a moment of your time?"

Not visible to her audience but to Cynara, Byron rolled her eyes. "Yes? What can I do for you?"

"We were wondering, well…if you could set us straight on something."

"If it is at all possible," Byron responded dryly.

Ginger smiled sardonically at the double entendre as did Cynara from her new vantage point at the arched entry. She leaned against the wall to observe.

"Well, it's about—" Ruth blushed and turned to Mark. "Go on. You're the one who brought it up."

Mark glanced uncertainly at his aunt, whose mouth was pinched in distaste.

"Well, I heard it from my cousin, Kenneth, who's traveled plenty and is honest as the day is long—"

"Yes, and what happens when the days grow short?"

Mark frowned, momentarily confused, as Ginger burst into laughter.

"Anyway, he got it on good authority that in Paris, well, in the ugly parts of the city that cater to the…well, how shall I put it…the bohemian population—"

"Oh, do you mean the writers and artists?" posed Byron.

"That there's all sorts of activity going on. People drunk and disorderly—"

"No!" Byron gasped in mock surprise.

"Why yes! And a lot of them Americans! Public nudity—" he stammered, "free love running rampant...all manner of combinations. Opium dens where people go stark raving mad."

Byron feigned dismayed astonishment.

"Well, I'm surprised you haven't heard this yourself—being there and all."

"Are you certain of your facts?"

"Oh, yes and much more. Or so Mark says," Ruth twittered at the edge of her seat.

"Absolutely," Mark declared. "I know we must seem quite provincial and inexperienced compared to New York and all the places you've been, but there is a limit. Why, if we all behaved like that, without any sort of structure, we'd have certain anarchy on our hands."

"Do you really think so?"

"I'm quite certain of it," Mark responded, pounding his knee with his hand. "So...is it?"

"Yes," Ruth repeated. "Is it true?"

Byron waited dramatically. "Absolutely not!"

Mark and Ruth's faces fell in obvious disappointment.

"It's much, much worse."

* * *

Byron walked in the isolated gray of morning and as she headed up the path she saw Cynara, atop her horse on a hill several hundred feet away, studying her. They regarded one another until Cynara pulled the reins and disappeared from Byron's view.

As Byron continued on her walk, she followed a path into a thatched area of evergreens. Cynara's horse approached from the trail ahead of her. When she reached Byron, Cynara sat appraising her from her vantage point.

"You'll never hear the end of it, you know," she said as she dismounted. "They'll be begging for all the tainted details."

Byron smiled and they walked in silence.

"Your father?" Cynara asked, her voice soft and encouraging.

Byron nodded, indicating that the worst had passed and they continued on in silence for some time, until Byron stopped.

"What are you doing here?"

"I was taking a ride —"

"No. I mean here. At Bay Cliff."

"Where else would I be?"

They came to an obvious fork in the path. Bay Cliff loomed in the distance. A moment of awkwardness ensued as Byron followed Cynara's view to the small cottage on the hill above them.

"You seem distinctly...misplaced."

Their eyes met briefly, then Byron headed down the hill.

* * *

The next evening Byron rapidly trailed down the stairwell, heading towards the door when Charles's voice boomed from the study. "Lilian? May I have a moment?"

Byron reluctantly headed to Charles's study. Charles had not only taken over running Bay Cliff, but her father's den—so much a part of who he was to her—that she was loath to enter. As she did so she was overwhelmed by the smell of Francis, the leather of his chair, the burning fire, even trace remnants of his cologne—all this belonged to her father; yet Charles sat at his desk as if he'd grown quite comfortable.

Charles motioned her to the chair opposite him. He shuffled papers at the finely detailed mahogany desk, then opened a cigarette case and casually pushed it toward Byron. She declined the offer and waited.

"Dreadful storm we're having." He took great pains to light his cigarette. "Do you think it's wise to go out?"

Her fingers tapped impatiently against her leg. "Surely we're not here to discuss the weather, Charles."

"Very well. This is difficult, but given the turn in Father's condition, well, as painful as it is"—his tone turned affectedly grave—"the inevitable will happen."

"Don't you think this is premature, Charles, even for you?"

"Lilian, you've always been a dreamer." His voice was slick with charm. "I, however, am practical. I assess situations, act accordingly and move swiftly. No matter how unpleasant, I do what needs to be done."

A shiver ran up the back of Byron's neck. She bit the inside of her lip and held her head steady.

"I'd like to know what your plans are. After—"

"My plans?"

"Yes. I mean after Father…passes…what do you plan to do?"

"Return to Paris, of course."

Charles was visibly delighted. "As I suspected. Well, you're more than welcome to stay for as long as you need. I will be traveling to Portland in the next few days and while there will visit Weatherby, Father's attorney, and inform him of your return to Paris."

"What possible interest could he have in my plans?"

"In order to facilitate the necessary paperwork." Charles inhaled his cigarette, his manner ever smug and satisfied. "You know. Settle things now, so we don't have to, ah, attend them at a more unsavory time."

"Fine. You tell him whatever it is you feel you need to, Charles, to 'facilitate' Father's demise."

She stormed from the den and ran from the house, aimless in her direction, anger propelling her forward, even as it became dark and she could no longer see. Breaking from the sand and racing up the hill, Byron felt the bramble of twigs tear against her ankles. Her pulse pounding in her neck, she struggled to an open pasture above Bay Cliff and began to realize that the path of her childhood had changed. Though she could barely see in the deep black forest she knew her bearings were off. Panting, she stopped, trying to find the stars through the tops of the trees. A low glimmer to her left—she headed toward it.

She walked to the lit cottage, hesitated only momentarily, then knocked. The door slowly opened, revealing Cynara, her face veiled in shadow. She lifted her lamp and peered into Byron's face.

"I…I'm," Byron sputtered, "lost."

Cynara took her by the elbow, and led her into her cottage.

Trembling, Byron retrieved a flask from her coat pocket. She tilted it back, taking a large swallow. Still shaken she went to stand by the hearth. As the liquid burned through her limbs and she warmed from the fire, Byron assessed the small, single-room cottage and saw that it was filled with comfort and grace, with books lining antique shelves and several feminine, but not flowery touches.

The single door in the room half-concealed a claw-foot tub and a Chinese silk screen stood as a barrier to a wrought-iron bed, behind which several boxes or crates were covered with blankets.

Byron offered Cynara the flask. "Don't worry, it's not bathtub gin."

Cynara hesitated and then took a sip. "Hmmm, very good."

"My dear friend Genet made sure I was fortified before I sailed home."

"From *The New Yorker*—the Letter from Paris."

Byron glanced at Cynara, surprised. "Then you know of her?"

"We're not all illiterate west of the Mississippi."

Byron took out her cigarette case, which she also offered to Cynara, and lit both cigarettes. She took a deep drag, still trying to steady her nerves.

"Are you all right?"

"Yes." Byron exhaled as if she had been revived. "I am now." She continued to warm her hands. After several moments, when her color returned, Byron sighed. "Ah…this could possibly be the first moment I've felt normal since I left Paris."

"Do you miss it terribly?"

"Desperately." Regaining her composure, Byron nonchalantly picked up a weathered piece of driftwood sitting on the mantel. "Tell me…what is it that you do around here?"

"Nothing terribly exciting." Cynara sat on an ottoman by the fireplace with a stillness Byron had rarely seen. She was clad in a rose peignoir, and her skin appeared an alabaster pink as the firelight played against it. "Keep to myself mostly."

"The recluse."

"I enjoy my solitude."

"Have you never traveled?"

"Aren't people pretty much the same everywhere?"

"Fundamentally, perhaps. But in terms of exposure to art, literature, philosophy, culture—all the things that make life worth living—these are hardly found in Cape Cannon."

"Yes. It's quiet." Cynara gracefully brushed a wisp of hair from her forehead. "Removed."

"How can you tolerate the void?" Agitation laced her voice. "The boredom?"

"I have my work."

"Your work?"

"Yes. I sculpt. Paint."

Byron glanced about her, and could not help but mask a condescending grin. "Well then. Where are your canvases?"

"I paint and sculpt for myself."

"A noble endeavor."

"Yes, well, by such an endeavor I am not faced with the burden of compromise."

Byron drew in a sharp breath. "Idealism is a luxury for the young and rich, but it hardly puts food in one's mouth."

"Or bathtub gin, cigarettes and other little pleasures."

"Is it all expatriates you feel so warmly toward or just myself?"

"I have nothing against you—"

Byron's eyes flashed in anger. "I guess I was mistaken. I thought we were getting on."

Cynara inclined her head in acknowledgment.

"But you feel compelled to point out all my shortcomings."

"I hate waste."

Suddenly Byron felt an ephemeral current weave between them—as if Cynara knew Byron without knowing anything about her—but it just as quickly evaporated. She assumed an air of cool disregard. "You know nothing about me."

"I know you are a gifted writer," Cynara said sadly, "who writes about nothing."

Byron turned from the fireplace, then, barely glancing at Cynara, thanked her for her hospitality and walked from the cottage.

* * *

The following morning Byron brooded over a cigarette, sullenly disconnected from the aimless chatter of Ruth, Mark and Miss Falstaff. Ginger listlessly flipped the pages of her magazine, equally disaffected.

"…and I'm not sure what the problem was but"—Ruth lowered her voice to hushed tones—"she was packed off to the cottage. Why, she's practically isolated from the whole world. Like she was a leper."

Byron snapped to attention.

"But why?" Mark asked. "What did she do?"

"Whatever she did is certainly none of our business," sniffed Miss Falstaff.

"Oh, I quite agree," Ruth said, "but still and all, it must have been something quite wretched to have been...well, excommunicated from her own sister's home."

"Ruth, shut up!" Ginger implored.

Ruth's jaw dropped. "Well, really, Ginger, you said yourself you thought it was strange she rarely sets foot in this house—"

"Ruth!" Ginger warned again as Mavis, who had silently entered the room, set down a plate of bacon, and then just as quietly retreated.

Ruth leaned to whisper before Mavis returned, "I'm just telling them what I heard in town. Why, she's her sister. You'd think she'd want to know what people are saying."

"That's really no concern of yours now is it, Miss Barrett?" Charles strode through the entryway, all eyes riveted on his powerful frame as he approached Ruth. "I'd instruct you in the future not to listen to idle gossip. And if you must, it's certainly not the earmark of a lady to repeat it."

Byron saw that his smile came at the cost of every bit of control he had. He then dismissed Ruth as he turned to Mavis, who entered bringing fresh coffee. "Have you finished my packing?"

Mavis smoothed a trembling hand over her skirt and silently shook her head.

"I haven't got all day. My train leaves at two."

Mavis rushed through the kitchen door. Charles cast a stern eye about the room. Satisfied the subject was closed, he followed his wife. A dead silence lay between those present.

"Well," Miss Falstaff finally addressed Mark and Ruth. "There will be no more talk about that poor unfortunate girl." She stood and quickly marched Ruth and Mark from the room.

"What was that all about?" Byron asked Ginger.

"I really couldn't tell you. All I know is Charles turns purple as an eggplant whenever it's mentioned."

* * *

As Byron headed to her room she noticed Mavis inside Charles's room packing for her husband. As she pushed the door open she caught Mavis frantically closing the cap on a flask which she shoved into her skirt pocket. She jumped when she saw Byron, opened her mouth to explain but Byron raised a hand.

"I've been doing a lot of that myself, lately." Byron walked in, closed the door behind her.

"Is there something you need?" Mavis asked, turning pink.

"No. I'm fine. Mavis—"

But Mavis was hurriedly gathering shirts and socks, brushing wild hair from her face. "So much to do…"

"About my father. I want to thank you for taking such good care of him."

Mavis stopped, lifted weary eyes to Byron. "Well, your father's a good man. A very good man."

"I appreciate all that you do for him."

"It's not a burden." She appeared confused and torn between someone paying her any attention and the task at hand. "Not a burden at all."

"Mavis, I don't mean to pry, but what is your sister—"

"His dinner shirt—that's what it was…she continued in a haphazard manner.

"What happened? What is she doing"—Byron lifted her hands in exasperation—"here, of all god-awful places."

But Mavis was a whirling dervish. "And yes…his tie…the blue one…no…yes, the blue tie."

Byron put a hand out to Mavis's arm. At the contact, Mavis closed her eyes and then regarded Byron intently, suddenly absent the frenetic manner. Now her eyes held a warning.

"What is it?"

"Please, Miss Harrington." Mavis's voice trembled. "You seem like a fine person. I suggest you keep to yourself. And not upset your brother."

"My brother," Byron spat.

Mavis's lips tightened and she did not utter another word. And then Byron saw something that shocked her. Although it was clear, for the time being, that Byron would get no further information from her, she recognized their common link: They both hated Charles.

For three days the stony silence filled every waking moment. The fourth day Spencer's secretary patched Lena through.

"I don't want to do this."

Spencer swallowed when she heard the soft hurt in Lena's voice. "I'm sorry, Lena. I...well, what can I say? I've been under a lot of stress? Nothing you haven't heard over and over again. I don't want to make excuses."

"I'm sorry too."

"Lena—" And before Spencer knew it, before she could stop herself she was saying, "I've been doing a lot of thinking. I'm right in the middle of this film and I'm just, well, you know, when I'm in it, I'm inside it all the way. I think I need to...need some space. Take some time to figure out...you know..."

"At least we're in agreement," Lena responded. This Spencer hadn't been prepared for. "That's why I was calling. MacKenzie and I are heading to Hawaii for a few weeks for the marriage vote. I thought it would be a good idea for us to do some thinking while we're apart."

"Oh…okay." Spencer's voice was small. Now it wasn't sounding like such a goddamn good idea after all.

"I'll call you when I get back."

"Sure." Spencer ran a hand over tired eyes. "Okay…well I've got to go. Jerry's been buzzing me for the past five minutes."

"Spencer? I just want to say one more thing. Don't let your fear destroy you." She paused. "I love you."

Another pause. Spencer couldn't say the words. She hung up.

* * *

What Lena didn't know, what Spencer was too humiliated to tell her, was that she had sold *May You* to Jerry. Sold her pride and joy. It had made sense to her at the time. She had rationalized that she was merely putting her own creative needs on hold to help Nina with her film. Nina, who was desperate to have a climactic daydream scene set against the Eiffel Tower.

During lonely, sleepless nights she kept reminding herself they were kindred spirits. Even though Spencer marveled as she watched Nina being the woman she wanted to be—Nina's searing focus as she sat at the editing bay, the sureness, the energy that radiated from her, the absolute disregard she had for the world—they continued to argue over the impossibility of the locations. Nina's tour de force had now become Spencer's crusade, but a budget was a budget.

"Nina, I'm sorry. We just don't have the money to send a unit with your leads to Paris for ten seconds of daydreaming. You're going to have to find somewhere else he can moon over her."

"But Paris is the city of love. It's the metaphor." Nina threw up her hands in anger. "You can't have him daydreaming in Bakersfield, for Christ's sake!"

"Look, you're talking to the ground zero romantic here, but there's no way in hell you can get this shot. This shot *is* your budget."

"There's not a romantic bone in your body," Nina spat contemptuously and walked out of the room.

Not a romantic bone in her body? By mid afternoon Spencer had let a good head of steam roll her into Nina's office. Between the deadening silence from Lena the past few weeks, lack of sleep, and more than a few panic attacks, Spencer was teetering on the precipice. She was primed for battle. She pushed past Nina's protesting assistant and stalked into the room.

"I'll have you know I cut my teeth on romance. I have lived…I have been…I know romance. Okay?" Spencer raised her hands to convince them both, then felt foolish. "I've seen more black and white films than you can count I was—"

"Hey, calm down." Nina walked over to her. Suddenly Nina's cruel mouth and deep set eyes reminded Spencer of Lermontov in *The Red Shoes* as she peered directly into Spencer's own, saying, "It is the small moments that make a movie. Like in life, it is in the small moments where the magic lies."

Spencer cleared her throat "Yes. I…I think…everything's fine. Just fine. We'll…figure something out." And she walked from her, all wobbly-kneed like Doris Day after Clark Gable kissed her in *Teacher's Pet*.

Alarmingly this episode set Spencer to indulging in one of Jerry's whims. He had been calling her for weeks telling her he needed to unload some money, quickly, for "uhum, tax purposes," but it was really to hide resources from his wife who, he had heard through the rumor mill, was planning to divorce him. He wanted to buy out *May You* with the assurance that Spencer could turn around and option it back from him. What if he didn't want to sell it back when all was said and done? But Scarlett wouldn't worry about that now because the funds would pay for Nina's Paris sequence. Her vision would be complete.

Ahhh, the heady responsibility, the gravity of aesthetic. Making *ahhhrt* was a compelling aphrodisiac.

Several nights later, after a sixteen-hour day, Thai take-out cartons littering Spencer's office, she clocked out the department heads, finalizing production boards while Nina tried to figure out what scenes she could cut.

"God, I just don't want to lose my Paris shot." Nina frowned painfully.

"Hans…thanks. Go home to your wife." Spencer ordered the rest of her tired crew to wrap for the evening. She would take care of whatever needed attending to, the cavalier Rosalind Russell *Girl Friday* type.

Alone, they both stared at the papers before them. Spencer glanced up, riveted by Nina's undeniable magnetism. She waited and picked her moment. "What would you say if I told you not to worry about your Paris dream sequence? That it was yours. That I would personally guarantee that you would absolutely get your shot?"

"I'd crawl to your toes and kiss them," Nina winked.

"Jerry's going to buy me out—temporarily mind you—on *May You.*"

"What?" Nina was impressed now.

"We can use the money to set up your scene."

"You'd be willing to do that?"

"I probably should have done it years ago. Maybe if he owns the damn thing he'll have the incentive to get it done. Besides, this way you can get to Paris, first class, and I'll be able to buy it back from him when we have a huge hit on our hands."

Nina stared at Spencer for a full three minutes, maneuvering between a frown and a smile, or maybe they were the same thing. She was difficult to read. Nina was known to prowl around the set, the crew waiting with bated breath, walking on eggshells as she bristled about on all fours. One never knew when she'd pounce on unsuspecting prey. Screaming epithets about incompetency the overworked crew's inability to get simple details straight—leaving Spencer to smooth over ruffled feathers. The next day Nina would arrive with doughnuts and smiles, teasing the gaffer, ruffling the hair of the key grip—joking and chatting as if the day before had never happened. Spencer, too, tiptoed carefully around Nina's fragile auteurship, something deeply familiar about the oft-tread ruts of danger.

"You sure are going to a lot of trouble for this movie."

"I believe in it." Spencer smiled and then turned self-conscious as Nina raised her right eyebrow. "I believe in you."

"I know. I can feel you. I can feel you every minute." Nina moved closer to her. "You're the reason this movie is going to work. I couldn't do it without you."

Spencer melted under the intensity of Nina's words. Not to mention her eyes.

"You are incredible," Nina continued and then moved in for the kill. "You're my very own angel, aren't you?"

Her lips were harsh and hungry, nothing like the soft exploration with Lena. But it was what Spencer needed. This hunger. This need, this blinding excoriation of everything in their path because they were making a movie, making magic, and nothing else mattered.

No tenderness or soft finesse lingered beneath Nina's aggression as they fell to the floor. It was hard, and rough, the carpet burned into Spencer's elbows—but she wanted to hurt, and be hurt. Needed Nina to wipe out the tender brown of Lena's eyes, the soft caresses of Lena's fingers smoothing Spencer's brow after a crazy day.

Underneath her Spencer felt herself fall, shuddering as Nina's mouth tore at her collar, teeth abrading the soft skin at her neck, her hands furiously running themselves up beneath Spencer's shirt, ripping at her bra. Nina's hands bruised her skin. Wrenching Spencer's arms behind her back, Nina bit a trail of lust over her body, up to Spencer's breast. Gasping at the pain from Nina's teeth upon her nipples, Spencer tried to push Nina from her.

"You wanted this." Nina's hand grasped the nape of Spencer's neck. "Didn't you…isn't this what you wanted?"

"Y…yes." Spencer could not tell if fear or arousal pushed her forward as she met Nina's mouth, lunging angry kisses into the deep of her, wiping everything away, the sensations obliterating Spencer's emptiness, her desperation to be inside Nina's dream to make her own come true.

Nina's hand found her pants. No taunting play, no delicate teasing —just the brutal business at hand, rubbing Spencer's clitoris too hard, thrusting fingers into her, a rampage of invasion. Spencer was hers. They both knew it.

Nina took her, angrily, hungrily, in frustration, in joy— everything that happened on the set those first couple of weeks was reflected in their mating. Spencer too wanted Nina, but not in the same way. She wanted to please her, to make her come, make her come hard and good and trembling and have to choke Spencer's name through clenched teeth.

Afterward, Spencer never understood how she made it through so many sleepless nights. Her panic attacks returned with a vengeance. She knew they were from the double-edged sword of guilt and stress. Drinking double mochas to make it through all-nighters. She constantly borrowed Nina's cigarettes, even though she had promised MacKenzie she would quit. She never knew if the sex she and Nina had before the crew got there in the morning, or during the lunch break, or even late at night, when their bodies twitched from exhaustion, was what held her together or what would ultimately break her.

* * *

The last morning they were shooting, Spencer woke and saw Nina sleeping beside her. The thought suddenly occurred to her that Nina was a stranger. She did not feel like she was waking next to her lover. She stared at the flared nostrils, angry even in sleep. Was she even really attracted to this woman? She touched Nina's chin, lightly, as if to make sure she was real, saw the faint edge of bitter lines at her mouth, looked at her muscular breasts and became desperate at how unmoved she really was. She shook her head. She could not afford to think Nina's charm had run out. Not after all she had given up. Not after Nina had wooed her with such cinematic ardor.

In a panic she woke her. She needed to see Nina's eyes. If she saw the light in her eyes, then she would feel...

"What?" Nina grumbled.

The dark brown eyes, squinty and irritable—the intense and angry demeanor she had once found so fascinating—now vaguely hinted at the bitterness in Jonathon's eyes. The crook of Nina's mouth now merely reminded her of Jonathon's sneer. The fear of Nina's angry tirades produced the same inner quiver; the sight of thick fingers reminded her of something she cared not to remember so she made sure never to look at them. *Rejection of the physicality that lies in blacked over memories...*

"Nothing...nothing." Spencer's heart was pumping her fully awake now. "Go back to sleep."

As Nina closed her eyes she slapped a hand out on the pillow. "Come back later and we'll fuck before dailies."

His hand slaps his lap.

Spencer withdrew, walking backwards as if she was afraid Nina might get her if she dared turn away. She gathered her clothes quickly and rushed to the bathroom. She sat, naked, trembling on the toilet, threw her shirt around her.

Sit next to me.

Heart pummeling in her ears now. Dizzy. Throat tightening.

I said sit next to me, goddamnit.

God, don't let me lose it, Spencer prayed as she wrapped her arms about herself, holding tightly. No. No. It couldn't be. How could she not see it? No...she was cracking because she had been working too hard—too far inside the art—becoming so lost inside her obsession that it was destroying her.

Sitting in the living room. He's over there. I don't dare look his way...begin to pull away inside myself.

Of course it was all bullshit. It had nothing to do with Nina's goddamn movie. It had...Jesus, she could barely stand to hear the words in her own mind—it had nothing to do with *May You*. Nina was Jonathon, right down to his thin-lipped sneer, jagged teeth and sinister eyes...and her repulsion, her acute discomfort with Nina's scent—*his scent*—for she smelled distinctly male, the bitter hard smell of men...

"I'll...I'll go get you another beer"—desperate not to sit next to him. Please don't make me...

Spencer vomited into the toilet.

"Sit next to me." The words crawl up the back of my spine...

"Sit next to me, goddamnit!" The covert innuendo...the hand inching forward...ever forward.

"I...I want to stay in the rocking chair."

"I said, get over here."

I pretend he hasn't said a word—

"One." Counting to one and a half, two—because he can and we are alone. My mother has long since stopped protecting me.

It is the night of the election returns. Nixon is winning. I feel our aloneness as I train my vision on the family portrait hung above our fire- place, thinking of The Waltons, Rockwellian dinner settings...Jilly Bean chewing her milk, awaiting her punishment.

I wait until he hits two and a half. Shuffle my feet, hesitate, glancing toward the door that leads out of the den, wondering if I dare try to make my escape—

"NOW!" His voice booms.

I sit on the couch.

"*Over here,*" *he demands. I inch over until he grabs me by the arm and slaps my body against his. Fetid and overbearing. The smells of his maleness, a clammy stench born of his own particular pungent odor, an oily dense concoction of BO, Integrin, and the rank stench of beer. I cringe at his smell, even as I do today when I see Jonathon, I must brace myself for the assault on my senses. "Please...I don't want to..."—I plead with him—"I...I'll get you another beer?" As if I could bargain my way out of our destiny.*

Then it begins.

The hands. Thick undefined fingers, calcium-flecked nails disappear as they slip into his jeans, always unbuttoned at the top...his hand inches down the inside to his thickening twisted desire—the same heavy hand on my shoulder, my breathing a tensed action as I see the movement of the lump in his pants. My throat is so tight I can't swallow as I watch his hand rub up against it, everything covert, nothing can be seen and if nothing can be seen, then it didn't happen, right?

Jonathon touching himself, his other arm slithering across my shoulders, his hand on my front, his hand in my shirt. And then the unthinkable as his fingers pry beneath my bra and his hands brand the tender flesh of my breasts.

The tyranny of the unexpected.

I never heard him utter the word Three.

I sit, enduring, and it goes black.

Byron scrambled through her trunk, tossing clothes and books out of the way. There it was. She stuck the object beneath her arm, and threw on her cloak.

She purposely strode from Bay Cliff to the worn path that led up the brambly hillside, pulling her cape close to protect her from the squalling winds. As she neared Cynara's cottage she saw smoke from the chimney. Heartened, she forged ahead, but when she got there, the door was ajar.

"Cynara? It's me, Byron."

She rapped one more time. As she pushed the door slightly forward, she saw a blazing fire and before it, Cynara, bent over in a strange rocking motion. And then, as she shifted to the side, revealing the work before her, Byron caught her breath.

Hands delicately traced the lines of a torso, kneading gently as they pressed into the smooth skin of the stomach…skimming hands tenderly caressed a ribcage, lingering at a tendon-strained neck… a fingertip lovingly graced a nipple. Byron's breathing quickened as she watched Cynara run her hands over and fully cup the breasts, her own palms tingling as she watched Cynara work the clay before her.

Byron slowly moved forward, transfixed by the extraordinary work in progress, the still wet clay forming the shape of a reclining female nude. An easel before the fireplace held sketch drawings of the figure, simple lines of a woman in sensual motion. Several variations on the same theme littered the floor, all the same strong woman of action, the body flowing, almost crusading off the paper.

"What are you doing here?" Cynara's terse voice rang out.

Byron's eyes radiated appreciation as she reached out, as if to touch a living image. "I owe you an apology," she murmured still mesmerized.

"What do you want?"

She was taken back by Cynara's anger, but again turned to the work in awe.

"Please." Byron retrieved the book from her cloak. "A peace offering."

Cynara hesitated.

"I could not have imagined…" Byron indicated the work before her, but Cynara quickly gathered up her drawings, and drew a cloth over the sculpture.

"Please don't. It's exquisite."

Cynara stood, not facing Byron. "It is not for viewing."

Byron walked up to her, gently laid a hand on her forearm. "What a rare gift you have. So clean, direct—honest."

Byron's tone was void of sarcasm or ridicule and though Cynara had stiffened at her touch, her hand remained on Cynara's arm as their eyes met. Like the night before, a sweet tension passed between them.

"I know how terrifying it is to have someone see your soul." Byron still did not take her eyes from Cynara's. "I want you to have this."

Cynara considered Byron's gift, a book, *The Parisian Artist*.

After a long moment Cynara smiled. Byron thought how the simple gesture transformed her face, how truly striking this woman was, cast out in the isolation of the woods. She belonged in a fairytale, so incongruous were her beauty and her environment. Or perhaps this was precisely where she belonged.

Cynara bowed her head in acknowledgment, and then said so low it was almost a whisper, "I guess I can accept this."

* * *

It was with no particular design, save the desire to share their hours with like-minded souls, that Byron and Cynara found themselves spending a great deal of time with each other. At first they might be found at breakfast in the dining room discussing the Oregon coast, its history and industry, and it would be some time before they realized that everyone else had left. Then, as they tentatively explored a friendship, they began to discuss other interests; an item in the newspaper, a book they had both read, a memorable line of poetry.

The initial shyness they had felt with each other soon abated as they began to take long, hearty walks together. Cynara shared her past with Byron, speaking of her father, a Presbyterian minister who had moved his family to Boston from England. How his and his prim wife's zeal for missionary work left Cynara and Mavis parentless from a tragic mining accident when they traveled to West Virginia. Mavis had raised her single-handedly from the time Cynara was seven until they moved to Oregon to live with their father's sister. It was during this time that Mavis sent her sister back east to Ballard's School for Enterprising Women in Boston.

"Its sole goal seemed intent upon finding the most enterprising manner in which to catch a husband," Cynara teased.

"But you mentioned you went to school in New York?"

"Yes, afterward I went to the University and studied art."

"When were you there?"

"From late nineteen-eighteen to twenty-one."

Byron laughed. "Nearly the same time I was there."

"Did you go to school there?"

"In a manner of speaking." Byron bent to retrieve a shell then diverted the conversation by leading Cynara up a path where they explored the wildlife.

It finally made sense to Byron why Cynara seemed to have dropped from the sky. Having lived in New York at roughly the same time, they found themselves eagerly discussing the restaurants, theaters—which plays they had attended and what they thought about them.

Cynara began inviting Byron to take tea at her cottage. Even began to work while Byron read. And as Cynara sculpted or moved her brush against canvas, the fire snapping in the background, they began to discuss various artists who made an impact on their own work and lives. Cynara spoke with authority about the deco work of architect Eileen Gray, the constructivist influence of painter Alexandra Exter, the portraits of Romaine Brooks, and Berenice Abbott's photography. Byron marveled at Cynara's knowledge of the cultural landscape and they argued, much as she had with Rabbit, over the modernist movement and what it meant to the arts.

They heartily disagreed about Picasso, Byron taking the stand she always did, that while she found his work "interesting, it is so esoteric—much like fractured panes...it leaves me cold."

"But do you not understand an artist's work is an extension of her inner self? We cannot help but to put to canvas what comes from within. It is what we are compelled to do."

"I guess I'm hopelessly old-fashioned. For me Picasso's work is disconcerting."

"Perhaps he sees the world as helplessly disconnected. It is only because we are told that things work and move along seamlessly that we believe it is true. What about all the instances when we feel disenfranchised? When we feel broken, our lives oftentimes not as 'whole' as desired."

"Are you speaking of yourself or Picasso?"

"I'm speaking from an artist's point of view. Surely you have felt like one of Picasso's paintings at times."

Byron pursed her lips, nodded in concession.

Every day they found new ways to spend more time together. Much to Charles's surprise, Cynara began taking an occasional meal in the dining room, where she and Byron were again often the last to leave. They spent late evenings taking turns reading to Francis. On days that held fair weather, they rode, Cynara on her palomino, and Byron on her father's aging sorrel. Hooves pummeled the sand, spraying fine silt behind them as the horses plunged against the ebbing waves, racing wildly down the beach, free as the birds above them, celebration in every movement.

They packed picnic lunches and hiked to Devil's Point—the haunt of Byron's childhood—where they were sprayed by the flying mist of the ocean as it roared against the jagged cliffs. From there they climbed up to the clearing where the rush of the water was less noisy, and they could talk as they ate their sandwiches and drank their wine.

One such afternoon, Byron leaned back, sated from their lunch, and shut her eyes.

"Tell me about Paris," Cynara asked sleepily, then teased, "Is it true it is filled with the drunk and disorderly?—'Opium dens where a person goes stark raving mad'?"

Byron laughed, then stopped, thinking of Marie. "Well, there is a bit of that, yes. But mostly it's...it's simply amazing." She sat up and enthusiastically began to share her Paris with Cynara. Shakespeare & Company, Natalie's and Gertrude's salons, the great works of her fellow female artists and how they were making a difference.

"It is as if the greatest women from all around the world—painters, photographers, writers—were all drawn by magnet to the only city that could answer their dreams. It seems no matter what you want to do, or try, you can succeed if you roll up your sleeves."

"And how is that? Because there is more freedom?"

"Yes, I suppose. But you would be surprised. Even though there are less social constraints put upon women, I think many of them are influenced by their heavy-handed Victorian predecessors. Actually, I have found the women in my circles to be primarily focused on their work. Look at Sylvia Beach—she practically bankrupted her own bookstore to publish Joyce."

"But that sounds a bit like the old view of women's work."

"How do you mean?"

"Well, it sounds like this Sylvia Beach subverted her own needs to meet those of Mr. Joyce."

Byron chuckled. "Sylvia was always the first to say she would not suggest another do as she did—it would be 'the death of publishing.' But in her mind, her sacrifices were equal to the brilliance of his masterpiece. I don't think she much considered the gender of the creator."

"It just happened to be male," Cynara countered. "It sounds too familiar."

"Are you thinking of your sister?"

"Yes. I suppose I am." Cynara shook her head and briefly shut her eyes.

"What happened?"

"Another tale of sacrifice. A lot of it was for me. I'm sure I was quite a burden to her. I was very curious as a child—always wanting what I couldn't have. I don't know how she did it, but she managed to send me to school. And left nothing for herself. Poor Mavis. She has never thought of herself as beautiful or intelligent, even when she was both. Back then, her eyes were soft and full of life, and they would shine with adventure when she read to me from the latest Jack London stories—"

"Adventure?" Byron laughed. "That's hardly a term I would apply to your sister."

"I tell you, Mavis is a shadow of the woman she once was." Cynara sat in silence, then finally said, "I love my sister very much, but I find…well, it's difficult to speak with her. She seems so frightened. When I approach her she spurns me."

"I was surprised to find you were sisters. You couldn't be more different."

"I could say the same for you and your brother."

"Yes, well…" Byron unconsciously tugged the skin at her forearm with her fingers. "How did they meet?"

"One day Charles and your father visited my aunt's shop to pick up supplies for Bay Cliff. Shortly thereafter, my sister's letters to me became uncharacteristically florid. She spent pages going on about this gentleman who had begun calling on her." Cynara sighed, twisting a piece of sea grass forcefully against her fingers. "It was shortly after they met that our money ran out and I was forced to leave school and return to live with my sister. From her descriptions I thought I would be meeting Heathcliff. When I met Charles I saw through his façade within minutes. I tried in a roundabout way to warn her that she was unused to flattery and that his words were nothing more than that—it was his actions that she should examine. How he often forgot she was in the room, how he rarely pulled out her chair at the dining table, how he watched me as if I were an animal he might hunt down some day…"

"Cynara—" Byron sat up abruptly.

"No, he never made an advance. I think he knew better. No, your brother—" Cynara stopped. "Quite frankly, your brother charmed her, seduced her into believing he was one of those dark-haired, misunderstood heroes from one of her novels."

"I'm sorry." Byron reached to touch her hand.

"She took my criticisms to heart." Cynara stared at the ocean. "My sister, whom I love more than anyone, wouldn't speak to me for months. She could barely share the same table with me, which afforded your brother no end of delight."

"So he played you off one against the other?"

"Yes." Cynara averted her eyes. "But after a time—after they were married—Mavis grew more nervous and tense. Though we never discussed it, I could see she had discovered for herself who Charles really was."

A long sigh followed as Cynara brushed the mangled grass from her skirt. "I shouldn't say these things if I didn't believe that you share my views."

"How well I share your views." Byron's voice cracked. She stood to pack up their picnic.

"Byron, are you offended? I'm sorry. I just assumed you cared as little for your brother as I do."

"I'm sure quite less."

They didn't broach the subject of their families again. Byron found herself regularly heading to Cynara's cottage, where she would sit reading a book while Cynara worked. Cynara, raptly attentive, would lovingly mold her sculpture, tender beads of sweat forming above her lip as she wiped a stray hair with a forearm, smudging her cheek with clay dust. It reminded Byron of her early days in Paris, where nothing, not food, hunger, daylight or a diminishing candle took her from her muse. As if sensing Byron's gaze, Cynara's mouth would settle into a grin and she would turn to her deliberately and catch Byron's eyes; entrancing, entreating, softly mysterious, then she would return to her work. Or as they sat in the open air, she might see Cynara's exquisite profile, as she did that first day, but now she saw another part of Cynara, the gentle, more vulnerable woman as she revealed eyes grown soft and misted.

As the sun beat into their bodies one particularly warm afternoon, the horses grazing lazily in a meadow behind them, the two new friends lay back on the earth staring at clouds and laughing as they described what they saw. Cynara's hand brushed against Byron's, and she did not bother to move it.

"Why have you come here?" she asked softly.

"For my father, of course."

"No. There is more to it than that."

"I thought…I—"

"To disrupt my life." Cynara smiled, teasing.

"I thought I might find something here for my writing."

"And have you?"

They turned to each other, their eyes meeting for a long moment. Then Cynara jumped up and challenged Byron to race across the flatlands.

Hooves pounded against the ocean's edge, as they galloped full out. Byron rode as much to escape her demons as she did to win the race. But then she saw the laughter in Cynara's eyes, hair flying madly behind her, the joy in her movement, and Byron forgot that she was even at Bay Cliff.

They walked the horses back to the stables to cool them down and then slowly ambled toward the house. It was late afternoon and everyone seemed to be gone or resting. They both lounged on the settee, lazy and cozy in the amber sunlight. Byron leaned back, stretched her feet out on the ottoman. Cynara smiled dreamily.

"What is it?"

"Hmmm?" Cynara turned to her and as she did her smile faded, her penetrating gaze growing more serious. Byron abruptly leaned forward to extract a cigarette from her case, offering one to Cynara.

"Actually I was thinking that you didn't answer. About your work," Cynara remarked.

"I…well, I've been dry as of late."

"Does that happen to you often?"

"From time to time. Hemingway said he would feel 'a death loneliness' at the end of a wasted day. I've always thought that was a perfect description. And I'm afraid I've had more than my fair share of days slipping by recently without a hint of meaning."

"Why, do you suppose?"

"Because my work has become stale."

"You're no longer enticed by your detective?"

"One day I was at Gertrude's salon and she pulled me aside and warned me in a stern voice, that once a writer compromised, she could only follow in one direction. She is a purist, mind you, and believes that one's work is forever changed once one has an audience."

"If that were the case I suppose there would be nothing whatsoever to read."

"Believe me, I don't think there is anyone who desires to be published more than Miss Stein."

"Her words are true for me, I suppose. Sometimes I wonder if I am a coward. I know that I would see my work differently if I were to put it out on display—fussing about what people thought, and then beginning to see it through their eyes. Now I need only to rely upon my own."

"Well you certainly live what she preaches. Your life and work are bound together by the virtue of integrity. My work, however, has become tarnished by its very lack of integrity."

"Byron," Cynara said softly, "I think you're taking this to the extreme. The fact of the matter is, the Venable mysteries are very entertaining."

"Entertaining," Byron snorted. "When I wrote poetry my life was my work. But over the years, my work has become my life. A life of the bon vivant. I play at being a writer. Write for an audience that has no idea as to how I really feel about anything. But they pay for the *me* they think they are getting. It's laughable. I don't know if I even have the ability anymore to write one pure sentence. One word of truth."

Cynara's hand brushed Byron's arm in sympathy.

"Dear me, I sound like one of Dorothy's dreaded plays." Byron gave a cavalier shrug. "All self-pity and sopping rot."

"You're being entirely too hard on yourself. And I shouldn't have been so hard on you either. I'm sorry, Byron."

"Don't be."

"I had no right."

"Certainly you did—to speak the truth."

Cynara smiled empathetically. She nonchalantly pulled a small twig that had woven itself into Byron's hair. As her hand trailed Byron's collar, the back of it grazed Byron's cheek.

Byron's eyes closed at the contact. When she opened them, Cynara's languid eyes seemed a brilliant blue as they peered into Byron's. Suddenly they seemed very close—a heartbeat away. Cynara leaned to her. Byron's heart thudded in her ears, her cheeks flushing as she found herself closing the distance between them.

A clamoring of footsteps broke the tension.

Charles and Mavis walked in from the entryway as Cynara quickly smoothed her riding pants, and Byron awkwardly lit a cigarette.

"I thought I heard voices in here." Charles cocked an eyebrow as he appraised Cynara and then his sister. "I should have known it was the two of you."

"Mavis," Byron greeted her.

"Why don't you fetch our two adventurers some tea," Charles ordered his wife and though Mavis appeared wary of leaving them, she quickly turned to attend to his demands.

"That's all right," Cynara said, then stood. "I was just about to leave."

"Oh, were you?" Charles spoke as if he didn't believe her. "What have you two been up to today? You seem inseparable these past weeks. Off on day-long explorations, and God knows what else…"

Charles moved to the hearth, lit a cigarette and tossed the match in the fireplace.

"What we do with our time is hardly your affair," Cynara tersely answered.

"I hope it stays that way."

Confused, Byron glanced from her brother to Cynara, both of them tense and combative.

"Very well." Charles exhaled then asked without conviction, "Will you be joining us for dinner?"

"No."

Cynara inclined her head toward Byron, then made her exit.

When Charles turned to his sister, a smirk punctuated the sick amusement residing in his eyes.

Jonathon. The name cloaks its tentacles about me, wrapping me in a final caress...To this day I cannot look at his hands without feeling them on my breast.

Was that the moment I began to tiptoe out of my frame—the moment Jonathon put his thick clammy hand on my twelve-year-old breast? The rocking chair where I had sat innumerable evenings on Jonathon's lap— Mom walking in, her voice pitched high in accusation—"You are too old to be sitting on your uncle's lap!" "She's fine, Elise. Let her be." And in the desire to please, I would wrap my arms around Jonathon's neck, and kiss the stubble of his cheeks. He had grown the mustache that year, and he became my Clark Gable, my first tenderhearted crush. How could I know that my slender pubescent body, sitting against him night after night, would eventually provoke moments of terror? Was it my fault? Don't we all ask that, in twelve-year-old voices choked out of our thirty-eight-year-old bodies?

There is no escape from the haunting of molestation. No matter how well you think you've dealt with it, therapized it, sanitized it. It rushes up against your skin when least expected.

"I don't even know what to call this," I explain to Therapist. *"He didn't rape me, after all. It…it could have been a helluva lot worse—"*

"Don't you dare minimize this." The first time Therapist raises her voice. *"It doesn't matter the extent of the crime when you're dealing with covert abuse. The fact is, twenty-five years later, you still tremble every time you mention his name, you still can't stand the smell of him, you still can't bear to see his hands. He didn't have to go to jail for the crime for you to be imprisoned all these years."*

She's right. I still see those crude fingers slip into his pants, his dough-boy stomach, the tendrils of hair that led…there…

All this time I have searched with the battered child's ache for approval in people, places and things. Never in myself. And now that I'm at the end, I can relate to him far more than I'd like. I know how difficult it is to negotiate the real world. He too, has to live with his choices. Fate makes strange bedfellows and we rarely choose our demons. Maybe, someday, he will get sober, look back, and make amends in his own way. Maybe he won't. He wasn't inherently mean. Just bitter. For having his hopes diminished, for never having become the writer, the Holden Caulfield of his dreams.

* * *

The path was finally complete and overall I was pretty impressed by my landscaping abilities, the symmetry to the design. I had fully lined it with ocean stones and run heavy cord up and down both sides of the trail for extra safety. The ice plant was thriving quite nicely, edging a blanket of purple against the verdant green. The swinging bench had been set precisely to take the best advantage of the sunset and the "caped lady" rock, and if one so desired they could make their way further down and be rewarded with two miles of exquisite private beach.

My beach. I surveyed the vast expanse and walked for a half an hour exploring, then returned to the bottom of my trail and smoked a cigarette, enjoying my now familiar view.

I read somewhere that it takes twenty-one days of consistent behavior to make something a habit. Or to break it. That it becomes less difficult to abstain from smoking or drinking after those three weeks. I guess it has something to do with the body's natural rhythms. On some level, I felt as if I had lived in the seaside cottage forever, that being a hermit was my most natural state—that being alone and isolated was the career to which I was best suited. Maybe it was because I was closest to what resonated with my soul, and I had only thought I wanted all those other things. The making of a career, movies, lights, action. Success.

Didn't I still want those things?

Don't I still want to make movies? Do I even have what it takes anymore?

Alas, personal integrity is like mercury, ever shifting, mercilessly unstickable. You try to have the right stuff. Be a mensch. How easy is it to give an inch that quickly becomes the most insidious mile? How softly we ease into non-confrontation, dunk ourselves below the murky plane of shame, until we're covered in "compromise."

Make excuses. Don't offend. Don't dare say how we feel. Machiavellian strategies. Good cop, bad cop. White lies—black lies. We betray and are betrayed.

But without compromise, how do we succeed? Even the small infractions that drift like single snowflakes—melting instantaneously in the palm of your hand and quickly brushed away—gather and become the proverbial snowball rolling down the mountain at breakneck speed.

And in the end all that compromise made me...made me what?

Over the years all those concessions chip away at your spirit—a slow erosion until you stare at your reflection in the mirror and like suddenly seeing a gray hair or a faint edged wrinkle, you are no longer the person you set out to be. And, finally, you no longer hope because you have lost the ability to hope—always waiting for the next shoe to drop. When you come to this conclusion you have but two choices. Fight like hell, or resign gracefully.

"Why is it that you write as a man?" Cynara asked one late afternoon as she and Byron walked along the tide's edge.

Byron smiled wistfully. "Because I thought a woman had no voice."

"But surely we do. Look at Willa Cather, Edna St. Vincent Millay—Edna Ferber."

"Yes. When we write in a style which pleases our publishers and doesn't ruffle feathers. Believe me, some of us cannot say what we wish."

"Did you ever enjoy writing your mysteries?"

"I suppose in the beginning." Byron straightened her shoulders, growing uncomfortable with the interrogation.

"You seem so weary," Cynara said. "You pretend at gaiety—as if you haven't a care in the world but —"

"Ah, yes, the cynic that—what was it you said?"

"Please forgive me. I spoke out of turn. But you seem—I don't know, now that I've had an opportunity to get to know you, much more serious than your books. And it's curious that you haven't written something in keeping with who you are."

"And how do you know that I haven't?"

Before Cynara could answer Byron began to walk up the stairs to Bay Cliff. They both heard music and wild laughter from inside. Byron turned to Cynara, baffled.

Pandemonium broke loose as they walked through the entryway. Jake pounded out ragtime on the old upright, Ginger clapped her hands to the music and Ruth and Mark laughed in uncontrolled excitement. And there was Rabbit lifting a flask to his lips. Her Rabbit. How desperately she had missed him. Only he could bring life to this sorry lot, Byron thought, as her face broke out in a joyful grin.

The music stopped. Byron drew Cynara into the room. Jake turned around, as did everyone else, while Rabbit approached dramatically and mocked a sweeping bow.

"Darling, how well you've kept in the frigid isolation of the great Northwest." Eyes full of mischief, he bent to kiss her hand, and then swallowed her in an all-encompassing embrace.

"We couldn't help ourselves." Jake came up behind him. "Hope you don't mind, Byron, but we missed you terribly. Besides, New York was becoming a bore—"

"—and we were simply starving for good company. Speaking of which"—Rabbit made an about-face to Cynara—"whom have we here?"

"Parnell Walbrook, better known as Rabbit, and Jake Wilmarth, allow me to introduce Cynara—"

"—'And I was desolate and sick of an old passion.'" Rabbit closed his eyes in rapture. " 'Yea, I was desolate and bowed my head: I have been faithful to thee, Cynara, in my own fashion.' *Exquis!*"

Cynara grinned, enchanted by Rabbit's performance.

"You made no mention your dreary landscape was filled with a shining star," Rabbit chided Byron.

"I see you've met my fellow boarders, then."

"A rare delight, I assure you." He winked at Byron.

"So, what are you really doing here?"

"Dear Lord, Byron, is that any way to treat your Rabbit, who has just endured three thousand miles of haggy, public transport?" Rabbit ushered Byron and Cynara into the sitting room. "Besides, rumor had it I was getting into a bit of a scrape."

Beneath the glib humor Byron could detect a trace of seriousness. But the gravity evaporated as Rabbit bowed to both Byron and Cynara, then swept Ginger to the center of the room.

"Hit it, Jake," Rabbit commanded.

Jake's fingers flew across the keys.

Rabbit whirled Ginger across the floor and the unusual sounds of laughter and life abounded in and around the walls of Bay Cliff. Byron caught the edge of movement at the entryway and realized Mavis watched from the shadows, a hand to her heart, her shoulders lifting and falling with an imperceptible sigh. Before Byron could fetch her, she turned and disappeared.

* * *

The next morning as Byron was finishing breakfast, Rabbit entered with a magazine tucked beneath his arm.

"Good morning, darling." He leaned over Byron and placed a kiss on her forehead. "I've been positively bereft without you."

Byron squeezed his hand and he then walked to the buffet, poured coffee. "Spare a smoke, old girl?"

Byron removed her cigarette case and slid it across the table as Rabbit tossed *The New Yorker* magazine to Byron. "I thought you might be homesick."

"More than you know."

"I think I have a fair idea." Rabbit cocked a brow as he assessed his surroundings.

"How did you manage to get away from that publisher of yours?"

"Well, old girl, to tell you the truth, Ross was a bit of a prig about the whole thing."

Byron could tell by Rabbit's tone that something was amiss, but as Cynara entered, clad in riding togs, he instantly transformed into his familiar nonchalance. "But I said, 'Ross, things are simply too fascinating in New York.' "

Cynara poured coffee as Rabbit continued. " 'There are simply too many trying plays, insightful books, and endless parties—far too much amok. We need something refreshingly banal for my Critic's Corner.' "

"I doubt your readers would enjoy our unassuming lives here in the west," Cynara observed.

"Then I shall have to put my imagination to the task. After all, I subscribe to Benchley's Elevated Eyebrow School of Journalism, which, when applied, has nothing whatsoever to do with the telling of a story—as long as it's penned while in evening attire."

"I see. Good manners camouflage bad taste."

"Ahh…" Rabbit smiled in approval.

"'To virtue, beauty, ne'er to find
In this wasteland of briny thought
Trips a maiden, fair and kind…
he raised his flask to Cynara,
'Except for when she's not.'"

Cynara accepted the double-edged praise with a smile.

"Darling, do tell me what you've been up to lately." He directed his speech to Byron, although his delighted eyes remained on Cynara.

"Decidedly, not much."

"But what about our dear lad, Venable? I hear through the grapevine that Monsieur Knopf grows restless waiting to deluge the masses with another tale of mysterious glamour."

Byron hedged, glancing from Rabbit to Cynara, who seemed quite intrigued by what she had to say on the subject. "I'm about up to here with Nate Venable."

"Courage darling, after all he does pay the rent."

Byron exhaled distastefully, stood up, and discarded her napkin upon the table, concluding the conversation. "Will you join us on our ride, Rabbit?"

"Dear Lord, no. It is far too early for physical activity."

* * *

Byron stood before the panoramic view offered by the sitting room bay window on the first floor, preparing to light her cigarette when a match flared from behind.

"May I join you?" Edward Dutton asked as he held the flame before her.

"Please do."

"Quite a group you have on your hands."

"Now that's an understatement."

"I'm familiar with Mr. Walbrook. Very witty," Dutton said. "I read his preview of *A Farewell to Arms*. I thought it was brilliant. He seemed to really understand the writer."

"More than you know," Byron grinned. "I've known Rabbit for years and he's truly a champion of the poor misguided artist, I being chief among his poor misguided artists."

"He is a very entertaining chap. I believe Cynara's quite enchanted by him."

Byron glanced at him, slightly perplexed. "Cynara?"

"Yes. Cynara," he said with reverence. "Her name sort of rolls off the tongue. Beautiful, isn't it?"

Byron's mouth curled to a smile. Now she understood. The good doctor was smitten.

"Yes. Do you know her well?"

Edward considered a moment. "Can anyone know Cynara well?"

They stood in companionable silence together.

"I rather think not," Byron concluded.

* * *

As Rabbit and Byron walked the tide, Byron could see that her dear friend was in a rare mode of serious consternation.

"Tell me what is bothering you, Rabbit," Byron asked as they walked along the tide.

"Silly goose, it's but naught," he said with an annoying wave of his hand.

She stopped him. "Rabbit, it's me."

"I've been found out," Rabbit said in a voice barely above a whisper.

"What?"

"It would be laughable if I could explain."

"But surely Ross will vouch for you."

"That's the rub of it." Rabbit tucked Byron's hand in his arm, continued to stroll.

"But he must certainly know about you by now."

"Of course he does. But he's been...well, he's being so difficult about it all. I suppose it's one thing for his key critic to be 'one of those flamboyant types' in Paris, but quite another walking the streets of New York, attending the plays with Park Avenue's *beau monde*. So I thought, might as well get out of town for a bit. Persona non grata and all that."

"But what happened?"

"I attended a play—an atrocious play at that—and over my flask and the two hours it took to put everyone to sleep in the theater, I fell tipsily in love with the hero. Dottie was absolutely flummoxed as to how the production ever got put up until we discovered quite by coincidence that the lead actor's wife had financed it as sort of a vanity production for her husband."

"Oh please, Rabbit, not the husband."

"Well, we had to celebrate that we'd survived the damn affair, so Dottie and I met up with Benchley and the gang at Frankie's, and wouldn't you know it—there sat my hero two tables down. He was such a darling. He told me they were celebrating *before* the reviews came out. We all knew it was going to be positively crucified. So I wrote an unabashed love affair of a critique—gushing in the purplest of prose mind you—extolling Albert Farnsworth as a thespian of such indisputable genius that they might as well close the show that very night because it was a performance that could never be topped."

"Let me guess."

"Yes, the show closed."

"And Ross let you have it for being the only rave review in town."

"Not to mention for consorting with the fair-haired Albert. Who knew his wife was one of *Vanity Fair's* new benefactresses?"

"I'll say one thing for you, Rabbit. When you blunder you do it up right."

"Yes, she called Ross, said she wanted that 'such and such' of a critic fired. Said I had made them the laughingstock of New York."

"She was right."

"I know. I just wanted Albert to have one review he could frame and put in his dressing room for all the ingénues to tremble over."

"So what are you going to do?"

"Look. I'd rather have him run me out of town and keep my reputation intact, than for all of New York to find out my propensity for the fairer sex is…quite less than fair."

"But you can't simply run away from it, Rabbit."

Rabbit tossed her a sly look. "Why, dear girl, when it's what I do best?"

* * *

The sounds of "hoofing" echoed through the boarding house as Rabbit, Ginger, Ruth and Mark bobbed to a frenetic Charleston. Byron laughed as she watched the four of them dance, all out of step with one another.

She proffered a flask to Jake and as he continued to play with one hand and swig with the other, Byron caught Mavis, again watching from beyond the archway. She walked to her, gently retrieved the folded laundry from Mavis's hands and set it on the dining room table.

"Everyone deserves a few moments of rest."

Mavis resisted, as afraid of the festivities as she was drawn to them.

"Come along," Byron whispered to her very gently as she led her into the sitting room. She grabbed a teacup from the setting and poured a hefty shot from her flask, then cajoled Mavis into acceptance. Mavis took a sip, visibly relieved.

"Oh." Her face lit delightedly. "It's very good."

Edward and Cynara entered the room at that moment. Cynara and Mavis exchanged hesitant glances.

"I thought your sister needed a break," Byron said.

Cynara walked to her sister and held out her arms. Mavis's stiff body leaned delicately into the embrace. Byron handed the flask and two tumblers to Edward who poured for them.

Cynara put a gentle palm to Mavis's face. "I'm so happy that you're joining us."

As the hours passed, the noise grew louder and more raucous. Rabbit flung Ruth from his hands and pulled the graceful and sanguine Ginger into her place.

"This girl's a natural!" he shouted to the onlookers.

As Ginger danced it was clear she was the only one among them who possessed a shred of talent. Her eyes blazed brightly with dreams long dormant, while her strawberry blonde hair tumbled in rhythm with her movements. Rabbit darted a hand out to Ruth, pins falling from her loosened hair as she stumbled in with gusto.

Byron turned to watch Cynara with her sister, who was clearly enjoying herself now. When Cynara lifted her eyes to Byron they were filled with gratitude.

"This is wonderful! It's simply grand!" Ruth sang out as Rabbit twirled her to Mark, who awkwardly took the lead, while Ruth flopped over his arms, dangling an empty teacup. "May I have some more? Yes…swi…swimmingly graaaaand—"

"Lilian!" Charles's voice thundered from the entry. "Mavis!"

All heads lazily spun to Charles, who loomed menacingly as he glared at the merry-makers. "What in blazes is going on here?!"

The music faded. Ruth belched loudly. Charles approached Mavis, grabbed the teacup from her hand and sniffed it.

"What in God's name are you doing?" His eyes burned into her until Mavis jumped and scurried from the room.

"May I have a word with you?" Charles addressed Byron and turned to the den before she could answer.

"My, my," Rabbit tsked.

Byron shrugged and followed her brother into the study, closing the door behind her.

"Lilian, this really won't do at all." Charles tried to keep his voice level, but his hands were clenched at his sides. "I've only been gone a week, and all hell's broken loose."

"A couple of my friends—"

"You mean your gin-sucking pals from New York."

"I had no idea they were coming —"

"And my wife!" He turned to her enraged. "Drinking!"

"Really, Charles, that shouldn't come as a shock to you."

"I will not have it."

"There's no harm in having some fun."

"I prefer things to be within the law."

"You prefer them dead. And there are some of us around who are still with the living."

Emboldened by the alcohol, Byron resolutely squared her shoulders as Charles tapped nervous fingers against the edge of the desk.

"They may stay the night, but then I must ask you to have them leave."

"You're the keeper of the inn. You ask them."

A knock at the door interrupted them, and Rabbit poked his head in before either could answer.

"Is there a problem, old boy?" He walked in without invitation. "Ah, you must be Charles."

Rabbit extended his hand forcing Charles to shake. "I've heard so much about you. All rotten of course—your sister's such a gossip!"

Charles's eyes narrowed in anger.

"My brother is concerned with your accommodations."

"Nonsense. They're fine ol' chap," Rabbit assured Charles. "Not the St. Regis, of course, but then your rooms have a charm all their own. Yes. 'Very quaint' is how I'd describe them."

Charles glared at Byron, then walked brusquely from the room. Rabbit turned to Byron in mock surprise. "Dear me, was it something I said?"

Journal of Parnell Walbrook
Bay Cliff: September 1928

They fight to keep their eyes from one another. If Byron was ready to hear it I might tell her she has formed a tragic infatuation for the beautiful Cynara, but I think it will be better to let her find out in her own good time. This setting has all the elements for a gothic drama with haunting misty sea-side, Cynara as the fair-maiden, Byron as our tormented hero and of course, Charles as the evil villain.

* * *

Rabbit was dressed to the nines, resplendent in tails and bow-tie. He entered the dining room with Ruth on one arm and Miss Falstaff on the other. As he graciously showed the dowager to her seat, and the old bat coyly flirted with him, Byron could not suppress a smile.

After feasting on a wonderful dinner of lamb, potatoes, asparagus and sweet pearl onions, Rabbit extracted a cigarette from his gold case as a serving maid removed his dish.

"Gauloises, anyone? The finest Turkish tobacco from Paris."

He passed the case around, lit his own cigarette and inhaled appreciatively. "Yes. The second best vice known to man."

Encouraged by Rabbit, Ruth gingerly extracted one. "And what is the first?"

"Why, gin, naturally. Of course there's nothing quite so fine as watching my dear friend, Byron, enjoy her cigarettes. It's like a symphony—full of passion, pathos—"

"Cigarettes are one thing," Miss Falstaff sniffed, "but gin is quite another. Tobacco helps the digestion, gin corrupts."

"Madame Falstaff." Rabbit bowed in deference. "I take it you're a strict observer."

"I am, indeed, a strict observer of the law."

Ruth began to cough.

"Most certainly the law of tract and deed," Rabbit replied. "But what of the law of the soul? I am of the opinion that the poor fools who devised the 18th Amendment were on a very short leash from those who fabricated organized religion."

"But whatever can you mean?" Miss Falstaff demanded.

"Why simply, Madame Falstaff," Rabbit exhaled elegantly, "that both are based on the premise that someone, somewhere, might be having a good time."

Miss Falstaff's lips pursed tightly and Ruth, gagging, handed her cigarette back to Rabbit, who wearily appraised his dinner companion.

"Darling," Rabbit whispered as an aside to Byron, "how do you fill up the hours?"

"Hey Byron," Jake said. "I've a smashing idea. How would you feel about Nate Venable taking a trip to Hollywood?"

"Oh marvelous!" Ruth agreed. "Oh, Ginger, don't you think that would be just marvelous?"

"Yes! That would be enormous fun!" Mark nodded.

"Actually, I think Nate Venable needs a rest," Byron answered.

"What?" Jake asked incredulously.

"Even stick figures deserve a vacation now and again." Byron subtly inclined her head toward Cynara.

"Well, I for one, would miss him." Rabbit winked at Miss Falstaff as he tossed his napkin aside. "He is so very clever, figuring out all those tedious clues, arriving at the least suspected villain."

"Come on Byron," Jake said. "He'd make great stuff for the new talkies."

"Really Jake," Rabbit sniffed disdainfully. "You've lost all sense of proportion."

"Mark my word man—there's money to be made and someday people will think of talkies as another form of art."

"Anything that imitates life so completely could never be mistaken for art. Let's talk of something less obscene." Rabbit then lowered his voice. "Like where's the nearest speakeasy?"

"In my room," Byron suggested. "But first I must check on Father."

"Quite right. I think we should all pay him a brief visit."

Rabbit stood, patted imaginary crumbs from his vest. "Then, shall we adjourn?"

Charles stood abruptly, tossed his napkin aside in disgust and dismissed himself.

Rabbit bowed to Miss Falstaff and took her hand. "I sincerely hope our opposing views will not affect our new friendship." His intensely brilliant eyes melted her in seconds and when she smiled he kissed her hand. "Wonderful."

As Cynara excused herself and began to walk from the dining room, Rabbit whisked from behind her and took her arm in his own.

"Darling you must join us as all the best people shall certainly be there," he teased.

Cynara smiled, accepting his invitation.

* * *

"... and then Mata Hari requested permission to have a salon audience upon an elephant no less!" Rabbit gesticulated wildly as he performed the tall-tales version of Paris literati for Francis. "To which Natalie replied she couldn't possibly have an elephant in her garden as she was serving little cakes and such."

"My lord, now that's some woman!" Francis tugged his beard.

"Not to be denied, Mata Hari arrived on a horse. Naked."

Francis laughed heartily, wildly entertained, and Byron was pleased with the color that had returned to his cheeks. But when his laughter turned to coughing, Byron rushed from her chair in alarm.

"Oh, Father…please, Rabbit, stop…you're making him sick. You must stop!"

They waited for the coughing to pass.

"No…no…do Miss Stein once more," Francis insisted. "You're even better at her than she is herself."

"One more, Byron, and then I promise we'll all leave like good little tykes." Rabbit chucked his tumbler and prepared himself for his next story.

* * *

Much later, the foursome retired to Byron's room. Jake built a fire in the grate and they all lounged close to the hearth feeling softer, slower. Jake soon slumped in the corner, nodding off now and again, while Byron sat at her desk and Cynara perched in a small sitting chair by the edge of the hearth.

Rabbit roamed freely around the room, stopped at the Victrola and placed the needle on the record that was already there. The seductive husk of a trumpet accompanied by a piano and violin set the mood.

"Much better." Rabbit sipped from the bottle at Byron's desk. "Why, this is Genet's cognac isn't it?"

"Yes. It is." Byron frowned, feeling more than a little drunk.

"She sent me off with some as well. Darling Genet and Solita, they're—"

"Uhum, Rabbit," Byron intervened, "tell me about the latest shows. I do miss them so much."

"Nonsense. She hates most theater." Rabbit pulled a flask from his jacket and sidled next to Cynara, "Howls at the tragedies and laments the comedies."

He regarded Cynara, who was bathed in the soft light of the embers. "My dear, did you know you positively glow?" Rabbit's voice was hushed reverence.

" '*She was a Phantom of delight,*
When first she gleamed upon my sight;

A lovely Apparition sent
To be a moment's ornament.'"

As Rabbit's words floated over them Cynara turned to Byron, feeling her eyes on her. She held Byron's gaze, challenging her.

"And have you never entertained the stage?" Rabbit asked.

Cynara slowly pulled herself from Byron's line of vision and watched as Rabbit poured her an extra shot.

"No. But I should certainly think you had."

Rabbit laughed. "Did I tell you how much I like you? No. I have no talent myself, which encourages my living on the coattails of others. Fortunately, I have been endowed with excellent taste. That is why I play my days out as a critic."

Byron raised her tumbler. "And a damn fine one at that."

"My greatest admirer. So darling, you interrupted me earlier... where was I?"

"You were going to tell her all about Genet and Solita's new living arrangements," Jake piped up from the corner, and then immediately slumbered off again.

"Ahh, yes the damndest thing I've ever heard of. Of course, Genet, she is a dear heart, but sometimes I don't know how Solita puts up with her. First—"

"Rabbit, where are your manners?" Byron quickly interrupted. "We have a guest who has no interest in the goings-on of people thousands of miles away."

"Nonsense! Cynara, do you mind?"

"I'm most interested," Cynara said softly.

"See, Byron. Well, now then...oh yes, she's gone completely daft over this Noel character, who's really quite dashing." Byron cast an apprehensive eye toward Cynara as Rabbit continued. "So where is Solita? Off in the country with another paramour. They keep house together in Paris, but visit one another like one big happy family. I mean really, no one ever knows whether she'll be home or prancing around the countryside with Noel."

"Noel's not so bad," Byron remarked as if concluding the conversation.

"Who is he?" Cynara asked.

Byron clenched her jaw, waiting.

"Darling, not he. *She.* Noel Murphy, a striking blonde, stunningly tragic, if that sort of thing appeals to you."

Byron saw Cynara blanche momentarily, then quickly recover as she looked up to Rabbit, unwaveringly.

"Anyway, why can't those girls behave themselves? At least the 'Steins' bicker monogamously amongst themselves." Rabbit lit a cigarette, tossed the match into the dying fire. "What about yourself, darling? Who warms the heart?"

Byron felt Cynara's eyes sharply upon her.

"I told you," Byron replied airily, "I've been working."

"Nonsense. How can you get anything done in a place so deadly silent?"

"Silence does have its merits," she remarked. "Now out, you two. I'm tired, and you're making too much noise."

"Oh, but darling, where shall we go? What shall we do?"

"I'll leave that to your impressive imagination."

"Then adieu, ladies." Rabbit mock bowed. "A delightful evening."

Rabbit retrieved Jake and they exited arm in arm. Byron closed the door behind them, then turned to Cynara, who put down her tumbler.

"I like your friends."

"I do too, despite the fact that they more often than not get… shall we say, carried away." Byron cleared her throat. "I hope you weren't offended by anything they had to say."

"Quite the contrary," Cynara answered, tilting her head as she boldly assessed Byron.

An uncomfortable silence edged into the room.

"I suppose I should be going." Cynara swayed as she stood.

"Are you sure you're all right?"

"I'm a little drunk, I think," Cynara spoke carefully.

"Would you like me to see you to the cottage?"

"Don't you think I can make it?"

Cynara stumbled as she moved forward and Byron grabbed her by the arms.

"I'm more drunk than I thought," Cynara laughed shyly, then glanced slowly up to Byron.

"That makes two of us." Byron's gaze was direct.

Byron realized her hands still held Cynara, but dropped them as she felt the weight of their exchange flood the room.

The record needle skipped into emptiness, but they continued to stand an interminable time, Byron's eyes searching, casting over the face she had watched for weeks now, seeing the other part of Cynara that she had only glimpsed in her work. And as they had a few days earlier, her eyes burned now with the same heat.

Cynara gingerly put a hand to Byron's chest to steady herself, her eyes heavy lidded. For some time they stood frozen, neither certain of the other until Cynara slowly raised her hand to Byron's throat, her fingers lingering as they caught a tendril of Byron's hair. She closed her eyes.

Byron leaned closer, feeling the tickle of Cynara's breath against her jaw, moving her face just to the side of Cynara's, their skin almost touching, her throat tightening, swallowing becoming a difficult measure. A strangled moan escaped Cynara's lips as her cheek grazed Byron's. Byron could feel the pulse in her neck, the pounding in her ears, dizzy with the smell of Cynara's hair.

Cynara abruptly pulled Byron's lips to her own, devouring, greedily consuming as Byron's hands swept up her back and into her hair. Byron's mouth traveled over Cynara's cheeks, her eyebrows, as she buried herself in the silk of her hair, yanking the nape of her neck so that Cynara was forced to meet her eyes before she kissed her again.

They tumbled to their knees, their union furious and savage. Frustration fueled a reckless hunger that drove them further, as they clung desperately to each other. And then Cynara pushed Byron to the side, anguish in her eyes.

"No...no," Cynara gasped, holding her stomach, her chest heaving as she struggled to her feet and rushed from the room.

It was, to say the least, difficult not to think of Lena when I felt the blossoming attraction between my characters. The writer's gift. I may relive those wonderful memories time and again, but it is painful to be sure. Within Byron's universe, though, I was able to fashion my characters' destiny—and express the love inside.

The hollow swell in my chest for Lena lives in me. I accept it.

Lena's simple act of loving me was the most potent and terrifying thing I had ever experienced. Simply more than I could bear. For as the old adage goes, if I could not accommodate my own self with that creature comfort, how could I accept it from others?

* * *

I picked up the phone. Put it down. Three times.
Dialed.
"Hello?" Her voice was cool, professional.
"Lena?" My voice cracked.
"Yes, hello?"
"Lena, it's me."

Charged silence.

"Spencer." Her voice was filled with—was it warmth, anger, resentment? "What are—are you okay?"

"Yes. I'm fine."

"Sarah told me you were up north. Are you back?"

"No. I'm still in Oregon."

"Oh." The voice, liquid and smooth. "Spencer?"

"Yes?"

"It's good to hear your voice."

And hers radiated strength and wisdom. My throat constricted. Thinking of how Lena was the only person in my life who remained fresh and ever-changing, new, yet always consistently Lena.

"It's great to hear yours too."

There was a pause. Where did we go from here?

"I...I tried to call you several times."

"Hmmm," I responded, feeling defensive.

"But you never called back."

"I guess...I guess I thought it was pointless."

"Pointless?" Lena repeated. "Why is that?"

"Just thought you'd rather not hear from me."

"No. That's not the case." Lena cleared her throat. "How did your movie go?"

"Well, I guess okay. Things got really crazy there for a while. We couldn't get any distribution. I think maybe three people ever saw it."

"I'm sorry."

"No. I'm the one who's sorry." I bit my lower lip. "Look, that's why I'm calling. I'm sure the last thing you want to do is dredge up ancient history, but I have something I need to ask you."

"Okay," she responded uncertainly.

It took me a moment to get it out: "Can you forgive me?"

Lena sighed.

"Lena, I...I was terrible to you and MacKenzie. You didn't deserve what I put you through. Hell, no one does, but the last person in the world I meant to hurt was you. It's just that I was—was a mess. I know I'm not telling you anything you don't know. But the problem is—*I* didn't know it. I thought I was simply being my tunnel-vision self, taking care of my career. It seemed so important at the time."

"And now?"

"Now?" I laughed. "Let's just say I've gotten a little perspective."

"Sarah says you're working on something."

"Not a project. Not for anyone. Just something I'm writing."

"What?"

"I guess it's what you'd call, 'writing the book I want to read.' "

"Spencer, that's wonderful. I'm glad. I really am. And I really appreciate your calling."

"Just one other thing. I know I couldn't see this then, back when we were together, and maybe I couldn't see it until I'd struggled long enough to know when to give up the fight—"

"That's just it, isn't it? It's always been a fight for you, hasn't it?"

"Yes. Pretty much. You'd think that would have tipped me off somewhere along the line. It's just you start out having your dreams—grand, small…whatever—thinking you're the architect of your own destiny. Some people understand their limitations better—"

"So many people don't even care to try, Spencer."

"Maybe. Or they give up before they start because it's not *responsible* or *mature* to run off to be a movie star, a writer, or an artist." For a moment I couldn't speak.

"Are you Okay, Spencer?"

"I wanted it so much—so much, Lena. I thought if I just suited up and worked it—if I was successful—it would make up for all the stuff I hated about me. For that bad little girl—the one who made Jonathon do those things to me. If I could just be this thing—this writer, director—a 'success'—it would make me clean. Make me okay. But no matter how close I got to it, I never felt any better. Until you. You and 'Kenzie were the only things that made me think I could look inside again. And even if I didn't really like everything I saw…I knew you did."

"And now?"

"Well, I've been thinking about what makes me happy. Really happy. How easily I used to be pleased—the little girl whose world bordered on perfection just from watching old schmaltzy romantic movies. It's not about what the world has to offer. It's about what I have to offer myself. And when it comes right down to it, all I want to do is write. Tell my stories. If I get to do that every day, then I'm damn lucky."

A silence spoke the answer.

"Do you have to go?" I asked, wishing I could see her, touch her hand.

"No—yes…I mean I have a few seconds, but I have to get MacKenzie to her art class."

"How is she?"

"She's great," Lena answered warmly. "She misses you. Asks about you all the time."

I couldn't speak.

"We don't have to do chit-chat here, Spence," Lena offered kindly.

"Thanks…I don't know that I can. I just wanted to tell you that I was sorry. I won't keep you."

"Thank you," Lena said graciously. "Will I hear from you again?"

"Do you want to?"

The longest silence of my life.

"Yes. I'd like that."

Byron's brow furrowed as she clumped down the stairwell in a daze.

"Byron. Good afternoon."

Distracted, Byron turned as Edward approached.

"How are you?"

"Apparently the worse for some wear," she faltered. "Excuse me. I have a devil of a headache. Have you been to see Father?"

"He's sleeping at the moment. I have some powders in my bag that should help you out. Please, join me for tea?"

Byron hesitated. The idea of consuming anything made her nauseous, but she didn't want to appear rude. "Certainly."

She followed him into the sitting room. He poured her a cup and then one for himself, studying her face as she took a sip.

"Are you well?"

"A bit tired."

"I know things are difficult here," he offered kindly. "If you ever need an ear…"

"Trying to save my soul, good Doctor?"

"No. Trying to be a friend. A person would have to be blind not to see your pain. And your father's only part of it."

Agitated, Byron glanced down at her boots, then back up to Edward. "I don't know…I…" She peered into his compassionate eyes for answers. "I only came here to take my father away, and now that I've been trapped, I feel as if I'm here for something entirely different."

His gaze shifted slightly and she followed his eyes to Cynara who had entered through the archway.

Edward stood. "Ah, there you are. Come join us."

Byron's hand trembled. She quickly set down her cup as Cynara walked slowly into the room, her eyes on Edward, and Edward only.

"I'm sorry I was late. I completely lost track of time."

"It's quite all right," Edward responded. "Byron and I have been getting better acquainted."

An awkward silence filled the room. Byron nodded in Cynara's direction, avoiding her eyes.

"Hello," Cynara said, just above a whisper.

"Perhaps we may continue this at another time," Edward said to Byron.

"Yes…yes, of course."

Edward lifted a hand to Cynara's elbow. "Well, then. We really should be off. Are you ready?"

She glanced in Byron's direction, then back to Edward. "Yes."

"We're having tea with my mother," Edward said. "She gets very cross when we're late."

"Please, don't let me keep you," Byron said weakly.

As soon as Edward and Cynara left the house, Byron released a long pent-up sigh. She reached for a cigarette and walked to the window to watch Edward gallantly escort Cynara to his Model T.

"They make a lovely couple, don't they?" Charles asked, creeping up from behind her.

Byron's jaw tensed. "What do you mean?"

"Didn't you know? I thought certainly she would have told you the exciting news. Especially since you've become the best of chums."

"Tell me what?"

He smiled nastily. "Why, they're to be married next spring."

Bay Cliff, Oregon: October 1928

Did I say melodrama? I feel like one of the understudy players in a dreadfully tense play. Earlier this evening I happened to be sitting in the dining room when Charles informed Byron that Cynara was to marry. I could see as well, from my vantage point, Mavis lurking behind the stairwell watching her husband deliver the tidy news.

I don't know yet what has transpired between Byron and Cynara, but it would not require Nate Venable's assistance to see the strong attraction growing between them. But this is not Paris. My Lord, how this is not Paris…

Long after I thought the dramatics were over I sat peacefully smoking a cigarette in the sitting room, when I again had the misfortune to overhear a conversation between Cynara and her gentleman caller when he returned her to the house. I could hear Dutton, I think his name is, nervously rubbing his hands together and then asking Cynara if she was feeling well.

"I'm just tired. I think we all stayed up a bit too late last night," she responded.

"Yes, I could see Byron was exhausted," Edward agreed. "She's quite a fascinating woman, don't you think? Traveled the world over, so sophisticated here in our neck of the woods, yet it hasn't made her mean-spirited or stuffy in the least."

Cynara did not respond.

"What's your take on her?" I could hear the strain in Edward's voice.

"My take?"

"Yes. What do you think of her."

"I…I don't really—I don't really spend my time thinking about her one way or another."

"But surely you must. You spend a great deal of time with her."

"She's, as you say, a very interesting person," Cynara hedged. "I've enjoyed talking with someone about art—"

"But her. What do you think of her?"

"I don't know what it is you want me to say, Edward," Cynara snapped.

"Darling, darling, please, I didn't mean to upset you."

"I'm sorry Edward, it's just that I feel you want me to…to," and then she stopped abruptly, apologized for being such poor company and said she must retire.

To say tensions permeate the walls of Bay Cliff is a gross understatement. I feel an ominous foreboding.

* * *

It was uncommonly peculiar for Rabbit to do so, but he took an early morning stroll to clear his mind and soon realized that the other lone figure, approaching from the south, was Cynara. He stopped just abreast of her, offered a cigarette. They smoked in silence as the sun rose then abruptly faded behind dark clouds. Rabbit tried to shield himself against a billowing gust of wind. Strands from Cynara's braid loosened as her hair flew wildly about her, and though her cheeks were pink from the cold, she seemed immune to the chill.

"I don't know how you stand it." Rabbit shivered, holding his coat close to his neck.

"It's actually quite warm for this time of year." Cynara smiled. "It's the dampness that gets you."

"Oh, so that's what it is. In any event, I don't know how much more of this fresh air I can take."

"What are you doing so far from Bay Cliff?"

"Well, I've come to find you, now haven't I?"

Cynara glanced up to him sharply.

"Yes, it's occurred to me, that swept away by my enthusiasm for telling stories, I may have gone a bit too far the other night and I've come to apologize."

"Did Byron ask—"

"Oh, dear Lord, no. She hasn't a clue that I'm even awake at this preposterous hour."

"You have nothing to apologize for."

"But something's wrong. You have been absent from the house ever since, and I'm afraid you're angry at Rabbit."

"No, truly." Cynara put her hand to his. "It has nothing to do with you. I've just been feeling a bit under the weather."

"Oh, my dear one, what seems to be the problem?" Rabbit asked tenderly.

Cynara turned to the ocean. "Sometimes when I come out here, all I have to do is look at this...all this, and anything that bothers me quickly disappears. But today it isn't working."

"Perhaps you need a wise old buzzard to lean on."

She smiled sadly.

"I'll have you know I'm not just any shoulder. Why, in Paris I'm famous for my wide lapels. Whenever *ma petit colombe* has a bad day, I sweep her up and help her fly again."

"And how do you manage that?"

"By making merry and wreaking havoc, of course."

She brushed the hair from her face, uncertain.

"Shall we?" He offered her his arm. "I've decided I should like to be a tourist today. Show me your fair land and tonight I shall take you to dinner and tell you of Paris. Perhaps we'll even sneak over to that shack Jake's been running off to these past days."

* * *

Tinny chords jangled from a broken piano through the din of voices in a shanty speakeasy. Rabbit's shocked amusement grew to dismay as he panned over the sea of regulars: toothless farmers, ragged lumberjacks, their beards stained with chewing tobacco, fishermen and several old Indians, ageless pioneers from a lost age.

"Good Lord! *Les Miserables.*"

In stark contrast, Rabbit stood impeccably attired as he scanned the crowd for Jake and Ginger. "I'm sure they're hidden somewhere about this colloquial, uhm...charm."

He spied them huddled in rapt discussion by one of the tables. As they made their way through the press of bodies, Byron could be seen staring dourly at the floor.

"I've come to wipe that tragic look off your face," Rabbit announced.

Byron's wry smile froze when Cynara stepped from behind Rabbit. He held out a chair for her to sit next to Byron as Jake and Ginger sat cozily alongside them.

Cynara folded her arms and made a show of studying her surroundings as Byron glanced her way.

"I thought these places only existed in the seedy minds of disillusioned writers," Rabbit decried.

"They do."

"I practically begged Cynara to join us. How could I have known?"

Byron pursed her lips and frowned.

"Well it's not Fouquets by any means. Never have I missed open hedonism more! Sunshine, sidewalk cafés, the smell of fresh croissant, a spot of *eau-de-vie a poire*—Ah you can take the bon vivant out of Paris..." He cast a distasteful look about him, "But why?"

"Hear, hear," Jake agreed.

Rabbit poured the whiskey, held up his glass in toast. *"Aux plus beaux jours!"*

Byron pounded back a shot, gasping heartily, while Cynara took a dainty sip and winced.

"Oh, no—that won't do at all!" Rabbit indicated to her as he poured himself another drink. "The only way one can possibly tolerate this swill is to have it pass the tongue so quickly one can't taste it." He knocked back his shot to demonstrate.

Cynara glanced at Byron but when she saw the anger and accusation in her eyes, she defiantly picked up the glass, and chucked the whiskey back like a pro.

"Bravo," Rabbit applauded. "You're a quick study, my dear."

Many such drinks later the shack was filled with smoke and the union of forced gaiety. Ribald laughter and loud music crescendoed toward a peak. Even Rabbit's collar had become loose.

"Oh, bother about Clay!" Rabbit pronounced.

"You don't understand," Ginger shouted over the din. "I couldn't possibly leave."

"But this is an incredible opportunity, Ginger," Jake insisted. "You're talented. You're wasting yourself here."

Byron studied Cynara as she watched Jake and Ginger argue.

"I know plenty of people in Hollywood. Hell, we could try and get you set up in a musical picture. You're a wonderful dancer."

"But I haven't really danced in years."

Rabbit took Ginger's hand and pressed it to his lips. "Modesty is so terribly unbecoming."

"Besides, Clay..."

Rabbit shook his head. "Isn't he rather beside the point?"

"And Ruth! She'd go blabbing to Mother."

"Ruth is inconsequential my dear," Rabbit replied. "The poor unfortunate subscribes to the religion of limitation, and as such will always meddle and obfuscate everyone's life around her. We, on the other hand"—he spread his hands to include those sitting at the table—"embrace the doctrine of abundance, where anything is possible—whether it presents itself as a radiant summer's day…"

He picked up a bottle, emptied it into Cynara's glass.

"…or the last dregs on the morning after. Speaking of which, excuse me while I seek new provisions." Rabbit unsteadily got to his feet and moved in the general direction of the bar.

"We'll work it out." Jake offered his hand to Ginger. "Come on."

He led her through the crowd to a small corner to dance to a sultry ragtime melody. Byron twirled her shot glass round and around.

"What are you doing here?" Byron finally asked.

"I need to talk with you."

Byron cocked her head, waiting.

"I want to explain—"

"Forget it."

"I want you to know—last night was not…was not—"

"I said forget it. Your secret's safe."

"I was…" Cynara searched for the right words.

"Carried away by Genet's wonderful cognac?" Byron held up her glass, downed the last of her whiskey. "Don't worry. Being under the influence is a sound defense."

"I don't understand you. Why are you so angry at me?"

"Timing is everything, don't you think?" Rabbit asked as he reappeared. "They've almost run out of this swill, thank God." He replenished their glasses then spotted Jake and Ginger on the floor. "Look at them. Finally. Something to toast. To new and illicit love."

"Ah yes, and to complicit union." Byron raised her glass as her eyes bore into Cynara. "There is nothing more poignant than two people in love. Love, which fills volumes of literature, from the sublime to the ridiculous—"

"Yes, well mostly ridiculous, darling," Rabbit concurred.

"And whatever is the relevance of love without the desire to couple in matrimony?" Byron tipped her empty glass toward Cynara, then swiveled to Rabbit. "Rabbit, do you remember Gerty's proverb? That one 'should only read what is truly good or what is frankly bad'? Well, I think one should only marry the truly pure, or the frankly wicked."

"Touché," Rabbit concluded.

"I've had enough." Cynara began to stand as Byron refilled her glass.

"But how can you leave now when I'm just about to make a toast?" Byron shoved the glass toward Cynara. "To the blushing bride."

Cynara grabbed her wrap and bent to Rabbit. "I want to go."

"Certainly." He stood, dismayed by Byron's performance. "Come along. It's time for you to go to bed."

"I'm not ready to go," Byron insisted.

"Oh, but I think you are." Rabbit's voice did not bridge protest. "Jake," he called, "Help me out here, man."

* * *

Supported by Rabbit on one side, and Cynara on the other, Byron was half-carried, half led up the stairs to her room.

"Ah, yes, 'Matrimonial devotion,' " Byron sallied. "'Doesn't seem to suit her notion.' That's Gilbert my good man—"

"Byron, do simmer down," Rabbit insisted.

"No…no…here's a good one from Dorothy: 'Accursed from their birth they be, Who seek to find monogamy—'"

"Damnit, Byron please keep quiet!" Rabbit pressed a finger over her lips. Byron closed one eye, on the lookout for whomever they were hiding from.

"'Pursuing it from bed to bed—I think they would be better dead,'" Byron whispered, and then announced in a baritone, "'What lies there are in kisses.'"

"Your brother will be out here any second," Rabbit hissed as they approached her room.

"Charles?" Byron's face crumpled, like a confused child's.

"Yes, so keep —"

"No! Rabbit, you mustn't let him come here." Byron's voice took on the timber of a young girl's.

Cynara saw the anguish in Byron's face as they laid her back against her pillow.

"Please…not…not Charles," she whimpered softly, her eyes heavy with misery and intoxication.

"He's not here," Cynara said softly. "Don't worry. It's just Rabbit and…"

Byron squinted at Cynara, and her face softened. "…And you. It *is* you isn't it? No. I'm dreaming. I dreamed it all. Thassit… dreams…dreams…"

She passed out.

Rabbit watched Cynara closely as she put a hand to Byron's forehead, brushing her hair aside.

"Spot of tea?" Rabbit asked.

"I'd love some."

They quietly crept to the kitchen. He poured her a steaming cup as she sat in a chair before the fireplace. He placed an afghan over her lap, then said, "I shall be back in a moment."

When he returned, he handed her a book, a wry expression covering his face. "Before you judge her too harshly."

Cynara looked down. She brushed fingers over the blue gilded letters of *Naked Truth* by Lilian Harrington.

* * *

Byron waited until everyone finished their breakfast before she entered the empty dining room. She unsteadily poured herself a cup of coffee, then sat at the table. Brushing a hand through her hair, she pressed cold fingers against aching temples.

Charles walked in, assessed her condition and smiled condescendingly. "I see your chums have given you wholesome examples by which to live your life."

She shakily lifted the coffee cup to her lips.

"I imagine you can't wait to get back to it all, after suffering the tedium of our provincialism," he remarked.

"Is there a point to this in my near future?"

"Yes, there is, actually. I would like you to come to the den—that is, when you think you are sufficiently recovered, to sign Father's papers. Everything is in order, with the exception of Bay Cliff."

"Charles, can't this wait until later?"

"No. It can't. And really, Lilian, by the way you've cleverly avoided me all this time, I don't think you want to deal with this at all." Charles approached her. "Bay Cliff belongs to me. It would be ridiculous to pretend it means anything to you. I rather doubt it holds any sentimental value for you and since Father's illness he has been virtually useless. It has been up to me to keep it prospering."

"And?"

"But don't you see? You are entitled to half of Bay Cliff and everything in it. I'm willing to pay you a handsome sum to acquire your share."

Byron shook her head in confusion. "Charles, I have no earthly interest in Bay Cliff or your money."

"Well, I am glad to hear that you are being so sensible." Charles appeared to be greatly relieved. "Finally something on which we see eye to eye."

Charles's ingratiating smile left Byron cold. As he walked from the room, she replaced the trembling cup on the table, spilling coffee over her hand. She heard Ginger and Ruth coming down the hall and, since she had no desire for further company, got up to make her exit out the back pantry door. But from there she could hear hushed urgent voices.

"I'm telling you, I don't care what he thinks. Or what he thinks he knows." Cynara's voice.

"Please, Cynara, you must listen to me." Mavis's voice. "If Charles —"

"No! I will not do this."

As Byron backtracked, Cynara came through the swinging door.

They stood in momentary shock until they heard Ruth, Ginger and Mark about to enter the dining room. Cynara brushed by Byron and ran out the front door. Byron wavered in indecision, then grabbed her cape, following Cynara. Byron could see the dark clouds gathering against the horizon. The storm would soon reach the shore.

She ran down to the beach after Cynara, tracing her footsteps. The sky grew darker, until a mist began to fall, and finally rain cascaded from the skies. There was only one place to seek refuge. As the drops became heavier Byron ran to the cave, shouting for Cynara to follow her.

Once inside they shook off the rain, both trying to catch their breath. Byron shook the rain from her hair, unfurled her cape. The longer neither spoke, the more difficult it became to break the silence.

"I rather suspect I have an apology to make," Byron began, finally.

"There's no need," Cynara stated emphatically.

"Look, I'm sorry. I...I got carried away last night." Byron reached inside her coat pocket for her cigarette case and offered it to Cynara.

"I don't wish to discuss last night."

"At least share a cigarette with me. What harm can there be in that?"

Cynara reluctantly accepted. As Byron lit their cigarettes and the flame danced between them, Byron could see the conflict in Cynara's eyes, the sad beauty, the lingering question.

"See? It's not so terrible, is it?" Byron smiled disarmingly.

"I meant to tell you." Cynara brushed raindrops from her cheek. "About Edward."

"But why hadn't you?" Byron asked. "We've spent hours in each other's company discussing everything under the sun, and yet—"

"I—"

"There must be some explanation for you to willingly keep such information from me," Byron insisted.

"I didn't want you to know."

"But why?"

"Because if you knew..." Cynara shrank into the recesses of the cave, her face partially hidden by the dark shadows.

Byron closed her eyes in understanding. Frustrated, she walked to her, not so gently pulled her into the light. When she saw that Cynara was trembling she cast her cloak over her shoulders.

"Cynara, I have been tormented—not shamed—by what I feel for you. Afraid you could never share my passion, never forgive—"

"Please don't—"

"Cynara, please hear me out."

"How can I?" Cynara's voice quivered. "When we have both been keeping secrets."

"Whatever are you talking about?"

Cynara stepped away from her and then said very quietly, "I read it."

Byron was bewildered.

"I read it, Byron. *Naked Truth*." Her voice was soft, almost as if she were talking to herself. "Words of such beauty...intimacy..." but then her tone sharpened in accusation. "All this time you have been hiding your true self. You'd rather parade that silly detective around—mimic his rakish charm—hide behind Rabbit and your drunken binges."

"Are my illusions any more ill-guided than your own?" Byron grabbed her by the arm, pulled her close.

"And now, it's nothing but a farce!"

"Farce?" Byron bent her lips to Cynara's neck, nuzzled kisses down the smooth skin. "You call this a farce?" Her lips found Cynara's forehead, her cheeks, as Cynara's hands grasped Byron's face, desperate for her mouth to touch her own.

Byron savagely pulled Cynara to her, crushing her lips, cruelly embracing her and Cynara succumbed, fully, willingly. Byron severed the contact this time, ragged, her voice strangled.

"Tell me. How will you share Edward's bed?"

"Don't—" Cynara's hand trembled at her bruised face.

"How will you blot me from your mind as his body lies on yours?" Byron's voice turned to ice.

"Stop—"

"Feel my heat when he demands your own—" Byron grabbed Cynara's hand bringing it to her chest. "Will your heart beat as strongly for him?"

"No!" Cynara wrenched free, walked to the opening of the cave, and watched the raging storm outside.

Byron was soon behind her, so close the words crawled down Cynara's neck. "Yes. A pretty little farce. I tried to protect you from my feelings. But you've already lived this particular scandal, haven't you?"

Cynara wouldn't answer.

"Haven't you?"

Cynara nodded, closing her eyes.

"Outcast from society—that makes it safe, doesn't it? But how do you escape yourself, Cynara?" The anguish in her voice was directed at them both. "How do you escape?"

Cynara could not speak.

"Yes, you were drunk. Drunk with passion."

She pushed past Cynara and walked into the rain.

* * *

Rabbit draped the last of Byron's wet clothes over the fireplace screen. Wrapped in one of Rabbit's smoking jackets, she sat trying to warm herself before the flames.

"Darling, you look positively bleak."

"Yes, well my head feels like a welling bruise." Byron took in Rabbit's smooth-shaven cheeks, his crisp appearance. "How do you do it? You look as fresh as the morning dew, with no evidence of our debauchery last night. I feel like a horse cart has dragged me from one end of the beach to the other."

"Simple." Rabbit withdrew a cigarette from his case and placed it between her lips. "It's called practice."

"This kind of practice I don't need." She carefully inhaled as Rabbit held the flame to her cigarette.

"If truth be told, dear one, my body long ago created an antidote to the ravages of alcohol. I rarely see the morning after through the haze of a hangover. And in the event I do, I exercise my inalienable right to a boxcar. No, when I awake, it's as if my mother tucked me in the night before and I slept a full twelve hours."

"Did we sleep?" Byron rubbed the side of her head, then exhaled in a long sigh. "This landscape is wearing thin."

"Well, one can bear only so much natural beauty."

"You don't know the half of it."

He removed his flask from his jacket, twisted the lid and handed it to her. She took a long swallow.

"Yes. Much better." He leaned against the mantel, studying her face. "This isn't just a bloody hangover, though, my darling."

Listless, Byron did not respond.

"Well, really, darling, your eyes are like struck flint every time she enters the room."

"You've been reading too much Colette."

Byron got up, walked to the window. Rabbit followed, so both their reflections faced one another.

"Does it never stop raining here?" she sighed.

Rabbit put an arm around her. "You need to forget this gloomy place and everyone in it. Come, Byron. Let's go to Portland, paint the town a veritable rainbow of colors. We'll make merry and wreak havoc, like in the old days. Doesn't Rabbit always help you to forget?"

She leaned her head gently against his shoulder and watched the pelting rain. Suddenly she straightened. "Rabbit?"

"What is it?"

"My father. Something's—"

Byron dashed from the room and stood uncertainly in the hallway. Bay Cliff felt as if all the life had been sucked from it. The silence was deafening. Byron glanced at the fixtures, the walls, the lights in her own home—they appeared to be cloaked in ominous portent. She rushed to her father's bedroom.

Francis lay against the pillow, pale as ash. When she saw Mavis's tearstained face she knew the end was near.

She held her father's hand for the next countless hours, during the long and lonely vigil. Later in the evening, someone gently touched her shoulders. She looked up, surprised to find the warmth in Mavis's eyes as she draped a shawl over her. Dutton remained calm and caring, although she could see the inevitable in his circumspect expression. Charles came and went. She saw the shadow of Cynara at one point and Rabbit stayed with her until late into the night.

As her father's life—the spirit of the man she knew him to be—slowly ebbed from Francis's body, time ceased to exist. Byron laid her head against her father's hand as she slept.

"Lilian...Lilian."

Byron woke, startled to hear his voice. "I'm here, Father."

"Dream...your mother...she was here...and you, when you were a baby."

"Shhh, Father, I'm here, just try to be still."

Francis's eyes widened in alarm. "Heart..."

Byron frowned. "What, Father?"

"My heart!"

"Father—" Byron tried to quell the panic in her voice.

"No...no...the heart." He pointed to the bed table. "Please... get it for me."

Byron found the worn carved heart, handed it to her father. His arm trembled as he held it before them.

"I made this for your mother. It was a symbol of pure... pureness in love. I...I want you...to have it, Lilian..." He paused, in pain. "I am so...so very sorry..." He shakily handed her the heart. "So very sorry I couldn't... protect you...protect —"

"Father, I —"

"I want you...to... have..." His head fell to the side. Byron clenched the heart and stared vacantly at her father's corpse.

* * *

She resolutely walked to her desk, turned on the lamp. She calmly took her writing paper and set it before her. Picked up her fountain pen. She studied it a very long time. And began to write.

The walls of old came tumbling down
Wept bitter tears, my shameful void
For I had slept as years did pass
And merely with my life had toyed

* * *

Rabbit, Jake and Ginger waited at the platform of the train station, still clad in the somber clothes of the funeral. Byron approached, pale and weary, but her eyes were clear and strong. She hugged Jake and Ginger. Rabbit took her arm, steered her to the side.

"I'm glad she's going with him," Byron said.

Rabbit assessed the blissful couple, then turned back to Byron. "Yes, well, I guess there are some happy endings. Sure you don't want me to stay?" Byron shook her head gently.

"What happens now?"

"I'll be fine. Don't worry."

"Ah, but, darling, I'd rather worry about you than breathe." Rabbit removed his flask, took a long swallow. "One for the road?"

"You have one for me."

Rabbit's eyes greeted Byron's in tender seriousness. "I won't see you again, will I?"

"Of course you will. You will always be my Rabbit. Don't be so melodramatic."

"Oh, I know I will 'see' you. But it won't be the same."

"No. It won't be the same."

He put an arm around Byron and as he led her to the others, drolly proclaimed, "I don't know how Jake can bear the idea of Hollywood, all those boorish mogul types. Perhaps I should join him—make certain he doesn't do anything too foolish. I think there may be a place for a critic in Hollywood—what do you think, darling?"

* * *

"I, Francis Peter Harrington, being of sound mind, do make and constitute this my Last Will and Testament, hereby revoking any and all Wills by me heretofore made," James Weatherby, the aging and rotund solicitor, droned on to the somber group.

Charles's eyes shone with avarice as he sat next to Mavis on the sofa in the sitting room. Byron barely listened, distracted and numb as Cynara sat quietly in the corner of the room.

"First: I give, devise and bequeath to Mavis Harrington, who was like a daughter to me, an annual stipend of one thousand dollars. Second: To Cynara Ashford, for her kindnesses and many hours of devotion, I give, devise and bequeath the cottage behind Bay Cliff, and all of its earthly contents."

Charles's jaw tightened as he glowered at Cynara, her head bowed.

"All the rest, residue and remainder of my estate, real, personal and mixed; of whatever nature, kind and description, including Bay Cliff and all its earthly contents, I give, devise and bequeath to my beloved daughter—"

Charles sputtered incoherently.

Weatherby glared at Charles as he continued. "To my beloved daughter, Lilian Harrington."

Charles jumped from his seat. "This is an outrage!"

"Charles. Sit down!" Weatherby commanded.

"This is a travesty! I was at your office not three weeks ago. You showed me Father's will —"

"Charles! Please!" Weatherby extracted two envelopes from his jacket. "Your father amended his will two nights before his death."

"No. No, you're wrong."

"He instructed me to give each of you this codicil at the time of this reading." Weatherby handed one to Byron, who sat unmoving, just as stunned as Charles.

Charles snapped the envelope from him.

Weatherby continued, "His codicil so reads: 'There is no way to recompense for the wages of sin, but I hope this will in some way make restitution for the unspeakable acts perpetrated upon you, my dear Lilian, by your brother—my son, Charles Harrington—who had no compunction in taking what wasn't his. And so now, what has been his, is taken from him.' "

"No!" Charles continued to shake his head, his hands curled to fists at his side. "*NO!*"

Cynara stared uncomprehendingly from Byron to Charles and back to Byron, who sat in a void.

"Goddamn you to hell, Lilian!"

He lunged at Byron and before anyone could stop him, savagely struck her to the ground. Weatherby, Mavis and Cynara rushed at him, but he threw them aside. He picked Byron up, knocked her against the wall.

"Bay Cliff is mine!" His rage spit in her face as he pummeled her body into the wall. "It's mine!"

Dutton rushed into the room. He, Weatherby and Mavis managed to drag Charles from Byron and contain him. Blood dripped from Byron's mouth as she stared at the hate in her brother's face.

Cynara hastened to Byron's side and led her from the house.

* * *

Cynara silently, gently undressed Byron and helped her into the claw foot tub. Steam wafted about them as Cynara tenderly sponged Byron in the hot bath. No words were spoken as she brushed a lock from Byron's forehead, continued her ministration, nurturing, healing. Byron allowed her aching limbs to relax, her bruised ribs to soak in the heat, leaned her head back against the ledge and closed her eyes.

"He's dead."

"He's out of pain now," Cynara responded quietly.

"He knew." She bit her bottom lip. "How did he know?"

"Shhhh." Cynara's voice was lulling. "You need to rest now. Rest…"

When the water grew tepid, Cynara wrapped Byron in a silk robe as she stepped from the tub and led her to the bed.

Byron gently moved a hand to her face, and tipped her chin so she could see Cynara's eyes.

"I want to thank you." Her voice had grown husky. She whispered, "Be with me."

"Byron, you've been hurt."

"I'm quite fine, really." Byron swept a tuft of Cynara's hair from her neck. "How beautiful you are."

"Please…" Cynara blushed.

"Cynara, be with me." It was a quiet command.

Cynara held Byron's gaze for a long questioning moment, and then her hands gently, but efficiently, began to loosen the knot until the robe hung open. Byron's breath quickened as Cynara's fingers traced the ribbing on the satin, moving to Byron's flesh. Byron shut her eyes. Could barely swallow as Cynara's hands slowly—maddeningly slowly—trailed her slender form with velvet fingertips, just past her breasts, stopping to gently rub Byron's chest, right at her heart.

She peered into Byron's eyes, cautiously taking her bruised face in both her hands, kissing her cheeks, forehead, eyebrows, eyelids, and traced with kisses the outline of her mouth, until she could hold back no longer, and flicked a tongue against Byron's upper lip. Byron's lips opened fully, tasting the full of her, delicate and sweet, the tip of her tongue and then more as she leaned deeper into the kiss, Cynara's hands deftly removing Byron's robe from her body.

As Byron stood before her naked, Cynara sighed. Removing her own dress, she stood beside Byron in a simple satin slip, and shyly leaned Byron back until they both lay upon the bed, Cynara straddling Byron's body, her braid falling over her left shoulder. Byron's hands untied the ribbon and slowly unfurled the braid, feeling the weighty silk in her hand. Her loosened tresses caressed Byron's body as Cynara's skin edged ever closer to her own, her lips traveling over Byron's collar bone, gently nibbling down the smooth dip between her breasts—spasms tightening her groin with every touch of Cynara's lips against her skin.

Byron reached up, her hands at Cynara's waist. "I must feel you."

Cynara sat up, slowly removed her slip. Byron released a low throaty gasp, riveted by Cynara's natural beauty as she cupped the gentle lull of Cynara's breasts. Cynara bowed her head.

"You are exquisite." Byron's voice was but a rasp. "Kiss me… kiss me, Cynara."

As Cynara's body fell over Byron's, she could feel Cynara's desire, wet upon her stomach, Cynara shuddering as she merged into Byron's silken body beneath her own, cradling her skin against Byron's, then melting into her.

Cynara held Byron still and with painstaking care began to kiss her, trailing a tongue down the tendon of Byron's neck, down over the sweep of her breast, and then grazing teeth over Byron's rigid nipples as Byron arched her own wet fullness against Cynara's thigh. Byron grasped Cynara's trembling fingers to her mouth but Cynara gently pushed her back and toured the lines of Byron's skin, her hair cascading over Byron's lean frame, dancing upon her nerve endings, fingers delicately massaging Byron's nipples, her mouth at the curve in Byron's pelvis, stopping at sweetly tussled hair. Cynara spread Byron open, smelling the delicate heat of her, piqued from the hot bath water, and moved her mouth to taste the woman beneath her, to captivate and own her, her tongue teasing and challenging Byron's need.

Each time Cynara brought her to the edge she withdrew, building the ache for release ever stronger until Cynara's mouth lay fully upon her suckling greedily as Byron came closer…closer… Byron choked Cynara's name, as her tongue stroked and caressed, until Byron was swollen to the point of pain…feeling as if all parts of her were about to break open. A flash of Cynara's eyes, and then everything went black as she came, and as Cynara lifted herself to Byron, laying her soft breast against her thudding release, she came again.

"Oh God…oh, God," Byron moaned as she felt Cynara's fingers gently resurrect a desire she thought must certainly be sated, only to discover as her fingers found Cynara, full and swollen wet, a final shuddering climax, this time Cynara gasping Byron's name as they fell into each other, having loved each other as well and dearly as if they had loved for a hundred years.

The pale blue of dawn caressed Byron and Cynara, wrapped in the other's soul. They slept, every inch of skin engulfed with the other.

* * *

Windswept, the two women stood, gazing intently at one another, unaware of the chill as they overlooked the ocean at the precipice of Devil's Point. Byron smiled and Cynara touched a finger to her lips. Byron laughed, and drew Cynara to her then, kissing her thoroughly, the raging ocean a backdrop for their brazen passion.

* * *

Muffled sounds could be heard against the crackling of a raging fire. The sounds of unbridled passion built to a crescendo as Byron's body lazily ground into Cynara's, their gaze fastened to each other, Byron's tempo quickening, her fingers thrusting inside Cynara as she moved faster, the rhythm more urgent. Cynara holding on as she watched in sweet anticipation, greedily kissing the tremor at Byron's lip, the flutter at her eyelids and then joining Byron as they both surrendered, their eyes never leaving one another.

Later they lay entwined as the fire's embers grew cold. Byron removed herself from Cynara, threw a blanket over her body to attend the fire. Once the flames rekindled, Byron lit a cigarette, and stood against the flickering light.

Cynara joined her, wrapping herself under the blanket until their bodies warmed. Then she moved apart from her, taking the blanket along. She stared unabashedly at Byron's form, leaned her head sideways, then grinned.

"I didn't have you far off at that," she commented.

"What do you mean?"

"I knew your body. Like I know my clay. I could feel you every time I worked, and as I held the clay beneath my hands I began to know your body—intimately."

Byron motioned Cynara back to her and together they sat on the rug, leaning against the settee and staring into the fire.

Byron touched her forearm. "Cynara, you have obviously known about yourself for some time."

"Yes. And you?"

"Let's just say my introduction to my nature was rather... extraordinary." Byron grinned now, thinking how little she had known about herself until that night with Marie. "What about you?"

"I don't really care to talk about it."

"But you have been with other women. Like us."

"No. Not entirely." Cynara's voice grew soft. "I've only dreamed of it. But what were the chances here that I would ever meet someone like myself?"

"And there I was in Paris, surrounded by the likes and I never really considered it until...well, not really until I met you. You make it real for me, these feelings."

Byron kissed Cynara until she pulled apart from her.

"What is it?"

"You speak of it so easily."

"And why not?" Byron frowned. "I know so many women like us in Paris."

"Perhaps in Paris, but not here. Not in my world."

"Cynara. Please, tell me."

Cynara sat very still and then began speaking in a low slow voice. "It happened shortly after I returned from New York. I was just nineteen and eager to know the world, myself and everything in it. A woman arrived one morning from San Francisco to board here at Bay Cliff. She, too, was a writer. She had an unusual name—Arianna. And she had this wild red hair; the color of a deep russet sunset." As Cynara spoke she sat rigidly, gazing into the fire.

"She was very urbane, very sophisticated. We immediately struck up a friendship. She was the only person I had been interested in talking with since leaving my friends in New York. As much as I loved the solitude of Bay Cliff, the beauty of the ocean, I missed the city, the lights, the excitement. I missed a culture of paintings, museums, theater. I was so lonely that I suspect I began to follow the poor woman around like a puppy dog.

"One night she invited me to her room. She wanted to share with me the latest Edith Wharton—*The Age of Innocence*. Arianna's intensity moved me. I had had similar feelings for a few of the girls at the University, and I'd heard rumors of women known as 'sapphists,' but I really didn't understand what it meant exactly. I was terribly naïve."

Cynara turned to Byron, leaned to her, and they exchanged a kiss.

"One evening, shortly before dinner, Arianna asked if I would sit on the bed and read to her while she lay down to rest? I gladly did so. It wasn't long before I felt her hand sweep the hair from my neck. When I turned to her she was crying. I felt terrible, as if I had done something bad. When I asked her what was wrong, she told me how she missed her youth and that I should cherish mine while I had the opportunity. I begged her not to cry and flung myself into her arms. I wanted to touch her face and feel her lips and… and I didn't know what. She pushed me from her, telling me I had mistaken her sisterly interest in me for something else entirely. But I knew what I was feeling and I was terrified I would never see her again—that I would never have the opportunity to express the feelings that I had lived with for years. So I kissed her."

Cynara shook her head, remembering. "I was so bold. I thought all that mattered was to answer the need inside. She didn't resist. We stripped ourselves of our blouses, fondled and caressed and I remember laughing, laughing in pure joy at the newness— the wonderful newness of sharing these feelings with someone."

Cynara shivered and Byron drew her closer.

"And then he showed up. I didn't even hear the door open. How he had the audacity to come into her room—but he must have known, must have been waiting for it. Arianna screamed, outraged, but Charles did not care about Arianna's anger. He grabbed my arm and threw me off the bed. He struck me again and again…dragged me down the hall, down the stairwell, while all the other boarders came from the rooms to witness the commotion. He threw me to the ground as I tried to gather what clothes I had about me.

"Everyone was staring at me. I've never felt such shame. As if no one could stand the sight of me. I was cast out. I finally stood up and walked to the forest."

Byron swallowed in pain, anger and bile crushing her throat.

"It was your father who found me. I had cried myself to sleep in the woods. He walked me to the cottage, took care of me. Never asked any questions. He must have ordered Charles to let me take my meals at Bay Cliff, but I couldn't eat. Charles took perverse pleasure in my sickness. I felt so ugly. He had finally gotten his revenge for my having spoken ill of him to Mavis."

Byron protectively tightened her arms around Cynara.

"And then?"

"Nothing. Here I am."

"But you've been here years since—"

"Yes. And for the most part have stayed quietly to myself in this cottage."

"And…the good doctor?"

Cynara stiffened, got up, aimlessly stoked the charred logs. Byron watched the firelight frame the woman she loved.

"Edward? Edward offered me salvation."

Byron watched Cynara a long moment, then joined her by the fire. She took Cynara's hand and recited,

> *"She walks in beauty, like the night*
> *Of cloudless climes and starry skies;*
> *And all that's best of dark and bright*
> *Meet in her aspect and her eyes."*

Byron lovingly brushed Cynara's hair from her face. "His poem came to me as I watched you tend the fire. It is precisely how I see you."

"Why him? Why Lord Byron?"

"His work epitomizes romance and beauty. That's why I went to Paris—to capture that essence—but I was captured instead… seduced, intoxicated. But you know that."

"Will you go back?"

"It seems so far away." Byron mused, staring at the fire as Cynara intently studied Byron's profile.

"Come with me." Byron turned to her. "Be with me there, Cynara."

"Oh, Byron. Our lives…our lives are so different. You need wild adventure, change, movement. You're always trying to fill the void."

"The void would be not having you."

"Perhaps for a time. I don't know if you could ever settle for less than—"

"Than what?"

"Than being on the edge of excitement. Danger. And I need to know my life will be solid. Safe. Not worrying every moment it might disintegrate and blow away into nothing."

Byron turned Cynara's face to her own. "Cynara, I can't see the future. But what are your options? To stay here and marry a man you will never love? To live as a hermit in this cottage away from humanity? All I can say with certainty is that I love you. But my life has never been, nor will it be, about safety."

Cynara hungrily pulled Byron to her.

* * *

Byron packed her books, skipping over some of her favorite titles she had read as a child—*Black Beauty*, *The Girl of the Limberlost*, and her Rudyard Kipling collection. She did not notice Charles peeking through her opened door until he entered without invitation. She glanced at him briefly, then dismissed him just as quickly.

"I want to talk to you Byron," Charles said as if it were his right. "I suppose I should apologize for my behavior the other night, but it came as quite a shock that you had gone round behind my back and coerced Father into giving you Bay Cliff."

"Don't be absurd." Byron found the books she was searching for and packed them into her trunk, then faced him. "I've come to a decision, Charles. I have decided to let go of Bay Cliff."

"But what—what can you be saying?"

"It's very simple. I'm selling Bay Cliff."

"But you can't!"

"I've arranged for Mavis to stay on for as long as she likes. You have thirty days to pack your things and get out."

"You have no right, Lilian. No right at all. I will fight you."

"With what, Charles? You're done."

"If I have to burn Bay Cliff to the ground—"

Byron continued to gather her things as if he wasn't there.

"You cannot take this away from me." Charles bit the words off in a tightly-controlled fury. "Where have you been all these years? Who took care of Bay Cliff? I have nurtured it, grown the business, made this one of the finest boarding houses on the west coast."

"Very accomplished," Byron stated offhandedly.

"It means nothing to you. How dare you think of taking it from our family."

"I'm sure you can find something else to attend to, Charles."

"No. I will not find *something else to attend to*. You are doing this to spite me. Bay Cliff is my life."

"That is your misfortune."

Charles's cheek twitched and his eyes narrowed as he moved toward his sister. "You have robbed me of my life!"

She turned to him then, and calmly stated, "Then we are even."

Charles's hands trembled, he gasped as if he could not breathe. He was about to say something more, but stopped quite suddenly, as if he remembered something he had forgotten. His eyes gleamed a little too brightly as he backed from the room.

Byron let out a long sigh, then swallowed, the tension draining from her body. Taking a deep breath, she finished her packing, latched her suitcase together. She glanced over the room, allowing her eyes to rest on the bed. She could move on now. But something—something was not right. She slowly moved her gaze from the bed to the window as she heard sounds below her. A seed of fear prickled at her neck. She ran to the window.

Byron flattened her palms against the pane, her face frozen in terror.

"*No!*" Byron ran down the stairwell, where Edward stood trying to calm a frantic Mavis, and pushed past them, then up the hill.

She ran as fast as her legs could carry her. Images floated through the darkened forest, imaginary creatures, demons at her heels. She saw herself as a young girl, saw her mother smoothing a brush through her hair, her father's strong hands on his pipe— the dark and angry eyes of her brother. She knew, knew what she could not see, the sanctimonious glare of restitution as Charles leaned over Cynara, the spit of rage as he mounted her, the gleam of victory as he took her—

"*NO!*" Byron screamed.

Charles's head snapped in the direction of his sister as he scrambled over Cynara on the floor near the bed. Byron saw that her dress was torn, blood at the corner of her mouth.

She attacked him in a cold rage, picked him up and threw him against the hearth. He grasped the fire poker, but Byron's fury was too great for caution. She hurtled into him before he could act, knocking him against the wall, flinging the poker to the side. She threw him to the ground, his head thwacking against the floor.

Byron stood over him gasping for breath, teetering precariously between salvation and hell as she raised the iron poker.

Edward appeared in the door frame, shocked and pale. Byron's eyes ricocheted from her brother to Edward, then to Cynara, who was pulling her clothes over her as she attempted to stand. She felt the black in her head—the hate, the unmitigating hate she felt for her brother—flood through her body. But she heard Cynara call her name and turned to her. In her eyes she saw truth and love. And no fear. The poker dropped.

She squared her shoulders and walked from the cottage.

* * *

Though her face was lined with fatigue, for the first time since she had arrived at Bay Cliff, Byron felt calm. Although Cynara hadn't been physically injured, she was shaken and distraught and now in Dutton's care. Charles was finally locked away in the county jail for assault.

She left her suitcase at the bottom of the stairwell and walked through the dining room where Mavis sat nervously binding a kerchief together. She rose as Byron entered the room.

"I've come to say goodbye," Byron said.

"Well, Miss Harrin—"

"Dear Lord, Mavis," Byron almost laughed. "Don't you think after all we've been through we deserve a given name basis?"

"I suppose we do," Mavis replied sheepishly.

"Have you decided to stay on then?"

"I rather think not. Please don't misunderstand. I appreciate your generous offer. And I love Bay Cliff. The grounds, the ocean. Your father was a wonderful man, and I will never forget how he helped us."

"But…"

"I don't think I could manage in this house," Mavis continued as she lowered her eyes.

Byron knew immediately that for Mavis Bay Cliff was filled with dark memories of abuse and terror. "I'm so very sorry, Mavis." Byron took her hand. "So very sorry."

Mavis said unequivocally, "I know you are."

"What?"

She looked Byron directly in the eyes, her own misted with tears.

"It was you." Byron brushed a hand through her hair trying to piece the evidence together. "You. You were the one who told my father."

Mavis's face turned pink as she bent her head.

"How did you know?"

"Because I know your brother. And he has to destroy anything that threatens him. And he as good as boasted his mastery of you when you returned. He thought by telling me, I would fear his power. It only made me loathe him all the more."

"Dear Mavis." Byron embraced her. "I shall never forget you for what you have done to make things right."

Mavis's lower lip trembled, and then she swiftly patted the pockets of her skirt. "Let's get you out the door or you will be missing your train."

* * *

She leaned against a rock ledge overlooking the ocean, her suitcase next to her.

She turned as Cynara approached her.

"Thank you for meeting me," Byron said quietly as she looked at the ocean. "This is the only thing I will miss about Bay Cliff." She gestured toward the view.

"Where will you go?"

"Home. To Paris."

"Byron, I—" Cynara fought back tears. "I…there's so much I want to say…but what is the sense in saying it?"

Pain and frustration lined Byron's face as she continued staring out to the ocean. "I will always be grateful to you, Cynara." She turned to her. "For giving me back my life."

"I'm not—our worlds are different. I…" She was crying more openly now "I love you. I love you, Byron…"

Byron gently opened Cynara's left hand, her gaze direct and loving, as she placed something in her palm, then closed it and held Cynara's hands tightly in her own. Without saying another word, Byron picked up her bag and walked away.

Cynara glanced down and opened her clutched fist. There in her palm lay the worn wooden heart.

* * *

Byron watched the long arc of ash about to fall from her cigarette. She sat on an empty bench waiting for the train. A shadow fell over her. She looked up to see Edward, who quickly removed his hat.

"May I have a word with you?"

Byron didn't respond.

"A moment, please."

Byron barely acknowledged him.

"You know she's been through this before. It almost destroyed her."

"And marrying you can remedy that?"

"I would never do anything against Cynara's wishes. I offered her marriage with the hope she might be able to heal. Lead a normal life."

Byron tossed aside her cigarette. "I'm sorry, but I don't feel disposed to this friendly farewell."

"Miss Harrington, I have nothing but the greatest respect for you," he began diffidently. "I saw you and Cynara on the hill the other day…embracing. I know I can never inspire the passion she feels for you. Forgive me, I'm bumbling awkwardly. I just want you to understand I have nothing against your love for one another. And if Cynara believed she could be happy with the social restrictions forced upon a relationship of your kind, I would release her. You see, I love her. In the truest sense, and I only want her happiness."

Byron tamped out her cigarette, then turned to him.

Edward sighed. "I promise you. I will keep her safe, and try to make her life as happy as possible."

A new respect for him glimmered in her eyes as she nodded in acceptance.

The train pulled in.

"Well, Godspeed. I wish you well." He tipped his hat and walked away. Byron watched him for a long moment. Her jaw tightened, her eyes remained dry.

As she boarded the train and settled in her berth, she thought back to over twelve years earlier, when she had fled in terror and shame. Now she was returning to her home, a new woman, with a new affinity and commitment to her work.

When she returned to Paris she was going to give Nate Venable his walking papers. She would return to the thing she loved most. Poetry. Its depth and nuance, its savagery and tenderness—she could feel all levels of the spectrum now because she had faced her worst fear and won. Charles was dead to her now. And Cynara, well, she truly had given her the gift to love.

Byron leaned back and closed her eyes. Sleep, yes, now she could sleep. And she did, a long, fitful, dreamless slumber.

It is amazing what happens when you realize you want to live. After so many years of not being sure one way or the other. And it is the little things in life you want to live for. Simple things— illustrated by Jilly Bean's and Heather's excursion from Portland after I lifted the no-visiting ban. Last weekend—the one before I found myself in the cave—the two came to visit me, on a mother and daughter adventure.

I still see Heather's face at her thirteenth birthday party. Unsullied and pure with her raging hormones and growing hostility. You are unblemished yet by what life will do to you, the compromises it will demand of you. When I ask, "What do you want this year to be about, Heather?"

You scream, "Fun!" So certain that in spite of your nagging moms and ornery sister, in spite of having to take out the garbage, having to brush through the waist-length tangles in your hair, that you will indeed have fun. For another year, and maybe a few after that. Then life will become more of a challenge, and you will face it with such ferocity and strength, determination and purpose, and time will whiz past you, a nippy wind at your cheek, and you'll wonder why all the fuss about aging?—

then find a gray hair, and by thirty-six you'll be dyeing your hair and wondering, like myself, what happened to the fun? When do I get to have fun?

* * *

Heather and I took a long walk while Jill took the rare opportunity to read a book. We watched a baby seal dipping in and out of the waves around its mother, stuck our fingers in sea anemones and then walked arm in arm while she told me about her friends in school, all the interpersonal dynamics of life at thirteen, and I remembered my hormone-drenched journals, how all the events in one's life at this age were of earth-shattering importance.

When we got back to the cottage, Jill sat stony-faced.

"What's the matter?" I asked.

"I love it, Spencer." She cracked a grin and then roughed me up—her version of affection.

"What are you talking about?"

"Hope you don't mind, but it was just sitting here on your table." Jill gestured to *Cynara*. I suddenly felt sick to my stomach.

"I'm sorry if I haven't been the most supportive of your work, but, well, it's hard for me to read things you write and not think, you know, that I know you. You're my sister."

"You shouldn't have done that. It's not ready."

"I don't know about that, but let me tell you—I didn't even think of you when I read it. I just felt the characters."

"Well, thank you. I think."

"It's the best thing you've ever done." Coming from Jill, this was a huge endorsement.

That night we built a big fire, played a ridiculously long game of Scrabble, which Heather won, and after she went to bed Jill and I actually talked with each other, something we were just learning to do after so many years of shouting to be heard, of hurting to be seen and of squabbling about who Mom liked best.

"I gotta tell ya, Spence, and don't take this the wrong way— you have your life and I have mine, but there are some days I just wish I could be you. You have this great life. Yeah, I know you've had some problems, but you've followed your dreams, you're not saddled with kids—who's gonna pick up Polly from day care, and pay for braces, yada, yada, yada. I sometimes envy the hell out of you."

"And don't you think I do the same? Seeing you and Kat and the kids—you've got the whole white picket fence thing sewn up. Who'd have thought, you ending up as the June Cleaver in our family?"

We looked lingeringly at each other and there was more peace between us than there had ever been.

"Speaking of June Cleaver, Spence, Mom is driving me goddamn crazy."

Jill rattled on for a while, and I listened knowing all the complaints, watching Jill. I would never dare tell her this, but since she had become a mother she had picked up so many of our own mother's traits and gestures. Suddenly I felt such a sweeping relief of forgiveness. God, how had Mom coped trying to protect us all those years when she had no idea how to protect herself?

"You know, Jill," I ventured, "you think Mom asked for this life? Hell no. I don't think when she put in her order to be a classical pianist, she thought she'd end up marrying a nut case, raising her children in poverty, and then marry man whose life was split in two. But that's what she got. She got us. And given the circumstances, I think she did a helluva job."

"Yeah, maybe." Clearly, Jill wasn't convinced.

"Remember all this when Heather is leaving the house."

"Shit, I'm not worried about her. Polly's the goddamn independent one."

We talked late into the night and as I watched my sister I knew how deeply connected I felt to her, how the cliché that blood was thicker than water was especially true with Jilly Bean.

The next morning I walked them to the car and we shared goodbye hugs all around.

"Hey, finish your goddamn book," Jill said eagerly. "I want to see what happens."

I grabbed onto Jill, and hugged her, holding on for dear life.

* * *

My pulse is slowing, it is faint and difficult to monitor...

I've grown accustomed to this cave—I think of it as my cave now. Who can lay claim to it better than I? After all, I have summoned my demons and spit-polished them for the salvation of my soul.

My breathing is slow. Calm. Strange how my breathing never bothered me here at the cottage. How panic has become a memory.

Untended tomorrows...

Malcolm and Sarah...sitting with you over cheesecake and cappuccinos at a sunny sidewalk café—all the laughs, the giggling, the silly philosophizing...the things best friends are made of

Momo, I do love you, when all is said and done, for all the things you did right, for giving me the gift of creative desire.

Little Jilly Bean, I feel you cuddling next to me in our tiny bunk bed, heads touching, knowing the love of a sibling is a strange and precious thing, that inexplicable bond that tests the endurance of patience and lifts the bar of loyalty.

And Jonathon, my sense memory still recoils at the thought of you, even in the face of death. Can I possibly forgive your betrayal? I too have committed the sins of the bereft, the broken of spirit, and I know how ugly it is to face one's shame, one's utterly flawed humanity. I choose instead to remember you as the man who held me in your arms, your low resonant voice telling stories—exposing me to the world of literature and critical thinking. Was it enough of a trade-off for instilling in me such a sense of dread that I lived a life based in fear? I don't know. I'm not your judge and jury.

My 'Kenzie-Bug—without you I would never know the gift of limitless love, pure love, in your pale cheeked skin, satin hair. I can smell your little child smell—your eagerness, hope and potential. I wish I could do it over—make you proud of me...

Lena, forgive me for betraying our future.

I suppose the cottage had become my last chance to build a path to a new life, to experience the smell of the sea and the wind in my face without the artifice of stage lights and wind machines. It has all been real. Reality. I have fled it all my life, and as with most things, it wasn't really so scary when I got here.

Cynara *sits printed by my bedside. I was going to read it tonight, to begin the never-ending process of editing. Perhaps no eye will ever touch the completed manuscript, but I feel the sense of accomplishment, nonetheless. How easily it came to me. Writing it brought me back to myself...to acknowledge, finally, that I was only really compelled by those things which touched my heart. Make me feel. That's all I ever wanted to do with my work. Perhaps I no longer fit in a world that has become so cynical. Yet I can't help but think—here I am, art imitating death.*

I am so tired now...I know...what were the chances of me actually living through such a night?

I see...a light...yes, it's MacKenzie's shiny Christmas bulb, the one in her dream. She is holding it up to me, and I see her pumpkin brows raise as her smile reflects back to me...but, no, that's not MacKenzie...it is me framed in the curving edges of the indigo blue...it is me in frame, and I...I can see me laughing...what? I can't hear you...I can't hear you, MacKenzie. Don't you remember, Aunnie Spinner? You can do anything you want.

Her laughter is the sweetest music I have ever heard and as she wraps her thin arms about my neck it is the force of her love I feel in my last moment, her big oval eyes, bright, the clearest joy as the light gets bigger, brighter, she whispers...you can do anything you want.

EPILOGUE

A brilliant spring morning surrounded Byron as she worked at an outside café deep within the Left Bank of Paris. She lit her Gauloises, and exhaling, scratched furiously on the pages before her. She was searching for a word...a precise word, and only that one would do. Then she smiled, and laughed out loud remembering the night before.

It was Sylvia who had sent word yesterday that Rabbit was returning by steamer that very night, and Byron had decided she would join their party to greet him. She had spent the day in giddy excitement, unable to contain herself at the thrill of seeing him again, as well as surprising him. When he had walked off the boat and seen her standing there, he'd dropped his hat.

"What? I don't believe it, dear lad," Sylvia sniped. "Is this our very own Rabbit, at a loss for words?"

He started laughing then, but his laughter turned to tears as he clasped Byron to him. "I was terrified I'd never see you again."

"Oh, don't be ridiculous," Sylvia chortled. "What is Le Pair without—" Her hands gestured to them both.

Rabbit put a palm to her cheek, quickly glanced about then murmured, "Is she—?"

"No." Byron felt the familiar twist in her gut, her eyes grow red.

"I'm terribly sorry, dear one."

"Well I'm not," Byron sniffed bravely, then shook her head and laughed. "Enough of that."

When Rabbit saw it was safe to return to what he knew best— seeing the world through his sense of the absurd—he gently squeezed Byron's arm and linked it to his own. "I was afraid you might have decided to set up housekeeping in a teepee or some such."

"And what about you? I thought I was going to see you pop up in one of the Bijou's matinees!"

Rabbit mocked fainting melodrama. "My dear, it is the most ghastly place I've ever been. Radiating sun, spindly palm trees, and the most exotic Spanish architecture. People run about in tennis togs all day drinking iced tea! Can you imagine?" He shook his head disdainfully. "Entirely, entirely too wholesome for me. Not to mention, everyone's stinking blond and they have no intellect whatsoever. No, I began to pine for the brooding Lavinia, the bleak rainy days, the chatter of women at Natalie's."

"Well, that's all that matters. You're home."

"We're both home," he had said, squeezing her. "What's say we head to the Dingo, make merry and wreak havoc."

The waiter approached with an espresso, breaking her reverie.

"*Merci,*" she said, furiously jotting a thought on the pages of poetry before her. She stopped a moment to enjoy her surroundings, inhaled once again, smiling wistfully, and returned to work.

When she finished, she strolled easily through the streets, the autumn leaves of the Champs Élysées nearly capturing the image of the Paris canvas she purchased so many years ago.

> *Maid of Athens, ere we part*
> *Give, oh, give me back my heart…*

The words of Lord Byron's poem ran through her mind, as she walked home to her new loft apartment. This place possessed the charm of her first attic, yet was large enough to comfortably house her bed, a sitting area, desk and chair. Books, files, and papers cluttered the cramped but charming flat.

Or, since that has left my breast,
Keep it now, and take the rest.

Inspired by her namesake, she sat at her desk, the soft patter of an afternoon rain enveloping her as she prepared to begin a new poem. She stretched, stood and lit a cigarette, pulled a bottle of Framboise from the cupboard and poured herself a glass, triumphantly raising it, so much happier to be rhyming verse than plotting complicated murder schemes. A hard-earned smile slowly spread across her face.

She was about to begin work when a loud clattering drew her attention to the window. A cacophony of vendors, café owners, patrons and pedestrians were arguing over a goat that had plowed into a table and knocked the dinner of two young lovebirds to the cobbles. The goat was now pushing his snout into a flower cart. The singing of their voices raised and lowered as they debated who should pay for the eaten posies and the ruined trout. Through the fray a woman draped in a long-hooded cape, quite out of character for her surroundings, stopped to ask a question of one of the onlookers.

Byron cocked her head to one side as she played with the incongruity of the images, then shook her head laughing as the patron told the café owner what he could do with his fresh trout.

A light mist now replaced the rain and the woman in the cape seemed unable to get her answers from one person to the next, until she stopped to ask a husky waiter, who was obviously still distracted by the wandering goat. They both leaned over the piece of paper in her hand until she looked up in the general area of the terrace where Byron was standing. Byron watched the lost character, amused.

The woman lowered her hood and Byron's amusement faded. A shiver wrenched through her. Her knees buckled and she grasped at the iron rail as shock replaced incredulity.

Cynara.

Disbelief mingled with joy. Byron could not take her eyes off the vision before her.

Cynara fairly glowed as the mists of rain fought with the final rays of sundown. Her eyes connected with Byron's as the faintest trace of a smile started at her mouth and moved over her beautiful face.

She had come home.

Bella Books, Inc.

Women. Books. Even Better Together.

P.O. Box 10543
Tallahassee, FL 32302

Phone: 800-729-4992
www.bellabooks.com